Praise for the novels of #1 *New York Times* bestselling author Debbie Macomber

"Debbie Macomber is the queen of laughter and love."

—*New York Times* bestselling author Elizabeth Lowell

"Popular romance writer Debbie Macomber has a gift for evoking the emotions that are at the heart of the genre's popularity."

—Publishers Weekly

"Bestselling Macomber…sure has a way of pleasing readers."

—Booklist

"Debbie Macomber tells women's stories in a way no one else does."

—BookPage

"Macomber is a master storyteller."

—Times Record News

DEBBIE MACOMBER

Rainy Day Meet Cute

Love 'n' Marriage and *Jury of His Peers*

MIRA

MIRA™

ISBN-13: 978-0-7783-06405

Recycling programs for this product may not exist in your area.

For questions and comments about the quality of this book, please contact us at CustomerService@Harlequin.com.

TM is a trademark of Harlequin Enterprises ULC.

MIRA
22 Adelaide St. West, 41st Floor
Toronto, Ontario M5H 4E3, Canada
MIRABooks.com

HarperCollins Publishers
Macken House, 39/40 Mayor Street Upper,
Dublin 1, D01 C9W8, Ireland
www.HarperCollins.com

Printed in U.S.A.

26 27 28 29 30 LBC 5 4 3 2 1

Contents

Love 'n' Marriage

To
Doris LaPort
and
Teresa Colchada
for helping me keep my life sane
and
my home beautiful

One

Stephanie Coulter sauntered into the personnel office at Lockwood Industries, the largest manufacturer of airplane parts in North America, carrying a brown paper bag. Her friend Jan Michaels glanced up expectantly. "Hi. To what do I owe this unexpected pleasure?"

In response, Stephanie placed the sack on Jan's desk.

"What's that?"

Stephanie sat on the corner of her friend's desk and folded her arms. "Maureen sent books. It seems I've been allotted the privilege of delivering your romances."

"I take it Potter is still sick?"

"Right." The entire morning had been a series of frustrations for Stephanie. Her boss was out with a bad case of the flu for the third consecutive day. For the first couple of days Stephanie had been able to occupy herself with the little things an executive assistant never seemed to find the time to do. Things like clearing out the filing cabinets, updating the on-line calendar and reorganizing her desk. But by the third morning she'd run out of ideas and had ended up writing a letter to her parents, feeling guilty about doing it on company time.

"Old Stone Face is out, as well," Jan informed her.

The uncomplimentary name belonged to the executive assistant to the company's president, Jonas Lockwood. In the two years Stephanie had been working for the business, she'd never known Martha Westheimer to miss a day. For that matter, Stephanie had never even visited the older woman's domain on the top floor and doubted that she ever would. Martha guarded her territory like a polar bear protecting her cubs.

The corner of Jan's mouth twitched. "And guess who's working with Mr. Lockwood in the interim? You're going to love this."

"Who?" Stephanie mentally reviewed the list of possible candidates, coming up blank.

"Mimi Palmer."

"Who?"

"Mimi Palmer. She's been here about a month, working in the mail room, and—get this—she's Old Stone Face's niece."

"I can just imagine how that's working out."

"I haven't heard any complaints yet," Jan murmured as she opened the paper bag. "But then, it's still early." She took out the top book and shot a questioning glance in Stephanie's direction. "Are you sure you don't want to read one of these? The stories are great, and if you're looking to kill time . . ."

Stephanie held up both palms and shook her head adamantly. "That would look terrific, wouldn't it? Can you imagine what Potter would say if he walked in and caught me reading?"

"Take one home," Jan offered.

"No, thanks. I'm just not into romances."

From the look Jan was giving her, Stephanie could tell that her friend wasn't pleased with her response. She knew that several of the other women at Lockwood Industries read romances, and often traded books back and forth. To be honest, she didn't see why they found the books so enjoyable, but since she hadn't read one she felt she didn't have any right to judge.

"I wish you wouldn't be so closed-minded, especially since—" Jan was interrupted when the door burst open and Mr. Lockwood himself stormed into the room like an unexpected squall. He was tall and broad-shouldered and walked with a cane, his limp more exaggerated than Stephanie could ever recall seeing it. She remembered the first time she'd seen Jonas Lockwood and the fleeting sadness she'd felt that a man so attractive had to deal with the twisted right leg that marred the perfection of his healthy, strong body. His appearance was that of a cynical, relentless male. As always, she couldn't take her eyes away from him. His dark good looks commanded her attention any time he was near.

He paused only a second while his frosty blue gaze ran over her in an emotionless inspection, dismissing her. She wasn't accustomed to anyone regarding her as though she were nothing more than a pesky piece of lint. His attitude infuriated her. She hadn't exactly been holding her breath waiting for the company president to notice her. Still, she found him intriguing, and subconsciously had expected some reaction from him once they met. He revealed nothing except irritation.

"Michaels, couldn't you find me a decent replacement for even one day?" he roared, completely ignoring Stephanie.

"Mr. Lockwood, sir." Clearing her throat, Jan got to her feet. "Sir, is there a problem?"

"I'd hardly be standing here if there wasn't," he gritted. "Why would you send me that nitwit woman in the first place?"

"Sir, Miss Westheimer recommended Miss Palmer. She told me that Mimi Palmer is highly qualified—"

"She's utterly incompetent."

He certainly didn't mince words, Stephanie mused.

"I specifically asked for a mature executive assistant. Certainly that shouldn't be such a difficult request."

"But, Mr. Lockwood . . ."

"Older, more mature women approach the office with businesslike attitudes and are far less emotional."

That had to be one of the most unfair cracks Stephanie had ever heard. She bristled involuntarily. "If you'll excuse me for interrupting, I'd like to point out that a qualified executive assistant is able to adapt to any situation. I sincerely doubt that age has anything to do with it."

His sharp eyes blazed over her face. "Who are you?"

"Stephanie Coulter."

"Miss Coulter is Mr. Potter's executive assistant."

"Do you always speak out of turn?" He eyed Stephanie with open disapproval.

"Only when the occasion calls for it."

"Can you type?"

"One hundred words a minute."

"Computer skills?"

"Of course."

"Follow me."

"But, Mr. Lockwood . . ." Stephanie felt like a tongue-tied idiot for having spoken out of turn.

Ignoring her, he imperiously addressed Jan. "I'm sure Ms. Coulter is willing to prove just how qualified she is. She can work for me today. What you tell Potter is no concern of mine." He turned abruptly, obviously expecting Stephanie to trot obediently after him.

Her gaze clashed with her friend's. "I guess that answers that."

Grinning, Jan pointed in the direction of the elevator. "Good luck."

Stephanie had the distinct feeling she was going to need it.

Walking briskly down the wide corridor, she arrived just as the elevator doors parted. She stepped inside, holding herself stiffly.

Jonas Lockwood moved forward and pushed the appropriate button, then stepped back. Stephanie noted that he leaned heavily on the cane. She had trouble remembering the last time she'd seen him use one. More often than not, he walked without it.

The elevator rode silently to the top floor, and the doors swished open to reveal his huge office, which occupied the entire top floor. Half of the area was taken up by an immense reception area with a circular desk in the center.

"This way," he said.

Speechless, she followed him, taking in the plush furniture in the gigantic office. The view of Minneapolis was spectacular, but she didn't dare stop to appreciate it. Mimi Palmer was sitting at the large circular desk, sniffling. A man Stephanie didn't recognize was pacing the area near the desk. He glanced up when Jonas and Stephanie approached, and frowned. He was ruggedly built and of medium height. She guessed his age to be around forty-five, perhaps a bit older.

"Jonas, I'm sure the young lady didn't mean any harm," the other man said, gesturing toward Mimi.

Jonas ignored the other man the same way he'd ignored Stephanie only moments earlier. He stepped in front of Mimi and shot a furious glance in her direction. "She may have ruined six months of negotiations with her incompetence."

"I'm sorry, s-so sorry," Mimi said, still sniffling. "I didn't know."

"Not only does she keep an important call on hold for fifteen minutes while she makes a pot of coffee, she insults the company president by demanding to know the nature of his business, and then claims I'm not to be bothered and hangs up on him."

Mimi covered her face with her hands. "I was only trying to help."

Jonas snorted, and Mimi let out a sob.

Stephanie moved forward. "Mimi, stop crying. That's not doing anyone any good. Unless you can help here, I'd suggest you go to the ladies' room and compose yourself." She turned to Jonas. "Tell me whom to contact and I'll do whatever is necessary to smooth matters over."

"Phinney," he said, not sounding at all pacified. "Edward Phinney."

"I tried to call him back, but I couldn't find his phone number," Mimi said on her way out of the office.

Jonas Lockwood glared at Mimi's departing back.

Stephanie had a fairly good idea what might have happened. "Under pressure, she might have had trouble spelling it." Sitting at the desk, she went through the Rolodex until she located the *Ph*'s. Within seconds she located the card. "I'll return Mr. Phinney's call and explain."

"I would prefer to do it myself," he barked.

"Fine." She pulled the card free and handed it to him.

"Now, how can I help you?" She directed her question at the middle-aged man who stood in the center of the room with his mouth hanging open.

"I'm Adam Holmes."

"Mr. Holmes," Stephanie acknowledged briskly. "As I'm sure Mr. Lockwood explained, his executive assistant is ill for the day, but I'll be happy to help."

He opened his leather briefcase. "I'm here to drop off a few papers for Jonas to read over."

Stephanie took them from his outstretched hand. "I'll see to it that he receives these as soon as he's free."

"I don't doubt that for an instant," he said with a low chuckle. "Tell Jonas to contact me at my office if he has any questions."

"I'll do that."

The phone beeped, and Stephanie reached for the receiver. "Mr. Lockwood's office," she said in a crisp, professional voice, then wrote down the message, promising that Mr. Lockwood would return the call at his earliest convenience.

While she was writing down the information, Adam Holmes raised his hand in salute and sauntered toward the elevator. She watched him go. There was a kindness to his features, and the spark in his dark blue eyes assured her that he was far from over the hill.

The phone rang twice more while she sorted through the mail. She wrote down the messages and put them in a neat stack, waiting for Jonas to be off the line so she could give them to him.

Mimi reappeared dabbing at the corner of her right eye with a tissue. "I made a mess of things, didn't I?"

"Don't worry about it." Stephanie offered the younger woman a warm, reassuring smile. "This job is just more than you're used to handling."

"I'm really not very good at this sort of thing."

"It's all taken care of, so don't worry."

"Aunt Martha said I wouldn't have any problems for one day."

"I think your aunt seems to have underestimated the demands of her position."

"I . . . think so, too," Mimi said. "Would it be all right if I went back to my job in the mail room? I don't think I'll be any good around here."

"That'll be fine, Mimi. I'll tell Mr. Lockwood for you."

At the mention of their employer's name, Mimi grimaced. "He's horrible."

Stephanie watched the young blonde leave, furious with Old Stone Face for having put her niece in such an impossible position. An hour later, however, Stephanie found herself agreeing with Mimi's assessment of their employer. He *was* horrible.

A couple of minutes after Mimi's departure, Jonas had called her into his office. She had taken the phone messages and the mail with her.

"Take a letter," he said, without glancing up from his huge rosewood desk.

She was too stunned by his cool, unemotional tone to react quickly enough to suit him.

"Do you plan to memorize it?" he said sarcastically.

"Of course not . . ." Stephanie didn't fluster easily, but already this arrogant, unreasonable man had broken through her cool manner. "If you'll excuse me a moment, I'll get a pad and pen." She hadn't used her shorthand skills in a very long while. But apparently this was the method he used with Martha and was most comfortable with, so she would adjust—just as she'd told him a good executive assistant would do.

"That's generally recommended."

No sooner had she reappeared than her employer began dictating his daily correspondence. He barely paused to breathe between letters, obviously expecting her to keep pace with him. When he'd finished, he handed her a pile of financial reports and asked her to update the computer records.

"How soon will you have the letters ready?" His expressionless blue eyes cut into her. The impatience in his gaze told her that as far as he was concerned, half the day was gone already, and there was business to be done.

"Within the hour," she replied, knowing she would have to draw on every skill she'd learned on the job to meet her own deadline.

"Good." He lowered his gaze in a gesture of dismissal, and she returned to the other office, disliking him all the more.

Her fingers fairly flew over the keys, her concentration total. Jonas interrupted her three times to ask about one thing or another, but she was determined to meet her own deadline. She would have those letters ready on time or die trying.

Precisely an hour later, smiling smugly, she placed the correspondence on his desk. She stepped back, awaiting his response. Meeting the deadline had demanded that she stretch her abilities to their limits, and she anticipated some reaction from her employer.

"Yes?" He raised his head and glared at her.

"Your letters."

"I see that. Are you expecting me to applaud your efforts?"

After all the effort she'd gone to, that was exactly what she had expected. After his derogatory remarks, she felt that her superhuman effort had shot holes in his chauvinistic view of the younger assistant's abilities, and she wanted to hear him say so.

"Listen, Miss Coulter, I'm paying you a respectable wage. I don't consider it my duty to pat you on the back when you merely do what you're paid to do. I have neither the time nor the patience to pander to your fragile ego."

Stephanie felt her face explode with color.

"If you require me to sing your praises every time you complete a task, you can leave right now. Is that understood?"

"Clearly," she managed, furious. This was a rare state for her; she thought of herself as even-tempered and easygoing. Never had she disliked any man more. He was terrible. An ogre. She pivoted sharply and marched into the reception area, so angry that she had to inhale deeply to control her irritation.

Rolling out her chair, she sat down and took a moment to regain her composure.

She hadn't been back at her desk more than fifteen minutes when the intercom beeped. For one irrational instant she toyed with the idea of ignoring him, then decided against it.

"Yes, Mr. Lockwood?" she said in her most businesslike tone.

"Take lunch, Miss Coulter. But be back here within the hour. I don't tolerate tardiness."

Stephanie sincerely doubted that this man tolerated much of anything. Everything was done at his convenience and at someone else's expense.

Grabbing her purse, she took the elevator down to the floor where Human Resources was located. Jan was at her desk, and she raised questioning eyes when Stephanie walked in the door.

"Hi, how's it going?"

Slowly shaking her head, Stephanie said, "Fine, I think." The lie was only a small one. "Is he always like this?"

"Always." Jan chuckled. "But he doesn't push anyone half as hard as he drives himself."

Stephanie wasn't entirely sure she believed that. "He gave me an hour for lunch, but I think I'm supposed to show my gratitude by returning early."

"I'll join you." Jan called a coworker to say she was taking her lunch hour, then withdrew her purse from the bottom drawer and stood.

Although Stephanie hated to admit it, she was full of questions about her surly employer, and she hoped that Jan would supply the answers. For two years she'd only seen him from a distance, and she had been fascinated. From everything she knew about Jonas Lockwood, which wasn't much, she wouldn't have expected him to be so surly. Those close to him were intensely loyal, yet she had found him rude and unreasonable.

By the time they arrived, the cafeteria was nearly deserted. Stephanie doubted that many employees took lunch this late.

They decided to share a turkey sandwich, and each ordered a bowl of vegetable-beef soup. Jan carried the orange plastic tray to a table.

Stephanie tried to come up with a way of casually introducing the subject of Jonas into their conversation without being obvious. She couldn't imagine any executive assistant, even Martha Westheimer, lasting more than a week. Finally she just jumped right in. "Why does Mr. Lockwood find young assistants so objectionable?"

"I haven't the slightest idea."

"You know—" Stephanie paused and took a bite of the sandwich "—he'd be handsome if he didn't scowl so much of the time."

Jan answered with a faint nod. "I think he must be an unhappy man."

That much was obvious, Stephanie thought. "Why does he walk with a limp?" The problem with his leg couldn't be age-related, since she guessed that he was probably only in his mid-thirties, possibly close to forty. Figuring out his age was difficult, since he'd worn a perpetual frown all morning.

"He had an accident several years ago. Skiing, I think. I heard the story, but I can't remember the details. Not that he'd ever let anyone know, but I'm sure his leg must ache sometimes. I can tell because he usually goes on a rampage when it hurts. At least that's my theory."

From the short time she'd spent with him, Stephanie guessed that his leg must be causing him excruciating pain today. She'd noted the way he'd leaned heavily on the cane while in the elevator. Maybe there was a chance that his temperament would improve if the pain eased. But at this point she doubted it would make any difference to her feelings toward the man.

Part of the problem, she realized, was that she was keenly disappointed in him. For two years she'd been studying him from a distance. Perhaps she'd even romanticized him the way that Jan and others romanticized men in the books they read. Whatever it was that had fascinated her from afar had been shattered by the reality of what a hot-tempered, unappreciative slave driver he was.

Jan finished off her soup. "Will you stop by after work?"

"So you can hear the latest horror stories?"

"He's not so bad," Jan claimed. "Really."

"He's the most arrogant, insufferable man I've ever had the displeasure of knowing."

"Give him a day or two to mellow out."

"Never."

Finished with lunch, Stephanie deposited their tray and refilled her coffee cup to take with her to the top floor. When she arrived, the door between the two offices was closed, and she hadn't the faintest idea if Jonas Lockwood was inside or not. Setting the coffee on the desk, she read over a stack of financial reports and cost sheets he'd left on her desk, apparently wanting her to update them. Taking a sip of coffee, she turned one sheet over, her eagle eyes running down the columns of figures.

"Welcome back, Miss Coulter." The gruff male voice came from behind her. "I see that you're punctual. I approve."

She bristled. Everyone who worked with the man seemed to think he was wonderful, but that certainly wasn't the impression she had. He made her furious, and she struggled to disguise it.

"I would suggest, however, that you stop wasting time and get busy."

"Yes, sir." She tossed him an acid grin. For just an instant she thought she caught a flicker of amusement in his electric-blue eyes. But she sincerely doubted that someone as cold as Jonas Lockwood knew how to smile.

As the afternoon progressed, the one word that kept running through Stephanie's mind was *demanding.* Jonas Lockwood didn't ask, he demanded. And when he wanted something, he wanted it that instant, not so much as one minute later. He tolerated no excuses and made no allowances for ignorance. If he needed a dossier, she was expected to know what drawer it was filed in and how to get to it in the most expedient manner. And she was to deliver it to him the instant he asked. If she was a moment late, he didn't hesitate to let her know about his disapproval.

The phone seemed to ring constantly, and when she wasn't answering it, she was tending to his long list of demands.

Just when she got back to updating the financial report, the buzzer rang.

"Yes." If she didn't get this finished before the end of the day, he would certainly comment. He didn't want a mere executive assistant, he required Wonder Woman. Her low estimation of Martha Westheimer rose quite a lot.

"Bring me everything you can find on the Johnson deal."

"Right away." She moved to the cabinet and groaned as her gaze located three files, all labeled Johnson. Not taking a chance, she pulled all three and set them on his desk. She noted that he was rubbing his thigh, his hand moving up and down his leg in a stroking motion. His brow was marred by thick lines. He seemed to be in such pain that she paused, not knowing what to say or do.

He glanced up, and the steely look in his eyes grew sharper. "Haven't I given you enough to do, Miss Coulter? Or would you like a few more tasks that need to be completed before you leave tonight?"

Rather than state the obvious, she returned to her desk. Sitting at the computer, she couldn't get Jonas out of her mind. There was so much virility in his rugged, dark features, yet for all the emotion he revealed, he could have been cast in bronze. No matter what, he wasn't a man she would be able to forget.

Five o'clock rolled around, and she still had two short reports to finish. It didn't matter how much time it required, she was determined to stay until every last item he'd given her was completed.

"Hi," Jan said, stepping off the elevator at five-thirty and greeting her. "I've been waiting for you."

"Sorry." Stephanie rested her hands in her lap. "I've only got a bit more to do."

"Leave it. I'm sure Old Stone Face doesn't expect her desk to be cleared when she comes in tomorrow morning."

"It isn't what she expects, it's what Mr. Lockwood demands. I've never met anyone like him." She lowered her voice. "Everything has to be done at his convenience."

"It *is* his company."

Stephanie shook her head. "Well, listen, I'll trade you bosses any day of the week."

"Is that a fact, Miss Coulter?"

Stephanie managed to swallow a strangled breath. She turned and glared at Jonas, despising him for eavesdropping on a private conversation.

"That will be all, Miss Coulter. You may leave."

She opened her mouth to argue with him but decided she would be a fool to give up the opportunity to escape when it was presented to her. "Thank you. And may I say it was a memorable experience working for you, Mr. Lockwood."

He'd already turned and didn't even acknowledge her statement.

"However—" she raised her voice, determined that he hear her "—I'd prefer working for a more mature male." She wondered if he even remembered his earlier derogatory comments about executive assistants. "A man over forty is far less demanding, and a thousand times more reasonable and patient."

"Stephanie . . ." Jan hissed in warning.

"Good day, Miss Coulter." He'd turned to look at her, and if possible, the icy front he wore like an impenetrable mask froze all the more.

"Goodbye, Mr. Lockwood." With that, she retrieved her purse and marched out of the office, Jan following in her wake.

"Wow, what happened this afternoon?" Jan asked the minute the elevator doors closed, her eyes sparkling with curiosity.

"Nothing."

"I can tell."

"He wasn't any less objectionable after lunch than he was before. Mr. Jonas Lockwood is simply impossible to work with."

"Obviously you two didn't start off on the right foot."

"I'm a fairly patient person. I tried to work with the man. But as far as I'm concerned, there's no excuse for someone to be so rude and arrogant. He has no right to take out his bad mood on me or anyone else. There's simply no call for such behavior."

"Right." But one side of Jan's mouth twitched as though she were holding in a laugh.

"You find that amusing?"

"No, not really. I was just thinking that you could be just the woman."

"Just the woman for what?"

"For ages the female employees of Lockwood Industries have been waiting for a woman exactly like you, and for the last two years you were right here under our noses."

"What are you talking about?"

"Jonas Lockwood needs a woman with nerves of steel who can stand up to him."

"Martha must be able—"

"Not in the office."

"Then what are you talking about?"

"Someone to bring him down amongst us mortals. A few of us feel what he really needs is to fall in love."

Stephanie couldn't help herself. She snickered. "Impossible. Rocks are incapable of feeling, and that man is about as emotional as marble."

"I'm not so sure," Jan commented. "He works so hard because this business is his life. There's nothing else to fill the emptiness."

"You don't honestly believe a mere woman is capable of changing that?"

"Not just any woman, but someone special."

"Well, leave me out of it."

"You're sure?"

"Absolutely, positively, sure." Although the thought of seeing Jonas Lockwood humbled was an appealing one, Stephanie was convinced it would never happen. He was too hard. A man like that was incapable of any emotion.

"Oh, I forgot to tell you."

"Tell me what?" From the look on Jan's face, Stephanie could tell she wasn't going to like her friend's next words—and that Jan hadn't forgotten at all.

"Martha Westheimer telephoned this afternoon. . . ."

"And?" Already Stephanie could feel the muscles between her shoulder blades tightening in anticipation.

"And she's apparently recovering."

"Good."

"But, unfortunately, not enough to return to work. It looks like you'll be working with Mr. Lockwood another day."

"Oh, no, you don't," Stephanie objected. "I'll quit before I'll work with that man for another minute."

Jan didn't speak for a moment. "In other words, you're willing to let him assume everything he said about younger assistants is true?"

Two

"Good morning, Mr. Lockwood." Stephanie looked up from her desk and smiled beguilingly. After a sleepless night, she'd decided to change her tactics. Her mother had always claimed that it was much easier to attract flies with honey than with vinegar. In working with Jonas Lockwood that first day, she'd been guilty of giving him a vinegar overdose. Today, she'd decided, she would fairly ooze with charm and drive the poor man crazy. With that thought in mind, she'd been humming happily as she'd dressed for work.

"Morning." He showed no reaction at all to her good-natured greeting.

"There's coffee, if you'd like a cup." She'd arrived an hour early to organize her desk and her day, and making coffee had been part of that.

"Please." He carried his briefcase into his office.

She realized that his limp was barely noticeable this morning. Jan's theory about his leg tying in with his disposition could well be proven within the next ten hours.

He was already seated at his desk, going through his mail, by the time she brought in his coffee. He didn't look up. "I would have thought you'd consider making coffee too menial a task for a woman in your position."

"Of course not. A good executive assistant is responsible—"

"I get the picture, Miss Coulter." He cut her off and continued to scan the mail, his concentration centering on the neat stack of letters she'd previously sorted. "I'll need you to accompany me to a luncheon meeting and take notes."

"Of course," she replied sweetly. "Are there any files I should read beforehand to acquaint myself with the subject?"

"Yes." He listed several names and businesses, but for all the notice he gave her, she could have been a marble statue decorating his office. "One last thing." For the first time he raised his eyes to hers. "Contact personnel and find out how much longer Ms. Westheimer will be out." His tone told her that day couldn't come soon enough to suit him.

It was on the tip of Stephanie's tongue to tell him that his precious "mature" executive assistant couldn't be back soon enough to suit her. "Right away." Her tone dripped honey.

The piercing blue eyes narrowed fractionally. "I think I liked you better when you weren't so subservient. However, I'm pleased that you finally realize the nature of the position."

She was so furious that she wanted to explode. Instead, she smiled until the muscles at the sides of her mouth ached with the effort. "It's my pleasure."

His eyes sharpened all the more if that was possible. "Good to know, Ms. Coulter."

It took every ounce of self-control Stephanie possessed to disguise her irritation. She'd never before had to deal with such a difficult man. But with everything that was in her, she was determined not to give in to his dislike of her.

They worked together most of the morning, dealing with the

mail first. If Jonas spoke to her, it was in the form of clipped requests. They had a job to do, and there was no room for anything else. Not a smile. Not a joke. No unnecessary communication. He seemed to look at her as a necessary piece of equipment, like the computer. She was there to see to the smooth running of his business—nothing else. She hated to sound egotistical, but that puzzled her. She knew she was reasonably good-looking, and yet Jonas treated her with as much emotion as he would his briefcase. She was both amused and insulted.

In every other office where she'd been employed, she'd seen herself as part of a team. With Jonas, she was keenly aware that she was only a small spoke in a large wheel, and Jonas Lockwood was the wagon.

Once back at her desk, she took a minute to contact Jan before tackling the long list of requests Jonas had given her.

"Jan? Stephanie here. I won't be able to meet you for lunch."

"Do you want me to bring you back something?"

"No, I'm attending a meeting with Mr. Lockwood."

"Hey, that's great. He's never taken Old Stone Face with him before. You must have impressed him."

"I sincerely doubt that. I don't think a rock could make an impression on him."

"Don't be so sure," Jan said, a smile evident in her voice. "By the way, did you give any thought to what I said yesterday?"

Stephanie could only assume Jan was referring to the challenge of making Jonas Lockwood fall in love. The idea caused her to smother a small laugh. "Yes, I did. You're nuts if you even think I'd attempt anything so crazy."

"He doesn't need to be put in his place as much as to find it. And from what I saw yesterday, you're just the woman to help him with that."

"Maybe." However, Stephanie sincerely doubted that someone as unemotional as Jonas Lockwood was capable of falling in love. Part of her wanted to rebel at the way he treated her. Rarely had a man been so indifferent toward her. With her even features, smooth ivory skin and soft golden hair, she was aware that men found her attractive. Jonas's blatant indifference was a surprise. When he looked at her, all she felt was a chill that cut straight through her bones.

"Steph? Are you there?"

"Oh, sorry, I was just thinking."

"I hope that means what I think it does. Listen, I'd like to get together with you soon. There's something we—I—want to talk over with you."

"If it has to do with you-know-who, forget it!"

Chuckling, Jan said, "I'll see you later."

"Right."

Replacing the receiver, Stephanie wheeled her chair to face the computer. She worked with only a few interruptions for the next two hours. Forty minutes before the scheduled luncheon, she read through the files Jonas had recommended in order to familiarize herself with the people she would be meeting, and tucked her tablet computer in her purse so she would be ready to take notes.

She felt mentally prepared and alert when he appeared. She stood wordlessly and followed him into the elevator. Well aware that he was a man who didn't appreciate unnecessary conversation, she kept her comments and questions to herself. She would have her answers eventually.

A limo and driver waited outside the building, and the driver held open the door for them as they approached.

She climbed inside, her fingers absently investigating the smooth leather interior of the limo. Almost immediately, Jonas opened his briefcase and took out a file.

She eyed him curiously. She might have a low opinion of him as a human being, but his knowledge and business acumen were beyond question. He was a man born to lead. In working with him these two days, she had witnessed his swift, decisive nature. When he saw something, he went after it by the most direct route. Life had no gray areas for a man of his nature—everything was either black or white, with no middle ground.

She found her gaze wandering to his hands. They were large, with blunt nails, and short wisps of dark hair curled out from the French cuffs of his shirt. He could be gentle—his hands told her as much. The thought of his large hands stroking her smooth skin did funny things to her breathing. The ridiculousness of the notion made her shake her head. A funny sound slid from the back of her throat, and he glanced up momentarily.

Quickly, she turned to look out the side window, wondering what was happening to her. She didn't even like this man.

As the limo pulled up to a huge skyscraper, Jonas announced, "As I said earlier, I want you to take notes during the meeting. When we return, format them for me and give me your impressions of what happened."

Stephanie opened and closed her mouth in surprise. She was his assistant, not his analyst. But she knew better than to question the mighty Jonas Lockwood. She would do as he asked and accompany it with a smile. She would give him no reason to find fault with her.

They rode the elevator to the twenty-first floor of the Bellerman Building. The heavy doors slid open, and Jonas directed her into the meeting room at the end of the long hallway. Ten chrome chairs upholstered in moss green were strategically placed around a long rosewood table. He claimed the seat at the end and motioned for her to take the chair at his side. She was faintly surprised that he wanted her so close at hand. Since she was an assistant and only there to take notes, she had expected to sit in a corner and observe the proceedings, not find herself right in the middle of them.

Lunch was served, and what followed was a lesson in business unlike anything she had learned in her four years as an executive assistant. There was a layered feel to the meeting. She took meticulous notes of everything that was said, but several times she wondered at the underlying meaning of the words. She was impressed by the role Jonas played. He appeared to be in complete charge of the subjects that were discussed, though he rarely spoke himself, determining the course of the meeting with a nod of his head or a small movement of his hand. At first glance, anyone looking in would assume that he was bored by the entire proceedings. The man was unnerving.

At precisely two, it was over. She looked up from her tablet and flexed her tired shoulder muscles. As the other men stood, the sounds of briefcases opening and closing filled the spacious room.

"Good to see you again, Lockwood." As the man sitting on Jonas's right spoke, his gaze slid over Stephanie with a familiarity that left a bad taste in her mouth. "Leave it to you to have the most beautiful woman in Minneapolis as your executive assistant."

Jonas's cutting blue gaze shifted to rest momentarily on her. "She's only a substitute. My regular assistant is ill this week." He didn't give her a moment more of his attention as he stood and reached for his cane, leaving her to follow him.

Fuming that he had treated her so dismissively, she reached for her purse. He hadn't noticed anything about her but her secretarial skills. She was a woman, and if Jonas Lockwood didn't recognize that, it was his problem, not hers. Even so, she was offended by his comment, and she stewed about it all the way back to Lockwood Industries.

The phone rang ten minutes after she was seated back at her desk. "Mr. Lockwood's office."

"Steph, it's Jan. I talked with Martha Westheimer this afternoon, and I have good news."

"I could do with some," Stephanie grumbled.

"She'll be back Monday morning."

"And not a minute too soon."

"How'd the luncheon meeting go?"

"I . . . I don't know." She hadn't yet sorted through her notes deeply enough to analyze what had transpired. "It was interesting."

"See, he's already having an effect on you."

"He?" she said, teasing Jan. "I can't possibly believe you mean who I think you do."

Jan's answer was a smothered giggle. "Don't forget to meet me at five-thirty. On second thought, I'll come up for you."

"Fine. And thanks for the very *good* news. I could do with a lot more."

The remainder of the afternoon was surprisingly peaceful. Stephanie fleshed out her notes and added her observations, then printed everything out and placed it on Jonas's desk.

He was writing something, but he paused and glanced up when she didn't immediately turn and walk away. "Yes?"

"I just wanted to tell you that Ms. Westheimer will be back on Monday morning. It's been an education working with you for the past couple of days."

He leaned back in his chair and looked at her steadily. "Not a pleasure? You filled in nicely. Quite a surprise, Miss Coulter."

She supposed that this was as much of a compliment as she could expect from such a man. "Now that's something I'm pleased to hear," she said, smiling despite the effort not to.

"I'm convinced you'll do well at Lockwood Industries."

"Thank you." She felt obligated to add, "And if ever you need a replacement for Ms. Westheimer . . ."

"I'm hoping that won't happen again any time soon."

Not as much as I am, Stephanie mused. "Good day, Mr. Lockwood."

He'd already returned to his work. "Good evening, Miss Coulter."

Her heart was pounding by the time she met Jan. For an instant there, she could almost have liked Jonas Lockwood. Almost, but not quite.

"I take it the afternoon ran smoothly."

"Relatively so," Stephanie confirmed.

"Are you ready to talk?"

"It depends on the subject. Jonas Lockwood is off-limits."

"Unfair," Jan objected. "You know I want to discuss our infamous boss. Come on, I'll buy you a drink and loosen your tongue."

"That's what I'm worried about."

"Stop complaining. Don't check the olive in a gift drink."

"What?" Stephanie asked, laughing.

"Oh nothing, I was just trying to make a joke. You know the old saying about checking the teeth in a gift horse? It's Friday, and it's been a long week." Folding her jacket over her arm, Jan led the way down the elevator and through the wide glass doors of the Lockwood Industries building. The Sherman Street traffic was snarled in the evening rush hour, and Jan wove her way to a small lounge a couple of blocks from the building.

Three women waved when they entered. Stephanie recognized one, but the other two were strangers.

"Hi, everyone. This is Stephanie."

"Hi." Stephanie raised her hand in greeting.

"Meet Barbara and Toni," Jan continued. "You know

Maureen." She sat down and looked at the others. "Well, what do you think, ladies?"

"She's great."

"Perfect."

"Exactly what we want."

Taking a chair, Stephanie glanced around the small group, shaking her head in confusion. "What are you guys talking about?"

"You!" All four spoke at once.

"Does this have something to do with Jonas Lockwood?" Already she didn't like the sound of this.

"You didn't tell her?" Toni, a brunette, asked Jan.

"I think we'd better order her a drink first."

Still shaking her head, Stephanie glanced from one expectant face to the other. Barbara had to be over forty, Toni in her mid-thirties, Maureen younger, and Jan, Stephanie guessed, was near her own age of twenty-four.

The waitress returned with five glasses of sparkling wine.

"Now, what's this all about?" Stephanie asked, growing more curious by the minute.

"I think we should start at the beginning," Jan suggested.

"Please," Stephanie murmured.

"You see, we all read romances. We're hooked on them. They're wonderful."

"Right. And Jonas Lockwood makes *the* perfect hero, don't you think?" Barbara added.

"Pardon?" To Stephanie's way of thinking, he made *the* perfect block of ice.

"Haven't you noticed his chiseled leanness?"

"And those craggy male features?"

"I suppose," Stephanie muttered, growing more confused by

the minute. To ease some of the dryness in her throat, she took a long swallow of her wine. It was surprisingly refreshing.

"He's got that cute little cleft in his chin."

Now that was something Stephanie hadn't noticed.

"The four of us have decided that Mr. Lockwood is really an unhappy man," Maureen, who was a redhead, continued. "His life is empty."

"He needs a woman to love, and who will love him," Barbara said.

"That's an interesting theory," Stephanie said, reaching for the wine for a second time. She had to watch how much she consumed, or the four of them would soon be making sense.

"It's obvious that none of us can be his true love," Toni added.

"What about you, Jan?" Stephanie pointed her drink in her friend's direction.

"Sorry, but you know I'm in a serious relationship. I'm expecting Jim to propose within the next year."

"Only Jim doesn't know it yet," Maureen piped in. Everyone laughed.

"But what has all this got to do with me?" Stephanie had to ask the question, even though she was sure she already knew the answer.

"You're perfect for him—just the type of woman he needs."

"The quintessential heroine. Attractive and bright."

"Spunky," Jan tossed in.

"I can't believe what I'm hearing," Stephanie protested. "I don't even like the man."

"That's even better. The heroines in the novels seldom do, either. Not at first, anyway."

"I think you ladies are confusing fantasy with reality."

"Of course we are. That's the fun of it. We're all incurable romantics, and when we see a romance in the making it's simply part of our nature to want to step in and help things along."

"We've even thought about writing one," Toni informed her.

"But why me?"

"You're perfect for Mr. Lockwood, in addition to being exceptionally attractive."

"Thanks, but . . ."

"And you don't seem to lord it over those of us who aren't," Barbara murmured.

"But that doesn't explain why you chose me to weave your plot around."

"Mr. Lockwood likes you."

"Oh, I hardly think—"

"All right, he respects you. We all noticed that this afternoon when you left for the meeting. He wouldn't take you along if he didn't value your opinion."

Stephanie shook her head wildly. "Do you know what he said? A man commented on what an attractive executive assistant he had, and your hero Lockwood told him I was only a substitute, as though he'd had to scrape the bottom of the barrel to come up with me." Finding the situation unbelievably hysterical in retrospect, she giggled. It took her a moment to notice that the other four were strangely quiet.

"What do you think, Maureen?" Jan asked.

"I'd stay he's definitely noticed her. He's fighting it already."

"Oh, come on. You've blown this all out of proportion."

"I don't think so." Jan reached for her purse, and withdrew a copy of Stephanie's employment application. "I did a bit of checking. You had two employers in the two years before you came to us. Right?"

"Right." Stephanie's hand tightened around her wineglass as she shifted uncomfortably.

"Why?"

"Well." She paused to clear her throat. "I've had some problems with the men I've worked with."

"What kind of problems?"

"You know." Embarrassed, she waved her hand dismissively.

"Men making advances?" Toni suggested.

"They all seemed to think I must be interested in off-duty activities, if you catch my drift."

"We do," Jan said. "Stephanie, there are laws against such behavior."

"I know, and I probably could have filed a lawsuit but it was easier to look for another job and avoid the hassle." She felt bad about that, but at the time it had seemed the more practical solution.

"It's always hard to know how to handle something like that," Jan said giving her shoulder a squeeze.

"I did make sure my replacement understood the reason I was leaving."

"Good move," Maureen said.

"Yes, she's heroine material, all right," Toni added with a nod.

Unable to hold back a laugh, Stephanie said, "You ladies don't honestly believe all this, do you?"

"You bet we do," all four concurred.

"But why does it matter to you if Jonas Lockwood is married or not? Maybe he's utterly content being single. Marriage isn't for everyone."

Jan answered first. "As I explained, we're all incurable romantics. We've worked for Mr. Lockwood a lot longer than you. He needs a wife, only he doesn't realize it. But we're doing this for selfish reasons, too. It would help the situation at work for everyone if Mr. Lockwood had a family of his own."

"Family?" Stephanie nearly choked on her wine. "First you have me falling in love with him, then we get married, and now I'm bearing his children." This conversation was going from the ridiculous to the even more ridiculous. To be honest, she was half tempted to practice her feminine wiles on Jonas Lockwood just for the pleasure of seeing if he would crumble at her feet. Then she would have the ultimate pleasure of snubbing him and walking away. But this clearly wasn't what Jan and friends had in mind.

"You see," Barbara inserted, "we feel that Mr. Lockwood would be more agreeable to certain employee benefits if he walked in our shoes for a while."

Dumbfounded, Stephanie shook her head. These women were actually serious. "I think a union would be the more appropriate way to deal with this."

"There isn't one. So we're creating our own—of sorts."

Stephanie still didn't understand. "What kind of benefits?"

"More lenient rules regarding maternity leave."

"Extra days off at Christmas."

"Increased health benefits to include family members."

Lifting the blond curls off her forehead, Stephanie looked around the table at the four intense faces studying her. "You're really serious, aren't you?"

"Completely."

"Utterly."

"We mean business."

"Indeed we do." Jan raised her hand and called for the waitress, ordering another round.

"I'm really sorry, but despite what you might think I'm not heroine material." The waitress delivered another round of sparkling wine, and Stephanie waited until the woman had left before going on. "A man like Mr. Lockwood needs a woman who's far less opinionated than I am. In two days, we barely said a civil word to each other."

"The woman who loves him will need a strong personality."

"She'll need more than that." Stephanie couldn't imagine any woman capable of tearing down Jonas's icy facade. He was too hard, too cold, too unapproachable.

"Say, I didn't know you spoke French." Jan glanced up from Stephanie's application, her eyes growing larger by the minute.

"My grandmother was French. She insisted I learn."

"Then you're bilingual?"

"Right."

All four women paused, regarding Stephanie as though she had suddenly turned into an alien from outer space. "Hey, why are you all looking at me like that?"

"No reason." Barbara lowered her head, apparently finding her drink overwhelmingly interesting.

"So your grandmother was French?" Toni asked.

"Yes, I just said so. And why do I have the feeling that you four have something dangerous up your sleeves?" She glanced from one grinning face to the other. "What does the fact that I speak French have to do with anything?"

"You'll see."

"I don't like the sound of this," Stephanie muttered.

"Be honest. What do you think of our idea?" Barbara asked bravely.

"You mean about finding a woman for Mr. Lockwood?"

The others nodded, watching her expectantly.

"Great. As long as that woman isn't me."

"I think it's fate," Jan said, ignoring Stephanie's words. "This couldn't be turning out any better than if we'd planned it."

"Planned what?"

"You'll see," all four echoed.

Monday morning Stephanie arrived for work early. She'd spent a peaceful weekend planting a small herb garden in narrow redwood planters and placing them on her patio. Living in a small apartment didn't leave much room for her to practice her gardening skills. The year before she'd rented a garden space through the parks department. This year she'd decided to try her green thumb on herbs.

Jan was at her desk when Stephanie arrived at coffee-break time. As much as possible, she had tried to blot out Friday evening's conversation with Jan and her friends. It appeared that the four had some hideous plot in mind. But she'd quickly squelched that. Even imagining Jonas Lockwood in love was enough to amuse her. It would never happen. The man had no emotions. That wasn't blood that ran through his veins—it was ink from profit-and-loss statements. He wasn't like ordinary humans.

"Oh, I'm glad you're here," Jan said.

"You are?" Already Stephanie was leery. "Ms. Westheimer's fully recovered, isn't she?"

"Yes, she's here. At least, I assume she is. I haven't heard any rumblings from above."

Stephanie felt a sense of relief. The less she saw of Mr. Jonas Lockwood, the better.

"I've made arrangements with your boss for you to be gone next week."

"Arrangements?" Stephanie repeated surprised. "What are you talking about?"

"Do you want to get together at lunch?" Jan asked, ignoring Stephanie's question.

"Jan, what's going on?"

"You'll see."

"Jan!"

"I'll talk to you later." She glanced at her watch. "I'd tell you, honest, but I can't . . . yet."

Disgruntled, Stephanie returned to her office, pausing on the way to question Maureen, who gave her a look of pure innocence. Stephanie didn't know what her friends had up their sleeves, but she was certain it involved Jonas Lockwood.

The remainder of the morning ran so smoothly that Stephanie was surprised to note that it was lunchtime. Truthfully, working for anyone other than Jonas Lockwood was a breeze. Mr. Potter, her grandfatherly boss, was patient and undemanding, a pleasant change from the man who'd barked orders at her as though she were a robot. And Mr. Potter was free with his praise and approval of her efforts. Getting a compliment from Jonas Lockwood was like pulling teeth.

She had lunch with Jan, Maureen and the two others she'd met Friday evening, so there wasn't an opportunity to corner Jan and ask her to explain her comment about arranging for her to be out of the office the following week.

The group was fun-loving, quick-witted and personable. Stephanie was grateful when no mention of their infamous employer entered the conversation. In fact, she was more than grateful. Despite all her intentions to the contrary, she had been thinking a lot about Jonas.

Later that afternoon, on her way back up to her office after delivering a file to accounting, she unexpectedly ran into the big boss himself. She was waiting for the elevator, checking her makeup with a small hand mirror, when the doors opened and she found herself eye to eye with him.

"Good day, Miss Coulter."

Caught entirely by surprise, she didn't even lower the tube of lipstick, her mouth open as she prepared to glide the color across her bottom lip. She was too stunned to move.

"Are you or are you not taking the elevator?"

"Oh, yes," she mumbled, hurrying in next to him. She quickly stuck her mirror and lipstick inside her purse, pressing her lips together to even out the pale summer-rose color.

He placed both hands on his cane. "And how are you doing, Miss Coulter?"

"Exceptionally well. Everyone I've worked with *lately* has appreciated my efforts."

"Perhaps your skills have improved."

She felt like kicking the cane out of his hands. The man was unbearable. "As you suggest," she said with a false sweetness in her voice, "things have definitely improved."

His mouth quirked upward in something resembling a smile. "I admit to missing your quick wit. Perhaps we'll have the opportunity to exchange insults again sometime soon."

A joke from Jonas Lockwood—all right, an almost joke. She couldn't believe it.

"Don't count on it." The elevator came to a halt at her floor, and the door swooshed open. As she stepped out she said, "Perhaps in another lifetime, Mr. Lockwood."

"You disappoint me, Miss Coulter. I was looking forward to next week." The doors glided shut.

Next week.

She'd let Jan get away without explaining earlier, but she wasn't waiting another minute. She hurried to Jan's office.

"All right, explain yourself," she demanded, placing both hands on the edge of her friend's desk.

"About what?" Jan was the picture of innocence, which was a sure sign she was up to something.

"I just saw Mr. Lockwood, and he said something about next week. I don't like the sound of this."

"Oh, I guess I forgot to tell you, didn't I?"

"Tell me now!" Stephanie straightened, a strange sensation, akin to dread, shooting up and down her spine.

"Mr. Lockwood's traveling to Paris on business."

Crossing her arms, Stephanie glared at Jan suspiciously. "That's nice."

"The interesting part is that he would like a bilingual assistant to accompany him."

Knowing what was coming, Stephanie tightened her jaw until her teeth ached. "You can't possibly mean . . ."

"When Mr. Lockwood first approached Human Resources about it, we couldn't think of anyone appropriate, but since that time I've gone through our personnel records, and when I found your application . . ."

"Jan, I refuse to go. The man and I don't get along."

"When I mentioned you to Mr. Lockwood, he was delighted."

"I'll just bet."

"Your flight leaves Sunday night."

Three

The jet tilted its wings to the right, slowly beginning its descent. Stephanie stared out the small window, fascinated by the breathtaking view of the River Seine far below. Her heart pounded with excitement. Paris. How her grandmother would have envied her. As a young French war bride, Stephanie's grandmother had often longed to revisit the charming French city. Now Stephanie would see it for her.

"If you would tear your gaze from the window for a minute, Miss Coulter, we could get some work done," Jonas Lockwood stated sarcastically.

"Of course." Instantly she was all business, reaching for a pad. This was obviously the only level on which she could communicate with him. Not once since they'd taken off from Minneapolis-St. Paul International Airport had her employer glanced at the spectacular scenery. No doubt he would have considered it a waste of valuable time.

"I've reserved us a three-bedroom suite at the Château Frontenac," he informed her coolly.

She silently repeated the name of the hotel. "It sounds lovely."

He glanced down at the report in his lap and shrugged one muscular shoulder. "I suppose."

It was all Stephanie could do not to shout at him to open his eyes and look at the beauty of the world that surrounded him. At times like these she wanted to shake him. The mere thought of anyone—much less her—even touching him produced an involuntary smile. He would hate being touched.

She looked across the aisle at Adam Holmes, who had accompanied them. His role in Jonas's plans had been left to conjecture, but she suspected that he was an attorney.

"It's looks like we're in for pleasant weather," he said conversationally. His dark blue eyes narrowed fractionally as he gazed out at the ground below. For most of the trip he had carried the conversation. He was both friendly and articulate, a blatant contrast to the solemn, serious Jonas.

A little surprised, Stephanie glanced up, unsure whether Adam was addressing his comment to her. Jonas didn't respond. Of course, she would have been shocked to learn that any type of weather interested her employer.

"I would guess early summer is the perfect time to visit Paris." In reality, she wondered how much of the city she had any chance of seeing. Her one hope was that she would be able to visit the Champs de Mars and view the Eiffel Tower, built for the 1889 World's Fair. High on her list were the twelfth-century cathedral of Notre Dame, and the Arc de Triomphe. She'd spent a year in France as an exchange student in high school, but apart from a quick trip through the airport, she hadn't seen anything Paris.

The plane began its final descent, and she clicked her seat belt into place. Casually Jonas put away his papers and closed his briefcase. As soon as they landed they would be going through customs and she would be expected to step into her role as translator. Although she spoke fluent French, it had been a while since she'd had the opportunity to use it, and she hoped she was up to the task.

To her surprise, everything went without a hitch at customs, and her confidence grew. They moved from the terminal to the waiting limo with only minimal delay.

The driver held the door open, and she climbed inside the luxurious automobile. Jonas and Adam followed her, and they were soon on their way.

At the hotel they were escorted to their rooms and their luggage was delivered promptly. While she unpacked her clothes, she heard Jonas and Adam discussing the project. Apparently they would be meeting a powerful financier in the hope of obtaining financial backing for a current project. Lockwood Industries, the largest North American manufacturer of airplane parts, was apparently ready to buy out their French counterpart. If the deal progressed as expected, Lockwood Industries would become the largest such manufacturer in the world. There also seemed to be the possibility of Lockwood establishing branches in several European cities.

"Miss Coulter."

"Yes." Responding instantly to the command in Jonas's voice, Stephanie stepped into the doorway of her room.

"We have a lunch reservation downstairs in ten minutes."

"I'll be ready. I just need a few minutes to freshen up."

"Of course."

He was already turning away, and she doubted that he'd even heard her. He'd often given her that impression. Returning to her assigned room, she glanced in the mirror. Several tendrils of soft blond hair had escaped from the coil at the base of her neck. Rather than tuck them back, she pulled out the pins and reached for her brush. Unbound, her hair curled naturally to her shoulders. Normally when she was working she preferred to keep her hair away from her face. It gave her a businesslike look, and she felt that was particularly important around Jonas.

"Miss Coulter."

Jonas again.

Her brush forgotten in her hand, she moved into the large living room, where Jonas and Adam were waiting.

"Yes?"

For a moment the room went still as Jonas caught her gaze. Their eyes met and locked. His narrowed, and an expression of surprise and bewilderment flickered across his face. Something showed in his eyes that she couldn't define—certainly not admiration, perhaps astonishment, even shock. His mouth parted slightly, as if he wanted to speak, then instantly returned to a stern line.

Adam's face broke into a spontaneous smile as his lingering gaze swept her appreciatively from head to toe. "I don't think I realized earlier how attractive your assistant is, Jonas."

The muscles in Jonas's jaw looked as though they were frozen solid. He ran an impatient hand through his hair and turned to reach for his briefcase.

"You wanted me?" It was hard to believe that breathless voice was hers. She sounded as though she'd been running a marathon. She couldn't be attracted to Jonas. He was the last person in the world she wanted to have any romantic feelings for. Normally she was a level-headed person, not the sort who let her emotions carry her away. Not that Jonas Lockwood was worthy of a moment's consideration. He was arrogant and . . .

"We'll meet you downstairs." He interrupted her thoughts, his voice cool and unemotional.

"I'll be there in a minute."

"Take your time," he said dismissively, clearly doing his best to avoid her.

She turned to go back into her room, but not before she caught the look Adam directed at them both, disbelief etched clearly on his smooth, handsome features.

After closing the door, Stephanie sank onto the edge of her bed. There must be some virus in the air for her to be thinking this way about Jonas Lockwood. For a moment she'd actually found him overwhelmingly, unabashedly appealing. She'd been genuinely physically attracted to him. She shook her head at the wonder of it. She was playing right into Jan's and the other women's hands.

The amazing thing was that Jonas had noticed her, as well—really noticed her. At least when Adam had complimented her, Jason hadn't told him that she was "only a substitute." A small smile tugged at the corners of her mouth. Maybe, just maybe, Jonas Lockwood didn't have a heart of ice, after all. Perhaps under that glacial exterior there was a warm, loving man. The thought was so incongruous with the mental picture she held of him that she shook her head to dispel the image. Without wasting further time inventing nonsensical fantasies about her employer, she finished styling her hair and changed clothes, then went downstairs to the restaurant.

Lunch passed without incident, as did the first series of meetings.

In bed that evening, Stephanie's thoughts spun. They'd called it an early night, but she wasn't able to sleep. The most beautiful city in the world lay at her doorstep, and she would be tied up in meetings for the entire visit. Sitting up, she wiped a hand across her face. She was undecided. They would only be in Paris another two nights. If this was to be her only opportunity, she was going to take it.

Dressing silently, she slipped the hotel key into her purse and carefully tiptoed across the carpet, letting herself out.

Since their hotel was in an older section of the city, she caught a taxi and instructed the friendly driver to take her to several points of interest. He escorted her through Les Halles, the mammoth central food market, which had once been located on the north of the river, but had been moved to Rungis, in the suburbs of Paris.

From there he drove her past Notre Dame cathedral, pointing out landmarks as he went. But she barely heard him. Her thoughts were focused on that moment in the hotel room earlier in the afternoon when Jonas had looked at her for perhaps the first time. Her hands grew clammy just thinking about it. At the time she'd been flippant. Now she was profoundly affected. Just remembering it caused her pulse to react. In those brief seconds he had seen her as a woman, and, just as importantly, she'd viewed him as a man. She was intensely attracted to him and had been for weeks, she just hadn't been ready to admit it.

The driver, chatting easily in French, pointed out the sights, but instead of seeing the magnificent beauty in the buildings that surrounded her, Stephanie's thoughts revolved around Jonas. She wondered about what he'd been like as a child, and what pain had snuffed out the joy in his life.

Straightening, she shook her head and said to him in French, "Please take me back to the hotel."

The driver gave her a funny look. *"Oui."*

Stephanie had hoped to see the Louvre, but it wouldn't have been open at this time of night, anyway. As it was, she didn't seem to be able to view any of the sights without including Jonas in what she saw. It was useless to pretend otherwise.

Back at the hotel, she gave the driver a generous tip and

thanked him. The lobby was quiet, and the soft strains of someone playing the piano sounded in the distance. She briefly toyed with the idea of stopping in the lounge for a nightcap but quickly rejected the idea. She needed to get some sleep.

Being extra-cautious not to make any unnecessary noise, she silently slipped into the suite. She was halfway across the living room when a harsh voice ripped into her.

"Miss Coulter, I didn't bring you to Paris so you could sneak out in the middle of the night."

She reacted with a startled gasp, her hand flying to her breast.

"Just who were you meeting? Some young lover?" The words were spoken with a cutting edge, mocking and bitter.

"No. Of course not." She could barely make out Jonas's form in the shadows. He sat facing her, but his features were hidden by the darkness.

"Surely you don't expect me to believe that. I understand you spent a year in France. Undoubtedly you met several young men."

The words to tell him what to do with his nasty suspicions burned on the tip of her tongue. Instead, she shook her head and replied softly, "I don't know anyone in Paris. I couldn't sleep. It may sound foolish, but I decided that I might not get the opportunity to see the sights, so I—"

"You don't honestly expect me to believe you were out sightseeing?" The shadow began to move, and as her eyes adjusted to the darkness she noted that he was massaging his thigh.

Against her will, her heart constricted at the pain she knew his leg must be causing him. With everything that was in her, she yearned to ease that pain. She took a tentative step in his direction, claiming the chair across from him. In low, soft tones, she told him about the historic buildings she'd visited and the chatty taxicab driver who had given her a private tour of the older sections of Paris, along with a colorful account of his own ancestry.

She watched as the cynical quirk of his mouth gradually relaxed. "It's really an exceptionally lovely city," she finished.

"Holmes is attracted to you."

"Adam?" Stephanie couldn't believe what she was hearing and quickly dismissed the suggestion. "I'm sure you're mistaken."

"Do you find it so surprising?"

"Yes . . . n-no."

"It's only natural that he thinks you're lovely. As you said, you're in one of the most beautiful cities in the world. It's springtime. You're single. Holmes is single. What's there to discourage a little romance?"

"I hardly know the man."

"Does it matter?"

"Of course it does." She sighed and dropped her gaze, sorry now that she'd made the effort to turn aside angry words and be friendly. The man was impossible.

"You could do worse. Adam Holmes is a bright attorney with a secure future."

"If I were buying stock in the man, I might be interested. But we're talking about *people* here. I find him friendly and knowledgeable, but I have no romantic interest in him. I'm simply not attracted to him."

"Who *does* attract you?"

Stephanie swallowed uncomfortably as she battled back the instinctive response. Jonas attracted her. She was still shocked by the realization, but she wasn't willing to hand him that weapon. "I don't believe my private life is any of your affair," she informed him crisply.

"So there *is* someone." Impatience surged through his clipped response.

"I didn't say that." Bounding to her feet, she stalked over to the window and hugged her waist. "There's no use even trying to talk to you, is there?" Her voice revealed her distress. "We seem incapable of maintaining even a polite conversation."

"Does that disappoint you?"

She could feel his gaze as it ran over her; it seemed to caress her with its intensity—and to demand an answer.

"Yes," she admitted gently. "Very much. I feel there's so much locked up inside you that I don't understand."

"I'm not a puzzle waiting to be solved."

"In some ways you are."

He rubbed a hand over his face. "I can't see that this conversation will get us anywhere."

She couldn't, either. She was tired, and he was unreasonable and in pain. The best thing she could do now would be to leave the conversation for a more appropriate time. "Good night, Mr. Lockwood." She didn't wait for his acknowledgement before she headed for her room.

"Good night, Stephanie."

It wasn't until she had changed into her cotton pajamas that she realized that for the first time since they'd met, he'd used her first name. No longer was she a robot who responded to his clipped demands. Somehow, in some way, she had become a woman of flesh and blood. The realization was enough to send her spirits soaring. Hugging the extra pillow beside her, she drifted into a sound sleep, content with her world.

"Good morning," Adam greeted her early the following morning. From the looks of the table, he and Jonas had already been working for hours.

"Morning." She walked across the room and poured steaming coffee into a dainty cup, then held it to her mouth with both hands.

"I trust you slept well, Miss Coulter," Jonas said.

So they were back to that. "Thank you, *Mr. Lockwood*, I slept very well."

He glanced up momentarily, and she recognized the glint of amusement in his eyes. A brief smile moved across his mouth.

"Would you like a croissant?" Adam asked, preparing to lift the flaky pastry onto a china plate with a pair of metal tongs.

"No, thanks." Actually, she might have liked one, but she was afraid that something as simple as accepting a breakfast pastry would encourage him. She hadn't noticed it the day before, but the eagerness glinting in his gaze revealed the truth of Jonas's statement. Adam Holmes really was interested in her.

As it turned out, it was just as well that she hadn't accepted the croissant, because she barely had time to down the coffee before Jonas stood. "We have a lot of ground to cover today."

He limped to the door without his cane. She knew that he preferred not to use it and did so only when absolutely necessary. His leg had kept him up last night and would soon be aching again without the cane.

"In that case," she said, "you'll want your cane."

Jonas expelled his breath. "Miss Coulter, I require an executive assistant and a translator, not a mother."

"Your leg was bothering you yesterday." She knew she was on dangerously thin ice. Not once had she ever mentioned his limp before. "I see no reason to aggravate it further."

He didn't answer her, but she noted triumphantly that he reached for his cane before they left the suite.

What followed was a day she was not likely to forget. The first meeting that morning was a marathon exchange of proposals and counterproposals. They adjourned briefly for lunch, then were at it again before she had the opportunity to take more than a bite or two of her salad.

The afternoon was just as jam-packed. No sooner had she finished translating one statement than Jonas gave her another. Much of the conversation went completely over her head, but in the weeks since meeting him, she had gained valuable insight into her employer. She could see that he was tense, although she was certain no one else noticed it. For the meeting, he almost seemed to wear a mask that revealed none of his feelings or emotions. This, like most of his life, was business, with no room for fun and games. If she had accepted what she saw on the surface, he would have frozen her out completely. But she'd seen a rare glimpse of the man inside, and she'd been intrigued.

Though the afternoon session was both complicated and challenging. She noticed that he was cool to the point of being aloof, as though what they were discussing was of little consequence to him. She suspected that, like a gambler, he placed his money on the line for the pleasure of tossing the dice. He enjoyed the thrill, the excitement, and had poured his whole life into pursuing it.

Throughout the afternoon Adam drifted in and out of the room, returning with one document and then another.

It was early evening when the meeting came to an end. Jonas and his French counterpart stood and shook hands.

"We're breaking until morning," Jonas informed Adam outside the conference-room door. "Did you locate that report on the export tax I asked about earlier?"

"I have it with me," Adam responded, tapping the side of his briefcase.

"I'll want to look it over tonight."

For her part, Stephanie was exhausted and hungry. After no

breakfast and virtually no lunch, her stomach was protesting strenuously.

Once they were back in the suite, she immediately slipped off her shoes. They were new, and pinched her heels. Sitting on the sofa, she crossed her legs and rubbed the tender portion of one foot, suspecting a blister.

On the other side of the room Jonas was drilling Adam about one thing or another. She couldn't have cared less. Then she noticed his gaze resting on her slender legs. When he realized she'd caught the direction of his glance, he turned his head. He looked tired, worn down. She wanted to suggest that he take this evening to rest, but after her comment that morning about his cane, she realized she would be pressing her luck. She was too weary to fight with him now.

"I'll get that statement for you as quickly as possible," Adam said, rising to his feet.

"Thanks."

The room seemed oddly quiet after Adam left.

"Miss Coulter, order a car."

She couldn't believe it. The man was a slave driver. Reaching for the phone, she contacted the front desk and asked that they have a car available. "How soon do you want it?" she asked, holding the receiver to her breast.

"Immediately."

She glared angrily at him. Not everyone was accustomed to his pace. She was tired, hungry and not in the most congenial mood.

"Will you be requiring my services?" She didn't bother to hide the resentment in her voice.

"Naturally, I'll need you to translate for me."

"Would you mind if I ate something first?" she asked as she reached for her shoes.

"Yes, I would."

Her gaze narrowed with frustration. "What is it with you? Maybe you can work all hours of the night and day, but others have limitations."

His mouth thinned, revealing his irritation; he picked up his cane. "Then stay here."

As much as she would have liked to do exactly that, she knew she couldn't. Reluctantly she followed him out of the suite. "Miss Coulter—" she mimicked his low voice sarcastically "—you've done a wonderful job today. Let me express my deepest appreciation. You deserve a break." She paused to eye him. The stone mask was locked tightly in place. "Why, thank you, Mr. Lockwood. Everyone needs a few words of encouragement now and then, and you seem to know just when I need them most. It's been a long grueling day, but those few words of appreciation seem to have made everything worthwhile."

"Are you through, Miss Coulter?" he asked sharply as they stepped into the elevator.

"Quite through." Her back was stiff and straight as they descended. She was tired, her feet ached, and she was hungry. For the last eleven hours she'd been at his beck and call. What more could he possibly expect from her now?

The driver was waiting outside the hotel when they approached. He held open the door, and she climbed inside. Jonas paused to speak to the driver, but what he said and whether the driver understood him didn't concern her at the moment. If he needed her to translate, he would tell her. "Telling" was something Jonas had no problem doing.

They'd gone only a few blocks when the driver pulled to the curb and parked. They were in front of an elegant restaurant. Tiny tables were set outside the door, and white-coated waiters with red cloths draped over their forearms stood in attendance, watching for the smallest hint of a request. Stephanie blinked twice. Exhausted and dispirited, she didn't know if she could bear another meeting now. And at a restaurant! Her stomach would growl through the entire affair.

"Are you coming, Miss Coulter?" Jonas said, climbing out of the car. "I did hear you say you were hungry, right?"

Stunned, she didn't move. "We're having dinner here?"

"Yes. That is, unless you have any objections?" He suddenly looked bored with the entire process.

"No . . . I'm starved."

"I believe you've already stated as much. Luckily I have a reservation—unless you'd prefer eating in the car?"

"I'm coming." This was almost too good to be true. Eagerly she made her way onto the pavement. As they walked into the plush interior, her gaze fell longingly on an empty table outside on the sidewalk.

Jonas surprised her by asking, "Would you prefer to dine outside?"

"Yes, I'd like that."

Jonas spoke to the maître d', who led them to the table and politely held out Stephanie's chair for her, then handed each of them a menu. She was so hungry that she quickly scanned the contents. "Oh, I do love vichyssoise," she said aloud, biting her lower lip.

Before she knew what was happening Jonas had attracted the waiter's attention. "A bowl of vichyssoise for the lady."

"Jonas," she said, shocked. "Why did you do that?"

"From the way you were acting, I was afraid you were about to keel over from hunger."

"I am," she admitted, her gaze going up one side of the menu and down the other. "Everything looks wonderful."

"What would you like?"

"I can't decide between a huge spinach salad or a whole chicken."

The waiter returned, hands behind his back as he inquired courteously if they would like to place their orders. Jonas asked for the bouillabaisse, and raised questioning eyes to Stephanie.

"I'll have one of those," she said, pointing to the meal another waiter was delivering and indicating a huge salad that was piled high with fresh pink shrimp. "And one of those." Her gaze flew to the dessert cart, which was laden with a variety of scrumptious, calorie-laden goodies.

"Will that be all?" Jonas asked wryly.

"Oh, heavens, yes." She felt guilty enough already. "This is what you get for depriving me of nourishment," she joked. "I'm a grouch when I get too hungry."

"I hadn't noticed." One side of his mouth lifted in an aloofly mocking smile.

"I guess I owe you an apology for what I said earlier."

Her soup arrived, and she eagerly dipped her spoon into it and tasted, closing her eyes at the heavenly flavor. "Oh, this is absolutely wonderful. Thank you, Jonas."

His eyes smiled into hers. "You're quite welcome."

"I really am sorry."

"My dear Stephanie, I've stopped counting the times you've let your mouth outdistance your mind."

She was so shocked that she stopped with her spoon poised halfway between the bowl and her mouth. Jonas joking? Jonas calling her *dear?* It was almost more than her numbed mind could assimilate.

No sooner had she finished the soup than her salad was delivered. The top was thick with shrimp. "I think I've died and gone to heaven."

"Then you're relatively easy to please. It was my understanding that women were more interested in jewels and other luxury items."

She eagerly stabbed her fork into a shrimp. "Personally, I prefer shrimp and lobster." She smiled. "I haven't eaten this well in months."

Jonas arched his eyebrows expressively. "So a man could win you over with cheesecake."

"Tonight he could." Unable to wait any longer, she ate the fat shrimp and closed her eyes at the scrumptious flavor. When she opened them, she discovered that Jonas was watching her. Tiny laugh lines fanned out from his eyes.

He was so handsome that she couldn't take her eyes from him. "Are you wooing me?" It seemed overwhelmingly important that she know where she stood with him.

"I will admit that you're the cheapest date I've had in a long time."

"Is this a date?"

"Think of it more as a token of appreciation for a job well done."

She pressed her hand dramatically to her forehead, and her bright blue eyes grew round with feigned shock. "Do my ears deceive me? Jonas Lockwood of Lockwood Industries has deigned to pay an employee a compliment? An employee who's a relatively young woman, at that—admittedly one with minor faults."

"I won't disagree with you there."

Despite herself, Stephanie laughed. "No, I don't suppose you will."

"You did very well today."

"Thank you." She felt inexplicably pleased.

"Where did you learn to speak French?"

He seemed eager to keep the conversation going, and she was just as eager to comply. For the first time since meeting the man, she didn't feel on guard around him.

"My grandmother was a French war bride, and she taught my mother the language as a child. Later, Mom majored in French at the University of Washington. I've been bilingual almost from the day I was born."

"You're from Washington State?"

"Colville. Ever hear of it?"

"I can't say that I have."

"Don't worry, most people haven't."

"I imagine you were the town's beauty queen."

"Not me. In fact, I was a tall, skinny kid with buckteeth and knobby knees most of my life. It wasn't until I was in my late teens and the braces came off that the boys started to notice me."

"I have trouble believing that."

"It's true." She reached for her purse, and took out her cell phone. "I carry this picture because people don't believe me." She brought it up and was about to show him when they were interrupted by the waiter, who was bringing a bottle of wine.

Jonas looked up and spoke briefly with the other man.

Stephanie's blue eyes widened with astonishment and surprise. The waiter nodded and stepped away.

"You speak French."

"Only a little."

"But very well."

"Thank you." He dipped his head, accepting her compliment.

A clenching sensation attacked her stomach. "You didn't really need me here at all, did you?"

Four

"I brought you along as a translator," Jonas answered simply.

Stephanie lowered her fork to her plate. Her thoughts were churning like water left to boil too long, bubbling and spitting out scalding suggestions she would have preferred to keep in her subconscious. He'd tricked her into accompanying him on this trip. The meal that had tasted like ambrosia only seconds before felt like a concrete block in the pit of her stomach. "You speak fluent French."

"My French is adequate," he countered, reaching for his wineglass.

"It's as good as my own."

"My linguistic abilities are not your business."

"But I don't understand. Why . . . ?" She couldn't understand the man. One minute he was personable and considerate, and the next he became brusque and arrogant. The transformation was made with such ease that she hardly knew how to respond to him.

"That I required a translator is all you need to know."

Rather than argue with him further, she stabbed another

plump shrimp. She ate it slowly, but for all the enjoyment it gave her she might as well have been chewing on rubber. "Letting the French company we're negotiating with believe you don't speak the language is all part of your strategy, isn't it?"

"Wine?" He lifted the long-necked green bottle of pinot noir and motioned to her with it.

"Jonas? Am I right?" she asked as he filled her glass.

He cocked his head to one side and nodded. "I can see you're learning."

She ate another shrimp and discovered that some of the flavor had returned. "You devil!"

"Stephanie, business is business."

"And what is this?" The wine was excellent, and she took another sip, studying him as she tilted the narrow glass to her lips.

He stiffened. "What do you mean?"

"Our dinner. Is it business or pleasure?"

The crow's-feet at the corners of Jonas's eyes fanned out as if he were smiling, yet his mouth revealed not a trace of amusement. "A little of both, I suspect."

"Then I'm honored. I would have assumed that you'd prefer to escort a much more *mature* woman to dinner." She felt the laughter slide up her throat and suppressed it with some difficulty. "Someone far less emotional than a *younger* woman."

"I believe it was you who commented that age has little to do with maturity."

"Touché." She raised her glass in salute and sipped her wine to toast his comeback. She felt light-headed and mellow, but she wasn't sure what was to blame: Jonas, her fatigue or the excellent wine.

She couldn't believe this was happening. The two of them together, enjoying each other's company, bantering like old friends, applauding each other's skill. As little as two hours ago, she would have thought it impossible to carry on a civil conversation with the man. She imagined that Jonas was about as relaxed as he ever allowed himself to be.

"I'll admit that the pleasure part comes from the fact that I knew you wouldn't be simpering at my feet," he commented, breaking into her thoughts.

"I never simper."

"You much prefer to challenge and bully."

"Bully? Me?" She laughed a little and shook her head. "I guess maybe I do at that, but just a bit." She didn't like admitting it, but he was right. She was the oldest of three girls, and did have a tendency to take matters into her own hands. "While we're on the subject of bullies, I don't suppose you've noticed the way *you* treat people?"

"We aren't discussing me," he said dryly.

"We most certainly are." She flattened her palms on either side of her plate and shook her head. "I've never known anyone who treats people the way you do. What I can't understand is how you command such loyalty."

He arched his eyebrows expressively, and his gaze swept her with mocking thoroughness.

She ignored him and continued. "It's more than just money. You pay well, but the benefits leave a lot to be desired." She felt obligated to mention that, since it had come up the other day and, she had to admit, the point was a good one.

"Is that a fact?"

"You're often unreasonable." She knew she was pressing her luck, but the wine had emboldened her.

"Perhaps others see it that way," he admitted reluctantly. "But only when the occasion calls for it."

For all the heed he paid her comments, they could have been discussing the traffic. "And I've yet to mention your outrageous temper."

"I wasn't aware that I had a temper."

Despite the fact he didn't seem to find their conversation the least bit amusing, Stephanie continued. "But by far, the very worst of your faults is your overactive imagination."

His gaze flew to hers and narrowed. "What makes you suggest something so absurd?"

She knew she'd trapped him, and she loved having the upper hand for the first time in their short acquaintance. "You actually believed I was meeting someone last night."

"With your own mouth you admitted as much."

She nearly choked on her wine, but she recovered and challenged his gaze with her own. "I most certainly did no such thing."

"You mentioned the taxi driver—"

"That's so farfetched, I can't believe you'd stoop that low."

"Perhaps, but you seemed to have enjoyed yourself. You sounded quite impressed by the sights you'd seen."

"If you want the truth, I hardly saw a thing. I was thinking about—" She stopped herself in the nick of time from admitting that her thoughts had been filled with him.

"Yes?" Jonas prompted.

"I was preoccupied with the meeting today. I was worried about how I'd do."

"Your French is superb. You needn't have been anxious, and you know it. What *did* occupy your thoughts? Or should I say who?"

Stephanie was saved from answering by the waiter, who reappeared to take their plates. She gave him a grateful smile and finished the last of her wine before the man returned with two steaming cups of coffee and her cheesecake.

A little while later Jonas asked for the bill, paused and looked at her. "Unless you'd like something more? Another dessert, perhaps?"

"No." She shook her head for emphasis and placed her hands over her stomach. After downing half of everything on the menu, she felt badly in need of exercise.

The sun had set, and the sky was darkening in shades of pink by the time they finished the last of their coffee.

"Shall we go?"

She nodded and stood. "Everything was wonderful. Thank you." The food *had* been marvelous—she freely admitted that—but it was this time with Jonas that had made the dinner so enjoyable. She didn't want the evening to end. For the first time since they'd begun working together, she felt at ease with him. She feared that once they arrived back at the hotel, everything would revert to the way it had been before. Jonas would immerse himself in the documents Adam was preparing for him, and everything would be business, business, business.

The maître d' was about to gesture for their waiting limousine when Stephanie placed her hand on Jonas's arm. "Would you mind if we walked a bit?"

"Not at all." He turned toward the maître d', who nodded and wished them a pleasant evening.

"I ate so much that I feel like a stuffed turkey at Thanksgiving. I'm sure a little exercise will help." She was conscious of his leg, but hoped that if it pained him, he would say something. His limp was barely noticeable as they strolled down the narrow sidewalk. "I see there's a park across the way."

"That sounds perfect."

They crossed the street and sauntered down the paved walkway that led them into the lush green lawns of a city park. Black wrought-iron fences bordered flower beds filled with bright red tulips and yellow crocuses. Row upon row of trees welcomed them, proudly displaying their buds with the promise of new life.

"I've always heard Paris in springtime couldn't be equaled," she said softly, musing that anyone happening upon them would think they were lovers. Paris in the spring was said to be a city meant for lovers. For tonight she would pretend—reality would crowd in on her soon enough.

They followed the walkway that led to the center of the park, where a tall fountain spilled water from the mouths of a ring of lions' heads.

"Shall we make a wish?" she asked, feeling happy and excited.

He snorted softly. "Why waste good money?"

"Don't be such a skeptic. It's traditional to throw a coin in a fountain, any fountain, and what better place than Paris for wishes to come true?" She opened her purse, digging for loose change. "Here, it's my treat." She handed him a dime, since she had only a few Euros with her.

"You don't honestly expect me to fall victim to such stupidity?"

"Humor me, Jonas." She noted the amusement in his blue eyes, and she ignored his tone, which sounded harsh and disapproving.

"All right." Without aim or apparent premeditation, he tossed the dime into the water with as much ceremony as if he were throwing something into the garbage.

"Good grief," she muttered beneath her breath. "I don't know of a single fairy in the entire universe who would honor such a wish."

"Why not?" he demanded.

"You obviously haven't given the matter much thought."

One corner of his mouth edged upward slightly. "I was humoring you, remember?"

"Did you even make a wish?"

He shrugged. "Not exactly."

"Well, no wonder." She shook her head dolefully and looked at him in mock disdain. "Try it again, and this time be a little more sincere."

His eyes revealed exactly what he thought of this exercise. Nonetheless, he reached inside his own pocket and took out a quarter.

Stephanie's hand stopped him. "That's too much."

"It's a big wish." This time his look was far more thoughtful as he took aim and sent the coin skipping over the surface of the water. The quarter made a small splash before sinking into the frothy depths.

She gave him a brilliant smile as she found another dime. "Okay, my turn." She turned her back to the fountain, rubbed the dime between her palms to warm it, closed her eyes and, with all the reverence due magical wish-granting fairies, flung it over her shoulder and into the fountain. "There," she said, satisfied.

"How long?" Jonas demanded.

"How long for what?"

"How long," he repeated with exasperation, "must one wait before the wish comes true?"

"It depends on what you wished for." She made it sound as though she had accumulated all the knowledge there was on the subject. "Certain wishes require a bit of manipulating by the powers that be. However, I'm only familiar with wishes made in American fountains. Things could be much different here. It could be that the wish fairies who guard this fountain work on a slower time scale than elsewhere."

"I see." It was clear from the frown that dented his brow that he didn't.

"Maybe you should just tell me what you wished for," she

suggested, "and I can give you an estimate of the approximate time you'll have to wait for it to come true."

"It's my understanding that one must never reveal one's wish."

"That's not true anymore." She laughed, enjoying the inanity of their discussion. "Science has proved that theory to be inaccurate."

"Oh?"

"Yes, I'm surprised you didn't read about it in the papers. It was all over the news."

"I must have missed that." He reached for her hand, and they resumed their walk. "But if that's the case, then perhaps you'd be willing to share *your* wish with *me*."

Color instantly flooded her cheeks. She should have known he would turn the tables on her when she least expected it.

"Stephanie?"

It was completely absurd. With everything that was in her she'd wished that Jonas would take her in his arms and kiss her. It was silly and hopeless and, as he'd pointed out earlier, a waste of good money.

When she didn't respond immediately, he stopped and turned, standing directly in front of her so that he could look into her eyes.

She felt the color rise in her face.

"I would think that a self-proclaimed expert on the subject of fountains and wishes would have no qualms about revealing her own wish, especially after sharing that latest scientific newsflash." He placed his finger under her stubborn chin, elevating her gaze so that she couldn't avoid his.

"I . . ."

"You still haven't answered my question."

"I wasted the wish on something impractical," she blurted out. The whole park seemed to have gone quiet. A moment ago wind had ruffled the foliage around them and hissed through the branches, but now even the trees seemed to have paused, as though they, too, were interested in her reply. She swallowed uncomfortably, convinced that he could read her thoughts and was silently laughing at her.

"I fear I wasted my wish, as well," he informed her softly.

"You did?" Her eyes sought his for the first time.

He placed his hands on the gentle slopes of her shoulders and bent toward her. "I'm seldom impractical."

"I . . . know."

His mouth descended an inch closer to hers, so close that she could feel his warm breath fanning her face. An inch more and their lips would touch. Stephanie moistened her lips, realizing all at once how very much she wanted to taste his mouth on hers. Her breath froze in her lungs; even her heart felt as though it had stopped beating.

"Could your wish have been as impractical as mine?" There was an unmistakable uncertainty in his voice.

She levered her hands against his chest, flattening one palm over his heart. His heartbeat was strong and even. "Yes." The lone word was breathless and weak, barely audible.

His arms went around her, anchoring her against him. Gently, he laid his cheek alongside hers, rubbing the side of his face over her soft skin as though he feared her touch, yet craved it. She closed her eyes, savoring his nearness, his warmth and the vital feel of him. A thousand objections shot through her mind, but she refused to listen to even one. This was exactly what she'd wished for, fool that she was.

Jonas turned his head and nuzzled her ear, and she noticed that his breathing was shallow. His arms tightened around her, and he whispered her name, entreating her—for what, she was afraid to guess.

It was at the back of her mind that she should break free, but something much stronger than the force of her will kept her motionless. He was her employer, she reminded herself. They argued constantly, battling with each other both in and out of the office. Jonas Lockwood was an arrogant, domineering chauvinist. But all her arguments were burned away like deadwood in a forest fire as his lips moved to her hair. He kissed the top of her head, her cheek, her ear, and then moved back to her hair. He paused, holding her to him as though it were the most natural thing in the world for them to be wrapped in each other's arms.

"Tell me, Stephanie," he asked in a hoarse whisper. "Did you wish for the same thing I did?"

Their eyes met hungrily and locked. She nodded, unable to answer him with words.

He caught her closer and lowered his mouth to hers, finally claiming her lips in a greedy kiss that left her weak and clinging. She felt herself responding as her arms slid around his neck. Their lips clung, and his tongue sought and found hers. Against her will, she arched against him, seeking to lose herself in his arms for all time.

Abruptly they broke apart, both of them moving of their own accord. She was trembling inside and out. She dared not look at Jonas. Neither of them spoke. For a moment they didn't move, didn't breathe. The world that only seconds before had been silent now burst into a cacophony of sound. Wind whistled through the trees. Car horns blared from a nearby street. An elderly couple could be heard arguing.

"Jonas, I . . ."

"Don't say anything."

She wouldn't have known what to say, anyway. She was as stunned as he was.

"It was the wine, and this silly wishing business," he said stiffly.

"Right."

"I told you wasting your money on wishes was foolish."

"Exactly," she agreed, though not very strenuously. Their wishes had come true; now they both wanted to complain.

She noticed on the way out of the park that he seemed to be keeping his distance from her. His steps were rushed. In order to keep up with him, she was forced into a half run. The instant they hit the main thoroughfare, he raised his hand and hailed the limo, which drove them directly back to the hotel.

"Well, how was Paris?" Jan asked the first day Stephanie was back at the office. They were sitting in the employee cafeteria. Jan had purchased the luncheon special, and Stephanie had brought a sandwich from home.

"Fine."

"Fine?"

"I was held captive in a stuffy room for most of the four days. This wasn't exactly a vacation, you know."

"How'd you get along with Mr. Lockwood?"

"Fine."

"Is that the only word you know?" Disgruntled, Jan tore open a small bag of potato chips and dumped them on her tray.

"I have an adequate vocabulary."

"Not today, you don't. Come on, Steph, you were with the man day and night for four days. Something must have happened."

The scene by the fountain, when Jonas had held her and kissed her, played back in Stephanie's mind in 3-D. If she were to close her eyes, she might be able to feel the pressure of his mouth on hers. She strenuously resisted the urge. "Nothing happened," she lied.

"Then why are you acting so strangely?"

"Am I?" Stephanie focused her attention on her friend, trying to look alert and intelligent, even though her thoughts were a thousand miles away in an obscure Paris park.

"Yes, very."

"What did you expect would happen?"

"I don't know, but the others thought you might have fallen in love with him."

"Oh, honestly, Jan, you're mistaking jet lag for love."

Disappointment clouded Jan's eyes. "This isn't going well."

"What isn't?"

"This romance. The girls and I had it all planned. We felt it would work out a whole lot easier than it is."

"How do you mean?"

"Well, in the books, the minute the hero and heroine are alone together for the first time, something usually happens."

"What do you mean, something happens?"

"You know, an intimate dinner for two, a shared smile, a kiss in the dark. Something!"

"We weren't exactly alone; Adam Holmes was with us." She avoided Jan's eyes as she carefully cracked a hard-boiled egg. If Jan could see her eyes, she would figure it all out. The egg took on new importance as she peeled the shell off piece by piece.

"At any rate," Jan continued, "we'd hoped that things might have taken off between you two."

"I'm sorry to disappoint you and the others, but the trip was a working arrangement, nothing else." Stephanie sprinkled salt and pepper on the egg.

"Well, I guess that's it, then."

"What do you mean?"

"If Mr. Lockwood was ever going to notice you, it would have been last week. You were constantly in each other's company, even if Adam Holmes was playing the part of legal chaperone. But if Mr. Lockwood isn't attracted to you by now, I doubt he ever will be."

"I couldn't agree more." Stephanie's heart contracted with a pang that felt strangely like disappointment. "Now can I get on with my life? I don't want to hear any more of your ridiculous romance ideas. Understand?"

"All right," Jan agreed, but she didn't look happy about it. "However, I wish you'd start reading romances. You'd understand what we're talking about and play your role a little better."

"Would you stop hounding me with those books? I'm not in the mood for romance."

"Okay, okay, but when you *are* ready, just say the word."

Stephanie took a look at her untouched egg, sighed and stuffed it in the sack to toss in the garbage, her appetite gone.

She couldn't decide how she felt about Jonas. Part of her wished the kiss had never happened. Those few minutes had made the remainder of the trip nearly intolerable. They had both taken pains to pretend nothing had happened, going out of their way to be cordial and polite, nothing less and certainly nothing more. It was as if Adam Holmes was their unexpected link with sanity. Neither Jonas nor Stephanie could do without him as they avoided any possibility of being trapped alone together. On the long flight home Jonas had worked out of his briefcase, while she and Adam played cards. For all the notice Jonas had given her, she could have been a piece of luggage. They'd separated at the airport, and she hadn't seen him since. It was just as well, she told herself. The incident at the fountain had been a moment out of time and was best forgotten.

"Steph?"

She shook her head to free her tangled thoughts. "I'm sorry, were you saying something?"

Jan gave her an odd look. "I was asking if you'd like to meet Jim's cousin, Mark. I thought we might double-date Saturday night. Dinner and a movie, maybe."

It took Stephanie a moment to remember who Jim was. "Sure, that sounds like fun." Anything was better than spending another restless weekend alone in her apartment.

"I knew Mark was interested, but I've held him off because I wanted to see how things developed between you and Mr. Lockwood."

Stephanie stared at her blankly and blinked twice, carefully measuring her words. She was saddened by the reality of what she had to say. "It isn't going to work between Jonas and me. Nothing's going to happen." The crazy part was that she was of two minds on the subject of the company president. He intrigued her. There wasn't a single man who interested her more. He was challenging, intelligent, pigheaded, stubborn and completely out of her league. Ah, well, she thought, sighing expressively, you won some and you lost some. And she'd lost Jonas without ever really having known him.

"Saturday at seven, then?"

"I'll look forward to it." She wasn't stretching the truth all that much. A date really did have to be better than staying home alone and moping.

"The three of us will pick you up at your apartment. Okay?"

"That sounds fine."

Jan groaned and laughed. "You're back to that word again."

Saturday evening, Stephanie washed and curled her hair, and spent extra time on her make-up. She dressed casually in slacks and a bulky knit sweater her mother had made for her last Christmas. The winter-wheat color reminded her of the rolling hills of grain outside her hometown.

The doorbell chimed, and she expelled her breath forcefully as she went to answer. She wasn't looking forward to this evening. All day her thoughts had drifted back to Jonas and their time in Paris, especially their stroll in the park. If she went out with anyone tonight, she wanted it to be with him. Wishful thinking, and not a fountain in sight. She wasn't especially eager to meet Jim's cousin, either. Jan had tried to build him up, but Stephanie knew from experience the pitfalls of blind dates. If she'd had her wits about her and been less concerned about revealing her attraction to Jonas, she would have declined the invitation. But it was too late now.

She needn't have worried about Mark, she quickly realized. He looked nice enough, although it came out immediately that he was newly divorced. Miserable, too, judging from the look in his eyes.

The vivacious Jan carried the conversation once the introductions were finished.

"Would anyone like some wine before we leave?" Stephanie asked. She'd set a tray with wineglasses on the coffee table, waiting for their arrival. "It's a light white wine."

"Sounds marvelous," Jan said, linking her fingers with Jim's. The two claimed the sofa and sat side by side. Mark took a chair, leaving its twin for Stephanie.

Still standing, she poured the wine. "What movie are we seeing?"

"There's a new foreign film out that sounds interesting," Jan said.

The doorbell chimed, and Stephanie got up to answer it. "I'm not expecting anyone," she said. "It's probably a neighbor looking for a cup of sugar or something."

She opened the door and stopped cold. It wasn't a neighbor who stood on the other side of her door. It was Jonas Lockwood.

Five

"Jonas!" Stephanie experienced a sense of joy so strong she nearly choked on it. Just when she'd given up any hope of seeing him again, he'd come to see her. But her joy quickly turned to regret as she heard the others talking behind her. "What are you doing here?" she whispered fiercely.

He stood stiffly on the other side of the door, his expression impossible to read. His grip on his cane tightened. "I came to see you. May I come in?"

"Yes . . . of course. I didn't mean to be rude." She stepped aside, still holding the doorknob. His timing couldn't have been worse, but she was so pleased to see him that she wouldn't have cared if he'd arrived unannounced on Christmas Eve.

"Mr. Lockwood, how nice to see you again," Jan said, tossing Stephanie a knowing look that was capable of translating entire foreign libraries.

Both Jim and Mark stood, and Stephanie made awkward introductions. "Jim, Mark, this is Mr. Lockwood."

"Jonas," he said, correcting her and offering them his hand.

"Would you care for a glass of wine?" Jan offered.

"Yes, of course," Stephanie hurried to add, her face filling with color at her lack of good manners. "Please stay and have some wine." Before he could answer, she walked into the kitchen for another glass, then came back, filled it and handed it to Jonas, who had claimed the chair next to Mark.

Resisting the urge to press her cool hands against her flaming cheeks, she took a seat on the sofa beside Jan, the three of them crowding together. The men were asking Jonas questions about the business as though it was the most interesting topic in the world. While they were occupied, Jan took the opportunity to jab Stephanie in the ribs with her elbow. "I thought you said he wasn't interested," she whispered under her breath.

"He isn't," Stephanie insisted. Glancing around, she wanted to groan with frustration. Although the small, one-bedroom apartment suited her nicely, she was intensely conscious that most of her furniture was secondhand and well-worn. She hadn't been the least bit ashamed to have Jan and her friends view her mix-and-match arrangement, but entertaining Jonas Lockwood was another matter entirely. Oh, for heaven's sake, what did she care? He hadn't stopped by to check out her china pattern.

"I can see that I've come at a bad time," Jonas said, standing. He set his glass aside, and Stephanie noted that he hadn't bothered to taste the wine.

She stood with him.

"We were about to leave for dinner," Jan explained apologetically. "But if you needed Steph for something at the office, we could change our plans."

"That won't be necessary." He shook hands with Jim and Mark again. "It was a pleasure meeting you both."

"I'll walk you to the door," Stephanie offered, locking her fingers together in front of her. He'd stopped in out of the blue, and she wasn't about to let him escape without knowing the reason for his impromptu visit.

Instead of stopping to ask him at her front door, she stepped into the hall with him. For a moment, neither spoke. She was trying to come up with a subtle way of mentioning that she'd only met Mark a few minutes earlier, that the blind date had been Jan's idea, and that she'd only accepted the offer because she didn't think that Jonas wanted to see her again. But she couldn't explain without sounding foolish.

"I apologize for not calling first," Jonas said finally.

"It . . . doesn't matter. I'm almost always home."

He cocked his brow as though he didn't quite believe her.

"It's true."

He glanced at his wristwatch. "I should be going."

"Jonas." Her hands were clenched so tightly that she was sure she'd cut off the blood supply to her fingers. "Why did you come?"

"It isn't important."

It was terribly important to her. "Is it something to do with work?"

"No."

"Then . . . why?"

"I believe there's someone in there waiting for you. It's not very polite of you to stand here with me, discussing my motives."

"What is this? Do you want to play twenty questions?"

He frowned.

"All right, you obviously want me to guess the reason you stopped by. Fine. Since that's the way you want it, let's start with the basics. Is it animal, vegetable or mineral?"

"Ms. Coulter." He closed his eyes, seemingly frustrated by her tenacity.

"I'm not going back inside until you tell me why you're here."

"This is neither the time nor the place to discuss it." His gaze hardened.

The look was one she knew all too well. "It's common courtesy to tell someone why you stopped by."

"The only manners you need concern yourself with are your own toward your friends. I suggest that you join them. We can discuss this later."

"When?" She wasn't about to let him off as easily as that.

"Monday."

She didn't want to agree, but she could hear the others talking and knew they'd long since finished their wine. "All right. Monday."

His gaze rested on her for a long moment. "It would be far better if you forgot I was ever here."

"I'm not going to do that." How could she? She hadn't been so pleased to see anyone in months.

"I didn't think you would. Enjoy yourself tonight." He said it with such sincerity that she wanted to assure him that she would, even though she knew the entire evening was a waste.

"Goodbye, Jonas."

"Goodbye." He hung the end of his cane over his forearm and turned away from her.

Stephanie watched him go, biting into her lower lip to keep from calling him back. If there had been any decent way of doing so, she would have sent Jan, Jim and Mark on their way without her. Reluctantly, she went back inside her apartment.

As she had known it would be, the evening was time misspent. Mark's conversation consisted of an account of how misunderstood he was by his ex-wife and of how terribly he missed his children. Stephanie tried to appear sympathetic, but her thoughts were centered on Jonas. They wavered between quiet jubilation and heart-wrenching disappointment. More than once she had to resist the urge to tell Mark to be quiet and go back to his wife, since it was so obvious that he still loved her. A thousand times over she wished she'd never agreed to this blind date, and she silently vowed she wouldn't do it again, no matter how close the friend who arranged it. She hoped Jan appreciated what she was going through, but somehow she doubted it.

After the movie the four of them returned to Stephanie's apartment for coffee. Jan offered to help as an excuse to talk to her alone.

"Well, what do you think?"

"Mark's nice, but he's in love with his wife."

"Not about Mark. I'm talking about Mr. Lockwood," she said. "I knew it from the first. I knew he was hooked!"

"Oh, hardly. Mr. Lockwood has no feelings for me one way or the other." Stephanie filled the basket with coffee and slipped it into place above the glass pot with unnecessary force.

"Don't give me that," Jan countered sharply. "I saw the way you two looked at each other."

"I don't even know why he came." Stephanie busied herself opening and closing cupboards, and taking down four matching cups.

"Don't be such a dope. There's only one reason he showed up. He wanted to see you again. He's interested with a capital *I*." Jan crossed her arms and leaned against the kitchen counter. "He's so into you that he can't look at you without letting it show."

"You're exaggerating again." Stephanie prayed her friend was right, but she sincerely doubted it. Jonas Lockwood wasn't the kind of man to reveal his emotions as easily as that.

"I'm not exaggerating."

"Come on," Stephanie said, refusing to argue. "The guys are waiting."

"Just do me a favor."

"What now?" Stephanie asked, desperate to change the subject. It was bad enough that Jonas had dominated her thoughts all evening. Now Jan was bringing him up, as well.

"Just think about it. Jonas Lockwood wouldn't have stopped by here for any reason other than the fact that he wanted to see you."

Jan's logic was irrefutable, but Stephanie still wasn't sure she could believe it. "All right, I'll think about it, but for heaven's sake, don't tell anyone. The last thing I need is for the rest of your Gang of Four to find out about this."

"I won't breathe a word of it." But Jan's eyes were twinkling. "I'll give you some time to think things through. You're smart. You'll figure Lockwood out." She held the door open for Stephanie, who carried the tray with the four steaming cups of coffee into the living room.

After a half hour of strained conversation, mostly about Mark's ex-wife, Jan and the men departed. Stephanie sighed as she let them out the door. It was only eleven, but she hurriedly got ready for bed. Amazingly, for all her doubts and uncertainty regarding Jonas, she slept surprisingly well.

Sunday morning Jan was at Stephanie's front door, smiling broadly and carrying a large stack of romances under one arm.

"What are those for?" Stephanie asked, letting her friend into the apartment. She was still in her house-coat, fighting off a cold with orange juice and aspirin, and feeling guilty for being so lazy.

"Not what—who."

"All right. *Who* are those for?" Stephanie's sore throat had taken a lot of the fight out of her.

"You."

"Jan, I've told you repeatedly that I'm not interested. You can't force me to read them."

"No, but I thought you might be interested in a little research." Jan paused, noticing Stephanie's appearance for the first time. "What's the matter—you look sick."

"I'm just fighting off a cold." And maybe a touch of disappointment, too.

"Great, there's no better time to sit back and read."

"Jan . . ."

Her friend held up a hand to stop her. "I refuse to hear any arguments. I want you to sit down and read. If I have to, I'll stand over you until you do."

Muttering under her breath, Stephanie complied, sitting on the sofa with her back against the armrest and bringing her feet up so she could tuck them under a blanket. Jan picked up the book on the top of the pile, silently read the back cover and nodded knowingly. "You'll like this one. The circumstances are similar to what's happening between you and Mr. Lockwood."

Stephanie bolted to her feet. "Nothing's happening between me and Mr. Lockwood."

"You called him Jonas the other day," Jan said, ignoring Stephanie's bad mood. "The funny part is, until then I'd never thought of him other than as *Mr.* Lockwood."

To the contrary, Stephanie had almost always thought of him as Jonas, but she wasn't about to add ammunition to her friend's growing arsenal.

"But I don't think we need to worry about his name."

"Thank heaven for that much," Stephanie muttered, sitting back down.

"Promise me you'll read these?"

"I would never have taken you for such an unreasonable slave driver." Stephanie fought back a flash of rebellion and shook her head. "All right, I'll read one, but I won't like it."

"And I bet you a month's pay you'll end up loving them the way the rest of us do."

"I'm reserving judgment."

Jan left soon after Stephanie opened the cover of the first book. To be honest, she was curious what the other women saw in the novels that they read with such fervor. What was even more interesting was the fact that they did more than just read the books; the whole group talked about the characters as though they were living, breathing people. Stephanie had once heard Barbara comment that she wanted to punch out a certain hero, and the others had agreed wholeheartedly, as though it were an entirely possible option.

The next time Stephanie glanced at the clock it was afternoon and she'd finished the book, astonished at how well-written it was. All along she'd assumed that romance heroines were sappy, weak-willed women without a brain in their heads. From tidbits of information she'd heard among the others, she couldn't imagine anyone putting up with some of the things the heroines in the books did. But she was wrong. The heroines in the first romance she'd read and the one she reached for next were strong women with realistic problems. Although she might not have agreed completely with the way they handled their relationships with the heroes, she appreciated why they acted the way they did. With love, she realized, came tolerance, acceptance and understanding.

First thing on Monday morning Stephanie stopped at Jan's desk. She dutifully placed three romances in Jan's Out basket, willing to admit that she had misjudged her friend's favorite reading material.

"What's that for?"

"I read them."

"And?" Jan's eyes grew round.

"I loved them, just the way you said I would."

Laughing, Jan nodded, reached for her phone and punched in Maureen's extension. "She read the first three and she's hooked." Once she'd made her announcement, she replaced the receiver and sat back, folding her hands neatly on top of the desk and sighing. "I'm waiting."

Stephanie groaned and shook her head lightly. "I knew I wasn't going to get away this easily. You want to hear it, so . . . all right, all right—you told me so."

Jan laughed again. "You look especially nice today. Any reason?"

Stephanie considered a white lie but quickly changed her mind. Like the heroines in the romances, she was a mature woman, and if she happened to be attracted to a man, it wasn't a sin to admit as much. "I'll be talking to Jonas later, and I wanted to look my best."

"You'll keep me up to date, won't you?"

Stephanie secured the strap of her purse on her shoulder. "I don't know that there'll be anything to report. Our relationship isn't like those romances."

"Maybe not yet, but it will be," Jan said with the utmost confidence.

"I'm not half as convinced as you are. Just keep this under your hat. I don't want the others to know."

"My lips are sealed."

But Stephanie wondered if Jan was capable of keeping anything a secret. Her coworker was much too friendly, and much too eager to see something develop between Stephanie and Jonas to keep the news to herself.

The day went smoothly although Stephanie was constantly on edge, expecting to hear from Jonas. Each time her phone rang she felt certain it would be him, issuing a request to join him in his office. He didn't call, and by five o'clock she felt both disappointed and frustrated. He'd said he would talk to her on Monday, and she'd taken him at his word.

Jan, Toni, Maureen and Barbara sauntered in together at quitting time. "Well? What did he say?"

Stephanie glared at Jan, who quickly lowered her eyes. "I couldn't help it," she murmured, looking miserable. "Toni guessed, and I couldn't lie."

"You didn't have any problem promising me your lips were sealed."

"She had to tell us," Maureen insisted. "It was our right. We're the ones who got you into this."

Stephanie straightened the papers on her desk. "I'm not sure I can find it in my heart to thank you. Jonas Lockwood has been a thorn in my side from the moment we met."

"Perfect," Barbara announced.

"Enough of that," Toni said. "We want to know what he had to say today."

"Nothing." Stephanie tried unsuccessfully to hide the disappointment in her voice.

"Nothing!" the others echoed.

"I haven't seen him."

"Why not?"

"Good grief, how am I supposed to know?"

Toni paused, and pressed her forefinger to her temple. "I

was thinking about what happened Saturday night, and in my opinion it wasn't necessarily such a bad thing that Jan's friend was there. It lets Mr. Lockwood know he's got competition."

"It might have been enough to scare him off, though," Barbara disagreed.

"Then he isn't worth his salt as a hero."

"Would you four stop!" Stephanie demanded, waving her arms for emphasis. She returned her attention to Jan. "Are they always like this?"

Jan shrugged. "It doesn't matter. What are you going to do?"

Stephanie had no idea. Jonas had said that he would talk to her on Monday, and there were still several hours left in the day. Maybe he intended to contact her at her apartment. No, she quickly dismissed the notion. He wouldn't be back; she'd seen it in his eyes.

"Steph?"

She looked up to notice that all four of her coworkers were studying her expectantly.

"I'm going up to his office," she said, the announcement shocking her as much as it did the others. The upper floor belonged to Jonas and was well guarded by his Martha Westheimer, who was reputed to have slain more than one persistent dragon.

Jan grinned. "Didn't I tell you she was heroine material?"

"The perfect choice," Maureen agreed.

The four of them followed Stephanie out of her office and to the elevator. Barbara pushed the button for her. Toni and Maureen stood behind her, rubbing her shoulders as though to prepare her for the coming confrontation. For a moment Stephanie felt as if she was getting ready for the heavyweight boxing championship of the world.

"Don't take any guff from Old Stone Face."

"Just remember to smile at Mr. Lockwood."

"And it wouldn't hurt to bat your lashes over those baby blues a time or two."

Armed with their advice, Stephanie entered the waiting elevator. Jan gave her the thumbs-up sign just before the heavy metal doors closed.

Now that she was alone, Stephanie felt herself losing her nerve. She sighed and leaned against the back of the elevator. The others had lent her confidence, but standing alone in the chilly, dimly lit elevator gave her cause to doubt. If there had been any way of disappearing from a moving elevator, she would have been tempted to try it.

The doors opened, and Martha Westheimer raised her eyes to frown at Stephanie's approach. A pair of glasses were delicately balanced at the end of the older woman's nose. She was near sixty, Stephanie guessed, tall and slender, with a narrow mouth. Just looking at the woman inspired fear.

"Do you have an appointment?" Martha asked stiffly, giving Stephanie a look that was not at all welcoming.

Stephanie stepped off the elevator and thrust back her shoulders, prepared for this first encounter. "Mr. Lockwood asked to see me." That was only a partial white lie.

"Your name, please?" With the eraser end of her pencil, Martha flipped through the appointment schedule.

"Stephanie Coulter."

"I don't see your name down here, Ms. Coulter."

"Then there must be some mistake."

There was challenge in Martha's dark brown eyes. "I don't make mistakes."

"Then I suggest you contact Mr. Lockwood."

"I'll do exactly that." The woman flipped on the intercom.

"There's a Ms. Coulter here to see you. She claims she has an appointment." Her tone made it clear that she was certain Stephanie had lied.

"I said," Stephanie corrected her through clenched teeth, "that Mr. Lockwood had asked to see me." The hand clenching her purse tightened. "There's a difference."

The silence on the other end of the intercom stretched out uncomfortably, and Stephanie was convinced she was about to be dismissed.

"Mr. Lockwood?"

"Send her in, Miss Westheimer."

Stephanie flashed Jonas's guardian a brilliant smile of triumph as she waltzed past her desk. The older woman had to know that Stephanie had stepped in while she was ill, yet she gave no indication that she was aware who Stephanie was, or even that she was employed by Lockwood Industries.

Stephanie let herself into Jonas's office and was instantly met by a rush of memories. She liked this room, just as she respected the man who ruled from it.

He was busy writing, his head bowed, and didn't bother to acknowledge her presence. She stood awkwardly as she waited for him to finish, not enough at ease to take a seat without being asked.

When he'd finished, Jonas put the cap on his pen and set it aside before glancing in her direction. "Yes?"

His crisp tone made her all the more uncomfortable, but she pushed on. "You said you would talk to me on Monday."

"About?"

He was making this difficult, and she drew a deep breath before continuing. "About Saturday night. You told me we'd talk."

"I don't recall committing myself to that."

"Please, don't play games with me. You stopped by my apartment on Saturday, and I want to know why."

The lines around his mouth deepened, but he wasn't smiling. "I happened to be in the neighborhood."

"But . . ."

"Leave it at that, Ms. Coulter. It was a mistake, and one best forgotten."

"But I don't think it *was* a mistake." He was closing her out; she could see it by the way he sat, his back stiff with determination. His eyes looked past her as though he wanted to avoid seeing her.

The silence was broken by Jonas. "Sometimes it's better to leave things as they are. In my opinion, this is one of those times."

Her hands trembled slightly but she stood her ground. "I disagree."

His mouth twisted in a cynical smile. "Unfortunately, you have little say in the matter. Now, if you'll excuse me, I have several reports to read over."

It was clearly meant to be a dismissal, and she wavered between stalking out of the office and trying to forget him, and staying and admitting that she was attracted to him and that she would like to know him better. But for all the attention he was giving her now, she might as well have been a stack of signed papers on his desk. Out of sight, out of mind, she mused ruefully. Her pride told her that she had better things to do than allow Jonas Lockwood to poke holes in her fragile ego.

Finally her pride won, and she gave him a small, sad smile. "You don't need to be rude, Jonas. I get the message."

"Do you?" He focused his gaze on her.

"Thank you for that wonderful night in Paris. I'll always remember that—and you—fondly."

His hard blue eyes softened. "Stephanie, listen . . ."

He was interrupted by the phone. "I'm waiting for a call," he said, almost apologetically, as he reached for the receiver.

She turned to leave, but he stopped her as he reverted to French. She could tell that he was speaking to a government official regarding his negotiations with Lockwood Industries' French counterpart, but the conversation quickly became too technical for her to understand fully.

A few minutes later Jonas hung up the telephone. His eyes revealed his excitement.

"Congratulations are in order," he said, standing. "Our trip to France was a success. Our bid has been accepted."

"Congratulations," she whispered. His happiness was contagious; it filled the enormous room, encircling them both.

He walked around the front of the large rosewood desk, his eyes sparkling. "It seemed for a while that this deal could go either way."

Stephanie noticed that his limp was less pronounced now than at any time she'd seen him walk.

"Do you know what this means?" He walked to the other side of the room, as though he couldn't contain himself any longer.

She nodded eagerly, pretending she did know, when in actuality she was ignorant of nearly all the pertinent information.

He came back over to her and locked his hands on her shoulders. "I can't believe it's falling into place after all the problems we've encountered." His arms dropped to her waist and circled her. With a burst of infectious laughter, he lifted her off the plush carpet and swung her around.

Caught completely off guard, she gasped and placed her hands on his shoulders in an effort to maintain her balance. "I'm so happy for you."

As if suddenly aware that he was holding her, he relaxed his grip. Her feet found the floor, but her hands remained on his shoulders, and her eyes smiled warmly into his.

He tensed, and the exhilaration drained from him as his gaze locked with hers. His hand slid beneath her long hair, tilting her head to receive his kiss. She had no thought of objecting. Since that night in Paris, she'd longed for him to hold and kiss her again. But she hadn't admitted how *much* she'd wanted it until now. He kissed her a second time, and his mouth was hungry and demanding. His lips moved persuasively over hers, hot and possessive. She was equally hungry and eager for him. A slow fire burned through her, and she melted against him. "Oh, Jonas," she whispered longingly.

He brushed his lips over hers again, as though he couldn't get enough of the taste of her. She opened her mouth to him, drugged by the sensations he aroused.

His mouth ravaged the scented hollow of her throat and began a slow meandering trail to her ear. He paused, took a deep breath, and waited a moment longer before releasing her. "Forgive me." He brushed the wisps of hair from her temple. "That shouldn't have happened."

She felt like a fool. She'd savored the feel of his arms, lost herself in the taste of his kiss and the rush of sensations that flooded her, and he was apologizing.

"No apology necessary," she murmured stiffly. "Just don't let it happen again."

Jonas hesitated, as though he wanted to say something more but then decided against it. He turned sharply and stalked back to his desk.

Six

"Well?" Maureen was at Stephanie's desk early the following morning. "Don't keep me in suspense. What happened?"

"Nothing much." Stephanie kept her gaze lowered, doing her best not to reveal her emotions. She'd been depressed and out of sorts from the minute she left Jonas's office.

"'Nothing much'? What does that mean?"

"It means I don't want to talk about it."

"You had an argument?" Toni joined her friend. The two of them placed their hands on the edge of Stephanie's desk and leaned forward, as if what she had to say was a matter of national importance.

"I wish," Stephanie muttered, sighing heavily. "No, we didn't argue."

"But you don't want to talk about it?"

"Very perceptive, ladies." Stephanie searched for something to do and finally settled for inserting a pencil in the sharpener. Despite the loud grinding sound, neither Toni nor Maureen budged.

"I think we need to talk to the others," Toni said.

"You'll do no such thing," Stephanie insisted, her tone determined.

"Hey, come on, Steph, we're all in this together. We want to help. At least tell us what happened," Maureen said.

It was apparent to Stephanie that she wouldn't have a minute's peace until she confessed everything to her romance-loving friends. "Meet me at ten in the cafeteria," she told them. "I'll get it over with all at once, but only if you promise never to mention Jonas Lockwood's name to me again."

Toni and Maureen exchanged meaningful glances. "This doesn't sound good."

"It's my final offer." Replaying her humiliation was going to be bad enough; she didn't want it dragged out any more than necessary.

"All right, all right," Toni muttered. "We'll be there."

After that Stephanie's morning went smoothly. Her boss, George Potter, was on a two-day business trip to Seattle, but there was enough work to keep her occupied for another week if need be.

When she arrived in the cafeteria promptly at ten she found the four women sitting at the table closest to the window, eagerly awaiting her arrival. A fifth cup of coffee was on the table in front of an empty chair.

"From that frown you're wearing, I'd say the meeting with Mr. Lockwood didn't go very well," Jan commented, barely giving Stephanie time to take a seat.

"There are no adequate words to describe it," Stephanie said by way of confirmation, reaching for the coffee. "I'm sorry to be such a major disappointment to you all, but anything that might have happened between me and Jonas Lockwood is off."

"Why?"

"What happened?"

"I could have sworn he was hooked."

"To be honest," Stephanie said, striving to be as forthright as possible, "I think he may be attracted to me, but we're too different."

"That's what makes you so good together," Barbara countered.

"And I saw the way he looked at her," Jan inserted thoughtfully. "Now tell us what happened and let *us* figure out the next step."

Stephanie swallowed and shrugged. "If you must know, he kissed me."

"And you're complaining?"

"No, *he* was!"

"What?" All four of them looked at her as if she'd been working too much overtime.

"He kissed me, then immediately acted like he'd committed some terrible faux pas. The way he was looking at me, anyone seeing us would have assumed that *I'd* kissed *him* and he didn't like it in the least. He was angry and unreasonable, and worse, he insulted me with an apology."

"What did you say?"

"I told him never to let it happen again."

A chorus of moans and groans followed.

"You didn't!" Jan cried. "That was the worst thing you could have said."

"Well, it was his own fault," Stephanie flared. She'd been furious with him *and* with herself. She'd enjoyed his kisses—in fact, she'd wanted him to continue.

"Did you like it—the kiss, I mean?" Toni looked at her hopefully.

Stephanie pretended to find her black coffee enthralling. "Yes."

"How do you feel about Mr. Lockwood?"

"I . . . I don't know anymore."

"But if he'd asked you to dinner, you would have accepted?"

"Probably." She remembered the exhilaration in his eyes when he'd found out his bid had been accepted. He'd worked so hard, and given so much of himself to the business, that she'd experienced a sense of elation just watching him. She'd been happy for him and pleased to have played a small part in his triumph.

"Then you can't give up."

"It was Jonas who did that," Stephanie said sharply.

"But he hasn't. Don't you see?" Toni asked, and the others nodded in agreement.

Stephanie glanced around the table, thinking her coworkers must be kidding. "No. Not at all."

"She hasn't read enough romances yet," Jan said, defending her friend. "She doesn't understand."

"Mr. Lockwood is definitely attracted to you," Barbara claimed with all the seriousness of a clinical psychologist. "Otherwise he wouldn't have reacted to kissing you the way you described."

"I'd hate to see how he'd react if he *didn't* like me," Stephanie said sarcastically. "I'm sorry, but this is getting just too complicated to understand. I'll admit to being disappointed—he's not so bad once you get to know him. In fact, I might even have enjoyed the chance to fall in love with him." She admitted this at the expense of her own pride.

"It's hardly over yet," Maureen told her emphatically.

"Whose move is next?" Jan asked, looking around the table, seeking an answer from her peers.

"Mr. Lockwood's," Toni and Maureen said together, nodding in unison. "Definitely."

"Then I'm afraid we've got a long wait coming," Stephanie informed them, finishing her coffee. "A very long wait."

"We'll see."

That same afternoon Stephanie was on the computer at her desk when Jonas entered her office. He leaned heavily on his cane, waiting for her to notice him before he spoke.

She was aware of him the second he entered, but she finished the line she was typing before she turned her attention to him. Ignoring her pounding heart, she met his gaze squarely, refusing to give him the satisfaction of knowing the effect he had on her.

"Good afternoon, Mr. Lockwood," she said crisply. "Is there something I can do for you?"

"Miss Coulter." He paused and looked into Mr. Potter's office. "Is your boss available?"

Jonas had to know that he wasn't.

"Mr. Potter's in Seattle."

"Fine. Take a letter." He pulled up a chair and sat beside her desk.

She reached automatically for her steno pad, then paused. "Is Miss Westheimer ill again?"

"She was healthy the last time I looked."

"Then perhaps it would be better if she took your dictation." She raised her chin to a defiant angle, thinking as she did that her behavior would upset her friends. But she didn't care. She wouldn't let Jonas Lockwood boss her around, even at the cost of a good job. Her hold on the pencil was so tight that it was a miracle it didn't snap in half.

"Address the letter to Miss Stephanie Coulter."

"Me?"

"Dear Ms. Coulter," he continued, ignoring her. "In thinking over the events of last evening, I am of the opinion that I owe you an apology."

As fast as her fingers could move the pencil, Stephanie transcribed his words. Not until her brain had assimilated the message did she pause. "I believe you already expressed your deep regret," she said stiffly. "You needn't have worried. I didn't take the kiss seriously."

"It was an impulse."

"Right." She felt her anger flare. "And, as you say, best forgotten." But she couldn't forget it, even though she wanted to banish it to the farthest reaches of her mind. He'd held her and kissed on two different occasions, and each time was engraved indelibly on her memory. She wondered if she would ever be the same again.

He scowled. "You're an attractive woman."

"I suppose I should thank you, but somehow that didn't sound like a compliment."

His frown deepened. "You could have any man you want."

She gave a self-deprecating laugh. "You clearly have an exaggerated opinion of my charms, Mr. Lockwood."

"I don't blame you for being offended that someone like me would kiss you."

"I wasn't offended." She was incensed that he'd even suggested such a thing. "If you want the truth, which you obviously do, I happened to find the whole experience rather pleasant."

"In Paris?"

"It was exactly what I wished for, and you know it." Even as she said it, she knew how true it was. Since leaving his office the night before, she'd been in a blue funk, cranky and unreasonable, and all because of him. As much as she'd disliked him those few days she'd spent filling in for Martha Westheimer, she admitted to liking him now. What she couldn't understand was why everything had changed. For days, angry sparks had flown every time they were in the same room. Sparks were still apparent, but now they set off an entirely different kind of response.

"What about my limp?"

"What about it?" Deliberately, she set the pencil aside.

"Does it trouble you?"

She noticed the way his hand had tightened around the handle of his cane. His knuckles were stark white, and some of her outrage dissipated. "Of course not. Why should it?"

"Some women would be repelled." He wouldn't look at her; his gaze rested on the filing cabinet on the opposite wall. "I want neither your sympathy nor your pity."

"That works out well, since you don't have either one." Her voice was crisp with impatience. She hated to believe that he had such a low opinion of her motives, but he gave her no choice but to think that.

"You could have your pick of any man in this company."

"Listen," she countered, her patience having long since evaporated. "It isn't like I've got a tribe of men seeking my company, and even if I did, what would it matter?"

"You're attractive, bright and witty."

"Such high praise. I don't know how I should deal with it, especially when it comes from you."

Jonas was still studying the filing cabinet. "I can see that our little talk has helped clear away some misconceptions," he said.

"I certainly hope so."

"Have a good day, Ms. Coulter."

"You, too, Mr. Lockwood."

Jonas had been gone for five minutes before Stephanie fully

accepted the fact that he'd actually been in her office. It took her another ten minutes to react. Her fingers were poised over the computer keyboard, ready to resume her task, when she realized she was shaking. She closed her eyes and savored the warm feelings that washed over her in waves. Then she felt chilled; nerves skirted up and down her spine. Jan and the others had been right about him. He was attracted to her, although he wore that stiff, businesslike facade like a heavy coat, not trusting her or the attraction they shared. He didn't have faith in her feelings for him, but she hoped that eventually he would realize they were genuine.

Unable to contain her excitement, she reached for her phone and dialed Jan's extension.

"Human Resources," Jan said when she answered.

"He was here."

"Who?"

"Guess," Stephanie said, laughing excitedly. "You were right. It was his move, and he made it."

"Mr. Lockwood?"

"Who else do you think I'm talking about?"

"I'll be right there."

Jan arrived a minute later, followed by Barbara, Toni and Maureen. "What did I tell you?" Jan said excitedly, slapping Barbara's open hand with her own.

"There isn't time for you to read more romances," Toni murmured, looking worried.

"The only thing she can do now is follow her instincts," Maureen said brightly. "He's interested. She's interested. Everything will follow its natural course."

"What do you mean 'natural course'?" Stephanie asked, concerned. This was beginning to sound a lot like kidney stones.

"Marriage." They said the word in unison, and looked at her as though her elevator didn't go all the way to the top floor. "It's what we're all after."

"Marriage?" Stephanie repeated slowly. Everything was happening too fast for her to take in.

"You like him, right?" Toni challenged.

"Hey, wait a minute, you guys. Sure, I like Jonas Lockwood, but liking is a long way from love and marriage."

"You're perfect together." Maureen sounded incredulous that Stephanie could question her fate. The four romance-lovers had everything arranged, and her resistance obviously wasn't appreciated.

"Perfect together? Jonas and me?" Stephanie frowned. The two of them did more arguing than anything. They were barely beginning to come to an understanding.

"You have to plan your strategy carefully."

"My strategy?"

"Right." Barbara nodded.

"You'll need to make him believe that love and marriage are all his idea."

"Don't you think we could start by holding hands?"

"Very funny," Jan said, placing her fist on her hip.

"I feel it's more important to let this relationship take its own time." Stephanie looked up at the four women who were standing around her desk, arms crossed, staring disapprovingly down at her. "That is, if there's going to *be* a relationship."

Together, they all shook their heads. "Wrong."

"So tell us, what are you planning next?" Jan asked.

"Me?" Stephanie held her hand to her breast. "I'm not planning anything. Should I be?"

"Of course. Mr. Lockwood made his move, now it's your turn."

This romance business sounded a lot like playing chess, or perhaps tennis. "I . . . hadn't given it any thought."

"Well, don't worry, we'll figure out something. Are you doing anything after work?" Jan asked.

"Depositing my check and picking up the bookcase I've had on layaway."

"Well, for heaven's sake, what's more important?" Jan gave her an incredulous look.

"You want the truth?" Stephanie glanced around at her friends. It didn't matter if she was with them or not; they were going to plot her life to their own satisfaction. "I'm going with the bookcase. If you four come up with something brilliant, phone me."

Several pieces of polished wood lay across Stephanie's carpet, along with a bowl full of screws. The screwdriver was clenched between her teeth as she struggled with the instructions, turning them one way and then another. The phone rang, and she absently reached for it, forgetting about the screwdriver.

"Hebbloo."

"Stephanie?"

"Jonas?" Her heartbeat instantly quickened as she grabbed the screwdriver from between her lips. For one crazy second she actually wanted to tell him he couldn't contact her—it was her move!

"I hope this isn't a bad time."

"No . . . no, of course it isn't. I wasn't doing anything." She stared at the disembodied pieces of the bookcase scattered across her carpet and added, "Important."

"I know it's short notice, but I was wondering if you were free to join me for dinner."

"Dinner?" She knew she sounded amazingly like an echo. She quickly toyed with the idea of contacting Jan before she agreed to do anything with Jonas, then just as quickly rejected that thought. Her coworkers were making her paranoid.

"If you have company or . . ."

"No, I'm alone." She picked up the instructions for assembling the bookcase and sighed. "Jonas, do you speak Danish?"

"Pardon?"

"How about Swedish?"

"No. Why?"

At that point she was so frustrated she wanted to cry. "It's not important."

"About dinner?"

"Yes, I'd love to go." Never mind that she had a pot roast in the oven, with small potatoes and fresh peas in the sink ready to be boiled.

"I'll pick you up in a few minutes, then."

"Great." She glanced down at her faded jeans, ten-year-old sweatshirt and purple Reeboks, and groaned. She picked up the receiver to phone Jan, decided she didn't have enough time and hurried into her room. The sweatshirt came off first and was flung to the farthest corner of her small bedroom. She found a soft pink silk blouse hanging in her closet and quickly slipped it on. Her fingers shook as she rushed to work the small pearl buttons.

She had the jeans down around her thighs when the doorbell chimed. She closed her eyes and prayed that it wasn't Jonas. It couldn't be! He'd only phoned a couple of minutes ago. She jumped, hauling her jeans back up to her waist, and ran to the door, yanking it open.

"Listen, I'm sorry if I sound rude, but I don't have the time to buy anything right now—" She stopped abruptly, wishing the earth would open up and swallow her. Her breath caught in her throat, and she closed her eyes momentarily. "Hello, Jonas."

"Did you know your pants are unzipped?"

She whirled around, sucked in her stomach and pulled up the zipper. "I didn't expect you so soon."

"Obviously. I called on my cell from across the street."

"Please come in. I'll only be a few minutes." If he so much as snickered, she swore, she would find a way to take revenge. Some form of justice fitting the crime, like a pot roast dumped over his head.

He glanced around at the pieces of wood strewn across her carpet. "You're building something?"

"A bookcase." She'd hoped to have that cleaned up before he arrived, but that had been her second concern. She'd wanted to be dressed first. He gave a soft cough that sounded suspiciously like a smothered laugh.

"Did you say something?" Her hands knotted at her sides, and she eyed the oven where the pot roast was cooking.

"I don't believe I've ever seen you flustered before." His look was amused, and his voice soft and gruff at the same time. "Not Stephanie Coulter, the woman who defies and challenges me at every turn."

"Try answering the door with your underwear showing. It has a humbling effect."

He chuckled, and the sound had a musical quality to it. Despite her embarrassment, she laughed, too, feeling completely at ease with him for the first time since Paris. "I'll only be a few minutes."

"Take your time."

She was halfway to her bedroom when she stopped, realizing that she'd forgotten her manners in her eagerness to escape. "Would you like something to drink while you wait?"

"No, thanks." He picked up the assembly instructions for the bookcase, which were on the end table by the phone. "Danish?" he asked, cocking both brows.

"I guess. It may be Swedish or Greek. I can't tell."

His gaze scanned the pieces on the floor. "Would you like a little help?"

"I'd like a lot of help." A wry smile curved her mouth. She'd spent the better part of two hours attempting to make sense of the diagrams and the foreign instructions.

"Do I detect a note of resignation in your voice, Ms. Coulter?"

"That's not resignation, it's out-and-out frustration, disillusionment, and more than a touch of anger."

"I'll see what I can do."

She started to leave, but when she saw him take off his suit jacket and reach for one long piece of shelving to join it to another, she paused. "That won't work." Soon she was kneeling on the floor opposite him. She began to feel like a nurse assisting a brain surgeon, handing him one part after another. In frustration, he paused to study the diagram, turning it upside down and around, just as she had done, but he still couldn't figure out which pieces linked together, either.

"Wait," Jonas said, shaking his head. "We've been doing this all wrong."

Stephanie, kneeling close to his side, groaned, then mumbled under her breath, "The man's a genius."

"If I was such a whiz, these bookcases would have books in them by now," he grumbled, his brow knit in a thoughtful frown. "Give me the screwdriver, would you?"

"Sure." She handed it to him.

He turned to thank her. Their eyes met, and they stared at each other for an endless moment. She blinked and looked away first. Never before had she been so aware of Jonas as a man. He looked different than any time she'd seen him in the office. Younger. Less worried. Almost boyishly handsome. He made no move to touch her, yet she felt a myriad of sensations shoot through her as though he had. He was so close that she could smell the spicy scent of his aftershave and feel the warmth of his hard, lean body chasing away the chill of her insecurities. She could feel his breath against her hair, and she welcomed it, swaying toward him.

She didn't know who moved first. It didn't matter. Before she was aware of anything, they were on their knees with their arms wrapped around each other. She closed her eyes and let the warm sensation of his touch thread through her limbs. His hands gripped her upper arms as he moved his mouth to hers. His kiss was tentative, exploring, as though he expected her to stop him. She couldn't. She'd been wanting him to hold and kiss her again from the moment he'd last released her and then apologized. His lips were warm as they covered hers. The tip of his tongue traced her lips, and she eagerly opened her mouth to his exploration.

Stephanie's fingers moved from his hard chest, and she slid her arms up and around his neck, flattening her torso to his. His hands were splayed across her back, drawing her as close as humanly possible. His kiss grew greedy, hungry and demanding.

She reveled in the feel of the hard muscles of his shoulders and the softness of the thick hair at the base of his neck. A delicious languor spread through her.

Jonas buried his face in the hollow of her throat and shuddered. "Stephanie?"

"Hmm." She felt warm and wonderful.

"I don't know what it is, but something smells like it's burning."

Her eyes flew open. She let out a small cry of alarm and jumped to her feet.

Seven

"Oh, Jonas, the roast!" She grabbed two pot holders and pulled open the oven to retrieve the pot roast. Black smoke filled the small kitchen, and Stephanie waved her hand to clear the air. "So much for that," she said, heaving an exasperated sigh.

"What is it?" He joined her, examining the charred piece of meat.

"What does it look like?" she said hotly, then stared at the crisp roast and slowly shook her head. "If you have any kindness left in your heart, you won't answer that."

Chuckling, he slipped his arm around her shoulders. "There are worse disasters."

"I imagine you're referring to an unassembled bookcase with instructions in a foreign language."

Amusement glinted in his blue eyes at the belligerent way her mouth thinned.

She couldn't help pouting. She was furious with herself for ruining a perfectly good piece of meat, and what was even worse was having to face the disgrace in front of Jonas.

"Come on," he prompted. "There's a fabulous Chinese restaurant near here. The kitchen can air out while we're gone, and when we get back, I'll finish putting that bookcase together."

"All right," she agreed, and her mouth curved into a weak smile. He was right. The best thing she could do was to draw his attention away from her lack of culinary skill. If he continued to see her, at least she would know for certain that it wasn't her talent in the kitchen that had attracted him.

It was not until she had buckled the seat belt in Jonas's Mercedes that she realized she was still wearing her faded jeans and tennis shoes. "This restaurant isn't fancy, is it?" She placed her hand over the knee that showed white through the threadbare blue jeans.

His gaze followed hers. "Poor Stephanie." He chuckled. "You're having quite a night, aren't you?"

She folded her hands in her lap and crossed her legs. "It's an average night." Better than most. Worse than some. It wasn't every day that Jonas Lockwood took her in his arms and kissed her until her world spun out of its orbit. Just thinking about the way he'd held her produced a warm glow inside her until she was certain she must radiate with it.

"You do enjoy Chinese food?"

"Oh, yes."

"By the way, do you often wear purple tennis shoes?"

She glanced down at her feet and experienced a minor twinge of regret. "I bought them on sale—they were half price."

Jonas chuckled. "I think it was the color."

"I usually only wear them around the apartment," she said, only a little offended. "They work fine for *The Twenty-Minute Workout.*"

"The what?"

"*The Twenty-Minute Workout.* It's on every morning at six. Don't you ever watch it?" She wasn't sure the neighbor in the apartment below appreciated her jumping around the living room at such an ungodly hour, but Mrs. Humphrey had never complained.

"I take it you're referring to a televised exercise program."

"Yes. Have you heard of it?"

"No, I prefer my club."

"Oh, the joys of being rich." She said it with a sigh of feigned envy.

"Are you complaining about your salary?"

"Would it do any good?"

"No."

"That's what I thought." Her gaze slid to him, and again she marveled at the man at her side. The top buttons of his starched white shirt were unfastened, exposing bronze skin and dark curly hair. The long sleeves were rolled up, a sign of the eagerness with which he'd helped her with the bookcase. He stopped at a red light and seemed to feel her watching him. His gaze met hers, and she noted the fine lines that feathered out from the corners of his eyes. The grooves at the side of his mouth, which she had so often thought of as harsh, softened now as he smiled. Jonas Lockwood was a different man when he grinned. It transformed his entire face.

Stephanie was astonished how much his smile could affect her. Her pulse slowed, then started up again, sending the blood pulsing hotly through her veins. If given the least bit of encouragement, she would have impulsively eliminated the small space that separated them and pressed her mouth to his, revealing with a kiss how much being with him had stirred her heart.

She reluctantly dragged her gaze from his and glanced down at her hands folded neatly in her lap. In that instant, as brief as it was, she'd recognized the truth. She was falling in love with Jonas Lockwood, and she was falling hard. Up to this point in their non-relationship, she had considered him an intriguing challenge. Jan, Maureen and the others had piqued her interest in their domineering, arrogant employer. The trip to Paris, and their time at the fountain in the park, had added to her curiosity. She'd glimpsed the man buried deep beneath the gruff exterior and had been enthralled. Now she was caught, hook, line and sinker.

Long after they'd returned from dinner and the finished bookcase stood in the corner of her living room, Stephanie recalled the look they'd exchanged in the car on the way to the restaurant. Briefly she wondered if Jonas had recognized it for what it was. Certainly the evening had been altered because of that glance. Before that they had been teasing each other and joking, but from the moment they entered the restaurant, they had immersed themselves in serious conversation. He'd wanted to know everything about her. And she had talked for hours. She told him about growing up in Colville, and what living in the country had meant to a gawky young girl. When he asked how she happened to move to Minneapolis, she explained that her godparents lived nearby, and had encouraged her to move to the area. There were other relatives close by, as well, and clinching the deal was the fact that there were precious few job positions in the eastern part of Washington State.

It wasn't until their plates were cleared away and the waiter delivered two fortune cookies that she realized that while she'd been telling him her life story, he had revealed very little about himself. She felt guilty about dominating the conversation, but when she mentioned it, he brushed her concern aside, telling her there was plenty of time for her to get to know him better. For hours afterward she was on a natural high, exhilarated and happy. She enjoyed talking to him, and for the first time since Paris, they'd been at ease with each other.

When Stephanie arrived at work the following morning, there was a message on her desk from Jan. The note asked Stephanie to join her and the others in the cafeteria on their coffee break. All morning she toyed with the idea of telling her friends about the evening she'd spent with Jonas, but she finally decided against it. The night had been so special that she wanted to wrap the feelings around herself and keep them private.

At midmorning she found the four women gathered around the same table by the window that they'd occupied earlier in the week. Again her coffee was waiting for her.

"Morning."

"You're late," Jan scolded, glancing at her watch. "We've got a lot of ground to cover."

"We do?" Stephanie glanced around the table at her friends and wondered if the Geneva peace talks had held more somber, serious faces.

"It's your move with Mr. Lockwood," Maureen explained. "And we've been up half the night discussing the best way for you to approach him."

"I see." Stephanie took a sip of her coffee to hide an amused grin.

"Subtlety is the key," Barbara insisted. "It's imperative that he doesn't know that you've planned this next *chance* meeting."

"Would it be so wrong to let him know I'm interested?" Stephanie let her gaze fall to the table so that her friends couldn't read her expression.

"That comes later," Toni told her. "This next step is the all-important one."

"I see." Stephanie didn't, but she doubted that her lack of understanding concerned her friends. "So what's my next move?"

"That's the problem—we can't decide," Jan explained. "We seem to be at a standstill."

"It's a toss-up between four different ideas."

One from each romantic, Stephanie reasoned.

"I thought you could wait until Old Stone Face has left her guard post for the day and then make up an excuse to go to his office. Any excuse would do—for that matter, I could give you one," Jan said eagerly. "You'd be on his turf, where he's most comfortable. Of course, you'd need to find a way to get close to him. You know, bend over the desk so your heads meet and your fingers accidentally brush against his. From there, everything will work out great."

"I don't like that idea," Maureen muttered, slowly shaking her head. "It's too obvious. Besides, Mr. Lockwood's too intelligent not to see through that ploy."

"George Potter is always taking one thing or another up to Jonas's office. I could volunteer to do it for him. I'm sure he wouldn't mind," Stephanie said, defending Jan's idea.

"Yes, but from everything I've read, it would be better if you force his hand."

"Force his hand? What do you mean?" Stephanie glanced at Maureen.

"Let him see you with another man."

"But that's already happened, with disastrous results," Jan argued. "Besides, where are we going to come up with another man?"

"My husband's brother is available."

"Ladies, please," Stephanie said, raising both hands to squelch that plan. "I've got to agree with any scheme you come up with, and that one is most definitely a *no.*"

"Sympathy always works," Barbara said thoughtfully. "I've read lots of romances where the turning point in the relationship comes when either the hero or the heroine gets sick or is seriously hurt."

For a moment Stephanie actually believed her friends were about to suggest she came down with the mumps or chicken pox just so she could garner Jonas's sympathy.

"I've got a cousin who works for an orthopedic surgeon. He could put a cast on Stephanie's leg so Mr. Lockwood would think she had broken it." Again Barbara glanced around the table, gauging the others' reactions.

Stephanie could just see herself hobbling to and from work for weeks in a plaster cast up to her hip while she carried out a ridiculous charade. After all, she couldn't very well arrive one day later without the cast and announce to everyone that a miracle had occurred.

"No go." She nixed that plan before anyone else could endorse it and she ended up in a body cast without ever knowing how it happened. "What's wrong with me inviting him over to my apartment for dinner?"

"It's so obvious," Barbara groaned.

"And the rest of your ideas aren't?"

"Actually, something like that just might work," Jan said thoughtfully, chewing on the nail of her index finger. "It's not brilliant, but it has possibilities."

"There's only one problem," Stephanie informed her friends, remembering the charred pot roast from the night before. "I'm not much of a cook."

"That's not a problem. You could hire a chef to come in. Mr. Lockwood would never have to know."

"Isn't that a bit expensive?" Stephanie could visualize the balance in her checkbook rapidly reaching the point of no return.

"It's worth a try." Barbara rapidly discounted Stephanie's concern.

"What was your idea, Toni?" Everyone had revealed their schemes except the small brunette.

Toni shrugged. "Nothing great—I thought you might 'accidentally on purpose' meet Mr. Lockwood by the elevator sometime. You could strike up a casual conversation and let matters follow their natural course."

"But Steph could end up spending the entire day hanging around the elevator," Barbara said, her voice raised at what she considered an unreasonable plan.

"Not only that," Jan added, "but who's to say that the elevator will be empty? She'd look ridiculous if there were other people aboard."

Stephanie's gaze flew from one intent face to the other. "Actually, I like that idea best."

"What?" Three pairs of shocked eyes shot to Stephanie.

"Well, for heaven's sake! With the rest of your ideas, I'm either going to have to subject myself to Martha Westheimer's scrutiny, date Barbara's brother-in-law, sheath my body in plaster or deplete my checking account to hire a chef to cook for me. Toni's idea is the only one that makes any sense."

"But *you* suggested inviting him to dinner," Jan informed her.

Maureen folded her hands on the table top and studied Stephanie through narrowed eyes. "You know, it suddenly dawned on me that you're not fighting us anymore, Steph."

"No," she said and reached for her coffee, curving her fingers around the cup. She took a drink and when she set it back down, she noted that the others had all fallen silent.

"In fact, if you've noticed, she's even contributing her own ideas." Jan's look was approving.

"Could it be that you've developed feelings for Mr. Lockwood?" Barbara asked.

"It could be that I find the man a challenge."

"It's more than that," Toni said, pointing a finger at Stephanie. "I noticed when you first joined us this morning that there was something different about you."

So it shows, Stephanie mused to herself, a bit irritated.

"What do you feel for Mr. Lockwood?"

"I'm not completely sure yet," she admitted honestly. "He makes me so angry I could shake him."

"But . . ."

"But then, at other times, he looks at me and we share a smile, and I want to melt on the inside." Stephanie knew her eyes must have revealed her feelings, because the others grew quiet again.

"Could you see yourself married to him?" Maureen asked.

Stephanie didn't need to think twice about that. "Yes." They would argue and disagree and challenge each other—that was a given—but the loving between them would be exquisite.

The unexpected shout of joy that followed her announcement nearly knocked her out of her chair. "Good grief, be quiet," she said, her hand over her heart. "We're a long way from the altar."

"Not nearly as far as you think, honey," Barbara said with a wide, knowing grin. "Not nearly as far as you think."

Stephanie left the cafeteria a couple of minutes later. In spite of everything, she had to struggle not to laugh. Her four romance-minded friends seemed to believe that a couple of dinners—one of which they knew nothing about—and a few stolen kisses in the moonlight practically constituted a proposal of marriage.

When she got back to her desk Stephanie placed her purse in the bottom drawer, sat down and turned on her computer, preparing to type a letter. She paused, her hands poised over the keyboard, trying to analyze her feelings for Jonas. The words on the screen blurred as she remembered his kisses. From the way he'd looked, he'd been as surprised as she was. The minute they'd met, she had disliked the man. He was so dictatorial and high-handed that he infuriated her. He enjoyed baiting her and challenging her. In some ways, Jonas Lockwood was the most difficult man she'd ever known. But at the same time, she suspected that the rewards of his love would be beyond any worldly treasure she could ever hope to accumulate.

At five that evening Stephanie cleared off the top of her desk, preparing to head home to her apartment. It had been so late by the time Jonas finished assembling the bookcase that she hadn't had the energy to fill it with the books that were propped against her bedroom wall. She'd learned as the evening progressed that he was an avid reader, and they'd had a lively discussion on their favorite authors. When he'd left her apartment, it had been close to midnight. She'd thanked him for dinner and his help, and had been mildly disappointed that he hadn't kissed her good-night. Nor did he arrange for another meeting. At the time she had been in such a happy daze that she hadn't thought too much about it. Now she wondered how long it would be before she saw him again. She was a bit discouraged not to have heard from him yet. All day she'd been half expecting him to pop in unannounced and dictate another letter to her. The entire afternoon had felt strangely incomplete, and she realized that she'd been wanting to hear from him since the minute she arrived that morning.

On her way to the elevator, she spotted him talking to Donald Black, head of the accounting department. Her pulse quickened at the virile sight Jonas presented. He was tall and broad-shouldered, and—she freely admitted it—a handsome devil. Her heart swelled at the sight of him, and when his gaze happened to catch hers, she smiled warmly, revealing all the pleasure she felt at seeing him again.

Jonas didn't respond. If anything, he almost looked right through her, as if she were nothing more than a piece of furniture. If any emotion showed on his taut features, it was regret. She swallowed, feeling as if she had a pine cone lodged in her throat.

When he did happen to glance in her direction, she read the warning in his eyes. What happened outside the office was between them, but inside Lockwood Industries she was nothing more than George Potter's executive assistant, and she would do well to remember that.

Humiliated and insulted, she stiffened and looked past him as though he were a stranger, pretending she had neither the time nor the energy to play his infantile games. She thrust her shoulders back in a display of anger and pride, and held them so stiffly that her shoulder blades ached within seconds.

From the minute he had left her the night before, she had been happy and content. Now her spirits plummeted to the bottom floor at breakneck speed and landed with a sickening thud. She turned her gaze to the front of the elevator and refused to look at him another moment.

She heard the two men walking behind her, but she ignored them both.

"Good evening, Miss Coulter," Jonas said in passing.

"Good evening," she responded tightly, her tone professional and crisp.

The elevator arrived, and without another word, Stephanie joined the others in the five o'clock rush. Five minutes later she caught Metro bus #17, which dropped her off a block from her apartment.

Affronted by his attitude, chagrined at how much she had read into the simple evening they'd shared, and upset that she'd allowed Jan and her friends to talk her into believing Jonas

Lockwood had a heart, Stephanie quickly changed clothes and decided to weed her miniature herb garden.

She hadn't been at it more than thirty minutes when the doorbell chimed. Glaring at her front door, she continued pulling up the weeds in the small redwood planters, then stared down at her garden gloves and realized she'd uprooted more basil than weeds.

She didn't need to answer the door to know it was Jonas who stood on the other side. When the doorbell rang sharply a second time, she impatiently set her trowel aside and stood up.

She muttered under her breath as she marched across the living room floor, and swore that if he commented on her purple tennis shoes one more time she would slam the door in his face. She jerked off a dirt-covered glove and pulled open the door.

"Hello, Stephanie."

"Mr. Lockwood," she responded tautly. "What an unpleasant surprise."

"May I come in?"

"No." She avoided his eyes. It took all her willpower not to close the door and be done with him. But she'd decided to play out this little charade. She might not come from a rich, powerful family like his, but she didn't lack pride. "As you can see, I'm busy," she finished.

"This will only take a minute."

"I'm surprised you're lowering yourself to come here," she said waspishly. "Your message this afternoon came through crystal clear."

"I'd like to explain that." Disregarding her unfriendly welcome and her unwillingness to allow him into her apartment, he stalked past her and into the living room.

"It seems I have no say in the matter. All right, since you're so keen to explain yourself, do so and then kindly leave."

"I honestly *would* like to explain—"

"Go ahead," she said. "But let me assure you, it isn't necessary."

Jonas leaned heavily on his cane as he walked to the center of the room. Stephanie stubbornly remained at the front door. She'd closed it but stood ready to yank it open the minute he finished.

He turned to face her and placed both hands on the curve of the polished oak cane, using it for support.

When long moments passed without him saying anything, she spoke into the heavy silence. "I realize the name Coulter may not cause a banker's heart to flutter, but it's a good name. My father's proud of it, and so am I."

"Stephanie, you misunderstood my intentions."

"I sincerely doubt that." Her voice trembled with the strength of her emotion. "I understood you perfectly."

His eyes were blue and probing as they swept her tightly controlled features. She wondered if a splattering of mud was smeared across her cheek but wouldn't give him the satisfaction of running her fingers over her face to find out. No doubt he would view that as a sign of weakness. She *was* weak, she realized, but only when he held her and kissed her, and she wouldn't allow that now.

"It wouldn't matter to me if your name was Getty or Buffet, or Gates, for that matter. Don't you understand that?"

"Obviously not," she returned stiffly. "You put me in my place this evening—and you did a good job of it, I might add. I'm a lowly assistant, and you're the big, mighty boss, and I shouldn't confuse the two. Since I'm not the mature woman you prefer, I would do well to bow low whenever your shadow passes near me. Isn't that what you meant to say?"

"No. I should have known you'd be unreasonable."

"Me? Unreasonable? That's a laugh. I've worked for Mr. Potter for nearly two years, and we've never exchanged a cross word. Two seconds in your company and I'm so angry I can hardly think."

"Would you stop with this lowly assistant bit? I wouldn't care if you were the first vice president," he said. "Anything that's between you and me has to stay out of the office!"

"Of course it does," she simpered. "It would do your reputation considerable harm if anyone knew you'd lowered yourself to actually date an employee."

"It's not me I'm thinking about."

"You could have fooled me."

"Stephanie, if you'd get off your high horse a minute, you'd see that it's good business. The fact is, I shouldn't even be seeing you now. I'm supposed to be at a meeting."

She jerked open the door. "Don't let me stop you." She recognized the flash of anger in his eyes and experienced a small sense of triumph.

He ran a hand over his face, wiping his expression clean as he fought for control of his considerable temper. "Don't you understand that I'm doing this for your own protection?"

"Forgive me for being dense, but quite frankly, I don't."

He continued as though she hadn't spoken. "Some no-good busybody is going to drag your name through the mud the minute they learn we're seeing each other. The next thing either of us knows, you'll be the subject of jealous, malicious gossip. You won't be able to walk into a room without people whispering your name."

Stephanie swallowed convulsively. "I hadn't thought of . . . that." Her friends were supportive, but they were only a tiny fraction of the staff at Lockwood Industries.

"A thousand times I told myself that seeing you would only

lead to trouble." A dark, brooding look clouded his eyes. "Even now, I'm not convinced it's right for either of us."

She had to swallow down the words to argue with him, because being with him felt incredibly right to her.

"If you're seeking my apology for what happened earlier," he said in a gruff, low-pitched voice, "then you have it. It has never been my intention to offend you."

She swallowed tightly, and nodded, embarrassed. "*I* owe *you* an apology, as well." With her hands clasped in front of her, she took a step toward him. "You're right about the office, Jonas, only I was too much of an idiot to see it."

He smiled one of those rare, rich smiles of his, a smile that she was convinced could melt stone. "I'm pleased we cleared up this misunderstanding," he said, and glanced at his watch, frowning. "Now I really must be going."

"Thank you for coming." Knowing that he'd found it important to explain meant a great deal to her.

He walked to the door, then suddenly turned to her. "Do you sail?"

"Sure." She'd never been on a sailboat in her life. "At least, I think I can, given the chance."

"How about this weekend?"

"I'd like that very much."

"I'll call you later," he said on his way out the door. Then he muttered something about her not making bankers' hearts flutter but doing a mighty fine job with his own.

She closed the door after him and leaned against it, grinning with a warmth that beamed all the way from her heart.

Eight

A stiff breeze billowed the huge spinnaker, and the thirty-foot sailboat heeled sharply, shaving the waterline with a razor-sharp cut. Stephanie threw back her head and laughed into the wind. The pins holding her hair had long ago been discarded, and her blond tresses now unfurled behind her like a flag, waving in the crisp air. "Oh, Jonas, I love this."

His answering smile was warm. "Somehow I knew you'd be a natural on the water."

"This is so much fun." She crossed her arms over her breasts as though to hug the sense of exhilaration she felt.

"You've really never sailed before?"

"Never." She noted the way he steered the boat from the helm, his movements confident, sure. "Can I do that?"

"If you'd like."

She joined him and sat down at his side. "Okay, tell me what to do."

"Just head her into the wind."

"Okay." She placed both hands on the long narrow handle that controlled the rudder and watched as the boat turned sharply. Almost immediately the sails went slack, but one guiding touch from Jonas and they filled with wind again.

"This isn't as easy as it looks," she complained with a smile. The day was marvelous. There wasn't any other way to describe it.

Jonas had arrived at her apartment early that morning, bringing freshly squeezed orange juice, croissants still warm from the oven and two large cups of steaming coffee. She had always been a morning person, and apparently he was, as well.

She had prepared her own surprise by packing them a picnic lunch. Included in her basket were two small loaves of French bread, a bottle of white wine, a variety of cheeses and some fresh strawberries that had cost her more than she cared to think about. But one look at the plump, juicy fruit and she couldn't resist.

The journey into Duluth was pleasant, as Jonas spoke of his family and their home on Lake Superior. His mother lived there now, and he said they would be joining her later that afternoon.

"You're quiet all of a sudden," Jonas mentioned as he reached over to correct her steering once again. "Is anything troubling you?"

"How could anything possibly be wrong on a glorious day like this one?"

"You were frowning."

"I was?" Stephanie glanced out over the choppy water. There wasn't another boat in sight. It was as though she and Jonas alone faced the mighty power of this astonishing lake. "I was thinking about meeting your mother. I guess I'm nervous."

"Why?"

"Jonas, look at me. I could be confused with a fugitive from justice in these old jeans. I only wish you'd said something earlier, so I could have brought a change of clothes along."

"Mother won't care."

Perhaps not, Stephanie mused, but *she* certainly did. If she was going to come face-to-face with Jonas's mother, she would have preferred to do it when she looked her best. Not now, with her hair in tangles and knots from the wind, and her face free of makeup and pink from a day in the sun. On the other hand, Mrs. Lockwood would be seeing her at her worst and would no doubt be pleasantly surprised if she met her again later. Her lazy smile grew and grew, and she glanced at Jonas.

His look was thoughtful. "Stephanie, I don't want you to fret about meeting my family."

"She must be an amazing woman."

"As a matter of fact she is, but you say that as if you know her, and that isn't possible."

Stephanie momentarily scanned the swirling green water in an effort to avoid meeting his intense gaze. "You're right. I could pass her on the street and not know who she is, but I'm sure she's a special person." The woman who'd born and raised Jonas would have to be.

Jonas placed his arm around her shoulder, and she leaned her head back against the solid cushion of his chest. Gently, he kissed the top of her head.

She turned so that her lips touched his throat where his shirt opened. His skin was warm, and she both felt and heard his answering sigh. His large hand was splayed against the back of her head, and he directed her mouth to his. She didn't need any more encouragement, and their mouths met in a gentle brushing of lips. She moved away from the helm and slipped her arms around his neck. He kissed her again, longer this time, much longer, but still he was infinitely gentle, as though he feared hurting her. He finally released her when the sails began to flap in the wind, but he did it with such reluctance that her heart sang.

"Are you hungry?" she asked, more for something to do than from any desire for lunch.

"Yes," he admitted hoarsely, but when she went toward the wicker picnic basket, he caught her hand, delaying her.

She raised questioning eyes to his. "Jonas?"

In a heartbeat, he gently pulled her back to him, his hand slipping around her waist. "It isn't food that tempts me." He kissed her again, his mouth moving on hers with an urgency as old as mankind itself. She threaded her fingers through his hair and held his head fast until she was so weak that she slumped against him.

"Jonas," she breathed.

He brought her down so that they were sitting side by side. He put his arms around her and fused his mouth to hers. Again and again he kissed her, tasting, nipping at her lower lip, until she thought she would go mad with wanting him. Her hand crept up his hard chest and closed around the folds of his collar. The kiss was long and thorough. This day with Jonas was the sweetest she had ever known.

With his arms wrapped securely around her shoulders, she swayed with the gentle rocking of the boat, lulled by the peace that surrounded them. He had somehow lowered the sails without her even knowing it. He continued to hold her, staring out over the rolling water. Not for the first time she noticed that his eyes were incredibly blue. As though sensing her scrutiny, he gazed down at her. For a long moment they stared at each other, lost in a world that had been created just for them and for this moment.

Sometime later Jonas reached for the picnic basket. He brought out a plump red strawberry, plucked the stem from the top and fed it to Stephanie. She bit into the pulp, and a thin line of juice ran down her chin. As she moved to wipe it away, his hand stopped hers. He bent his index finger, and with his knuckle rubbed the red juice aside. Then, very slowly, as though he couldn't resist, he lowered his mouth to hers. Their lips met and clung. His grip tightened as his tongue sought and found hers. When he lifted his mouth from her lips, he smiled gently. Moisture pooled in her eyes, and a tear slipped from the corner of her eye and rolled down her cheek.

A puzzled frown furrowed his brow. "You're crying."

"I know."

"Did I hurt you?"

"No."

"Then why?"

She turned her head into his shoulder, convinced he would laugh once he knew.

"Stephanie?"

"It was so beautiful. I always cry when I'm this happy." Feeling foolish, she rubbed her hands against her eyes. "It's a family curse. My mother cries every Christmas."

Jonas reached for the wine, opened it and poured them each a glass.

"Alcohol won't help," she said, sniffling, but she didn't refuse the glass Jonas offered her.

"Are there any other family curses I should know about?"

"I have a bit of a temper."

Jonas chuckled. "I've encountered that."

Laughing lightly, she straightened and took her first sip of wine. It felt cool and tasted sweet, reminding her that she was hungry. "Some cheese and bread?" she asked, looking at him.

He leaned forward to reach for it, and as he did, a look of pain shot across his face, widening his eyes. He sat back quickly.

"Jonas?" Concerned, she turned to him. "What is it?"

"It'll pass in a moment."

"What will pass?"

"The pain," he managed, his voice grating, stroking the length of his thigh in an effort to ease the agony. He closed his eyes and turned away from her.

She bent in front of him, nearly frantic. "Tell me what I can do."

"Nothing," he said through clenched teeth. "Go away."

"No," she said. "I won't . . . I couldn't." Because she didn't know what else to do, she put her hand on his, kneading the knotted flesh that had cramped so viciously. She could feel the muscles relax when the spasm passed.

"What happened? Did I do something?"

"No." He moved away from her, reaching for the ropes, preparing to raise the sails.

"Talk to me, for heaven's sake," she demanded, grabbing his forearm. "Don't close up on me now. I care about you, Jonas. I want to help!"

His hard gaze softened, and he tenderly cupped her cheek. Relieved, she turned her face into his palm and kissed it.

"Did I frighten you?" he asked her softly.

"Only because I didn't know what to do to help you." She sighed, feeling weak and emotionally drained. "Does that happen often?" The thought of him enduring such pain was intolerable.

"It happens often enough to make me appreciate my cane."

In spite of the circumstances, she bowed her head to hide a smile.

"You find that amusing?"

Her head shot up. "No, of course not. It's just that everyone in the office claims they know when your leg is hurting, because you're usually in a foul mood."

"They say that, do they?"

"It's true, isn't it?"

He shrugged. "To be honest, I hadn't given it much thought."

She reached inside the picnic basket for the two loaves of bread. She set them out, along with a plate of cheese, avoiding looking at Jonas as she asked him the question that had been on her mind since Paris. "How'd it happen?"

"My leg?" His gaze sharpened.

"You don't have to tell me if you'd rather not."

He hesitated, and when he finally spoke, she realized that telling her the story was an indication that he trusted her. "It happened several years ago, in a skiing accident. I was on the slopes with a . . . friend. There isn't much to say. She got in trouble, and when I went to help her, I fell."

"Down the slope?"

"No, off a cliff."

"Oh, Jonas." She felt sick at the thought of him being hurt. She closed her eyes to the mental image of him lying in some snow bank in agony, waiting for help to arrive.

"The doctors say I'm lucky to still have my leg. In the beginning I wished they had amputated it and been done with it. Now I'm more tolerant of the pain. I've learned to live with it." He grew silent, and Stephanie sensed that there was a great deal more to the story that he hadn't revealed, but she accepted what he had told her and didn't press him further.

"Thank you, Jonas," she said softly.

"For what?"

"For bringing me with you today. For relating what must be a difficult story for you to tell. For trusting me."

"No, Stephanie," he whispered, lifting her mouth to his. "Thank you."

Later that day, when Jonas pulled up to the large two-story brick mansion overlooking Lake Superior, Stephanie's breath caught at the sight of his magnificent family home. "Oh, Jonas," she said, awed. "It's beautiful." Imposing, as well, she thought, attempting to subdue her nervousness. Her hand went to her hair, and she ran her fingers through the tangled mass.

"You look fine," he told her.

She lowered her arm and rested her clenched hand in her lap. "Just you wait," she threatened. "I'm going to introduce you to my father. He'll be in mud-spattered coveralls, sitting on top of a tractor. You'll be in a thousand-dollar pin-striped suit, and you'll know what it feels like to be out of your element."

To her amazement, Jonas laughed. He parked the car at the front of the house, or perhaps the back—she couldn't actually tell which—and turned off the engine. "I look forward to meeting your family."

"You do?"

He climbed out of the car and came around to her side, opening her door for her. "One thing, though."

"Yes?"

"Don't introduce me to your mother at Christmas. I have a heck of a time dealing with crying women."

Stephanie got the giggles. They were probably a result of her nervousness, but once she started it was nearly impossible to stop. He laughed with her, and they were still laughing as, with his arm linked around her waist, he led her through the wide double doors of the house.

The minute they were inside her amusement vanished. The marble floor of the entryway had probably cost more than her family's farm in Colville. Marble that was probably imported from Italy. Maybe Greece. A large winding stairway angled off to the right, its polished mahogany balustrade gleaming in the sun.

"Jonas, is that you?" An elegantly dressed woman appeared. She was tall and regal-looking, with twinkling blue eyes that were the exact image of Jonas's. Her hair was completely gray, and she wore it in a neatly coiled French roll. She held her hands out to her son. He claimed them with his own and kissed her on the cheek.

"Mother."

They parted, and his mother paused to greet Stephanie. If she disapproved of Stephanie's attire, it wasn't revealed in the warmth of her smile. "You must be Stephanie."

For one crazy second Stephanie had the urge to curtsy. "Hello, Mrs. Lockwood." Even her voice sounded awed and a bit unnatural.

"Please call me Elizabeth."

"Thank you, I will."

"I can see you've had a full day on the lake." Elizabeth glanced at her son.

"It was marvelous," Stephanie confirmed.

"I hope you're hungry. Clara's been cooking all day, anticipating your arrival."

Jonas placed his hand along the back of Stephanie's neck and directed her into the largest room she had ever seen in a private home.

"Who's Clara?" she asked under her breath.

"The cook," he whispered. When his mother turned her back, he kissed Stephanie's cheek.

"Jonas," she hissed. "Don't do that!"

"Did you say something, Stephanie?" Elizabeth turned around questioningly.

"Actually . . . no," she stuttered, glowering hotly at Jonas, who coughed to disguise a laugh. "I didn't say anything."

"Would either of you care for a glass of wine before dinner?" Elizabeth asked, taking a seat on an elegant velvet sofa.

Stephanie claimed the matching chair across from her, and Jonas stood behind Stephanie.

“That would be fine, Mother,” he said, answering for them both. “Would you like me to serve as bartender?”

“Please.” Elizabeth folded her hands on her lap. “Jonas has spoken highly of you, Stephanie.”

“He . . . has?” she sputtered.

“Yes. Is there something unusual about that?”

Jonas delivered a glass of wine to his mother before bringing Stephanie hers. He sat beside her on the arm of the chair and looped his arm around her shoulder.

“Clara will never forgive you if you don’t say hello, Son,” Elizabeth informed him. “While you do that, I’ll show Stephanie my garden. It’s lovely this time of year.”

“I’d like that,” Stephanie said, standing. She continued to hold her wine, although she had no intention of drinking it. All she needed was to get tipsy in front of Jonas’s mother.

“I’ll be back in a minute,” he whispered as he left the room.

A small, awkward silence followed. Stephanie looked down at her soiled jeans and cringed inwardly. “I feel I should apologize for my attire,” she began, following Jonas’s mother out through French doors that led to a lush green garden. Roses were in bloom, and their sweet fragrance filled the air.

“Nonsense,” Elizabeth countered. “You’ve been sailing. I didn’t expect you to arrive in an evening gown.”

“But I don’t imagine you expected jeans and purple tennis shoes, either.”

Elizabeth laughed; the sound was light and musical. “I believe I’m going to grow fond of you.”

“I hope so.” Stephanie studied her wine.

“Forgive me for being so blunt, but are you in love with my son?”

Stephanie raised her eyes to Jonas’s mother’s and nodded. “Yes.”

Elizabeth placed her hand over her heart and sighed expressively. "I am so relieved to hear you say that."

"You are? Why?"

"Because *he* loves *you,* child."

Stephanie opened her mouth to argue, but Elizabeth stopped her.

"I don't know if he's admitted it to himself yet, but he will soon. A few minutes ago, when you came into the house, I heard Jonas laugh. It's been years since I've heard the sound of my son's laughter. Thank you for that."

"Really, I didn't do anything . . . I—"

"Please forgive me for interrupting, but we haven't much time."

Stephanie's heart shot to her throat. "Yes?"

"You must be patient with my son. He's been hurt, terribly hurt, and he is greatly in need of a woman's love. He probably hasn't told you about Gretchen. He loved her deeply, far more than the wretched woman deserved. She left him after the accident. She told him that she couldn't live with a cripple, even though it was she who had caused the accident with her carelessness."

Jonas's mother didn't need to say a word more for Stephanie to hate the fickle, faceless woman.

"That was nearly ten years ago, and he hasn't brought another woman to meet me until today. Knowing my son the way I do, I'm sure he'll battle what he feels for you. He's reluctant to trust again, so you must be patient and," she added, gently touching Stephanie's hand, "very strong. He deserves your love, and although he may be stubborn now and again, believe me, the woman my son loves will be the happiest woman alive. When Jonas loves again, I promise you it will be with all his heart and his soul."

Stephanie felt moisture gather in her eyes. "I don't know if I deserve someone as good as Jonas."

"Perhaps not," Elizabeth Lockwood said, her soft voice removing any harshness from her words. "But *he* deserves *you*." She glanced over her shoulder. "He's coming now, so smile, and please don't say anything about our conversation."

"I won't," Stephanie promised, blinking back tears.

"There you are," Jonas said as he joined his mother and Stephanie. "Did Mother let you in on any family secrets?"

"Several, as a matter of fact," Elizabeth said with a small laugh.

"Clara wants me to tell you that dinner is ready any time you are."

"Wonderful," Elizabeth replied with a warm smile.

"She cooked my favorite dessert," Jonas said, sharing a secret smile with Stephanie. "Strawberry shortcake."

Stephanie could feel the heated color seep up her neck, invading her cheeks.

"I don't recall you being particularly fond of strawberries," Elizabeth commented as she led the way into the dining room.

"It's a recent addiction, Mother," Jonas said, reaching for Stephanie's hand and linking her fingers with his. He raised her knuckles to his mouth and lightly kissed them.

The meal was one Stephanie would long remember, but not because of the food, though it could have been served in a four-star restaurant. Jonas was a different person, chatting, joking, teasing. He insisted that Clara join them for coffee so Stephanie could meet her. Although Stephanie liked the rotund woman instantly, she could feel the older woman's distrust. But by the end of the evening all that had changed, and Stephanie knew she could count Clara as a friend.

When it came time to leave, Elizabeth hugged Stephanie

and whispered softly in her ear, "Thank you, my dear, for giving me back my son. Remember what I said. Be patient."

"No. Thank *you,*" Stephanie whispered back. They joined hands, and Stephanie nodded once. "I'll remember."

It was dark by the time they left Duluth, and Stephanie was physically drained from the long day. She yawned once and tried to disguise it. "I like your mother, Jonas."

"She seemed to be quite taken with you, too."

They talked a bit more, and she began to drop off, giving way to her fatigue. He woke her when they reached the outskirts of Minneapolis.

"I'm sorry to be such terrible company," she said, yawning.

"You're anything but," he said, contradicting her. He eased to a stop in front of her apartment building and parked the car, but he kept the engine running.

"Do you want to come in for coffee?" she asked.

"No, you're exhausted, and I have some work that I need to look over."

"Jonas, don't tell me you're going to work on a Saturday night." She glanced at her wristwatch, shocked to find that it was after eleven.

He chuckled, and leaned over to press his mouth lightly to hers. "No, but it was the best excuse I could come up with to refuse your invitation."

"Good, I was worried there for a minute. You work too hard." She yearned to tell him how much the day had meant to her, how much she'd enjoyed the time on the sailboat, and meeting his mother and Clara. But finding the right words was impossible. "Thank you for everything," she said when he helped her out of the car. "I can't remember a day I've enjoyed more."

"Me, either," he murmured, his gaze holding hers.

* * *

"We've got it!" Jan announced Monday morning, as she, Maureen, Toni and Barbara circled Stephanie's desk like warriors surrounding a wagon train.

"Got what?" Stephanie looked up blankly. She'd only arrived at the office a few minutes earlier and hadn't even turned on her computer. "What are you talking about?"

"Your next move with Mr. Lockwood."

"Oh, that," she returned with a sigh. She hadn't told her friends about the weekend sailing jaunt, but then she'd been keeping quite a few secrets from them lately.

"We've got it all worked out."

"Answer me this first," Stephanie said. "Will I need to wear a cast? Date someone's brother-in-law? Hire a French chef?"

"No."

"It's working out great. We've got a contact in the janitorial department."

"A what?"

"All you have to do," Maureen explained excitedly, "is get in the elevator alone with Mr. Lockwood."

"Yes?" Stephanie could feel the enthusiasm coming from her coworkers in waves. "What will that do?"

"That's where Mike from maintenance comes into the picture," Toni explained patiently.

"He'll flip the switch, and the two of you will be trapped alone together for hours."

"Isn't that a marvelous idea?" Barbara said.

"It works in all the best romances."

"It's a sure thing."

"You're game, aren't you, Steph?"

Nine

"No, I'm not game for your crazy schemes," Stephanie informed her friends primly. It wasn't that she objected to being alone with Jonas for hours on end—in fact, she would relish that—but to plot their meeting this way went against everything she hoped for in their relationship.

Jan, Maureen, Toni and Barbara exchanged an incredulous look.

"But it's perfect."

"Jonas and I don't need it," Stephanie said, knowing that the best way to appease her friends was with the truth.

"What do you mean, you don't need it?" Jan asked, her eyes narrowing with suspicion.

"You been holding out on us, girl?" Maureen barked, her hand on her hip.

"I do believe she has been," Barbara said before Stephanie had a chance to answer.

"Let's just say this," Stephanie said with a conspiratorial smile. "The romantic relationship between Mr. Lockwood and me is developing nicely."

"How nicely?" Jan wanted to know. "And put it into terms we understand."

"Like on a scale of one to ten," Barbara added.

"What's a ten?" Stephanie glanced up at her friends, uncertain.

"If you need to ask, we're in trouble."

"Right." Hot color blossomed in Stephanie's cheeks.

"If he phoned once or twice and showed up at your apartment—that's a four, a low four."

"But if you shared a couple of romantic evenings on the town, I'd call that a six."

"I'd say meeting his family is an eight," Toni murmured thoughtfully, her index finger pressed against her cheek. "Maybe a nine."

The four romantics paused expectantly, waiting for Stephanie to locate her relationship with Jonas on their makeshift scale. "Well?" Jan coaxed.

"An eight, then, maybe a nine," she admitted softly, waiting for her friends to break into shouts and cheers. Instead, she was greeted with a shocked, dubious silence.

"You're not teasing, are you?" Barbara murmured. "You really aren't joking?"

"No. Jonas introduced me to his mother this weekend. She's a wonderful woman."

"It's going to work," Maureen whispered in awe, her face revealing her surprise. "It's really going to work!"

"Speaking of work . . ." Stephanie said reluctantly, glancing at her watch. She was relieved not to be subjected to an endless list of questions from her coworkers, but she was so grateful to her romance-loving friends that she wanted them to share some of her happiness.

As though in a daze, Jan, Maureen, Toni and Barbara turned and walked away as if in a trance.

"Do you think the janitor will give us a refund?" Barbara asked no one in particular as they moved out the door.

"Who cares?" came the reply from the others.

Stephanie's boss, George Potter, arrived at the office a couple of minutes later, his first day back from Seattle. They exchanged a few pleasantries, and he handed her some notes from his briefcase. "If you get the chance, could you take these receipts to Donald Black?"

He said the name stiffly; Stephanie knew from experience that there was little love lost between the two men. She couldn't imagine her amiable boss disliking anyone, so she was quite certain he had a good reason for his animosity.

"I'll do it as soon as I finish this report," she said with a welcoming smile. There was so much to be happy about that she felt like humming love songs. She wondered briefly how Jonas's day was going, her thoughts wandering naturally to the man who just happened to be in sole possession of her heart.

The morning whizzed past. Stephanie was so close to finishing the report that she skipped her midmorning coffee break. Five minutes later, with the floor all but deserted and Mr. Potter in a meeting, she walked down the hallway to give the receipts to Donald Black.

"Good morning, Mr. Black," she said, knocking politely on his open door. "Mr. Potter asked me to bring these over."

"Put them over there," he said, indicating a table on the other side of the room.

Stephanie placed the envelope where he'd requested and turned to leave, but the middle-aged, potbellied man stood and blocked her way.

"You and Jonas Lockwood seem to be seeing a great deal of each other."

A plethora of possible answers crowded her mind. Jonas had

mentioned that he would prefer to keep their personal relationship out of the office, but she wasn't in the habit of lying. Nor was it her custom to discuss her personal relationships with a stranger.

"We're . . . friends," she said, since apparently Jonas himself had mentioned her to the other man.

"I see." With slow, deliberate movements, Mr. Black placed his pencil on the edge of his desk. "How willing are you to be . . . friends with other Lockwood employees?"

She stiffened at the insulting way he uttered the word *friends.* "I'm not sure I understand the question."

"I'm quite certain you do."

She didn't know what game this middle-aged Don Juan was playing, but she had no intention of remaining in his office. "If you'll excuse me."

"As a matter of fact, I won't. We're having an important discussion here, and I'd consider it a desertion of your duties to this company and to me personally if you left."

She wasn't much into office gossip, but she was starting to understand why George Potter had no respect for Donald Black. As the head of the accounting department, Black had been through three assistants in the two years Stephanie had been employed by Lockwood Industries. From her own dismal experience with her former employers, she could guess the reason why he had trouble keeping a decent employees.

"I'll desert my duties, then," she replied flippantly. She turned to go, but didn't make it to the door. He reached out and gripped her shoulder, spinning her around. She was so shocked that he would dare to touch her that she was momentarily speechless.

"Everyone in the company knows you're being generous with Lockwood. All I want is a share in the goods."

Still breathless with shock, she slapped his hand aside. "You sicken me."

"Give me time, honey, I promise to improve."

"I sincerely doubt that."

He drew her closer, obviously intent on kissing her, but she managed to evade him. With everything that was in her, she pushed against his chest with both hands and was astonished at the strength of the man.

Her eye happened to catch the clock, and she realized it would be another five minutes before anyone returned to the department. Crying out would do no good, since there wasn't anyone there to answer her plea for help.

"All I want is a little kiss," Mr. Black said coaxingly. "Just give me that and I'll let you go."

"I'd rather vomit!" she cried, kicking at him and missing.

"You stupid—"

"Let her go."

The quietly spoken words evidenced such controlled anger that both Stephanie and her attacker froze. Black dropped his arms and released her.

With a strangled sob she turned aside and braced her hands against the edge of the desk, weak with relief. Her neatly coiled hair had fallen free of its restraining pins and hung in loose tendrils around her flushed face. It took her several deep breaths to regain her strength. She didn't know how or why Jonas was there, but she had never been so glad to see anyone.

"Clear out your desk, Black." The emotionless, frigid control in Jonas's voice sent a chill up her spine. She'd never heard a man sound more angry or more dangerous. Acid dripped from each syllable. An unspoken challenge hung over the room, almost as if Jonas was hoping for a physical confrontation.

"Hey, Jonas, you got the wrong idea here. Your lady friend came on to me." Black raised both hands in an emotional plea of innocence.

Stephanie spun around, her eyes spitting fire.

"Is that true?" Jonas asked evenly.

"No!" she shouted, indignant and furious. "He grabbed me—"

"You didn't hear her crying out, did you?" Black shot back, interrupting Stephanie. "I swear, man, I'm not the kind of guy who has to force women. They come to me."

"I said clear out your desk." Jonas pointed the tip of his cane at the far door. "A check will be mailed to you tomorrow."

Donald Black gave Stephanie a murderous glare as he marched out of the office. "You'll regret this, Lockwood," he muttered on his way past Jonas.

Stephanie could see the coiled alertness drain from Jonas the minute Black was out of the room. "Did he hurt you?"

"No . . . I'm fine." She closed her eyes. She was too proud to allow a man like Donald Black to reduce her to tears.

Jonas's arm slipped around her, comforting and warm, chasing away the icy, numbing chill that had settled over her. "I'm fine," she whispered fiercely, burying her face in his shoulder. "Really," she insisted as she shuddered against him.

"Let's get out of here." He led her into the hallway and toward the elevator. She didn't recall anything of the ride to the top floor, but when the thick door glided open, Jonas called to Martha Westheimer.

"Bring me a strong cup of coffee, and add plenty of sugar."

"Jonas, really," Stephanie said, her voice wavering slightly. "I'm fine, and I'm certainly not in shock."

He ignored her, leading her into his office and sitting her down in a heavy leather chair. He paced the area directly in front of her until the ever-efficient Martha appeared with the coffee, carefully handing it to Stephanie. The older woman gave her a sympathetic look that puzzled her. She couldn't understand why the other woman would regard her with such compassion, but then she remembered her hair, which was certainly evidence of a sort. She smiled back as Martha quietly left the room, softly closing the door behind her.

"I won't ever have you subjected to that kind of treatment again," Jonas seethed, still battling his rage.

She stared up at him blankly as he paced. He marched like a soldier doing sentry duty, going three or four feet, then swiftly making a sharp about-face. She realized his irritation wasn't directed at her.

"We're getting married," he announced forcefully.

Her immediate response was to take a sip of the syrupy coffee, convinced she'd misunderstood him.

"Well?" he barked.

"Would you mind repeating that? I'm certain I heard you wrong."

"I said we're getting married." He said it louder this time.

She blinked twice. "If I wasn't in shock before, I am now. You can't possibly mean that, Jonas."

"My name will protect you."

"But, Jonas—"

"Will you or won't you be my wife?" he demanded.

"Stop shouting at me!" she cried, jumping to her feet. The coffee nearly sloshed over the edges of the cup, and she set it down before she ended up spilling it all over the front of her dress.

"Anything could have happened down there," he continued. "If I hadn't arrived when I did . . ." He left the rest to her imagination.

She went still, her gaze studying this man she loved. "Isn't marriage a little drastic?"

"Not in these circumstances." He looked at her as though she were the one being unreasonable.

"Jonas, do you love me?" She asked the question softly, almost fearing his response.

"I'd hardly be willing to make you my wife if I didn't."

"I see."

He hesitated, looking uneasy. "How do you feel about me?"

"Oh, Jonas, do you really need to ask?" Her gaze softened, and her heart melted at the pride and doubt she read in his hard expression. He was more vulnerable now than at any time since she'd begun working for him. "I've been in love with you from the moment we stood in front of the fountain in Paris—only it took me a while to realize it."

His eyes looked deeply into hers, and when he spoke, the burning anger had been replaced by tenderness. "Stephanie, I love you. I never expected to fall so hard, and certainly not for a woman who is so proud and forthright. But it's happened, and I'll thank God every day of my life if you'll agree to marry me."

"Oh, Jonas." She battled back the tidal wave of emotion that threatened to engulf her. Then she sniffled and turned around, desperately seeking a tissue.

He handed her one and paused to cup her face in his hands, smiling at her gently, lovingly. "We're going to have a wonderful life together," he said as he lowered his mouth to hers. His kiss was tender and sweet. The wonder of being in his arms, knowing he loved her, made her knees grow weak.

She locked her arms around his neck as his mouth meandered over her lips to her ear. "You're a crazy woman."

"Crazy about you," she admitted, loving the feel of him rubbing against her, knowing that their lovemaking would be exquisite.

"A man attacks you and you're a fireball. I ask you to marry me, and you burst into tears."

"I'm happy."

"You will, won't you?"

"Marry you? Oh, Jonas, yes. A thousand times yes."

"Do you want children?"

"A dozen, at least," she said with a happy laugh. Fresh tears misted her eyes at the thought of their raising a family together.

"A dozen?" He cocked his brows and grinned sheepishly. "I'm willing, but you may change your mind after three or four." Still holding her, he flipped the switch to the intercom. "Miss Westheimer?"

"Yes," came the tinny-sounding reply.

"Contact Mr. Potter and tell him that Miss Coulter won't be in for the remainder of the day."

"Jonas," Stephanie whispered. "I told you, Black didn't hurt me. I'm fine, really."

He ignored her, but his grip on her shoulder tightened. "And cancel my appointments for today, as well."

"Yes, of course," Martha said, but the reluctance in her voice was evident even to Stephanie.

"Is that a problem, Miss Westheimer?"

"Adam Holmes is scheduled for four-thirty, and he'll be leaving town this evening."

Jonas closed his eyes and sighed with frustration. "All right, I'll make a point of being back before four-thirty, then."

When he'd finished speaking, he released the switch and turned Stephanie into his arms. "We have some shopping to do."

"Shopping?" For some reason her mind flashed to the grocery store. She hadn't eaten breakfast and had hoped to pick up something on her coffee break, but she'd been so involved working on the report for Mr. Potter that her plan had fallen by the wayside.

"Shopping for a ring. A diamond, preferably, and so large anyone looking at it will know how special you are and how much I love you."

"Jonas," she said slowly, measuring her words carefully, "a plain gold band would do as long as I'm marrying you."

"I can afford a whole lot more, and I have every intention of indulging you from this minute to the end of our lives."

She swallowed her objections. She loved Jonas, and not for the material wealth he could give her. She remembered Elizabeth Lockwood's words. His mother had told her that when Jonas admitted that he loved her, he would make her the happiest woman alive. For now he equated bringing her joy with adorning her with riches. And diamonds *were* wonderful, but her happiness came from being loved by Jonas and nothing more. It wouldn't matter to her if he made sandwiches at the corner deli; she loved the man. In time he would learn that her happiness was linked to his. He was all she would ever need to be content and whole.

His look grew sober and thoughtful. "What do you think about making Potter a vice president?"

Stephanie was both stunned and thrilled. She was surprised and complimented that he had asked her opinion. "George Potter is a wonderful choice."

"Then consider it done," Jonas said with a decisive nod. "Now that I'm going to be a married man, I don't want to spend nearly so much time at the office. Not when I have more important matters to concern myself with."

"Right," she said with a wide grin, thinking of all the years they would have to build a life together. She could see them thirty-five years from now, teaching their grandchildren to sail.

"Jonas," she said suddenly, remembering her own happy childhood. "I want you to meet my parents and my sisters."

"We can fly out next week," he answered matter-of-factly.

"When do you want to have the wedding?" she asked. He was moving so fast he was making her head spin.

"Is next month too soon?"

"Oh, Jonas," she said, wrapping her arms around his neck and hugging him fiercely. "I wonder if it will be soon enough."

From that point the afternoon took on the feel of a circus ride. Their first stop was the jewelers, where Jonas bought a lovely diamond solitaire. When he slipped it on her finger, she felt emotion tighten her chest. She bit into her lower lip to keep her feelings at bay, not wanting to embarrass either of them with a display of tears. From the jewelers, Jonas drove to an exclusive French restaurant in memory of their trip to Paris. They dined on veal, sipped champagne and shared secret glances with eyes full of love.

At four, he glanced irritably at his watch. "I may be tied up with Holmes for several hours, and then I've got a dinner engagement."

"Not with another woman, I hope," she teased.

He looked startled for a moment. "There will never be another woman for me, Stephanie. Never."

"Jonas, I was only joking."

"You need never doubt me on this. All my life I've been intensely loyal. I'm sure my mother can give you several examples from my boyhood, if you want to hear them."

"Jonas, please, I didn't mean to imply . . ."

"I know, love." He paused to caress the side of her face tenderly. "I knew I was falling in love with you, too, you know—perhaps even as early as Paris—but I fought it. I thought I was in love once before, and I was thoroughly disgusted with myself, given how things turned out. But this morning, when I saw Black pawing at you—I've never experienced such overwhelming rage. I knew in that moment that the feelings I hold for you could be nothing less than love."

She found his hand and squeezed it gently.

His blue eyes darkened by several shades, and she realized that had they been anywhere other than a restaurant, he would have taken her in his arms and kissed her until she begged him to stop.

From the restaurant they drove back to the office. She was about to burst with happiness, and if she didn't share it with Jan and the others soon, she was convinced she would start screaming that Jonas Lockwood loved her from the top floor for all of Minneapolis to hear.

Her first stop after they parted at the elevator was Human Resources. Jan looked up from her desk and blinked.

"Hey, where were you at lunchtime? I have a feeling you were trying to avoid questions. You can't do this to us, Steph. We're all dying to find out what's happening."

"I wasn't avoiding anyone."

Jan looked at her more intently. "You've got that saucy grin again. Would you care to tell me the reason you look like a contented cat with feathers in his mouth?"

In response, Stephanie held out her left hand. The large diamond solitaire sparkled in the artificial light.

Jan gasped, and her eyes shot to Stephanie's. "Mr. Lockwood?"

"Who else would it be?"

Jan's hand flew to her breast. "I think I'm going into cardiac arrest. You did it! You actually did it!" Even as she spoke, she was reaching for the phone.

"Tell the others to meet us at that place you took me to that night. The drinks are on me this time," Stephanie said happily. "I owe all of you at least that."

An hour later the five of them were gathered around a table, sipping wine and munching on an assortment of appetizers.

"How did you get him to propose?" Barbara wanted to know.

"I didn't do anything. I was more surprised than any of you."

Jan refilled Stephanie's glass, and they all raised their drinks in a silent salute to their illustrious boss.

"To years and years of happiness," Maureen said.

"And romance," Stephanie added, a believer now. She recalled the first time she'd met with her coworkers and how they'd claimed to have recognized her as the perfect match for Jonas. At the time she had been shocked, even appalled. She wouldn't have given the man a free bus ticket. Now, at the very mention of his name her knees turned to butter, she was so much in love with him. Truly head over heels in love, for the first time in her life.

"Who guessed today?" Toni asked.

"No one," Jan answered.

"Today? What are you talking about?" Stephanie glanced around the table at her friends. True, they'd all had their share of wine—and she'd had a bit more than her share, since she'd also had champagne at lunch with Jonas. But until this moment, everything her friends said had made perfect sense.

"Have you decided on a date for the wedding yet?"

Stephanie noticed how intense their faces became as they awaited her reply. "I'm not answering your question until you answer mine," she said, crossing her arms stubbornly. "What's all this about guessing the day?"

"The marriage pool."

"The what?" Stephanie cried.

"You know, like a football pool, only we had a bet going on when Lockwood was going to pop the question."

Stephanie took another swallow of her wine. "I can't believe I'm hearing this."

"A lot of people bet that you wouldn't be able to carry this off. They lost out big time." Jan and Maureen slapped hands high above the table.

"Money?"

"Three hundred dollars is riding on your wedding date."

Stephanie placed her elbows on the table and cradled her head in her hands. "So that's how Black heard about me and Jonas," she mumbled under her breath.

"Say, do you know what happened to him today?" Jan asked.

"How would I know?" Stephanie didn't look her friend in the eye. She hoped that by asking the question she could avoid lying outright.

"I got a call from Old Stone Face shortly after I returned from break this morning. She told me that Donald Black had been terminated, and to arrange for his check to be mailed to him at his home."

"How unusual," Stephanie commented, struggling not to reveal any of her involvement with the situation.

"I don't know anyone who's sorry to see him go," Maureen added. "He was a real—"

"We know what he was," Toni inserted quickly.

"So what else has been going on today?" Stephanie tried to steer the conversation away from the unpleasant subject of Donald Black.

"You mean other than you and Mr. Lockwood getting engaged, and Donald Black biting the dust? I'd say that was enough to make it one crazy Monday."

"Can you imagine what Tuesday's going to be like?" Maureen asked.

From there the five of them went to dinner at a Mexican restaurant, and by the time Stephanie got home it was close to nine o'clock. She hoped Jonas hadn't tried to get in touch with her and felt a little guilty for staying out so late. As it was, her head was swimming, so she took a quick shower and hurried to bed.

The following morning she was at her desk bright and early, hoping Jonas would stop in on his way up to his floor. She didn't know how she was going to be able to work when all she could think about was how much she loved him and how eager she was to share his life.

Before George Potter arrived, Stephanie received a call from Jan. "Can you come to my office?"

"Sure, what's up? You don't sound right."

"Just get here."

Stephanie couldn't think of a reason why her friend should sound so upset, and she hurried to her office. She took one look at Jan's red eyes and grew worried. Her friend reached for a tissue and loudly blew her nose.

"What's wrong?" Stephanie asked, taking a chair. She'd never seen Jan cry.

"Mr. Lockwood contacted me first thing this morning."

"Jonas?"

"You've been terminated."

Alarm filled Stephanie for an instant, but then she sighed and offered Jan a reassuring grin. "Of course I have. Jonas and I are getting married. I can't very well continue to work here." They hadn't talked about it specifically, but she was sure that was it.

"I don't think so," Jan said. She reached for another tissue, blinking back fresh tears.

"You're not making any sense. What did he say?"

"He said . . ." Jan paused to wipe her eyes. "He said to mail you your check just the way I was instructed to do with Mr. Black, and . . . and he asked that you give me the engagement ring. He doesn't want you on Lockwood property again. He was clear as glass on that subject."

Stephanie felt as though someone had kicked her in the stomach. For a moment she couldn't breathe. Her heart constricted with an intolerable pain.

"Steph, did you hear me?"

She nodded numbly. "Why?" The word came from deep within her throat, low and guttural.

"He . . . he didn't say, but he was serious, Steph. Very serious. I've never heard him more angry. You'd better give me the ring."

Ten

Stephanie's right hand covered the large diamond engagement ring protectively. "I don't understand. That doesn't make any sense."

"He was very precise when he contacted me."

Pacing the carpet in front of Jan's desk, Stephanie folded her arms around her waist and pondered her friend's words. "Call Barbara, Toni and Maureen, and ask them to get here right away."

"What?"

"Just do it," Stephanie snapped, impatient now. "And tell them to hurry."

Momentarily dumbfounded, Jan hesitated, then reached for the phone. A few minutes later their coworkers rushed into the office.

"What is it?" Maureen, the first to arrive, asked breathlessly.

Toni followed on her heels. "Hey, what's so important?"

Barbara came in last, paused, glanced around and said, "All right, I'm here, what's the big deal?"

Jan gestured toward Stephanie. "You called them here, you explain."

"Apparently," Stephanie began, swallowing past the thickening in her throat, "Jonas wants to call off the engagement."

"What?" All three newcomers cried out simultaneously in disbelief.

Barbara recovered first. "What happened?"

"I . . . don't know," Stephanie admitted honestly, her stomach churning as she considered the incredible situation. "I arrived at the office this morning, and Jan contacted me. She told me I had been terminated by Lockwood Industries, and I was to return the engagement ring to her."

Barbara, Toni and Maureen turned accusing eyes on Jan.

"Hey," Jan said. "It wasn't *my* fault. I'm as shocked as the rest of you."

Stephanie twisted the diamond around and around on her finger, almost believing that she would prefer to lose the appendage than surrender the ring that had been a token of Jonas's love. "You four are the self-proclaimed experts on romance. You're the ones who convinced me that Jonas and I were meant for each other. I need your advice now more than ever." Stephanie spoke quietly, doing her best to keep the emotion from her voice. "What can I do now?"

"Did he give any reason?"

"None," Jan answered. "But he was so angry . . . worse than I can ever remember hearing him."

"Can you think of anything?" Maureen turned to Stephanie, her brow creased in a frown that revealed the depth of her bafflement.

"Nothing. Absolutely nothing." She turned her palms to them in a gesture indicating her own confusion. Unless Donald Black had somehow convinced Jonas that she hadn't been speaking the truth . . . but that wasn't possible, she decided. Jonas knew her better than that. At least she prayed he did.

"Are you going to give him back the ring?" Toni asked quietly, her voice dejected and unhappy.

"I . . . don't know yet."

"It's obvious he doesn't want to face you," Jan said, her expression thoughtful.

"Probably because he's afraid of what would happen."

"But I would never hurt him," Stephanie returned, appalled at the suggestion that she would do anything to cause him pain.

"Not physically, silly," Barbara explained with a long sigh. "It's obvious that he loves you—that isn't going to change overnight—so breaking off the engagement is bound to be emotionally painful."

"Maybe even impossible, if he's forced to face you."

"Then that's exactly what's going to happen." For the first time Stephanie thought she could see a glimmer of hope. She wouldn't make things easy for Jonas. "I'm not going to hand over this ring without an explanation."

"You shouldn't," Maureen stated emphatically.

"He isn't going to let you leave," Toni said.

"He isn't?" Stephanie wasn't nearly as convinced as her friends.

"Oh, he might let you get as far as the door—"

"Maybe even the elevator," Jan interrupted.

"But he'll come for you once he realizes you really mean to leave."

"He'll stop me?" Stephanie was doubtful.

"Oh, yes, the hero always rejects the heroine, and then at the very last second he realizes that he couldn't possibly live without her."

"He may even quietly plead with you and say 'Don't go' in a tormented voice. You'd be crazy to walk away from him then."

"It's like that in all the best romances," Maureen said, nodding sharply.

"But Jonas hasn't read any romances." Stephanie wanted desperately to believe that what her friends said was true, but she was afraid to count on it. Jonas was too proud. Too stubborn. Too Jonas.

"He's enough of a hero to know when he's turning away from the best thing that's ever happened to him. He loves you."

Barbara's words were the cool voice of reason cutting through the fog of doubt that clouded Stephanie's troubled mind. Even Elizabeth Lockwood had told her how much Jonas needed her love. She couldn't doubt his mother.

"He must love you, or he wouldn't have asked you to marry him." Toni was equally convincing.

"So the next move is mine, right?" Stephanie glanced around at her friends' intent expressions.

"Most definitely."

The four followed Stephanie out of Jan's office, moving in single file like troops marching into battle. Down the hallway they paraded, finally coming to a halt in front of the elevator. Jan pushed the button for Stephanie, while the others offered words of encouragement.

"Fight for him," Barbara advised her. "If he's going to do this to you, then don't make it easy on him."

"Right," Toni concurred. "Let him know what he's missing."

"Good luck," Jan said as Stephanie walked into the elevator. Just before the thick steel doors glided shut her friends gave her the thumbs-up sign.

All the confidence Stephanie had felt when she stepped into the elevator deserted her the minute she faced Martha Westheimer. The woman barely looked in her direction. It was apparent the dragon was prepared for this confrontation.

For a full, intolerable minute Stephanie stood in front of the dragon's desk while Martha ignored her.

"Excuse me, please," Stephanie said in a strong, controlled tone. "I'm here to see Mr. Lockwood."

"He's in a meeting."

"I don't believe that."

"It is not my concern what you believe. Mr. Lockwood has no desire to see you."

"Now *that* I believe."

For the first time since Stephanie had known her, Martha Westheimer smiled. Well, almost smiled, Stephanie corrected herself. She wasn't completely convinced that the woman was capable of feeling amusement, much less revealing it.

"I'd like to help you, but . . ."

"I'll simply tell him you weren't able to stop me."

"Mr. Lockwood would know better," Martha said quietly. "If I can persevere against pesky attorneys and keep persistent salesmen at bay, one female employee is a piece of cake."

But Stephanie could see that Martha was weakening, which was in itself a sight to behold. She held her ground but didn't speak.

"He's in a rare mood," Martha whispered under her breath. "I don't remember ever seeing him quite like this."

"Is it his leg?"

"I beg your pardon?" The horn-rimmed glasses that balanced so precariously at the tip of the woman's nose threatened to slide off. Martha rescued them in the nick of time. "I don't understand your question."

"Jonas is often irritable when his leg is hurting him."

"No, it's not his leg, Ms. Coulter. It's you. First thing this morning, I asked about you. When Mr. Lockwood brought you up to his office yesterday it was apparent there'd been some trouble. You were shaking like a frightened rabbit and . . . well, the minute I said your name this morning, he nearly bit my head off. He said if I cared about my job I was to forget I'd ever met you. I've been with Mr. Lockwood for a good number of years, and I have never seen him like he was this morning. From the looks of it, I'd say he didn't go home last night."

A sense of urgency filled Stephanie. "It's imperative that I talk to him."

"I have my instructions, but quite honestly, Ms. Coulter, I don't believe I can go through—"

"Ms. Westheimer." Jonas's voice boomed over the intercom, startling both women. "Just how much longer am I to be kept waiting for the Westinghouse file?"

Stephanie's heart pounded frantically at the cold, hard sound of Jonas's voice. She'd thought she'd seen him in every mood imaginable. He could be unreasonable and flippant, but she had never known him to be deliberately cruel. Judging from the edge in his voice, she didn't doubt he was capable of anything today.

"Right away, sir," Martha answered quickly. She raised her head and whispered to Stephanie, "It would be better if you came back another day . . . perhaps tomorrow, when he's had a chance to mull things over."

"No," Stephanie countered, and shook her head for emphasis. "It's now or never." Squaring her shoulders, she picked up the file he'd requested from the corner of Martha's desk. "I'll take this to him."

Martha half rose from her chair, indecision etched on her pointed features. "I . . . can't let you do that."

"You can and you will," Stephanie told her firmly.

Slumping back into her chair, Martha shook her head slowly and shut her eyes. "I hope I'm doing the right thing."

With her hand on the knob of the door that led to Jonas's office, Stephanie hesitated for a second, then pushed open the door. With quick firm steps, she marched across the plush carpeting and placed the file on his desk. He was busy writing and didn't glance in her direction.

"I believe you asked for this," she said softly.

His head flew up so fast that for a moment she wondered if he'd given himself whiplash.

"Get out!"

The harsh words cut through her, but she refused to give in to the pain. "Not until you tell me what's going on. Jan Michaels gave me the most ridiculous message this morning. If you want to end our engagement, I have the right to know why."

He pointed viciously at the door. "I've had a change of heart. Leave the ring with Ms. Westheimer and get out of my sight."

She winced at the cold, merciless way he looked at her. "It's not that simple, Jonas," she said quietly, fighting back her anger and pain. "I have a right to know what happened. This doesn't make any sense. One afternoon you love me enough to ask me to share your life, and the following morning you despise me."

Jonas lowered his gaze, and it looked for a minute as though he was going to snap the pen he was holding in half. His hands clenched and unclenched.

"Does it have anything to do with Donald Black?"

His eyes shot to hers and narrowed. "No, but perhaps I was hasty in firing the man."

She decided to let that comment slide. "Then what possible explanation could there be?"

He rose slowly from his chair and braced his hands on the side of the desk, leaning forward. His eyes were as blue as a glacier and just as cold. "An interesting thing happened on my way out of the office yesterday afternoon. I heard howls of laughter coming from a group of male employees. By pure chance I happened to overhear that Stephanie Coulter had managed to pull off the feat of the century. A mere executive assistant had won the heart of the company president. Apparently some money was riding on just how quickly you could make a fool of me."

Stephanie blanched. "Jonas, I . . ."

"I didn't believe it at first," he went on, his voice as sharp as a new razor blade. "At least not until I saw the betting sheet posted on the bulletin board. You did amazingly well. The odds weren't in your favor. Several of the women seemed to have underestimated you. But I noticed the men were quick to trust your many charms. But only three hundred dollars? Really, Stephanie, you sold yourself cheap." His eyes narrowed as he mentioned the money.

"I didn't have anything to do with the marriage pool."

"Not according to what I overheard. You've been in on this little setup from the beginning. You and half the office were plotting my downfall as if I was some puppet on a string. Tricking me into falling in love with you was all part of the plan, wasn't it?"

"I—"

"Don't bother to deny it. At least have the decency to own up to the truth."

"I never had any intention of falling in love with you," she admitted.

"I suppose not. All you wanted—all anyone wanted—was to see me make a fool of myself."

Stephanie inhaled sharply. "You want the truth, then fine, I'll tell you everything."

Jonas reclaimed his chair and reached for his pen. "I have no desire to hear it."

He started writing, ignoring her, but she refused to walk away from him now. He had to understand that it had never been a game with her. She'd fallen into her coworkers' plan as an unwilling victim.

"Several weeks ago, a few of the women from the office

approached me. It was right after I'd worked for you when Ms. Westheimer was ill." She waited for some response, but when he didn't give her any, she continued undaunted. "They believed . . . that you worked so hard and demanded so much of everyone else because you needed a wife and family to fill your time. They thought you and I would be perfect together."

He snickered.

She did her best to ignore his derision. "Anyway, I laughed at them and told them it was a crazy idea. I didn't want any part of it."

"Obviously something changed your mind."

"Yes, something did!" she cried. "Paris. I met the real Jonas Lockwood at a fountain in a French park, and I knew then that I'd never be the same. For just a fleeting instant I glimpsed the man beneath that thick facade and discovered how much I could come to love him."

"More's the pity."

"I had no intention of falling in love with you. It just . . . happened. Even now, I don't regret it, I can't. I love you, Jonas Lockwood. I apologize that their game got carried to that extent, but please believe me, I didn't have anything to do with the marriage pool. I didn't even know anything about it until yesterday." She paused, her chest heaving with the tension that coiled her insides like a finely tuned violin. "I'd never do anything to hurt you. Never."

He dropped his gaze again. "Okay, you've had your say, and I've listened. It's what you wanted. Now kindly do as I request and leave the ring with Ms. Westheimer. Whatever was between us, and I sincerely doubt it was love, is over."

She felt as though she'd been hit physically. Tears burned in her eyes, but she refused to give in to the emotion. "You put this ring on my finger," she said softly, slowly. "If you want it off, you'll have to remove it yourself." She held her hand out to him and waited.

Although he refused to look at her, she could sense his indecision. "If it isn't love between us, I don't know what it is," she added softly.

"I saw you last night," he said, in a voice so low that the words were barely audible. "You came out of some lounge, laughing and joking with a group of women, and I knew it was a victory celebration. You'd achieved the impossible. You'd brought me to my knees."

"Not that . . . never that." She didn't know how to explain that she'd simply been happy and had wanted to share her joy with her friends. Words would only condemn her now.

"Keep the diamond," he said finally. "You've earned it."

"Jonas, please—"

"Either you leave quietly, or I'll call security and have you thrown out." His tone left little doubt that the threat was real.

Stunned almost to the point of numbness, she turned away from him. Tears blinded her as she headed for the door. Her hand was on the knob when she paused, not daring to look at him. "Did you say something?" she asked hopefully.

"No."

She nodded and, leaving the door open, moved into the foyer and to the elevator. Something came over her then. A sensation so strong and so powerful that she could barely contain it. With a burst of magnetic energy she whirled around and stormed back into his office, stopping at his desk. "Well?" she cried, her hands on her hips. "Aren't you going to stop me?"

Jonas glanced up and snarled. "What are you talking about?"

"They said you'd stop me."

"Who?"

"The others. They said if you really loved me . . . if anything between us was real, that you wouldn't be such an idiot as to let me leave." She'd improvised a bit, but that had been the gist of their message.

"I can assure you that after yesterday I have no feelings for you. None. At this point, my only intention regarding you is to sever our relationship and be done with you once and for all."

"You fool," she said, swallowing a hysterical sob. "If your pride is worth so much to you, then fine—so be it. If you want your ring back, then here it is." She paused long enough to slip it off her finger and place it on his desk. "It's over now, and all the trust and promise that went with it: the love, the joy, the laughter, the home, the family." She sucked in her breath at the unexpected pain that gripped her heart. "Our children would have been so special."

Jonas's mouth went taut, but he said nothing.

"It may surprise you to know that you're not the only one with an abundance of pride." Although she said each word as clearly as possible, the tears rained down her face. She turned and pointed to the elevator. "It's going to tear my heart out to walk out that door, but I'm going to do it. From here on, you'll live your life and I'll live mine, and we'll probably never meet again. But I love you, Jonas, I'll always love you. Not now, and probably not soon, but someday you'll regret this. My love will haunt you, Jonas, all the way to your grave."

"I suggest if you're going to leave you do it quickly," he said tonelessly, "before security arrives."

"Stop trying to hurt me more," she said, her voice cracking. "Isn't this humiliation enough?"

Again he refused to answer her.

"Goodbye, Jonas," she said softly, her voice trembling violently.

She turned and walked away from him, telling herself over and over again not to look back. It wasn't until she was in the elevator that she realized she was speaking out loud.

As the elevator carried her to the bottom floor, she felt as though she were descending into the depths of hell. She paused in the washroom to wipe the tears from her face and repair the damage to her makeup. Unable to face anyone at the moment, she took the bus directly home and contacted Jan from there.

"What happened?" Jan demanded. "Everyone's dying to know."

"The engagement is off," Stephanie announced, doing her utmost to keep her voice from cracking. "I'm going to call my parents. I'm letting go of the apartment and flying home at the end of the week. The sooner I leave Minneapolis the better."

"Steph, don't do anything foolish. It'll work out."

"It's not going to resolve itself," Stephanie said, pressing her fist against her forehead. "Jonas made that very clear, and I refuse to remain in this city any longer." Not when there was a chance she would run into him again. She could bear anything but that.

"I feel terrible," Jan mumbled, "Really terrible—I was the one who got you into this."

"I got myself into it, and no one else. I love him, Jan, and a part of me always will."

"Are you crying?"

"No." Stephanie tried to smile, but the effort was a miserable failure. "The tears are gone now. I'm not saying I didn't cry—believe me, this morning it was Waterworks International around here. But my crying jag is over. I'll recover in time. That's the best thing about being a Coulter—we bounce back."

Jan sighed with a hint of envy. "I can't believe you—you're so strong. If this were to happen to me and Jim, I'd come unglued."

Family was the sticking agent that would hold Stephanie together. Her parents would help her get through this ordeal.

Now, more than at any time since she'd left home, she felt the need for their comforting love and all that was familiar. The wheat farm, the old two-story farmhouse with the wide front porch. The half-mile-long driveway with rolling fields of grain on either side. Home. Family. Love.

"Is there anything I can do for you?" Jan wanted to know.

"Nothing. If . . . if I don't see you before Saturday, say goodbye to everyone for me. I'll miss you all."

"Oh, Steph, I hate to see it come to this."

"I do, too, but it's for the best."

For four days Stephanie tried to pick up the pieces of her life. She packed her bags, sold what furniture she could and gave the rest to charity. None of it was worth much, since she'd bought most of it secondhand. The bookcase was the most difficult to part with, and in the end she disassembled it and packed the long boards with the rest of the things she was having trucked to Colville. The expense of doing so was worth more than three similar sets of bookshelves, but it was all that she would have to remember Jonas by, and even though she was doing everything humanly possible to purge him from her life, she wanted to hang on to the bookcase and the memory of that night together.

Late Friday afternoon, her suitcases resting in the barren apartment, she waited for Jan to pick her up and drive her to a hotel close to the airport. She half expected Maureen, Toni and Barbara to arrive with Jan, and she mentally braced herself for the drain on her emotions. Goodbyes were always difficult.

When the doorbell chimed, she took a deep breath and attempted to smile brightly.

"Hello, Stephanie." A vital, handsome Jonas stood in the doorway.

"Jonas." Her fingers clutched the door handle so tightly that she thought the knob would break off. All week she'd been praying for a miracle, but finally she had given up hope. Jonas was too proud, and she knew it.

"May I come in?"

She blinked twice and stepped aside. "As you can see, I can't offer you a seat," she said, leaning against the closed door.

He stepped into the middle of the bare room and whirled around sharply. "You're leaving?"

"I'm expecting my ride in a few minutes—I thought you were Jan."

"I see."

"You wanted something?" She tried to keep the eagerness from her voice. In her dreams, he'd had her in his arms by now.

"I've come to offer you your job back."

Her hopeful expectations died a cruel death. "No, thank you."

"Why not?"

"Surely you know the reason, Jonas."

He hesitated, ambled to the other side of the room and glanced out the window to the street below. "You're a good executive assistant."

She held her ground. "Then I shouldn't have a problem finding work in Washington."

"I'll double your salary," he said, not bothering to turn around.

She was incredulous. She could see the expression on his face; he looked weary and defeated. "Jonas, why are you really here?" she asked in a soft whisper.

He smiled then, a sad smile that didn't reach his eyes. "I'm afraid I have a mutiny on my hands."

"A what?"

"Five of my top female employees are threatening to quit their jobs."

"Five?"

"Perhaps more."

"I . . . I don't understand."

"For that matter, I'm having a problem comprehending it myself." He wiped a hand over his face. "This afternoon Martha Westheimer, and four others I barely know, walked into my office."

"Martha Westheimer?" Every bad thought she'd ever entertained about Jonas's executive assistant vanished in a flood of surprise and pleasure.

"Was she in on this from the beginning?" His gaze captured Stephanie's but quickly released it.

"No . . . just Jan, Barbara, Toni and Maureen."

His mouth formed a half smile. "They accused me of not being hero material."

"They didn't mean anything by it—they're still upset."

"I take it that being rejected as a hero makes me the lowest of the low?" He cocked his thick brows questioningly.

"Something like that." Despite the seriousness of the conversation, she was forced to disguise a smile. "This whole thing started because Jan and the others thought I was heroine material—but they were mistaken about me, as well. I did everything wrong."

"How's that?" He turned and leaned against the windowsill, studying her.

She shrugged, lowered her gaze and rubbed the palms of her hands together nervously. "You kissed me once in your office, and I told you never to let it happen again. I was forever saying and doing the worst possible thing."

"But I did kiss you again."

This was a subject she wanted to avoid. "What else did they say?"

"Just that if I let you go I would be making the biggest

mistake of my life, and that they refused to stand idly by and let it happen."

"What did they suggest you do?"

"They said if I didn't do something to prevent you from leaving they were handing in their resignations effective that minute."

Looking at him was impossible; it hurt far too much. "So that's why you offered me my old job back—you were seeking a compromise?"

"No," he said harshly. "I figured if you agreed to that, then there would be hope of you agreeing to more."

"More?"

"The ring's in my pocket, Stephanie." He brought it out and handed it to her. "It's yours."

The diamond felt warm in her palm, as though he'd been holding on to it. She raised her eyes to his, not understanding. "Jonas," she whispered past the tight knot that formed in her throat. "I can't accept this ring."

He went pale. "Why not?"

"For the same reason I refuse to go back to Lockwood Industries."

"I love you, Stephanie."

"But not enough to truly want me as your wife," she said accusingly, feeling more wretched than the day he'd fired her. "Don't worry about Jan and the others. I'll explain everything. You needn't worry about them quitting. That's the reason you're here, isn't it?"

"No," he said huskily, then paused and seemed to regain control of his emotions. "I don't want you to leave. I thought about what you said, and you're right. If you go, everything I've ever dreamed about will disappear with you. I have my pride, Stephanie, but it's been cold comfort the last few days."

"Oh, Jonas, don't tease me, I don't think I could bear it—are you saying you *want* me for your wife?"

"Yes." He raised his eyes toward heaven as if to plead for patience. "What did you think I meant?"

"I don't know. That they'd blackmailed you into proposing again, I guess."

He reached for her, drawing her soft body to his and inhaling the fresh sunshine scent of her hair. "I've been half out of my mind the last few days. To be honest, I was glad Ms. Westheimer and the others came. It gave me the excuse I needed to contact you. Right after you left it dawned on me that I'd been an idiot. I'd overreacted to that stupid marriage pool. Why should any of that silliness matter to me when I've got you?" He pressed his mouth hungrily down on hers.

Stephanie melted against him and sniffled loudly. "I love you so much."

"I know." He rubbed his chin against the top of her head. "I think we fooled the odds makers this time."

"How's that?"

"Odds were three to one that we'd get back together again."

"Three to one?"

"You know what else?"

"No," she said with a watery smile.

"There are other odds floating around the office. They say you'll be pregnant by the end of the year."

"That soon?" She wound her arms around his neck and moved her body against his, telling him without words her eagerness to experience all that marriage had to offer them.

"I say they're way off," he growled in her ear. "It shouldn't take nearly that long."

* * * * *

Jury of His Peers

To
Ted Macomber, our son,
the wonderful negotiator

One

There was something vaguely familiar about him. Caroline Lomax's gaze was repeatedly drawn across the crowded room where the prospective jury members had been told to wait. He sat reading, oblivious to the people surrounding him. Some were playing cards, others chatting. A few were reading just as he was. It couldn't be Theodore Thomasson, Caroline mused, shaking her head so that the soft auburn curls bounced. Not "Tedious Ted," the childhood name she had ruthlessly given him because of his apparent perfection. The last time she'd seen him had been the summer he was fifteen and she was fourteen, just before her father's job had taken them to San Francisco. It wasn't him; it couldn't be. First off, Theodore Thomasson wouldn't be living on the West Coast and, second, she would have broken out in a prickly rash if he were. Never in her entire life had she disliked anyone more.

Determined to ignore the man completely, Caroline picked up a magazine and idly flipped through the dog-eared pages. If that was Theodore, which it obviously couldn't be, then he'd changed. She would never openly admit that he was handsome back then. Attractive, maybe, in an eclectic way. But this man . . . If it was Theodore, then his eyes were the same intense blue of his youth, but his ears no longer had the tendency to stick out. The neatly trimmed dark hair was more stylish than prudent, and if Tedious Ted was anything, he was sensible, levelheaded and circumspect. And rational. Rational to the point of making her crazy. Admittedly, her own father was known to be rational, practical, discriminating and at times even parsimonious. As the president of Lomax, Inc., the fastest growing computer company in the world, he had to be.

The thought of her stern-faced father produced an involuntary smile. What a thin veneer his rationality was, at least where she and her mother were concerned. He loved his daughter enough to allow her to be herself. Caroline realized that it was difficult for him to accept her offbeat lifestyle and her choice to go to culinary school with the intent of becoming a chef, not to mention that she'd opted for a lower standard of living than what she was accustomed to. She knew he would rather see her in law school. Regardless, he supported her and loved her, and she adored him for it.

A glance at the round clock on the drab beige wall confirmed that within another fifteen minutes the prospective jurors would be free to go. Her first day of jury duty had been a complete waste of time. This certainly wasn't turning out as she'd expected. Her mind had conjured up an exciting murder trial or at least a dramatic drug bust. Instead she'd spent the day sitting in a room full of strangers, looking for a way to occupy herself until her name was called for a panel.

Fifteen minutes later, as they stood to file out of the room, Caroline toyed with the idea of saying something to the man who resembled Theodore, but rejected the idea. If it was him, she decided, she didn't want to know. In addition, she needed to hurry to the Four Seasons Hotel. Her dad had a business meeting in Seattle with an export agency, and her mother had come along to visit Caroline, a plan that was derailed when fate decreed that Caroline would spend the day in a crowded, stuffy room being bored out of her mind. Tonight the three of them were going out to dinner. From the restaurant they would take a cab, and she would see her parents off on a return flight to San Francisco.

At precisely five, she walked down the steps of the King County Courthouse and glanced quickly at the street for the bus. She swung her backpack over her shoulder and hurriedly stepped onto the sidewalk. Thick, leaden-gray clouds obliterated the March sun, and she shook off a sensation of gloom and oppression. This feeling had been with her from the moment she'd walked into the jury room, and she suspected that it didn't have anything to do with the early spring weather.

A few minutes later she smiled at the doorman in the long red coat who held open the heavy glass doors of the posh hotel. Moments later she stepped off the elevator, knocked, and was let into her parents' suite.

Ruth Lomax glanced up from the knitting she was carrying, and her eyes brightened. Her bifocals were perched on the tip of her nose, so low that it was a wonder they didn't slip completely free. "How'd it go?" she asked as she sat back down.

"Boring," Caroline answered, taking the seat opposite her mother. "I sat around all day, waiting for someone to call my name."

A smile softened her mother's look of concentration. There was only a faint resemblance between mother and daughter, which could be attributed mostly to their identical hair color. Although Ruth's was the deep combination of brown and red that was sometimes classified as chestnut, Caroline's was a luxuriant shade of brilliant auburn. Other similarities were difficult to find. A thousand times in her twenty-four years, Caroline had prayed that God would see fit to grant her Ruth's gentle smile and generous personality. Instead, she had been pegged a rebel, a nonconformist, bad-mannered and unladylike—all by her first grade teacher. From there matters had grown worse. In her junior year she was expelled from boarding school for impersonating a nun. Her father had thrown up his hands at her shenanigans, while Ruth had smiled sweetly and staunchly defended her. Ruth seemed to believe that Caroline could have a vocation for the religious life and the family shouldn't discount her interest in this area. Caroline was wise enough to smother her giggles.

"You know who I thought I saw today?"

"Who, dear?" Folding her glasses, Ruth set them aside and gave her full attention to her daughter.

"Theodore Thomasson."

"Really? He was such a nice boy."

"Mom!" Caroline exclaimed. "He was boring."

"Boring?" Ruth Lomax looked absolutely shocked and smiled gently. "Caroline, I don't know what it is you have against that boy. You two never could seem to get along."

"Being with him was like standing in a room and listening to someone scrape their nails down a blackboard." Irritated, Caroline yanked the backpack off and tossed it carelessly aside. "I suppose you're going to want me to wear a dress tonight." Her usual jeans and T-shirt had been a constant source of aggravation to her father. However, tonight Caroline wanted to keep the peace and do her best to please him.

Ruth ignored the question, her look thoughtful as she set aside her knitting. "He was always so well-mannered. So polite."

"'Stuffy' is the word," Caroline interjected. "It's the only way to describe a fifteen-year-old boy who takes dancing lessons."

"Lots of people take dance lessons, dear."

Caroline opened her mouth to object, then closed it again, not wishing to argue. As a boy, Theodore had been so courteous, charming and full of decorum that she'd thought she would throw up.

"He was thoughtful and introspective. As I recall, you were dreadful to him that last summer."

Caroline shrugged. Her mother didn't know the half of it.

"Sending him all those mail-order acne medications was outrageous." She wasn't able to completely disguise a smile. "C.O.D. at that. How could you, Caroline?"

"I wanted him to know what it was like not to be perfect in every way."

"But his skin was flawless."

"That's just it. The guy didn't have the common decency to have so much as a pimple."

Slowly, her mother shook her head. "And you had pimples and freckles."

"Don't forget the braces."

"And he teased you?"

Caroline tossed her jacket over a chair without looking at her mother. "No, he wouldn't even do that. I'd have liked him better if he had."

"It sounds to me as if you were jealous."

"Oh, really, Mother, don't get philosophical on me. What's there to like about a kid whose favorite television program is *Meet the Press*? Believe me, there's nothing to envy."

Although her mother didn't comment, Caroline felt her frowning gaze as she busied herself, pulling out a skirt and sweater from the backpack. "What ever became of him, Mom, do you know?"

"The last I heard, he was working for the government."

"Probably the Internal Revenue Service," Caroline said with a mocking arch of her brow.

"You may be right."

That secret smile was back again, and Caroline wondered exactly what her mother was up to. "He's the type of guy who would relish auditing people's tax returns," Caroline mumbled under her breath, running a brush through her thick hair until it curled obediently at her shoulders.

"By the way, Caroline, your father and I are definitely getting you a bed for your birthday."

"Mom, I don't have room for one."

"It's ridiculous to pull that . . . thing down from the wall every night. Good grief, what would you do if it snapped back into place in the middle of the night?"

Caroline smiled. "Cry for help?" It wasn't that she didn't appreciate the offer, but her apartment was small enough as it was. Having a fold-up bed was the most economical use of the limited space. The apartment was cozy—all right, snug—but its location offered several advantages. It was close to the Pike Place Market and the heart of downtown Seattle. In addition, her school was within walking distance. As far as she was concerned, she couldn't ask for more.

"You need a decent bed," her mother argued. "How do you expect to find a job if you don't get a good night's rest?"

"I sleep like a baby," Caroline returned, hiding a smile. "Now, about dinner tonight. Would you prefer to take a taxi to meet Dad, or are you brave enough to try the backseat of my scooter?" She only suggested this for shock value. The scooter was safely tucked away in the basement of her apartment building.

"Your scooter?" Ruth's voice rose half an octave as she turned startled eyes toward her daughter.

"Don't worry, I can see you'd prefer the taxi."

Since Charles Lomax was tied up later than expected in a meeting, Caroline and her mother took a taxi directly to La Mer, an elegant Seattle restaurant that overlooked the ship canal connecting Lake Union with Puget Sound. A large stone fireplace with a crackling fire greeted them. As they checked their coats, Caroline glanced around the expansive room, seeking her father's burly figure. When she caught sight of two men rising from a table in the middle of the room, her heart dropped. Next to her father was the same man she'd seen in the jury room, and something told her it really was Theodore Thomasson. So this was the reason for her mother's strange little smiles. Everything fit into place now. This business deal with the export outfit was somehow linked to Theodore.

"Ted, how nice to see you again." Ruth Lomax embraced him and stepped back to study him. "You've grown so tall and good looking."

"The years have only enhanced your beauty." He looked beyond Ruth to Caroline. "I wondered if that was you today."

So he had noticed her. Caroline's throat felt scratchy and dry. On closer inspection, she was forced to admit that Theodore had indeed changed. The boyish good looks of fifteen had matured into strikingly handsome sculpted features that were the picture of both strength and character. Theodore Thomasson was attractive enough to cause more than a few heads to turn. And Caroline was no exception. Her bemused thoughts were interrupted by his deep male voice, which was as intriguing as his looks.

"Hello, Caroline." His eyes moved with warm appraisal from her mother to rest solidly on her. Then the friendliness drained from the brilliant blue gaze as they sought and met hers. "It's good to see you again, Hot Stuff."

Caroline fumed at the reference to that last summer and the

incident she sincerely hoped her parents never connected with her. With an effort, she managed to shrug lightly and smile. "Touché, Tedious Ted."

With a hearty laugh, Charles Lomax pulled out a chair and seated his wife. Before Ted could offer her the same courtesy, Caroline seated herself.

"I see you're not intimidated by my daughter," her father told Ted with a smile.

Silently, Caroline gritted her teeth. Theodore Thomasson wasn't getting the best of her that easily. Her chance would come later.

Her gaze was drawn to the huge windows that provided an unobstructed view of the ship canal. Sailboats, their sails lowered, glided past, with the brilliant golden sun setting in the background.

Inside the restaurant, the tables, covered in dark red linen, were each graced with a single long-stemmed rose. La Mer was rated among the best restaurants in Seattle. She had never eaten here before, but the elegance of the room assured her that no matter what the food was like, this was going to be a special treat.

"I understand you work for the government. The Internal Revenue Service, is it?" Caroline asked Ted with mock-sweetness, then turned away to study the elaborate menu. She hoped the dig hit its mark.

"And exactly what is it that *you* do?" From beneath dark brows he observed her with frank interest. She noted that he hadn't answered her question. Although his eyes didn't spark with challenge, there was an uncompromising authority in the set of his jaw that wasn't the least bit to Caroline's liking.

Her mother spoke up quickly. "Caroline graduated cum laude from—"

"I'm training at the Natalie Dupont School," Caroline interrupted. Unsure that he would recognize the name of the nationally famous culinary school, she added, “I’m a chef—or I will be shortly. I’ve just completed a year’s apprenticeship.” Her father had had a difficult time accepting the fact that she’d chosen a career as menial as cooking. Ambition and hard work had driven Charles Lomax to the top of his profession. Caroline didn’t doubt that she would have to work just as hard making a name for herself, but though he rarely argued the point with her, she knew her father didn’t agree.

The aggressive vitality in Ted’s eyes demanded that she look at him. “So you didn’t grow up to be a firefighter,” he said with a smile.

Caroline felt a cold sweat break out across her upper lip. Her family knew nothing of the fireworks display she had rigged outside his bedroom the night of July third.

“No.” She forced her voice to sound as innocent as possible, as if her memory had blotted out that unfortunate chain of events that had set the balcony on fire.

“Shame,” he responded casually. “You displayed such a talent for pyrotechnics.”

“What’s this?” her father asked, his gaze swinging from Caroline to Ted.

“Nothing, Dad.” She gave him her most engaging smile. “Something from when we were kids.”

Ted’s mouth quirked in a half smile.

Caroline tilted her chin and haughtily returned his gaze. “You were such an easy target,” she whispered.

“Not anymore, I’m not.”

Smoothing the starched linen napkin over her lap, Caroline gave him a cool look. “I never have been able to turn down a challenge.”

“Am I missing something here?” her father demanded.

"Nothing, Dad," Caroline answered. "Tell me, Theodore, what brought you to Seattle? I always thought you'd think of Boston as home."

"Most people call me Ted."

"All right . . . Ted."

"Seattle's a beautiful city. It seemed a nice place to live."

"Are you always so vague?" Caroline's voice was sharp enough to cause her mother to eye her above the top of the menu. Unbelievable! She actually found Theodore—Ted—as irritating now as she had when they were teenagers. Worse, even.

"Only when I have to be," he taunted lightly, doing a poor job of disguising a smile.

Caroline itched to find a way to put him in his place and was surprised at the intensity of her feelings.

The meal was an uncomfortable experience. Countless times Caroline found her gaze drawn to Ted. In astonishment, she noticed the way his eyes would warm when they rested on her mother and immediately turn icy cool when they skimmed over her. He didn't like her, that much was obvious. But then, he had little reason to do anything but hate the sight of her.

Through the course of the conversation, Caroline learned that though Ted might have worked for the federal government at one time, he didn't now. From the sound of things, her guess had been right and he was employed by the export company that had brought her father to Seattle. She didn't want to ask for fear of sounding interested.

The meal was as delicious as she'd been led to believe it would be, so she focused on that and made only a few comments, spoke only when questioned and smiled demurely at all the appropriate times.

"So you two are both serving jury duty this week," her father said after an uncomfortable pause in the conversation. "What a coincidence."

Caroline's and Ted's eyes met from across the table.

"I call it bad luck," Caroline answered. She toyed with the last bit of baked potato as she dropped her gaze.

"And neither of you was aware that the other lived here?"

"No." Again it was Caroline who answered, then mumbled under her breath that moving to California was looking more appealing by the minute. If she expected a reaction from Ted, he didn't give her one. He'd heard her, though, and one corner of his mouth jerked upward briefly. Somehow she doubted that the movement was in any way related to a smile.

"Never served on a jury myself," her father continued. "Don't know that I ever will."

"It must have been twenty years ago when I was called. You remember the time, don't you, Charles?" Ruth chimed in, and detailed the account of the robbery trial on which she'd sat.

When Caroline did chance a casual look Ted's way, she was rewarded with a slightly narrowed gaze. Outwardly, he looked as if he hadn't a care in the world and was thoroughly enjoying himself. She couldn't imagine how. He couldn't help but feel her obvious dislike. Occasionally she would catch him studying her and flush angrily. His pleasant, amused expression never varied, which only served to aggravate her more. He should be the uncomfortable one. Instead, he exchanged pleasantries with her parents, then spoke affectionately of his own family. When the bill was presented, Ted insisted on paying, and in the same breath offered to drive her parents to the airport.

"But I thought I was taking you," Caroline objected.

"Your father and I can hardly ride on the back of your scooter," her mother said with a teasing glint in her eye.

"Scooter?" Ted repeated with a curious tilt of his head.

Caroline bristled, waiting for a cutting remark that didn't come.

"It's the most economical way of getting around," she supplied and granted him a saccharine smile.

"It's a shame my daughter has to be economical about anything," her father said with a rumbling chuckle. "She's taking this cooking business seriously. Living within her means. I give her credit for that."

Caroline had to bite her tongue to keep from reminding him that she was training to be a chef, not a short-order cook. A year of schooling, plus another year's apprenticeship, proved that this was serious business. In four years of college she hadn't worked as hard as she had in the last two years.

"It will work out fine to have you drop us off at the airport," her father continued.

"I'll take a taxi from here," Caroline said. The thought of getting stuck alone with Ted Thomasson on the return ride from the airport was more than she could tolerate.

"Nonsense. I'll see you home," Ted said smoothly, one dark brow rising arrogantly, daring her to refuse.

"Theodore, you were always so polite," Ruth said, smiling at her daughter as if to point out that Caroline had indeed misjudged him all these years.

Personally, Caroline doubted that. He might have matured into a devilishly handsome man, but looks weren't everything.

From the restaurant, the foursome returned to the Four Seasons Hotel so the Lomaxes could collect their luggage. The ride to the airport took an additional uneasy twenty minutes. Caroline buried her hands deep inside her pockets as she walked down the concourse at Sea-Tac International. She dreaded the time when she would have to face Ted without her parents present to buffer the conversation.

Her father and mother hugged her goodbye and Caroline promised to email more often. In addition, they promised to pass on her love to her older brother, Darryl, who lived in Sacramento with his wife and two young sons. All the while they were saying their farewells, Caroline could feel Ted's eyes studying her.

He didn't say anything until her parents had disappeared into the security line.

"The cafeteria's open."

She cast him a curious glance. "We just ate a fantastic meal. You couldn't possibly want another."

One brow arched briefly. "I'm suggesting coffee."

"No thanks."

"Fine." His long stride forced her to half walk, half run in order to keep up with him. By the time they were in the parking garage, she was straining to breathe evenly. Not for anything would she let him know she was winded.

The ride back into the city was completed in grating silence. It wasn't until they were near the downtown area that she relayed her address. Even then, she said it in a mechanical monotone. Ted glanced at her briefly and his fingers tightened around the steering wheel. This was even worse than she'd imagined.

When he pulled into a parking lot across from her apartment, turned off the engine and opened the car door, butterflies filled her stomach. "I didn't invite you inside," she said indignantly.

"No," he agreed. "But I'm coming in anyway." A thread of steel in his voice dared her to challenge him. In disbelief, she watched as his slow, satisfied smile deepened the laugh lines at his eyes. Too bad. Whatever he had in mind, she wasn't interested.

"Listen," she said, striving for a cool, objective tone. "If you want an apology for what happened that summer, then I'll give you one."

Ted acted as if she hadn't spoken. Agilely, he stepped out of the car and slammed the door closed. Caroline climbed out on her own before he could walk around to her side. Opening a lady's car door was something he would obviously do, given the kind of man he was.

She stopped and looked both ways before stepping off the curb. A hand at her elbow jerked her back onto the sidewalk. "What are you doing?" he demanded.

Caroline stared at him speechlessly. "Crossing the street," she managed after a long moment.

"The light's this way."

Ted hadn't changed, not a bit. Good grief, he didn't even jaywalk. She clenched her jaw, hating the thought of him invading her home.

"Did you hear what I said earlier?" she asked. "I owe you an apology. You've got one. What more do you want?"

His hand cupped her elbow as they stopped at the traffic light. She pulled her arm free, angrier with her body's warm response to his touch than the fact that he'd taken her arm.

The light changed, and they crossed the street. The brick apartment building was four stories high. Caroline's tiny apartment was on the third floor. All the way up the stairs, she tried to think of a way of getting rid of Ted. She realized that arguing with him wasn't going to do any good. She might as well listen to what he had to say and be done with it.

The key felt cool against her fingers as she inserted it into the lock. A flip of the light switch bathed the room in a gentle glow.

Standing just inside the apartment, Ted made a sweeping

appraisal of the small room. Caroline couldn't read the look in his eyes. Hooking her backpack over the doorknob, she turned to him, hands on her hips. "All right," she said in a slow breath. "What is it you want?"

"Coffee."

Seething, she marched across the room to the compact kitchen. With anyone else she would have ground fresh-roasted beans. As it was, she brought down one earthenware mug, dumped a teaspoon of instant coffee inside and heated the water in the microwave.

"Satisfied?" she asked sarcastically as she handed him the steaming mug.

"Relatively so." His half smile was maddening.

Pulling out a chair, he sat and looked up at her standing stiffly on the other side of the narrow room. "Have a seat."

"No thanks. I prefer to stand."

He shrugged as if it made no difference to him and blew on the coffee before taking a tentative sip.

Stubbornly, Caroline crossed her arms in front of her and waited.

"I want to know why," he said at last.

"Why what?" she snapped.

"Why do you dislike me so much?"

"Have you got a year?"

"I have as much time as necessary."

"Where would you like me to begin?" Her voice was deceptively soft, but her feelings were clear. By the time she was finished, his ears would burn for a week.

"That last summer will do." He still refused to react to the antagonism in her voice.

"All right," she said evenly. "You were perfect in every way. Honest, sincere, forthright. What kind of kid is that? Darryl and I had stashed away fireworks for weeks, and you acted as if we'd robbed a bank."

"They were illegal. You're lucky you didn't blow your fool head off. As it was—"

"See." She pointed an accusing finger at him. "If you didn't want any part of it, that was your prerogative, but tattling to my dad was a spiteful thing to do. It's that goody-goody attitude I couldn't tolerate," she continued, warming to the subject.

Ted looked genuinely taken back. "What? I didn't say a word to your family."

Caroline's lungs expanded slowly. Ted Thomasson probably hadn't stretched the truth in his life. She couldn't do anything but believe him. "Then how did Dad find out I had them?"

"How am I supposed to know?" His eyes nearly sparked visible blue flame.

"At least he never found out how I got rid of them."

"What were my other crimes?"

Uneasy now, Caroline shrugged weakly.

"Well?" he demanded.

"You wouldn't go swimming with me." The one afternoon she'd made an effort to be nice, Ted had flatly rejected her offer of friendship.

A brief smile touched his eyes. "True, but did you ever ask yourself why?"

"I don't care to know. What was the matter? I was trying to be nice. Were you afraid I was going to drown you?"

"Knowing your past history, that was a distinct possibility."

"It wasn't my fault the brakes on that golf cart failed."

"Don't lie to me, Caroline. You never hid what you thought of me before."

Guilt colored her face a hot shade of red. "Okay, I'll admit it. I never liked you. And I never will." She crossed her arms again to indicate that the conversation was closed.

"Why didn't you like me?" he asked softly, setting his coffee aside. The chair slid back as he suddenly stood.

Caroline pinched her mouth tightly closed. When he moved so that he loomed over her, she clenched her jaw.

"Why?" he repeated.

"I . . . just didn't . . . that's all." She detested the way her voice shook.

"There's got to be a logical reason." His eyes cut through her.

"Your hair was always perfectly trimmed." Her gaze locked with his in a fierce battle of wills. "It still is," she added accusingly.

"Yours is still the same fiery red." As if he couldn't resist, he reached out and wove a thick strand around his index finger. "I remember the first time I saw it and wondered if your hair color was the reason you were so hot-tempered."

"A lot you know." Her voice gained strength and volume. "My hair is auburn."

He laughed softly, as if he found her protestations amusing.

"You've probably never done anything daring in your life," she went on. "You were always afraid of one thing or another. You're the most boring person I ever met."

"And you're a hellion."

"But I've never bored anyone in my life," she snapped defensively.

"Neither have I. You simply didn't give me the chance to prove it to you." He released her hair to slide his fingers around her nape in a slow, easy caress.

Caroline drew in a sharp breath and tried to shrug his hand free. A crazy whirl of sensations caused her stomach muscles to tense.

"Take your hand off me." She grabbed his arm in an effort to free herself.

He ignored her protests. "Was there anything else?"

"You . . . took dancing lessons."

Nodding, he laughed softly. "That I did. Only I hated them more than you'll ever realize."

"You—never wanted to do anything fun." Desperately her mind sought valid reasons for her intense dislike of him and came up blank.

"I want to do things now," he drawled in a voice that was barely perceptible. Ever so slowly, he lowered his mouth to hers.

Mesmerized, her heart pounding like the crashing waves upon a sandy shore in a storm, Caroline was powerless to stop him. When he fitted his mouth over hers, she made a weak effort by pushing against his chest. No kiss had ever been so sweet, so perfect, so wonderful. Soon her hands slid around his neck as she pressed her soft figure to his long length, clinging to him for support.

When they broke apart, she dropped her arms and took a staggering step backward. The staccato beat of her heart dropped to a sluggish drum roll at the wicked look twinkling in Ted's eyes. He'd wanted to humiliate her as she'd done to him all those years ago. And he'd succeeded.

"I bet you didn't think kissing 'Tedious Ted' could be so good, did you, Caroline?"

Two

Caroline woke with the first light of dawn that splashed through her beveled-glass window. The sky was cloudless, clear and languid. Her first thought was of Ted and her overwhelming response to his kiss. Silently, she seethed, detesting the very thought of him. To use sensory attraction against her was the lowest form of deceit. He'd wanted to humiliate her and had purposely kissed her as a means of punishment for the innocent crimes of her youth. And what really irritated her was that it had been the most sensual kiss of her life. Her cheeks burned with mortification, and she pressed cool palms to her face to blot out the embarrassment. Ted Thomasson was vile, completely without scruples, and that was only the tip of the iceberg as far as she was concerned.

The morning was chilly, but Caroline had her anger to keep her warm. If she'd disliked Ted Thomasson at fourteen, those feelings paled in comparison to the intensity of her feelings now. Yet she had to paint on a plastic smile and sit in the same room with him today, pretending she hadn't been the least bit affected by what had happened. If she were lucky, she would be called out early for a trial, but at the rate her luck was running, she would end up stuck sitting next to him for the next four days.

The brisk walk to the King County Courthouse helped cool her indignation. She bought a cup of coffee from a machine and carried it with her into the jury room. The bailiff checked off her name and gave her a smiling nod. Caroline didn't pause to look around, afraid Ted would see her and think that she was seeking him out. As far as she was concerned, if she saw him in another eighty years it would be a hundred years too soon.

The coffee was scalding, and she set it on a table to cool while she reached for a magazine—an outdated copy of *Time.* Flipping through the pages, she noted that the stories that had captured the headlines six months ago were still in the news today. Little had changed in the world. Except Ted—he'd changed. His aggressive virility had captured her attention from the minute they'd stepped into the restaurant. Forcibly, she shook her head to reject the thought of him. She detested the way he'd invaded her mind from the minute she'd climbed out of bed.

She caught a movement out of the corner of her eye and turned to see. Ted stood framed in the doorway of the large, open room. He wore an impeccable three-piece gray suit with leather shoes. Italian, no doubt. After spending a restless day lounging in the jury room, almost everyone else had dressed more casually today. She herself had slipped on dark cords and an olive-green pullover sweater. But not Mr. Propriety. Oh, no, his long legs had probably never known the feel of denim. Angrily she banished the image of Ted in a pair of tight-fitting jeans.

"Morning." He claimed the empty chair beside her. "I trust you slept well. I know I did."

Wordlessly, she took her cup of coffee and moved to a vacant seat three chairs down.

Without hesitating, Ted stood and followed her. "Is something wrong?"

Despite her anger, she managed to make her voice sound calm and reasonable. "If you insist on pestering me, then you leave me no option but to report you to the bailiff."

"Did I pester you last night, Caroline?" he asked in a seductive drawl that sent shivers racing down her spine.

"Yes." She felt like shouting but made an effort and kept her voice low.

"Funny, that wasn't the impression I got."

"You're so obtuse you wouldn't recognize a—"

"Your response to me was so hot it could have set off a forest fire."

She drew a rasping breath. She tried and failed to think of a comeback that would wipe that mocking grin off his face.

"From the time we were children, I've disliked you," she murmured, her gaze fixed on her coffee. "And nothing's changed."

His soft chuckle caught her off guard. She'd expected something scathing in retaliation, but certainly not laughter. In hindsight, she realized that Ted had probably never raised his voice to a woman.

"That's not the impression you gave me last night," he taunted.

Seething, Caroline closed her eyes. Her mind groped for a logical explanation of what had happened. She'd only had one glass of wine with the meal, so she couldn't blame her response on the influence of alcohol. Telling him that her biorhythms were out of sync would make her sound like an idiot. "Knowing that you've always been perfect in every way, I don't expect you to understand a momentary lapse of discretion on my part," she finally said.

"I don't believe that any more than you do," he said with cool calm.

Crossing her arms in front of her, she refused to look at him. "Fine. Believe what you want. I couldn't care less."

"You care very much," he returned flatly.

Pinching her mouth tightly closed, she refused to be drawn further into the conversation.

"You intrigue me, Caroline. You always have. I've never known anyone who could match your spirit. You were magnificent at fourteen. With that bright red hair and freckles dancing across your nose, I found you absolutely enchanting."

Slowly, she appraised him, searching each strongly defined feature for signs of sarcasm or derision. She was so taken aback by the gentle caress of his voice that any response died in her throat. "How can you say that?" she managed at last. "I was horrible to you."

"Yes," he chuckled, "I know."

"You should hate me," she said.

"I discovered I never could."

The bailiff began reading the names on the first panel of jurors, and Ted paused to listen, along with the hundred and fifty other people seated in the room. Periodically during the day, the court sent requests down to the jury room and names were drawn in a lottery system, and this same hush fell over the crowd every time.

Caroline's name was one of the first to be called. At last, she thought, she was going to see some of the action. A few seconds later she heard Ted's name. They were being called along with several others for the same trial.

They were led as a group into an upstairs courtroom and seated outside the jury box. Caroline sat down on the polished mahogany pew, uncomfortably distracted by the knowledge that Ted was behind her. Their conversation lingered in her mind, and she wanted to free her thoughts for the task that lay before her. She looked up and noticed that several people were studying the potential jurors. The judge, in his long black robe, sat in the front of the courtroom, his look somber. The attorneys were at their respective tables, as was the defendant. She found her gaze drawn to the young man who stared at the group with a belligerent sneer.

Everything about him spoke of aggressive antagonism—his looks, his clothes, the way his eyes refused to meet anyone else's. His slouched posture, with arms folded defiantly across his chest, revealed a lack of respect for the court and the legal proceedings. The defense attorney leaned over to say something to him, but the defendant merely shrugged his shoulders, apparently indicating that he didn't care one way or the other. What an unpleasant man, Caroline thought, holding back her instant feelings of dislike. Above all, she wanted to be impartial and, if she were chosen for the jury, base her decision on the evidence, not the look of the defendant.

The judge spoke, announcing that the defendant, Nelson Bergstrom, was being tried for robbery and assault. Twelve of the panel members were led to the jurors' box. Caroline was the last to be seated in the first row. A series of general questions was addressed to the prospective jurors. No one answered out loud, instead raising their hands if their response was positive. No one on the jury knew the defendant personally. Several had heard of this case through the media, since there had been a string of similar late-night assaults against female clerks. No one had an arrest record of their own. Three members had been the victims of crime. After the general questions, each juror was interviewed individually.

The attorney who approached the box smiled at Caroline, who thought that Ted was dressed more like a lawyer than this lanky guy with an easy grace and charming grin. One by one, he asked the prospective jurors specific questions regarding friends, attitudes and feelings. When he was finished, his opposite number stepped up and had his own questions for them. Neither attorney challenged Caroline for cause, but she was surprised at the number of available jurors who were dismissed for a variety of reasons, none of which seemed important to her. The two lawyers went through the first twelve-member panel and called for another. In the end, she, Ted and eleven others were chosen. The thirteenth member was an alternate who would listen to all the testimony. However, he would be called into the deliberation only if one of the jurors couldn't continue for some reason, a procedure intended to prevent the need for a retrial.

The trial began immediately, and the opening statements made by each attorney filled in the basic details of the case. A twenty-three-year-old clerk, a woman, had been robbed at gunpoint at a minimarket late one night shortly before Thanksgiving. Terrified, the woman handed over the money from the till, as requested. The thief then proceeded to pistol whip her until her jaw was broken in two places. Although the details of the crime were relayed unemotionally, Caroline felt her throat grow dry. The defendant revealed none of his feelings while the statements were being made. His face was an unyielding mask of indifference and hostility, a combination she had never thought was possible. Again and again she found her gaze drawn to him. In her heart she realized that she fully believed Nelson Bergstrom was capable of such a hideous crime. As soon as she realized that she was already forming an opinion, she fought to cast it from her mind.

By the end of the first day, Caroline's thoughts were troubled as the jurors filed from the courtroom. Serving on a jury wasn't anything like what she'd anticipated. When she'd been contacted by mail with her dates of service, her emotions had been mixed. This was her first free week after completing her apprenticeship, and she'd hated the thought of spending it tied up in court. Now that she was sitting on a case, the reality of the crime genuinely distressed her. The victim was no doubt sitting in the courtroom. Caroline hadn't picked her out of the small crowd, but she knew she had to be there. Absently she wondered how the poor woman could endure the horror of that night.

"Are you all right?" Ted asked her once they hit the steps outside the courthouse.

"Of course," she said, struggling to sound offhand. It had been another stroke of bad luck to have Ted on the same trial. She hadn't seen him in ten years, and now, in a mere two days, he had become an irritating shadow she couldn't shake.

The jury had been warned against discussing any of the details of the case with each other. Caroline yearned to ask Ted what his impression of the proceedings had been but bit back the words. She felt strangely, unaccountably melancholy. Bemused, she frowned at the brooding sense of responsibility that weighed her down. This was only the beginning of the trial, and already she felt intimately involved with the victim *and* the defendant.

"Let's go have a drink," Ted said, taking her elbow. "We both need to relax."

She felt as if she'd been anesthetized and didn't argue—another clear sign of her confusion.

It wasn't until they entered the bar that Caroline realized she was acting as docile as a lamb being led to the slaughter.

"The Tropical Tradewinds?" She raised questioning eyes to Ted.

"You look like you're in the mood for something exotic."

She shook her head and released a slow sigh. Honestly, it was just like Ted to bring her somewhere like this. Oh, the Tropical Tradewinds had a wonderful reputation, but it certainly wasn't her style. She doubted that a place like this even carried something that didn't call for at least six ingredients. "What I'm in the mood for is a good ol' fashion beer."

"Fine, I'll order you one," he returned, pressing a hand to the small of her back as he directed her toward a vacant table. Politely, he held out a chair for her, and, struggling to hold her tongue, she took a seat. She never could understand why men found it necessary to seat women. They seemed to assume that the weaker sex was incapable of something as simple as sitting without assistance. Obviously Ted felt she needed his help, and this once she would let it pass; she simply wasn't in the mood to get into a fight with him.

The waitress arrived, and before Caroline could open her mouth, Ted placed their order. Unable to restrain her reaction, her blue eyes clashed with his as the waitress headed to the bar.

"What did I do wrong now?" he asked quietly, his gaze studying her.

"Does it look as if I've lost control of my tongue?"

"No, but I was hoping." His devilish grin served only to aggravate her further.

"Incidents like these irritate the hell out of me," she said, crossing her legs.

"Incidents like what?"

"Pulling out my chair, ordering my drink, opening a car door. Do I honestly look so helpless?"

"A gentleman always—"

"Can it, Thomasson. I'm not up to hearing a dissertation on the proper behavior of the refined adult male."

"Caroline," Ted replied curtly, "in this day and age a man

is often placed in an unpleasant position. Half the time I don't know which a lady prefers. If I don't hold out her chair, I'm considered a creep, and if I do, I'm a chauvinist. It's a no-win situation."

"I suppose you'll pay for this with a gold-plated credit card, too."

"What's that got to do with anything?" His mouth hardened with displeasure, then softened into a faint smile as their waitress approached. She placed two thick paper coasters on the round tabletop, and set down Caroline's beer and Ted's scotch.

One look at his drink and Caroline rolled her eyes.

"Now what?" The acid in his voice was scathing.

"You're drinking scotch?"

"I would have thought that much was obvious when I ordered." He started to say more, then stopped, as if he couldn't trust himself to speak.

Remorse brought a flush of guilt to Caroline's cheeks. Ted was only trying to be nice, and her behavior was inexcusable. "Listen, Ted, I apologize for . . . I don't mean to be so rude. It's just that we're so different. We'll never be able to agree on anything."

Her casual apology didn't seem to please him either.

"If it's any consolation, you turned out about a thousand times better than I ever imagined," she continued. More than his good looks prompted the statement. He really wasn't the bore she would have expected. He was a little too concerned with propriety, but some women would appreciate that quality. Not her, but someone else.

His blue gaze frosted into an icy glare as he stared at her.

"See," she murmured triumphantly, catching his look. "You and I grate against each other. I prefer a beer out of a can."

"And I enjoy the finest scotch."

"Exactly." She supposed she should be pleased that he agreed with her so readily. "I'm a morning person." She looked at him questioningly.

"I do my best work at night."

"Baseball is my favorite sport." She leaned back in the chair and took a drink of the cold beer. It helped ease the dryness in her throat. "I suppose you enjoy polo."

"No." He shook his head and lowered his gaze to his glass. "Curling."

"Of course." She did her best to disguise a smile.

"I'm certain that if we looked hard enough we'd discover several common interests."

"Such as?" Her look was skeptical.

The beginning of a smile added attractive brackets to the corners of his mouth. "You're a chef, and I definitely enjoy eating."

"Well, you didn't deny working for the Internal Revenue Service at one time, but I don't enjoy paying taxes."

"Caroline," he muttered with obvious control, "I was employed for a brief time by the federal government, but that was years ago. I'm in exports now."

He regarded her steadily with sky-blue eyes. He really had wonderfully expressive eyes. The thick lashes were the same dark color as his hair. If she allowed it, she realized, she could watch him forever. She lowered her own eyes, fearing what he might read in them.

"We should concentrate on the interests we share."

"Good idea." She scooted closer to the table. "Do you play cards?"

"I'm a regular shark."

"Great." Perhaps the real problem between them was something as simple as her own attitude. They were bound to find several things to enjoy about each other if they looked hard enough.

"How about bridge?" he asked.

"Bridge?" Caroline spat out the word. "I hate it. It's the most boring game in the world. I like poker."

Ted stared at her in amazed disbelief. "Okay, we'll forget cards."

"What about music?" At the cynical arch of his brow, she added, "My tastes may surprise you."

"Everything about you surprises me."

"Ha!" She was beginning to enjoy this. "I already know your tastes. You appreciate Michael Bublé, I bet."

"Talented guy," Ted agreed.

"And," she paused to give some thought to his tastes, "I imagine you enjoy some of the early rock and roll stars like Buddy Holly. I'll throw in the Kingston Trio just to be on the safe side. In addition, I'm sure you're crazy about classical."

"Very good." His smile was devastating. "I'm impressed."

"All right." Gesturing with her hand, she offered him the opportunity to add his own speculations regarding *her* musical tastes. "Do your worst—or best, as the case may be."

He chuckled, and amusement flickered across his features. "I couldn't begin to venture a guess. You are a complete enigma to me and always have been. That's what makes you such an enchantress."

Caroline's smile was filled with confident amusement, sure she was about to surprise him. "I adore Mozart, Gene Autry and Billy Joel."

"Not Kermit the Frog?"

"Don't tease," she replied cheerfully. "I'm serious."

"So was I."

For the first time that evening, she felt completely at ease.

She lounged back in the chair and tucked one foot under her. "Shall we dare venture into television?"

"Speaking of which, did you see the recent PBS special on fungus?"

For a moment she assumed he was teasing, but one look assured her that he was completely serious. All her energy was expended in an effort not to laugh outright. "No, I must have missed that. I was watching old reruns of *I Love Lucy.*"

"From the sounds of this, perhaps it would be best to move on to something else."

"What was the last book you read?"

He shifted uncomfortably and took a sip of his drink. "I think we should skip this one, too."

"Ted," she whispered saucily, "don't tell me you're into erotica."

"What? *No,*" he responded emphatically, obviously uneasy. "If you must pursue this, I recently finished Homer's *Iliad.*"

Caroline pushed the errant curls from her forehead. "In the original Greek?"

He nodded.

"I should have known," she muttered under her breath. Absolutely nothing about this man would surprise her anymore. He was brilliant. She wanted to resent that fact, but instead she found a grudging respect taking root.

"What about you?"

"I enjoy romances and science fiction and Dick Francis."

"Dick who?"

"He writes horse-racing mysteries. You have to read him to believe how good he is. I'll lend you some of his books if you'd like."

"I would."

Caroline offered him a bright, vivacious smile as she polished off her beer. "You realize we haven't found a single interest we share."

"Does it matter?" Just the way he said it sent a chord of sensual awareness singing through her, igniting an answering reprise within her heart. She couldn't believe that she was looking at Theodore Thomasson and hearing music. That was something reserved for novels. Romances. No, science fiction.

"Caroline . . ."

She shook her head to clear her thoughts. "Sorry, what were you saying? I wasn't listening."

"I was asking you to have dinner with me."

"Here?"

His look was one of tolerant amusement. "No, you choose."

"Great." Mentally she discarded her favorite Egyptian restaurant and asked, "Is Italian okay?"

"Anything's fine."

She sincerely doubted that but managed to hide her knowing grin. "There's a seafood place within walking distance if you'd rather."

"The choice is yours," he said.

"Don't be so accommodating," she said, raising her voice. "There's only so much of that I can take."

With a wide grin, Ted stood. She noted that he didn't offer her his hand as she got out of her chair, a small courtesy for which she was disproportionately grateful.

Dusk had settled over the city as they moved onto the sidewalk. Streetlights were beginning to flicker around them.

"Your dad said you went to college. What's your degree in?"

"Biochemistry." She watched the surprise work its way over his features and marveled at the control he exhibited.

"Biochemistry," he repeated in bewilderment. "And now you're in culinary school?"

"Yup. I felt that of all the majors I could have chosen, biochem would be the most value to me."

Confusion shone from his expressive eyes. "I don't think I care to follow your line of reasoning."

"It's not that difficult," she answered brightly. "You see, Dad never was thrilled with my ambitions in the kitchen. I am, after all, his daughter, and he didn't feel I was aiming high enough, if you catch my drift."

"I understand."

"So instead of constantly arguing, we made an agreement. I'd go to college and get my degree, and in exchange he'd continue to support me while I went to culinary school afterwards."

"That sounds like a fair compromise. Did you come up with it?"

"Who, me?" She pressed her palm to her breast. "Hardly. I was too involved in defending my individual rights as a human being to see any solution. Mom was the one who suggested that course of action."

"But why did you choose biochemistry?"

"Why not?" she tossed back. "I'd like to think of myself as a food scientist. There's a whole world out there that has only been touched on."

"I'm surprised your father didn't insist on sending you to Paris, if you were so sure that cooking was what you wanted to do."

"He offered." The frustration remained vivid in her memory. "Only the best for his little girl and all that rot. But I didn't want to go overseas. The Natalie Dupont School here in Seattle is one of the best, and it offers a focus on baking. I'd like to focus my efforts in the area of breads. The average person looks at a loaf and thinks of sandwiches or toast. I see lipids, leaveners, proteins and biological structures. Yeast absolutely fascinates me."

"Obviously I'm a less complicated soul. What fascinates me most is you."

The tender look in his eyes nearly stopped her heart. "Me?" She stared at him, hardly believing the pride and wonder in his gaze. His blue eyes were full of warmth, and he was smiling at her with gentle understanding in a way she never would have suspected.

"Have you noticed your sense of timing is several years off?"

"My what?" Caroline's look was bewildered. "How do you mean?"

"At a time when most women are happy to get out of the kitchen, you're battling your way in."

Smiling, she nodded and placed her hand in the crook of his arm. Within the span of one day, she felt as if Ted and she had always been the closest of friends. True, they didn't share a lot of common interests, but there was a bond between them that was beyond explanation. The knowledge stunned her, and she paused, wanting to speak, but not knowing what to say or how to say it.

Caroline knew when he lowered his head that he intended to kiss her, and her eyelids slowly fluttered closed with eager anticipation. When nothing happened, her eyes shot open to discover him staring down at her. Reluctantly, it seemed, he kissed the top of her head and took her hand as they continued to stroll down the street.

Mortified, she felt the embarrassment extend all the way to her hairline. Seconds earlier they'd experienced a spiritual communication that left her breathless with wonder, and now . . . The traffic light changed, and a long series of cars whizzed past.

In a flash, Caroline understood that as much as he might want to, Ted wouldn't kiss her on a busy Seattle street. Not with the possibility of them being seen.

Their meal was wonderful. It could have been the wine, but she doubted it. In spite of their many differences, they found several subjects on which they shared similar opinions. They both enjoyed chess and Scrabble and, most surprisingly, shared the same political affiliation, though Ted's sense of humor was more subtle than her own. By the time they left the Italian restaurant, Caroline couldn't remember an evening she'd enjoyed more. She'd laughed until her stomach ached.

Ted's hand at the back of her neck warmed her spine as they lazily strolled toward her apartment.

"I had a good time," she said casually, reaching over and entwining her fingers with his.

"Don't sound so surprised." His chin nuzzled the crown of her head.

"I can't help it. Darryl would keel over if I told him I'd spent an enjoyable evening with you."

She basked in the warmth of his slow, easy smile.

"I never did understand how your parents could possibly have two such completely different children. Darryl's exactly like his father, and you . . . well, it's just hard to believe you're his sister."

Caroline pulled her hand free. Disappointment and anger burned through her. "I've already apologized for my childhood bad behavior. You're right, I treated you terribly. I tricked you. I lied about you. I nearly burned the house down in an effort to undermine you. But that was ten years ago." Whirling, she marched away.

"Caroline?" Hurried footsteps sounded behind her. "What did I say?"

"You know exactly what you said." She tried to walk faster, her pace just short of an outright jog.

"I *don't* know," he countered. His hand on her shoulder stopped her. Turning her around, he held her shoulders while his bewildered gaze roamed her face. A frown drew his thick brows together. "I've hurt you."

"What you said about not knowing how . . . how I could possibly be Darryl's sister, when you know good and well that I'm not."

A stunned look drained the color from his face. "Are you saying you're adopted?"

Her narrowed, fiery glare answered the question for him.

"That's impossible," he whispered.

Three

"Just what exactly do you mean by that remark?" Hands on her hips, Caroline stared into his face.

"You look—"

"Like my mom? No I don't."

"The hair—"

"That's the only thing, but otherwise we're nothing alike. Mom's gentle, patient, forgiving. Every day of my life I've wanted to be exactly like her. I've honestly tried, but I'm—"

"Stubborn, quick-tempered and often impertinent," Ted supplied for her.

She opened her mouth to argue, then thought better of it. "Yes," she admitted, then rammed her hands inside the pockets of her cords and began shuffling backwards. "Thank you for tonight, I'm sorry it has to end this way."

"Come on, Caroline. I can't be blamed for an innocent mistake. I didn't know."

"You do now."

"What difference does it make?"

"Think about it," she snapped. "You're a smart man. You'll figure it out."

"Since we're tallying your faults, you can add unreasonableness to your growing list. I've never met a more frustrating woman."

Turning, Caroline made her escape, running up the three flights of stairs that led to her apartment. She knew she was behaving badly, but she couldn't help it. From childhood, Ted had been Mr. Prim-and-Proper and she had ridiculed him for it. But that wasn't the real reason she'd disliked him so intensely. The truth was, he was everything she wanted so badly to be.

If she were even half as refined as Theodore Thomasson, her mother would have been so proud. If only she could have maintained high grades and managed to stay out of trouble, everything would have been so grand. But no matter how hard she tried or how many promises she made, she simply couldn't be something she wasn't. Her temper flared with the least provocation, her poise was as fragile as fine china, and her self-confidence was shattered by every grade school teacher who was unfortunate enough to have her in class. Perhaps she could have accepted herself more readily if her mother hadn't been so tolerant and forgiving. She'd wanted to cry and beg her mother's forgiveness for every minor blunder, but her mother would never allow that. She loved her daughter exactly the way she was. Often when Caroline was sent to her room without dinner by her father—the ultimate punishment—her mother would smuggle in fruit and cookies. More times than Caroline could count, her mother had calmly intervened between her and her father. Amazing as it was, she shared a strong relationship with her mother. There wasn't anything Caroline felt she couldn't share with her. No mother could have been more wonderful.

Each year, on Caroline's birthday, her mother told the story of how she'd longed for a daughter. Darryl was her son and she loved him dearly, but she wanted a daughter and had prayed nightly that God would smile upon her a second time and grant her another child—a girl. After five years it became apparent that she wouldn't have more children, and they'd decided to adopt. On their first visit to the caseworker, Ruth had seen a picture of a fiery-haired, two-year-old toddler and known instantly that this was just the little girl she wanted. At that point in the tale her father always interrupted to add that the caseworker had discouraged them from adopting the tiny hellion. But Ruth had persisted until the caseworker relented and brought the four of them together for the first time. Usually at this point her brother, Darryl, would insert that the first time he'd seen Caroline, she'd bitten him on the leg. He claimed she'd marked him for life and had the scar to prove it. So she had been adopted into this family who loved her in spite of her rambunctious behavior. For their love, Caroline would be forever grateful, but in her heart she would never really feel a part of them. Theodore Thomasson was a constant reminder of exactly how different she was. Next to him, her imperfections were magnified a hundred times.

An air of expectancy hung over the proceedings early the following morning. The jury was seated in a closed room adjacent to the courtroom, but Caroline arrived in time to see the defendant being brought into the court and seated. Again she noted his apparent lack of concern. It was almost as if he didn't care what the jury or anyone else thought. He was purposely making himself unlikable, and she couldn't understand that.

She stepped into the room reserved for the jury and sat beside a grandmotherly woman who paused in her knitting and said hello.

"I want to talk to you," Ted whispered.

Caroline smiled apologetically to the older woman, who had already gone back to her knitting. "I don't know that man. Would you kindly tell him that if he continues to pester me, I'll be forced to report him to the bailiff?"

"I can't understand what's the matter with these young men today." The metal needles clicked as they wove the fine strands of yarn in and out. She had been knitting through the entire proceedings the day before, and Caroline had dubbed her Madame La Farge.

Now Madame La Farge turned and gifted Ted with what Caroline was sure was a scathing look. "Kindly leave this young lady alone."

"Caroline . . ." Ted ground out her name, his voice ringing with frustration.

Ignoring him, she scanned the faces of her fellow jurors, thinking that they resembled a fair cross section of society. All the men were dressed casually, except Ted, who wore a pinstriped suit. There were an electrician, a real estate broker, an engineer and others whose occupations Caroline couldn't recall. The other four women on the jury were all middle-aged.

"All rise, this court is now in session," the bailiff announced, and a rustling sounded in the jury room as those in the courtroom rose to their feet.

Within minutes the door opened and the jury was led in and seated. The prosecutor stood to present his case, calling several witnesses. The defendant, Nelson Bergstrom, had been tried and found guilty of assault and robbery five years before, and had been on parole only six weeks at the time of the minimarket robbery. His parole officer testified that Nelson had been living within ten blocks of the market. Another witness testified that he had seen Nelson at the store the day before the robbery.

The arresting officer followed with his report.

The next witness, Joan MacIntosh, was called. Caroline saw a young woman slowly enter the courtroom. Obviously nervous and shaky, Joan cast a pleading glance to the large man who had walked in with her. He gave her an encouraging smile and squeezed her hand, then took a seat. From the fear in the woman's eyes, Caroline realized that Joan MacIntosh must be the woman who had been assaulted. She was petite, barely five feet, with a fragile, delicate look. If she weighed over a hundred pounds, it would have been a surprise. The woman was terrified, that much was obvious. She hesitated once and glanced back. The man who'd come in with her nodded reassuringly several times, and Joan squared her shoulders before continuing forward.

The scene was poignant. Whatever physical harm had been done her had apparently healed, but it was obvious that the psychological damage had been far greater. Caroline looked at Joan and was overcome with sympathy. They were close in age, and from the address, Caroline knew they didn't live more than three miles apart. It could have been her instead of Joan who had been treated so brutally.

After being sworn in, Joan took the witness stand. Following a series of perfunctory questions, the prosecutor leaned against the polished banister. "Joan, to the best of your ability, I'd like you to tell the court the events of the night of November twenty-third."

Joan's voice had been weak and wobbly, but as she began speaking, she gained confidence and volume. "I was working as a clerk for the market for only two weeks. There—really isn't much to tell. I was alone, but that didn't bother me, because there had been a steady stream of customers in and out most of the night."

The prosecutor gave her an encouraging smile. "Go on."

"Well . . . it must have been close to eleven, and things had slowed down. I noticed someone hanging around outside, but I didn't think much of it. A lot of kids hang around the store."

Caroline noticed that Joan's hands were tightly clenched, and that a tissue she was holding was shredded.

"Anyway—he . . . the man who had been outside, came into the store. He went to the back by the refrigerator unit. I assumed he was going to buy beer or something. But when he approached the register I noticed that he had a ski mask over his face. And he had a gun pointed at my heart." Joan's voice grew weak as she remembered the terror. Briefly, she closed her eyes.

"Go on, Joan."

"He . . . he didn't say anything to me, but he pointed the gun at the cash register. I wanted to tell him he could have everything, but I couldn't talk. I was . . . so scared." She blinked, and Caroline could see tears working their way down her face. "I would have done anything just so he wouldn't hurt me."

"What happened next?"

"I opened the till to give him the money." She hesitated and bit her trembling bottom lip. "He told me to put all the money in a sack. I did that—I even gave him the change. I was so frightened that I dropped the bag on the counter. All the time I was praying that someone would come. Anyone. I didn't want to die. . . . I told him that over and over again. I begged him not to hurt me." Her voice cracked, and she placed a hand over her mouth until she'd regained her composure. "Then he looked inside the sack and told me it wasn't enough."

"What did you tell him?"

"I said I'd given him all the money there was and that he could take anything else he wanted."

"How did he react to that?"

"He told me to give him my purse, which I did. But I only had a few dollars, and that made him even angrier. He started waving the gun at me. I begged him not to shoot me. He told me to get more money. He shouted at me over and over that he needed more money. Then he started hitting me with the gun. Again and again he hit my face, until I was sure I'd never live through it. The pain was so bad that I wanted to die just so it would stop hurting."

Caroline could barely make out the words, because Joan was sobbing now. The man who'd accompanied her stood and clenched his fists angrily at his sides. The bailiff pointed to him, indicating that he should sit down again. The man did, but Joan's testimony was obviously upsetting him.

Caroline doubted that anyone could remain unaffected by the details. Joan MacIntosh was a delicate young woman who had been brutally attacked and beaten for less than twenty dollars. Caroline felt that any man who could beat someone so much smaller and virtually defenseless—or anyone, for that matter—should rot in prison.

After a few more questions, the prosecutor stepped back and sat down, and the defense attorney came forward. Joan sat up and eyed him suspiciously.

"Can you describe to the court what the man who attacked and robbed you looked like?" he asked in a calm, cool voice.

"He . . . he was average height, about a hundred and sixty pounds, dark hair, dark eyes. . . ."

"Did you ever get a clear view of his face?" the defense attorney pressed. "I noted in your testimony that you claim that the man who beat you had been hanging around outside the store."

"Well, I . . ."

"It seems to me that you would have had ample opportunity to clearly see his face," he pressed.

"Not entirely. He wore a ski mask."

"What about before, when he was outside the store? When he first came in?"

"He . . . he averted his . . . I only saw his profile."

"Before you answer the following question, Ms. MacIntosh, I want you to think very carefully about your answer. Is the man who attacked you in this courtroom today?"

Caroline's eyes flew from Joan to the defendant. Nelson Bergstrom was sneering at the young woman in the witness box, all but challenging her to name him.

"Is that man in the courtroom today?" the defender repeated.

"I . . . think so."

The attorney placed the palms of his hands on the banister and leaned forward. "A man's entire future is at stake here, Ms. MacIntosh. We need something more definite than 'I think so.'"

"Objection." The prosecutor vaulted to his feet.

Caroline listened as the two men argued over a fine point of law that she didn't entirely understand, and then the defense attorney went back to questioning Joan. When the cross-examination was complete, the judge dismissed the court for a one-hour lunch break.

After the defendant was led away, the courtroom emptied into the hall. Ted was standing outside the large double doors waiting for Caroline. She paused, and their eyes met and held. Listening to the morning testimony had drained her emotionally and physically. She waited for the rising tide of resentment she'd so often experienced in his presence, but none came. After last night she realized that it would be best to keep their relationship strictly impersonal.

His look was long and penetrating, as if he were reading her thoughts. A full minute passed before he spoke. "Are you going to talk to me, or am I going to be forced to send you notes through your bodyguard with the knitting needles?" The quiet tenderness in his deep voice softened her struggling resolve to remain detached. He hadn't done anything to provoke her, not really. She could hardly blame *him* for the circumstances of her birth.

"We can talk," she said, and looped the long strap of her purse over her shoulder. "Really, I should be the one who does the talking."

Ted touched her elbow, guiding her in the direction of the elevator. As if forgetting himself, he quickly lowered his hand. Caroline managed to hide a secret smile. He was trying so hard to please her. She simply couldn't understand why he would want to go to that much trouble.

"Once again, I find myself in the position of having to apologize to you," she began as they paused on the outside steps. "I realize now that you didn't know I was adopted. In fact, I find it a compliment that you hadn't guessed years ago."

"Apology accepted," he said, smiling down at her. Together they walked down the long flight of stairs that led to the busy sidewalk. "I don't know what made you so angry, but then, I've given up trying to understand what makes you tick."

In spite of herself, Caroline laughed. "Dad said the same thing to me when I as ten."

"I'm a slow learner," Ted admitted and slipped an arm around her shoulder. "It took me until late last night to realize that I'll probably never understand you. With that same thought came the realization that you mattered enough to me to keep trying."

"Why would you even want to?" His reasoning was beyond Caroline. And he thought *she* was difficult to comprehend!

His expression softened, and he looked at her with an unbearable gentleness. He traced a finger along the delicate curve of her jaw and down her chin to linger at the pulse that hammered wildly at the base of her neck. The muscles of her throat constricted, and she swayed involuntarily toward him.

"I'm not exactly sure why," he admitted, slowly shaking his head. "Maybe it's as simple as the magnetic attraction between opposites."

"No one is more opposite than you and I."

"That is something we can definitely agree on," he said, and led her across the street.

"Where are we going?"

"There's an excellent French restaurant a couple of blocks from here." There was a guarded edge to his voice as he studied her. "You don't like French food." It was more statement than question.

"It's fine. It's just I'm not very hungry. I was thinking of walking down to the waterfront and ordering clam chowder from Ivar's."

"Listening to the testimony this morning bothered you, didn't it?"

They had been strictly warned against discussing any of the details of the trial. Fearing that once she answered she would blurt out the opinions she was already forming, Caroline simply nodded. "I could feel that poor woman's terror."

"I don't think there was a person in the room who wasn't affected by it," he agreed.

She dragged her eyes from his, wanting to say more and knowing she didn't dare. "Jury duty is so different from what I thought it would be. Monday morning I was hoping I'd get on an exciting murder trial. Today I'm having difficulty dealing with the emotional impact of an assault and robbery. Can you imagine what it's like for the jury on something as horrible as a murder case?"

"I don't think I want to know," Ted murmured with feeling.

They strolled down to Seattle's busy waterfront. The smell of salt water and seaweed drifted toward them. A sea gull squawked as it soared in the cloudless blue sky and agilely landed on the long pier beside the take-out seafood stand.

Caroline insisted on paying for her own lunch, which consisted of a cup of thick clam chowder, a Diet Pepsi and an order of deep-fried mushrooms. Ted ordered the standard fish and chips.

They sat opposite each other at a picnic table. As much as she tried to direct her thoughts into other channels, her mind continued to replay the impassioned testimony she'd heard that morning.

"Are you seeing anyone?" Ted's question cut into her introspection.

"Pardon?"

"Are you involved with someone?"

Caroline stared at him and noted that his dark brows had lifted over inscrutable blue eyes. That he didn't like asking this question was obvious.

But even if he didn't like asking it, ask it he had, and she wasn't all that pleased to be answering it. "Not this month," she said flippantly.

"Caroline," he said with a sigh. "I'm serious."

"So am I. Romance is a low priority right now. I'm more interested in finding a job."

He didn't even make a pretense of believing her. "Who was he?" he asked softly.

"Who?"

"The man who hurt you."

She laughed lightly. "And people say *I* have a wild imagination."

"I'm not imagining things. The minute I asked you about a man, a funny, hurt look came over you."

Still? Caroline expelled her breath in a slow, even sigh. Clay had broken up with her over two months ago, but the memory of him was still as painful as it had been the night they'd finally split. She opened her mouth to deny everything, then realized she couldn't. The only person who knew the whole story was her mother. Caroline had enjoyed being with Ted the last couple of days, but that didn't mean she was up to sharing the most devastating experience of her life with him. And yet she couldn't stop herself from speaking.

"His name was Clay," she began awkwardly, repeatedly running her index finger along the rim of her cup. "There's not much to say, really. We dated for a while, decided we weren't suited and went our separate ways."

Ted's smile was sympathetic but firm. "You're not telling me the half of it."

"You're right, I'm not," she confirmed hotly. "Who said you had the right to butt into my personal life? What makes you think I'd share a painful part of my past with you? Good grief, I'm not even sure I like you. At any minute you're likely to turn back into 'Tedious Ted.'" Tension and regret were building within her at a rapid rate. She regarded him with cool disdain. How dare he put her in this position? "What would you know about love? In your orderly existence, I doubt that you've . . ." She stopped before she said something she would regret. "I didn't mean that," she finished, feeling wretched.

He took her hand, his fingers folding around hers. "I'm sorry I asked."

She refused to lower her gaze, although it demanded every

ounce of her willpower. “It was over several weeks ago. . . . I don’t know why I reacted like that.”

“Are you still in love with him?” he asked meaningfully.

Caroline pasted a smile on her mouth and glanced his way with a false look of certainty. “No, of course not.” Not if she could respond to Ted’s kiss the way she had. Her overwhelming reaction to him had been a complete shock. His mouth had claimed hers and it was as if Clay had never existed. However, that night, that kiss, had been a fluke. It had been so long since a man had kissed her with such passion that it was little wonder that she’d responded.

An uneasy silence stretched between them, until Ted slid off the bench and stood. “We should think about getting back.”

“Yes, I suppose we should,” she replied stiffly. She rose. Pausing, she turned her eyes toward the long row of high-rise structures, her gaze seeking the courthouse. A sinking sensation landed in the pit of her stomach. “I have the funniest feeling about this case,” she murmured, and stopped, surprised that she’d spoken out loud.

Ted was giving her a look that said he was experiencing the same mixed feelings. “Come on, let’s get this afternoon over with.” He reached for her hand, and Caroline had no objection.

The jury entered the courtroom using the same procedure as they had that morning and sat down to hear testimony.

The defending attorney presented his defense by recalling two of the morning’s witnesses for an additional series of questions.

Caroline kept expecting Nelson Bergstrom to take the stand in his own defense, but it soon became obvious that he wasn’t going to be called. It didn’t take much to understand why. With his attitude, he would only hurt his own chances.

The closing arguments were completed by three o’clock, and the jury entered into deliberation at three-fifteen. By the time they were seated at the long jury table, Caroline's thoughts were muddled. She didn't know what to think.

The first order of business was electing a foreman. The first choice was Ted, which surprised her. She decided to attribute it to his crisp business suit, which made him look the part. He declined, and the engineer was elected.

A short discussion followed, in which points of law were discussed, and then they went on to the evidence. This was the first time any of the jury members had been given the opportunity to discuss the trial and voice their opinion.

"If looks count for anything, that young man is as guilty as sin," Madame La Farge said, her knitting needles clicking as her fingers moved with an amazing dexterity.

"They don't," Ted said in a flat, hard voice.

"Everything that was said today, every piece of evidence, was circumstantial." Caroline felt obliged to state her feelings early. From the looks of those around her, everyone else had already made up their minds.

"As far as I see it," the real estate agent inserted, "it's an open-and-shut case. That man repeatedly hit that poor girl, and nobody's going to convince me otherwise."

"None of the money was recovered."

"Of course not," Madame La Farge inserted, planting her needlework on the tabletop. "That boy was desperate. Obviously he spent it as fast as he could on drugs. Crack, no doubt. One look at that man and anyone can tell he's an addict. No one in his right mind would act the way he did otherwise."

"He was wearing the same jacket as the assailant. What more evidence do we need?" someone else piped in.

"He was wearing a Levi's jacket, which is probably the most popular men's jacket in America. We can't convict a man because of a jacket," Caroline added heatedly.

"He lived in the neighborhood, and he had been seen there the day before."

"I know," Caroline agreed, backing down. She looked at the faces studying her and realized that she could well be standing alone on this. "I am as appalled by what happened to Joan MacIntosh as anyone here. I would like to see the man who did this to her rot behind bars. But even stronger than my sense of righteousness is the fact I want to be certain we don't punish the wrong man."

"That's everyone's concern," the foreman told her.

"The evidence is overwhelming."

"What evidence do we really have?" Ted asked.

"She identified him," Madame La Farge commented as if she were discussing the weather, pausing to cover her mouth when she yawned. "I really would like to be home before five today. Do you think we could have a vote?" She directed her question to the foreman.

"I'm not ready," Caroline insisted. "And she *didn't* identify him," she added, contradicting the older woman's statement. "Joan MacIntosh said that she *thought* it was him. In her mind there was a reasonable doubt. There's one in mine, too."

Half the room eyed her balefully. An hour later Caroline was convinced they would never reach a unanimous decision. Caroline felt taxed to the limit of her endurance. The only other person in the room who had voiced the same doubts as she was Ted.

"I have misgivings, as well," he said now.

"Maybe these two are right," one woman said softly. Groans went up around the room.

"Are we going to let that . . . that beast walk out of here after what he did?" The real estate agent rolled his pencil across the table in disgust. "Come on, folks. The sooner we agree, the sooner we can go home."

"Listen, everyone," Ted said, squaring his shoulders as he sat straighter. "I'm as anxious to get home as the next person, but we can't rush these proceedings."

A half hour later the judge sent in a note, asking if they were anywhere close to reaching a verdict.

"See?" the real estate agent fumed. "Even the judge is shocked at how long this is taking. We should have been out of here an hour ago."

The foreman wrote out a reply and sent it back to the judge. Within fifteen minutes they were dismissed and told to return in the morning.

This time it was Caroline who was waiting in the hallway for Ted. Her hands were clenched at her sides as waves of intense anger washed over her. He paused and grinned at her, but she waited until they were alone to speak, then struggled to make her voice sound normal. "Just what do you think you're doing?"

"Doing?" he asked in confusion.

"Listen, I don't need anyone to defend me, so step off your shining white horse and form your own opinions. I don't appreciate what you're doing." She caught his startled look and ignored it.

"What are you talking about?"

"This case. Don't you think I know what you're doing? It's that chauvinistic attitude of yours. The fanatical gentleman in you who refuses to let me stand alone against the others."

A look of sorely tried patience crossed his face. "Believe what you will, but I happen to share your sentiments regarding the case."

"Ha!" she snapped.

The controlled fury in his eyes was enough to knock the breath from her lungs. She noted the red tinge that was working its way up his neck and the tight, pinched look of his mouth. "I can assure you, Miss Lomax, that I consider it a miracle that we share any opinion. I would appreciate it, however, if you'd afford me the intelligence to decide for myself how I feel about this case without making unwarranted assumptions."

Suddenly drowning in resentful embarrassment, she murmured, "If I've misjudged your actions, then I apologize."

"From the time you were a girl your mouth has continued to outrun your brain," he said with deadly calm. "I have endured your anger, your lack of manners, even your temper. But I have no intention of being further subjected to your stupidity."

Hot color invaded her cheeks, and Caroline experienced an unwanted pang of misgiving. "Maybe I spoke out of turn."

The look he gave her would have frozen rainwater. Without a word, he pivoted sharply and left her standing alone in the wide hall. She pushed the curls from her face and forcefully expelled her breath. Tendrils of guilt wrapped themselves around her heart. She'd done it again. And this time she'd messed it up good. Ted wouldn't have anything to do with her now. She should be glad, but instead she discovered a sense of regret dominating her thoughts. Maybe they could settle things after the trial. Maybe, but from his look, she doubted it.

Four

"Has the jury reached a verdict?" the stern-faced judge asked the foreman. The engineer rose awkwardly to his feet. The courtroom was filled with tense silence. Every face in the crowded room turned to stare expectantly at the twelve men and women sitting in the jury box.

The foreman shifted uneasily, casting his gaze to his nervously clenched hands. "No, we haven't, Your Honor."

Low hissing whispers filled the room. Caroline lifted her gaze to the young victim and watched angry defeat dull her eyes as she cupped her trembling chin. Joan MacIntosh gave a small cry before burying her face in the shoulder of the man Caroline suspected was her husband.

After long, tedious hours of holding her ground, repeating the same arguments over and over until she longed to weep with frustration, Caroline was unsure about the evidence and how she should vote. As much as anyone, she wanted the man who had so brutally attacked Joan MacIntosh punished. But as much as she yearned for justice, she also needed to feel sure that she was sending the right man to prison.

Holding her ground hadn't been easy. Neither she nor Ted had wavered from their earlier stand, although others had made some persuasive—and heated—arguments. Still, Caroline couldn't change what she believed simply because someone else saw things differently. A mistrial was the worst possible outcome, as far as the courts were concerned. The jury members had been warned earlier that if it were possible to make a decision, one should be made. But since they couldn't agree unanimously, there had been no choice but to return to the courtroom and the judge.

"What was the vote?" The deepening frown in the judge's weathered face revealed his displeasure.

"Ten to two," the foreman returned, pausing to clear his throat. "Ten of us felt the defendant was guilty, the other two," he hesitated and swallowed, "didn't."

The judge studied the twelve jury members, then called for a jury poll.

When her turn came, Caroline slowly, reluctantly, said, "Not guilty." Unable to meet the judge's penetrating glare, she lowered her eyes. Unexpectedly her gaze clashed with the surly defendant's. A ghost of a grin hovered around his mouth, as if he were silently laughing at everything that was going on around him. Caroline was reminded again that Nelson Bergstrom had already been proven capable of such a hideous crime.

"You leave me with no option but to declare a mistrial." The judge spoke in a solemn voice, and it seemed to Caroline that his tone was sharp and angry. "The defendant is free on ten thousand dollars bond. A new court date will be set at the end of the week. The jurors will return tomorrow to fulfill the rest of their obligation to serve."

Joan MacIntosh burst into tears, her sobs reverberating against the hallowed walls. A dark shroud of uncertainty wrapped around Caroline's tender heart. She felt tears prickle the corners of her eyes, and she pinched her lips tightly together as the gavel banged down and the jurors were dismissed.

It seemed as if everyone in the room was accusing her with their eyes. She wanted to stand by Ted, lean on him for support, but since their last argument, he had barely spoken to her. Even her greetings had been met with clipped, disinterested replies. Ted wasn't the sort to get angry easily, and to his credit, he'd put up with a lot from her over the years. But when she'd questioned his integrity, she had committed the unforgivable. A hundred times since, she'd wished she could have pulled back the thoughtless words, but the truth was, defending her decision was just the kind of thing Ted would think chivalrous. If anything, she was pleased they shared the same opinion. If ever she needed a friend, it had been today, standing against the fellow members of the jury. Yet even when their decisions concurred, they were treating each other as enemies.

The line of accusing faces didn't fade when Caroline and Ted entered the wide hallway outside the courtroom. The man who had sat with Joan MacIntosh was waiting for them, as were photographers from the local newspapers.

The moment Caroline appeared, the presumed Mr. MacIntosh started spewing a long list of obscenities at her with the venom of a man driven past his endurance. At first she was stunned, too shocked to react, and then she couldn't believe anyone would talk to her that way. She had been called some rotten things in her life, but nothing even close to this.

"I didn't mean to upset you," she pleaded, yearning desperately to explain. "I'm so sorry," she went on, "but if you only understood why I voted the way I did—"

She wasn't allowed to finish, as another tirade of harsh, angry words broke across her explanation. Bright lights flashed as the press took in the bitter scene.

"Caroline," Ted said sharply, coming to her side. "It won't do any good to reason with him. Let's get out of here."

"But he needs to understand. Everyone does," she insisted, turning toward the reporters. "Ted and I agonized over the decision."

"Ted?" one reporter tossed back at her.

"Ted Thomasson," she clarified.

"And you are?" the reporter pressed.

"Caroline Lomax."

"Caroline," Ted snapped angrily, "don't give them our names."

"Oh." She swallowed quickly. "I didn't mean . . . Oh dear." She felt utterly and completely confused.

Without allowing her to speak further, Ted took her hand and led her away. Even as they briskly walked down the wide corridor, they were followed by the reporters, who hounded them with a series of rapid-fire questions.

To every one, Ted responded in a crisp voice, "No comment."

"What about you, Miss?"

Still reeling from the shock of the encounter outside the courtroom, she opened and closed her mouth, unsure what to say. A fiery glare from Ted convinced her to follow his lead. "No comment."

Because his stride was so much longer than her own, she was forced to trot to keep even with him. "Where are we going?" she asked breathlessly as they raced down the steps and sped toward the parking lot.

"I'm taking you home."

"Home," she echoed, disappointed. Tonight she would have enjoyed a leisurely drink or a peaceful dinner out.

He stopped in front of his car, took out his key and pressed the button to unlock the doors. Before he had a chance to open the passenger door for her, Caroline climbed inside. Ted stared at her for a long moment, then opened his own door and slid in. He braced his hands against the steering wheel and exhaled sharply. She understood his feelings. She had never been so glad to be out of a place in her life. Not even when she'd been caught raising prissy Jenny Wilson's gym shorts up the flagpole had she felt more glad to escape a situation. The leather-upholstered seat felt wonderful, almost comforting. The tension eased from her stiff limbs, and she slowly expelled a long sigh of relief as she leaned her head back. It felt like heaven to close her eyes.

Wordlessly, Ted started the engine and pulled out of the narrow space.

The silence was already grating on her as they pulled onto the busy Seattle street, which was snarled with rush-hour traffic. She searched her mind for something casual to say and came up blank. When she couldn't stand it any longer, she gave in and asked the question that had been paramount in her mind.

"Are you still angry with me?" she asked tentatively, surprised by how much the answer mattered to her.

"No."

"Good." For the life of her, she couldn't come up with something more clever to say. She was too drained emotionally to be original and come up with some witty remark that would restore the balance to their relationship. The funny part was that though she wasn't entirely sure they were capable of being friends, a whole day of hostility had left her decidedly upset. Previously, she'd delighted in tormenting him, had taken pride in coming up with ways to needle "Tedious Ted." Lately, though, she'd been hard-pressed to know who was tormenting whom.

Instead of pulling into the parking lot across the street from her apartment building, Ted eased to a stop at her curb.

"You aren't coming in?"

"No."

"Why not?" He made no move to turn and look at her, which only served to upset her further.

"It's been a long day."

"It's barely four-thirty," she countered. In her mind she'd pictured spending a quiet evening together. She'd even thought of cooking a meal for him, so she could impress him with her considerable culinary skills. After a day like theirs, they needed to talk and unwind.

"Another time, maybe."

Just the nonchalant way he said it grated on Caroline's nerves. She knew a brush-off when she heard one. What did she care if he came inside or not? She wasn't desperate for a man's companionship. She didn't even like Theodore Thomasson, so it wasn't any skin off her nose if he preferred his own company. At least that was what she told herself as she swallowed back the unpleasant taste of disappointment.

"All right. I'll see you tomorrow, then," she said, tightening her hand around the door handle. Still she hesitated, not wanting to part. "Thanks for the ride."

"You're welcome."

If he didn't stop being so polite, she was going to scream. Finally she got out, and when she was safely on the sidewalk and had closed the car door, he pulled away. He didn't even have the common decency to speed. She would have liked him better if he had. For a long moment she didn't move. He might claim that he'd forgiven her, but she knew he hadn't. His sleek Chevrolet was long out of sight when she finally sighed with defeat and entered her apartment building.

As it turned out, she didn't even bother cooking a meal. After years of schooling to be a cordon bleu chef and countless arguments with her father over her chosen vocation, she ate a bowl of corn flakes in front of the television. The mistrial was barely given a mention on the local news, leaving her relieved. She felt as if she were wearing a scarlet letter as it was.

Tucking her bare feet beneath her, she leaned her head back and closed her eyes as a talk show came on after the national news. The next thing she knew, the sound of shrill ringing assaulted her ears, jolting her into full awareness. Straightening, she searched around her for the source. The phone pealed again, and she reached for it.

"Hello."

Hollow silence was followed by an irritating click.

Although she'd had a long nap, she slept well that night and woke refreshed early the next morning. She dreaded another day at the courthouse. There was a possibility she could be called to sit on another trial. The thought filled her with apprehension.

As she was grabbing her raincoat, the phone rang. She answered it on the second ring, and once again the caller immediately disconnected. Slowly Caroline replaced the receiver, perplexed.

Ted was already seated in the jury room when she arrived. She felt a sense of relief at seeing him and took the vacant chair next to him. He glanced up from his crossword puzzle but didn't greet her.

"Did you try to phone me last night?" she asked, sipping coffee from the steaming cup she'd picked up on her way in. It burned her mouth, and she grimaced.

"No." He gave her a look of condescension, as if to say she

ought to know enough to let her coffee cool before trying to drink it. But that was the sensible thing to do, and she had never been sensible.

“What about this morning?” she asked.

“I didn’t phone you this morning, either.”

He didn’t need to sound so pleased with himself. So he hadn’t phoned. Deep down, she’d hoped it had been him.

“The reason I asked,” she hurried to explain, “is that twice now someone has phoned and hung up when I answered. Caller ID just said private caller.”

“Surely you don’t think I—”

“No,” she interrupted. “Listen, I’m sorry I asked. It was a mistake. Okay?” Irritated, she crossed her legs and studied his crossword puzzle, amazed that it was nearly complete. She hated the ones that gave the average solution time. It took her twenty minutes just to sharpen her pencil, find a comfortable position and figure out one-across. Since she was lousy at them, it naturally meant that Ted was a whiz at crossword puzzles. If the one he set aside now was any indication, he could win competitions.

The morning passed slowly. Several panels were called out for jury selection, but her name was not among them. That was more than fine with her.

At lunchtime Ted left the building without suggesting they eat together. She’d expected that, although she couldn’t help feeling a twinge of regret. Without meaning to follow him, she discovered that they’d chosen the same place along the waterfront where they’d eaten a few days earlier. As usual, the outdoor restaurant was crowded, and once her order had been filled, there wasn’t a place to sit. She could ask some strangers if they would mind sharing a table with her, but no one looked that interesting.

"Do you mind if I sit down?" she finally asked, standing directly in front of Ted.

"Go ahead." He didn't sound welcoming, but at least he didn't sound unwelcoming, either.

"I didn't follow you here," she announced, pulling out the bench opposite him. Vigorously she stirred her thick clam chowder.

"I didn't think for a minute that you had." He avoided her eyes and sat looking out over the greenish waters of Puget Sound.

"Are you always like this?"

"How do you mean?" He turned his gaze to her for an instant, then looked back to the choppy waters, seeming to prefer the view of the busy waterway to her.

"Are you always sullen and uncommunicative when you're angry with someone?" She considered it her greatest weakness that she really was miserable when someone was upset with her. In the past, this personality quirk had only applied to people she cared about, which meant that her current uneasiness over Ted was troubling her more every minute.

"Usually," he agreed.

"How long does it last?"

"That depends," he said, nibbling on a French fry.

"On what?"

"On how offended I am."

"How much have I offended you?"

"On a scale of one to ten," he stated casually, "I'd say a solid nine."

A thick lump worked its way down Caroline's dry throat. She had done some regrettable things in her life, and pulled enough shenanigans to cause her father a headful of gray hair. But there hadn't been a time when she regretted any words more than she regretted the ones she'd spoken to Ted. She'd felt recently that they had been on the brink of something special. She didn't know how to explain it. She wasn't even sure she liked him, but she felt a strange and powerful attraction to him. "I can't do anything more than apologize."

"I know." A sad smile touched the edges of his mouth. He didn't say anything when she slid off the bench and stood. She wanted to ask him how long he planned to be this way but didn't. They only had one more day of jury duty, and from the looks of things it would take far more time than that.

If the morning was dull, the afternoon was doubly so. Caroline intentionally sat as far away from Ted as possible, doing her best to ignore him. Yet again and again, as if by a force more potent than her own will, her gaze was drawn to him. He was by far the most attractive man in the room. There was a quiet authority about him that commanded the respect of others. The masterful thread in his voice hadn't gone unnoticed, either. From her experience being on the jury with him, she knew that he was quick, sure and decisive. If it hadn't been for his strength against the others, she sincerely doubted that she would have been able to withstand the concerted pressure to change her vote.

Later that afternoon she returned to her apartment, which didn't feel as welcoming as it usually did. Sluggishly she removed her backpack and looped it over the closest doorknob. She was physically drained and mentally exhausted, and thoroughly disgusted with life. Once again her sense of timing had been off-kilter. She didn't know how to explain her life in better terms. It was as if everyone else was marching "left, right, left, right," and she was loping along her merry way—"Right, left, right, left." Another woman would have looked at Ted Thomasson and immediately recognized what a devastatingly attractive man he was. She saw it, didn't trust it and chose to insult him. Only when it was too late did she recognize his appeal. At least after tomorrow their forced proximity would be over and she could go about her life, forgetting that she'd ever had anything to do with Tedious Ted Thomasson.

The phone started ringing at six that evening. The first time she was scrambling eggs for dinner and reached for it automatically. The pattern was the same. She picked up the phone, heard some distant breathing and then the caller disconnected. Obviously some weirdo had gotten her number and was determined to play games with her. Fifteen minutes later it happened again. After the third time, she unplugged her phone.

Refusing to give in to fear, she told herself that calls like these were normally harmless. What she needed to stir her blood was a little exercise. She changed into her jogging outfit and ran in place. She stopped only when the tenants below her began pounding on their ceiling. Panting, she turned off the record and slumped onto the sofa, panting.

Feeling invigorated and secure, she plugged her phone back in. It rang immediately. She practically jerked the receiver up to her ear. "If you don't stop bothering me, I'm calling the cops." That should frighten the jerk who was playing these games.

A moment of stunned silence followed. "Caroline, is that you?"

It was her mother.

"Oh, hi, Mom." She laughed in relief and briefly explained what had happened as she slumped against the thick sofa cushions. "I thought you were my prank caller."

"I'm so relieved," her mother said, and laughed softly. "You know how I live in fear of the police." Then she said, excitement brimming in her voice, "I have news. Your father and I are taking off for a little while." She paused, then added, "To China."

"China!"

"We leave tomorrow, and we're both very pleased. You know this is just the market he's been wanting to reach."

"How long will you be gone?"

"Two weeks. It's going to be a wonderful trip."

"It sounds like it." Caroline would miss her mother. Although they lived several hundred miles apart, they talked at least twice a week.

"Have you seen Theodore again?" The question had been asked casually, but she knew her mother well enough to sense the interest she was struggling to disguise.

"I see him every day in the jury room."

"He's grown up into someone pretty impressive, don't you think?"

"Yes, Mom, I do."

"You do?" Her mother was clearly having trouble disguising her surprise, and the line went silent for a moment. "You like him, don't you?"

"I insulted him. I didn't mean to, but it just slipped out, and now I doubt that we're capable of anything more than a polite greeting."

"He'll get over it," her mother said knowingly.

"Sure, just as soon as the moon turns blue."

"Caroline, I saw the way he looked at you. He'll come around, don't worry."

Caroline wished she had as much confidence as her mother, but she didn't.

The next morning it was Caroline who arrived at the federal courthouse first. She'd brought along a book to occupy her time—a best-seller that was said to be irresistibly absorbing. She certainly hoped so.

When Ted entered the room, she pretended to be immersed in the thrilling plot of the book, though she couldn't even remember its title, let alone the characters or the story.

He took the seat beside her. "Morning." The greeting was clipped.

"Hello." She continued reading, proud that she'd resisted the urge to turn and smile at him, then cursed her heart for pounding because she was so glad he'd chosen to sit beside her.

"Did you try to phone me last night?" he questioned dryly.

So that was it. "No."

He leaned back in his chair and rubbed a hand over his face. "Someone was playing tricks on me half the night. Phoning, then hanging up."

"Surely you don't think I would do something like that?" She snapped her book closed and stiffened. "I'll have you know—"

"Caroline," he said, and gently placed a hand over hers to stop her. "Weren't you telling me the same thing was happening to you?"

"Yes," she said, still angry that he would think she'd done something so childish and trying not to remember that she'd all but accused him of the same thing just yesterday.

"Did it happen again last night?"

"Yes." She turned frightened eyes to him as she felt her facial muscles tense. "I thought it was a prankster . . . a joker, but now it's happening to you, too?"

"I don't think it's anything to worry about."

"Probably not," she agreed, but in truth she was frightened out of her wits. "But I think there has to be some connection between the phone calls and the trial."

"Still . . . a friend of mine is a detective. It might be a good idea if we have a chat with him."

"Do you think it's necessary?"

"I don't know, but I'd feel better if we knew where we stood."

"We're not standing anywhere. We're sitting ducks."

"Caroline, we're not. Whoever is doing this is angry because of the mistrial, but it will blow over in a day or two." His face revealed none of his thoughts.

"Right," she said, crossing her legs and starting to nibble on her bottom lip. She wished he hadn't said anything about the calls he'd gotten. Ignorance really was bliss.

"Listen," he announced a minute later. "I'm sure I'm just overreacting. We've both gotten a few harmless phone calls, but there's no need to contact the police."

She wasn't nearly as convinced, but she let the subject drop.

They sat together for the rest of the day, though they barely spoke. At lunchtime they bought sandwiches and ate in the cafeteria.

"I'll drive you home," Ted announced at the end of the day.

Caroline didn't argue. Silently they walked toward the parking lot. Her hands were tucked deep within the pockets of her light jacket. She had a sinking feeling that something was about to happen, which caused chills to run up and down her spine. She would never lay claim to possessing any supernatural insight, not in the least, but her imagination had flipped into overdrive.

Ted stopped abruptly and released a mumbled curse.

"What's wrong?"

He pointed to his car, which had been smeared with raw eggs.

Caroline's earlier chill became so intense that she feared frostbite. "The person who did this has to be the same one who's making the phone calls," she murmured, struggling to disguise her alarm. If he was doing this to Ted, then something was bound to happen to her, as well.

"We don't have any proof of that."

He sounded so calm and reasonable that she wanted to shake him. "What are we going to do?"

"For starters, we'll head for a car wash."

"And then?"

"And then my friend's office."

"Okay." She was more than ready to agree.

Detective Charles Randolph was a brown-haired, clean-shaven man whose mouth widened with a ready smile when Ted walked into his office. Caroline followed closely on his heels and nodded politely when introduced. She resisted shaking hands, since hers were clammy with fear.

Ted briefly explained the reason for their visit. Detective Randolph sympathized, but he told them that chances were good their tormentor would stop his games in a day or so, and then he added that there was little he could do. He did offer some helpful suggestions, and assured them that the minute they could pinpoint a suspect or prove anything, he would do everything within the limits of the law to put an end to the problem.

Afterward Ted escorted Caroline to her apartment, and this time he accepted her invitation to go up for a cup of coffee. This time she ground the beans and went through elaborate steps to prolong the process to keep him with her as long as possible.

"You're not frightened, are you, Caroline?" he asked, his eyes dark and serious as he studied her.

"Who, me?" She laughed bravely and claimed the overstuffed chair across from him, her hands cupping her steaming mug.

"I agree with Randolph. Whoever is doing this is unlikely to hurt either one of us."

"Right." *Wrong,* her mind countered.

Ted didn't take more than a few sips of his coffee before he stood. Caroline sent him a pleading glance, but she wasn't about to ask him to stay if he was intent on leaving. She might be frightened half to death, but she still had her pride.

"Don't let any strangers into your apartment," he cautioned.

Was he kidding? Her own brother would have to break down the door.

"Call me if anything happens. Okay?" he went on.

Wonderful. She had to wait until her life was in danger before contacting him. "Define 'happens.'" Her eyes were begging him to stay, to move in if necessary, at least until this craziness passed.

Ted appeared to be weighing her question. "You'll know."

"That's what I'm afraid of."

He hesitated in the open doorway. "You're sure you'll be all right?"

"I'll be fine." She was shocked that she could lie with such ease, but if he was determined to leave her to an unknown fate, then she would let him. No wonder she'd disliked him so much all these years. Maybe this was how he'd chosen to take his revenge.

He waited on the other side of the apartment door until she turned the lock and it clicked into place.

After he left, she managed to push the crank caller to the back of her mind by keeping busy. She baked bran muffins and ate one with a slice of bologna and cheese for dinner. Everything on television bored her, so she picked up the book she'd tried to read earlier that day with no success. By ten-thirty her eyelids were drooping. Chastising herself for being afraid to go to sleep, she slipped into her nightgown and started humming the national anthem. Her duty as a patriotic citizen had gotten her into this mess.

She crossed the room to pull the drapes closed when she noticed a burly figure of a man standing on the sidewalk below. He looked like the same man who had accompanied Joan MacIntosh. The resemblance was enough to cause her heart to flutter wildly and panic to fill her.

Ted had told her to wait until something happened. But she wasn't waiting until the commando below decided to break into her apartment.

Her fingers were shaking so badly that she could barely punch out Ted's telephone number.

He answered on the first ring.

"Ted." She heard the nervous tremor in her voice and tried unsuccessfully to calm herself.

"What is it?" He was instantly alert.

"A man . . . The man from the trial . . . He's here."

"In your apartment?"

"Not yet. He's standing outside my building. I . . . went to close the drapes, and I saw him staring up at my window."

"Did he see you?"

"I don't know," she said sarcastically. "Do you want me to stick my head out the window and ask him?"

"Are you sure it's him? Nelson Bergstrom?"

"Not Nelson, Joan MacIntosh's husband. At least I think it's him. He was standing in the shadows, but it looked like it was him, and . . ."

"Caroline," he said her name so gently that she wanted to cry. "You're worrying too much. It's probably nothing."

"Nothing?" she echoed, hurt and angry. "I'm locked in an apartment with a man seeking revenge outside my door. In the meantime you're probably sitting there in front of a cozy fireplace, smoking your pipe and . . . and you have the nerve to tell me I'm overreacting."

"Caroline—"

A loud knock sounded against her door and echoed like a taunt around the room.

"What was that?" Ted asked.

"He's here," she whispered, so frightened she thought she was going to faint.

Five

"Caroline!" Her name was followed by frantic pounding on her front door. "Caroline! Are you all right?"

"Ted?" His name was wrenched from the stranglehold of shock and fear that gripped her throat. Her hands were trembling so hard that she could barely unlatch the door and open it. A shock wave shuddered through her bones at the sight of him. His eyes were narrowed and hard, and flickered possessively over her like tongues of fire, checking to see that she was unharmed. She had never seen a more intense expression. At that moment, she didn't doubt that he would have seriously hurt anyone who'd hurt her.

"Thank God." He closed the door and swept her into his arms, crushing her slender frame to his with such force that the oxygen was knocked from her lungs. She didn't care how hard he held her. He was here, and she was safe. She wanted to tell him everything that had happened, but the only sounds that escaped her fear-tightened throat were gibberish.

The unexpected strength of his kiss forced her head back so that she was pressed against the apartment wall. He moved his hands to cup her face, and his mouth pillaged hers with such hunger that her knees gave way. Her grip on his shoulders was the only thing that kept her upright. Consuming fear gave way to delicious excitement as she opened her mouth to him and met his lips with burning eagerness. His touch chased away the freezing cold of stark fear, and she nestled closer to his warmth, trembling violently. When his mouth trailed down her throat to explore her neck, Caroline fought her way through the haze of engulfing sensations. For days she'd wanted Ted to kiss her. She'd planned to treat him as he'd done her and make fun of him with some cutting remark. But one kiss and she'd melted into his arms. Her resistance amounted to little more than wafer-thin walls. Of course, the circumstances undoubtedly had something to do with the strength of her response. And now, instead of rejecting him, she held him as if she wasn't sure she could survive if he let her go.

"He didn't hurt you?"

"No." Her voice wavered, betraying the havoc he was causing to her self-control.

"When I saw the blood, I think I went a little crazy."

"Blood?" He wasn't making any sense. She hadn't answered the knock, and whoever wanted in had been content to make a few strange noises outside her door before leaving.

"The door," Ted muttered. His hands roved gently up and down her spine, molding her closer to him, as though he couldn't let her go.

"I didn't let him in." She still wasn't sure what he was talking about, but it didn't seem to matter when he was touching her with such tenderness.

"Caroline." He lifted his head long enough for the intimate look in his sapphire eyes to hold her captive.

"Yes?"

He shook his head from side to side, as if he couldn't bring himself to speak. Ever so slowly he lowered his mouth to hers again. She breathed deeply to control the excitement that tightened her stomach. If his first kiss had shocked her into melting bonelessly, this kiss completely and utterly devastated her.

Her hands strained against his shirt, clenching and bunching the material, but she didn't know if she meant to push him away or pull him closer. After a moment she didn't care.

"I would have hurt him—a lot—if he'd touched you," Ted growled against her lips.

Remembering the feral light in his eyes earlier, she didn't doubt his words.

His breath filled her lungs. It felt warm and drugging, muddling her already-confused thoughts. "But he didn't, and I'm fine." Or she would be once her blood pressure dropped, but she didn't know who to blame for that—the lunatic or Ted.

Relaxing his hold, Ted slid his arm around her waist and securely locked the front door. "All right, my heart's back where it belongs. Tell me what happened."

His heart might have been fine, but hers wasn't. She felt as if she was standing on a dangerous precipice where the view was heavenly and heady, and stepping off looked like a distinct possibility. But she had only to look down the deep abyss below to realize what dangerous ground she was standing on. Mentally she took a step in retreat.

"Caroline," he coaxed, tenderly guiding her to the cushioned chair and sitting her down. He knelt in front of her, his hands clasping hers. "Tell me what happened. Tell me everything."

"Nothing happened, really. He—or whoever it was—knocked a few times. I . . . I didn't answer, and after a little while and a few weird noises, he went away." She didn't add that she'd stood stock-still, deathly afraid that whoever was doing this would come back. Not knowing if she should run from the apartment or stay put, she had waited, praying that Ted would arrive before her tormentor decided to return.

Ted expelled his breath. "I think I broke the land speed record getting here. If anything had happened to you, I never would have forgiven myself."

"I wouldn't have forgiven you, either," she said, rallying slightly, remembering how he'd abandoned her to an unknown fate earlier. "Why didn't you stay with me before? I was frightened and you knew it, yet you chose to leave."

"I couldn't stay." He raised his head, but he refused to meet her gaze. "I had another commitment."

"Another commitment." She spoke the words with all the venom of a woman scorned. So Theodore Thomasson had some hot date that was more important to him than her welfare. How incredibly stupid she'd been not to have guessed it sooner. No wonder he hadn't been able to get out of her apartment fast enough.

Raging to her feet, she stalked to the other side of the room as two bright spots of color blossomed in her cheeks. He'd left the arms of another woman to rescue her, then had the nerve to kiss her like that. She felt as if she was going to be sick. The worst part was that she'd kissed him back, encouraged him, and, yes, wanted him. Her throat ached as she battled back stinging tears.

"Well, as you can see, I'm unscathed." She did her best to sound normal. "Now that you've assured yourself of that, you'll want to go back to the ready arms of your calendar girl. I apologize if I inconvenienced your plans in any way."

"My calendar girl? What are you talking about?" he asked in confusion. "Have you taken leave of your senses?"

"Yes," she said. She had indeed abandoned sanity the minute

he'd pulled her into his arms. "And don't you ever . . . ever—" She whirled on him, pointing her index finger at him like a weapon. "Don't you ever touch me again."

A weary glitter shone in his eyes, as if he were attempting to make sense of her words. "From the impression you gave me, I'd say you were enjoying my kiss."

"I was in shock," she countered, her expression schooled and brittle. "I didn't know what I was doing."

He ran his fingers through his hair, mussing it all the more. "All right, all right, we both didn't know what we were doing. Chalk it up to the unpleasant events of the last week. I'll admit kissing you was a mistake."

"I don't want it to happen again."

His frown deepened into a dark scowl. "It won't. Does that soothe your outrage?"

She swallowed past the lump that was choking her throat. Her answer was little more than a curt nod. "You can go now," she finally managed. She shivered, then wrapped her arms around herself to ward off the sudden chill. Ted opened her closet and took out a bulky-knit cardigan. It cost her more pride than he knew to let him drape it around her shoulders.

"Where's a bucket?" he asked, taking off his coat and rolling up his shirt sleeves.

"A bucket?"

"A couple of rags, too, if you have them?"

"Why?"

"Why?" he repeated, glancing at her as though she'd lost her mind. "Because of the blood."

Her face went sickly pale as she suddenly remembered what he'd said earlier. "What blood?"

"You didn't see your door?"

"No. What's wrong with it?" She marched across the room,

but Ted stopped her before she made it halfway to the door. Their eyes locked in a battle of wills. "Ted?"

"There are a few unsavory words painted on it. I'm sure you've read them before."

"He—he wrote something on my door . . . in blood?"

"It's probably spray paint, but I thought . . . Never mind what I was thinking."

"But . . ."

"Just get me a bucket, Caroline."

Numbly, she complied, leading the way into her kitchen and taking out a yellow plastic pail from beneath her sink. "Why would he knock if all he wanted to do was write some ugly words on my door? That doesn't make any sense."

"After spending this week in your company, there's little left in this world that does. How do I know what he was thinking? Maybe he wanted to know if you were home before he defaced your property," he said, and his mouth thinned with irritation. He took the plastic pail from her hands and filled it with soapy water. "And for that matter, who knows what he would have done if you *had* opened the door."

"There was no chance of my doing that. Maybe he would have gotten scared if I answered and gone away."

"There's no way of knowing that." Preoccupied, he pulled open a kitchen drawer and withdrew a couple of clean dishrags.

"There's no need for you to clean up. I'm perfectly capable of washing my own front door. Besides, you probably want to get back to your hot date."

"My hot date?"

"Would you stop repeating everything I say?"

His gaze seized hers in a hold that felt as physical and punishing as if he'd grabbed her arm. Pride demanded that she meet his eyes, but it wasn't easy. Never had Caroline seen anyone look so angry. His dark blue eyes were snapping with fire. "You certainly have a low opinion of me."

"I— You were the one who said you had an earlier commitment."

"And you assumed it was with a woman."

"Well . . . yes." She wished her voice would stop wavering. "You mean it wasn't?" Each word dropped in volume until they emerged in little more than a low whisper.

He didn't answer her. "Why don't you change your clothes while I wipe down your door?"

"Change my clothes?" For the first time she realized that she was wearing a five-year-old flannel nightgown that had faded from a bright purple to a sick blue from years of washing. As if that wasn't bad enough, the hem had ripped out and was dragging against the floor. Complementing her outfit was a pair of glorious, scarlet knee-high socks.

"For once in your life, don't argue with me," he said in a voice that told her his patience was gone.

"I wasn't going to."

Ted's expression revealed surprise, but he said nothing more as he carried the yellow pail full of soapy water out her front door.

While he was about his task, Caroline changed into deep burgundy-colored cords and a fisherman's knit sweater. She knew that with her hair she shouldn't wear colors like burgundy, but such taboos had always been mere challenges to her. How she wished she didn't have this penchant for being so contrary.

Her hair was combed and tied at the base of her neck with a pale blue nylon scarf by the time Ted returned. She followed him into the tiny kitchen and watched as he emptied the bucket, rinsed it out and placed it back under the sink. When he turned, he looked surprised to find her close.

"You might want to pack a few things."

"Pack a few things?"

"Now who's sounding like a parrot?"

In other circumstances she would have laughed, but there wasn't any humor in the look Ted was giving her.

"Why should I pack?"

"I'm taking you home with me."

"Why?" He made her sound like a puppy dog that needed a place to stay.

"Because I refuse to spend the rest of the night worrying about you." Each word was dripping with exasperation.

"It didn't seem to bother you earlier."

"It does now." Apparently that explanation was supposed to satisfy her. "Don't argue with me, Caroline. It won't do you any good."

From the scathing look he gave her, she could see that he was right. She could put up a valiant argument, but she was tired and afraid, and the truth was that she wanted to be with Ted so much it actually hurt. The lunatic on her doorstep was only an excuse for enjoying his company. She'd been bitterly disappointed when Ted had left her earlier that evening. She'd longed to spend a quiet evening alone with him. There was a peacefulness about him that attracted her, an inner strength that drew her to him naturally. Yet all she'd managed to do was offend him. She reminded herself that he wasn't taking her to his apartment to enjoy her tantalizing company but out of a sense of duty. She swallowed her pride and followed him. She was going for more reasons than she cared to analyze.

Ted's apartment wasn't anything like what she'd imagined, though she *had* been right about the fireplace, which dominated the living room, with tan leather furniture positioned in front of it. Brass light fixtures were accentuated by the cream-colored carpet. Several paintings adorned the walls. Compared to her tiny apartment, Ted lived in the lap of luxury.

"I'll take your coat."

With a wan smile, she gave it to him. He'd barely spoken to her on the way over, and she once again sought for a way to tear down the concrete walls she'd erected between them with her thoughtless accusations. "Your apartment is very nice."

He looked as if he were about to answer her when the phone rang.

Her eyes widened with apprehension as he crossed the room. His back was to her, and although she couldn't hear much of the conversation, she saw Ted's shoulders sag in defeat. She had felt as if she'd been slowly crumpling under the oppressive weight of the pressure they'd been under these last few days, but Ted hadn't once revealed in any way that the trial and its outcome had affected him, so whatever was being said now must be far worse than anything they'd experienced so far.

Replacing the receiver, he turned to her. His eyes showed both anger and defeat.

"What is it?"

He rubbed his eyes and pinched the bridge of his nose. "That was Randolph."

"And . . . ?"

"He just wanted me to know that there's been another assault against a woman in a mini-mart."

"Nelson?"

"They don't know, but the MO's the same. Assuming our problems are tied to the trial, that can only inflame whoever's been harassing us, so he thinks it might be a good idea if we got out of town for a few days until the heat blows over."

Six

"Leave town? Whatever for?" Caroline watched with concern as Ted rubbed a hand across the back of his neck, looking as if the weight of the world were pressing against his shoulders.

"Don't you understand what I'm saying?" he barked. "Another young woman—a mini-mart clerk just like Joan MacIntosh—has been brutally assaulted. Pistol whipped in the same way as Joan, and from what Charles said, the cops are betting the same man who attacked Joan struck again tonight. And once again it was within walking distance of Nelson Bergstrom's address."

Caroline felt the strength leave her legs, and she slowly sank into a leather chair. Her voice wobbled as the tears that had hovered near the surface broke free. "And . . . and we set him free." Sniffling, she pressed her fingers to her eyes, but that did little good and the moisture ran unheeded down her ashen cheeks.

"We did what we thought was right," Ted countered. "We still don't know if Nelson Bergstrom is guilty or not. No one does."

"But it must've been him."

"Apparently the newspapers have gotten hold of this, and according to Randolph, the morning paper is doing a story about the mistrial in connection with this latest assault." He gave her his handkerchief and lowered himself into the chair beside hers. "Listen carefully, Caroline. The press have our names, and our addresses aren't exactly top-secret. They're going to have a field day with this, and we could be stuck in the middle of it."

"So we have to leave?"

"We don't *have* to, but Randolph advises it. I've been meaning to visit your parents anyway, and this seems like the perfect opportunity."

"We can't go see them. They've gone to China."

Ted nodded. "What about your brother?"

"No." She was just beginning to formulate her thoughts. She had a key to her parents' home. There wasn't any reason why she couldn't steal away there for a few days. "It shouldn't matter if Mom and Dad are gone. I'll take a couple of days and drive home, lounge around for a day or two, and head back. By then this thing will have been settled."

"You?" He gave her a disgruntled look. "We're in this together. Wherever *you* go, *I* go."

"You?" Caroline would have thought from the way he had been acting that the last person in the world he wanted to spend time with was her.

"Don't look so pleased," he murmured sarcastically, propelling himself out of the chair. "Believe me, I'm not all that thrilled to waste my time in *your* company, either."

"Then why do it?" she asked, feeling hurt and unreasonable. "I don't need you to escort me to San Francisco. I'm perfectly capable of taking care of myself."

"Listen, Miss High and Mighty, I had enough of you when

I was fifteen to last any man a lifetime." He paused and pointed out the window. "But some loon is out there, seeking revenge because our actions set a guilty man free. You can bet that once this latest development hits the papers it's going to be more phone calls and messages smeared on doors—and maybe worse." His look cut right through her. "Now get this through that thick, stubborn skull of yours. I'm not sending you any place where I can't keep an eye on you. We're in this thing together, whether you like it or not."

Caroline had never seen Ted's eyes so flinty. Each word forced her deeper into the chair, until she felt as though she were physically embedded in the leather cushion. She crossed her arms in front of her in an attempt to ward off the hurt his words were inflicting, instead hugging the warm memory of his kiss to her heart. The burning heat from her cheeks dried her tears.

"Well?" he challenged, standing over her, apparently expecting an argument.

"When do you want to leave?"

Some of the diamond hardness left his eyes. "First thing in the morning."

"My clothes . . ."

"We'll pack tonight, catch what sleep we can, and leave first thing in the morning." He spoke impersonally, and Caroline had the impression that his thoughts were elsewhere. She could be a slab of marble for all the notice he gave her.

It took what felt like half the night to make the necessary preparations for the trip. Once she was packed and her apartment securely locked, they returned to his place. She offered to help and was refused without so much as a backward glance. When he went to get his things together, she sat on the sofa. She only meant to close her eyes and give them a rest, but the next thing she knew Ted was gently shaking her awake.

She sat up with a start. "What time is it?"

"Five-thirty. It might be a good idea if we left now."

"Okay." A headache was pounding at her temple, and she pressed her fingertips to it and inhaled deeply.

"There's coffee, if you'd like a cup."

She nodded, since conversation felt as if it would require a monumental effort. He stepped into the kitchen, then returned a moment later with a steaming mug. Her smile of appreciation drained her of strength, and she sagged back against the sofa cushions. He gazed at her, and she lowered her eyes, unwilling to let him see how miserable she felt. She could hear him moving around the apartment, and she took another sip of coffee, feeling the need for caffeine to inspire her to get moving.

"Here." Ted pried off the safety cap from a bottle of aspirin and shook two tablets into her palm.

"Thank you," she mumbled, accepting the glass of water he offered next. The tablets slid down the back of her throat easily. He had ranted at her earlier with an anger that had shocked her. Now he was tenderly seeing to her aches and pains. "Did you get any sleep at all?" she asked.

"No."

He didn't elaborate, but Caroline realized that, like her, he was feeling the heavy burden of responsibility for this latest assault case. Rationally, she recognized that they'd done what they felt was right by sticking to their convictions. But the fact they had felt the shadow of a doubt over Nelson Bergstrom's guilt didn't matter now. Every piece of evidence against the man had been circumstantial; they hadn't felt confident enough to hand over a guilty verdict. But this latest assault had jerked the rug out from under Caroline's feet. In her heart, she was sure that she had set a guilty man free.

"Did—did your friend at the police station mention how

badly the latest victim was hurt? I mean . . ." She let the rest of the words fade, not wanting to know, yet realizing she must.

"She's in the hospital. Randolph said she's in pretty bad shape."

Caroline felt like weeping again, but she managed to hold back the tears with a suppressed shudder.

Twenty minutes later they were heading south on Interstate 5. Neither spoke and the air between them hung ominously heavy and still.

"How's the headache?" Ted asked as they approached the outskirts of the state capital in Olympia.

"Better." Her hand tightened on the armrest of the car door. She doubted that the headache would go away until Nelson Bergstrom was in jail where he belonged—where she should have put him.

When Ted exited the freeway onto a secondary highway, she gave him a surprised glance. He answered her question before she voiced it.

"We're both drained. I thought we'd spend the day in Ocean Shores. I have a cabin there."

"That sounds like a good idea." She shifted to a more comfortable position in the seat, and his dark blue eyes slid briefly to her.

"When we get to the cabin we can catch up on some sleep, then leave again when it's dark and we won't be seen."

"Leave tonight? Why?" The idea of spending a relaxing day on the beach was appealing to her. She needed the peace and solitude of a windswept shore to exorcize the events of the past week from her heart.

"I thought we should probably do our traveling by night," Ted explained. "It will be to our advantage to attract the least amount of attention possible."

Staring out the window at the lush green terrain, Caroline swallowed down a ready argument. The world outside the car window looked serene and peaceful, with its pastoral farms and grazing animals. The day was glorious, especially now in the light of early morning, as they raced down the highway with the rising sun that stood boldly out to greet them in hues of brilliant orange. She didn't want to argue with Ted, not now when she felt so tired and miserable. Telling him that he'd been watching too many cop shows wouldn't be conducive to an amicable journey.

More silence followed, but it wasn't harsh or grating; it was almost pleasant. Without being obvious, Caroline studied Ted. The image of him sitting in an office all day seemed strangely out of sync. His shoulders were too broad and muscular for a man who was tied to a desk. His jawline was solid, and there was a faint bend to his nose, as if it had been broken at one time. She couldn't picture him fighting, though she was sure he would if necessary. The last few days had taught her that. Another thing that amazed her was that he had never married. Fleetingly, she wondered why. He was more than attractive, compellingly male, and he stirred her blood as no one else ever had.

"You're looking thoughtful," Ted commented, his gaze momentarily turning toward her.

Caroline continued to study his handsome profile for a thoughtful second. "I was just wondering why you'd never married."

"No reason in particular." Amusement gleamed briefly in his eyes. "I've been too busy to settle down. To be honest, I've wondered the same thing about you."

"Me?" She half expected him to add a comment that she would be fortunate if any man wanted to put up with her. He had never seen the softly feminine part of her that yearned for a family of her own. No, he had only been witness to the shrewish part of her nature. "I've been too busy to think about a husband and home." The lie was only a small one.

"Your career is more important?"

Proving to her father that she could be the best cook in America had been more important. Her pride demanded it, but she couldn't tell Ted that. He would scoff and call her stubborn, and add a hundred other unsavory adjectives. And he would be right.

"Yes, I guess it is," she answered finally.

They didn't speak again until the road signs indicated that they were entering the community of Ocean Shores. Although she had heard a great deal about the resort town, with its rolling golf courses and luxurious summer homes, she had never been there. For herself, she would have chosen a less populated area, one with wide open spaces and room to breathe. She wouldn't want to worry about nosy neighbors or invading another's privacy. But her tastes weren't Ted's, and every minute together proved how little they shared in common.

When he turned off the main street and took a winding, narrow road that led down a secluded strip of windswept shore, then turned down his drive, Caroline was pleasantly surprised. His log cabin was far enough off the road so that it couldn't readily be seen.

He parked on the far side of the house, so that his car wouldn't be easily visible from the road, either, and turned off the engine. He rested his hands on the steering wheel for a long moment as he closed his eyes.

"You must be exhausted."

They were less than three hours out of Seattle, but it felt as if they'd traveled nonstop to California.

"A little," was all he would admit.

The fireplace was the only source of heat inside the cabin, and Ted immediately started a fire. The place was small and homey, with only a few pieces of furniture.

Caroline looked around and came up with enough odds and ends from the kitchen cupboards to fix them something to eat. They were both hungry, and ate the soup and canned fruit as if it were ambrosia. While she washed and put away the few dishes they'd used, he sat on the sofa, staring into the fire, and promptly fell into a deep slumber. For a time she was content to watch him sleep. A pleasant warmth invaded her limbs, and she yearned to brush the hair from his brow and trace her hands over his strongly defined masculine features. Finding a spare blanket, she spread it over him, lingering at his side far longer than necessary.

A walk along the deserted beach lifted her heart from the doldrums and freed her eager spirit. Even when the sky darkened with a threatening squall, she continued her trek along the windy beach, picking up odds and ends of sea shells and bits of rock. The surf pounded relentlessly against the smooth beach. Crashing waves pummeled the sand until the undertow swept it away into the swirling depths. Caroline felt her own heart being lured into the abyss that only a few hours before had seemed so frightening. She was half a breath from falling in love with Ted Thomasson, and it frightened her to death.

Ted found her an hour later, building a sand castle with an elaborate moat and a bridge made from tiny sticks.

"I wondered where you'd gone," he said, and sat on a dried-out driftwood log. "You shouldn't have let me sleep so long."

"I figured you needed the rest." She glanced up into his warm gaze. Quickly she averted her eyes.

"We should be leaving soon."

"No." She shook her head for emphasis, her cloud of auburn curls twisted with the strength of her conviction.

"What do you mean—no?"

"I refuse to run away." She leaned back, sitting on her heels. Her hands rested on her knees as she met his puzzled gaze with unwavering resolve. "I realize that I've probably had a lot more experience in dealing with guilt than you have, and the first thing I've learned is—"

"Caroline—"

"No, please listen to me. We—*I*—did what I felt was right even when the decision wasn't easy. I refuse to punish myself now because I may have made the wrong choice. If there's someone out there who wants me to suffer because of that, then I'd prefer to meet him head-on rather than sneak around in the dark of night like a common thief. I simply won't do it."

The expression that crossed his face was so like her father's when she'd utterly exasperated him that Caroline suppressed the urge to laugh.

"You know I won't leave you," Ted admitted slowly.

"I'm hoping you won't, but I wouldn't stop you," she said, feeling brave. She hadn't planned on him driving off without her—she hadn't seen the necessity. He was much too much of a gentleman.

"It would be a simple thing for anyone looking for us to learn about this cabin. Our coming here makes sense."

"Don't worry, I've got that all figured out. We'll sleep on the beach tonight."

"We'll do *what?*" he exploded. "It's cold out here."

Caroline did an admirable job of holding back her laugh of pure delight. In the last twenty hours Ted had taken great pains not to touch her. Of course, she'd asked him not to, but that shouldn't matter. If they pitched a makeshift tent here on the sandy beach, he would be forced to seek her body's warmth. Although he would have every intention of avoiding it, he would wake up holding her in his arms. The mental image was one of such delight that she experienced a tingling warmth up and down her arms.

"I'll keep you warm," she promised under her breath, smiling.

He wasn't pleased with the rest of her ideas, either, so she was astonished that he did as she asked. For dinner they roasted hot dogs on sticks and melted chocolate bars over graham crackers. By the time they'd eaten their fill, the first stars were twinkling in the purpling sky.

"I thought it might rain earlier this afternoon," she mentioned conversationally.

"If it did, maybe you'd listen to reason."

"Maybe," she said with a gleeful smile. "But I doubt it. I've always loved the ocean."

"It's cold and windy, and it's only a matter of time before everything smells like mold," Ted grumbled, tossing another dried piece of wood on the fire.

"Yet you bought a place by the beach, so you must not dislike it half as much as you claim."

His answer was a soft snort as he wrapped a blanket more securely around his shoulders. "I don't need to worry about anyone hunting me down. One night with you and I'll be dead from pneumonia."

"Stop complaining and look at how beautiful the sky is."

"Bah humbug!" He rubbed his hands together and stuck them out in front of the sputtering fire.

The pitch-black night darkened the ocean, while the silvery beams of a full moon created a dancing light on the surface of the water.

"When I was a little girl I ran away to the sea. I was utterly astonished when they told me I couldn't board the ship."

Ted chuckled. "I remember my parents telling me about that. How old were you? Ten?"

"About that. I'd pulled one of my usual shenanigans—I can't even remember what it was anymore—but I knew that once again I'd embarrassed my mom and dad, so I decided to go to sea. I'll never forget when they came down to the docks to pick me up. My mother burst into tears and hugged me close. For the first time in my life, I realized how much she loved me."

"Had you doubted it before?"

"No, I'd simply never thought about it. No matter how I tried, I could never do things right. There would always be one reason or another why my marvelous schemes failed and I ended up with egg on my face. When I ran away I thought it was for the best, so I wouldn't embarrass Mom again. That night I learned that it didn't matter how many escapades I got myself into, she would always love me. I was her daughter."

"Did you ever try running away again?"

"Never. There wasn't any need. My home was with her and Dad." She centered her concentration on the bark she was peeling from an old stick. She didn't often speak of her youth, chagrined by her behavior.

"You were marvelous, Caroline Lomax. Full of imagination and sass. Your parents had every reason to be proud of you." He spoke with such insight that she raised her head, and their gazes met over the flickering fire. The mesmerizing quality in his eyes stole her breath. Her heart pounded so loud and strong that she was convinced he could hear it over the crashing of the ocean waves. When his attention slid to her softly parted lips, she was certain he was going to reach for her and kiss her. She held her breath in helpless anticipation, yearning for his touch.

Abruptly, he stood and tossed the blanket to the sandy ground. "I've had enough of this wienie roast. You can sleep out here if you want, but I'm going inside."

She tried to hide her disappointment behind a taunting laugh. "You always were a quitter."

He ignored her derision and shook his head. "I don't have your sense of adventure. I never did."

"That's all right," she mumbled, standing. She brushed the sand from the back of her legs. "Few men do."

"You're coming with me?" He looked stunned that she'd conceded so easily.

"I might as well," she grumbled, mostly to herself. Ted helped her put out the fire, and haul the blankets and left-over food back to the cabin.

If she was disgruntled with his lack of adventure, the sleeping arrangements irritated her even more. "You go ahead and take the bed." He pointed to the bedroom, and the lone double bed with the thick down comforter and two huge pillows.

She had to admit it looked inviting. "What about you?"

"Me?" His Adam's apple worked as he swallowed convulsively. "I'll sleep out here, of course."

"But why?"

"Why? Caroline, for heaven's sake think about it."

"You can sleep on top of the covers if it will soothe your sense of propriety. I read once that if we each keep one foot on the ground, it's perfectly fine for two unmarried people to sleep in the same bed."

Clearly flustered, he waved his hand toward the bedroom. "You go on. I slept most of the day. I'm not tired."

A smile curved Caroline's full lips. She was enjoying riling him and, true to form, Ted was easy to rile. "I trust you."

"Maybe you shouldn't," he barked, and rubbed the back of

his neck in a nervous gesture. "I can't believe you'd even suggest such a thing."

"Why? It only makes sense to share, since there's only one bed."

"Good night, Caroline." He crossed his arms, indicating that the discussion was closed, and turned his back to her, standing stiffly in front of the fireplace.

"Good night," she echoed, battling to disguise her amusement.

She had no trouble falling asleep. The bed was warm and comfortable, and after only a few hours' sleep the night before, she slipped easily into an untroubled slumber.

Ted woke her at dawn and brought her in a cup of coffee. "Morning, bright eyes."

"Is it morning already?" she grumbled, yawning. Propping herself up on an elbow, she brushed the hair off her forehead. "How'd you sleep?"

"Great. You were right. Spending the night on the sofa was silly when there was a comfortable bed and a warm body eager for my presence."

She bolted upright. "You slept in this bed?"

"You're the one who suggested it."

"Here? In this bed?" she said again, too amazed to come up with anything else.

"Is there another one I don't know about?"

"You didn't really!"

"Of course I did. Honestly, Caroline, have you ever known me to tease?"

She hadn't. Her mouth dropped open, but a shocked silence followed. For the first time in recent history, she was stunned into speechlessness.

"I'd like to leave in twenty minutes," he said, and set the steaming coffee mug on the dresser top. "Will that be a problem?"

She answered with a shake of her head, still not quite believing his claim about sleeping with her. Mystified, she watched him leave the room and gently close the door, offering her privacy.

Biting her bottom lip, she cocked her head as an incredulous smile touched her eyes. Faint dimples formed at the corners of her mouth. Maybe this trip wouldn't be such a disaster. It could turn out to be the most glorious adventure of her life. Even now, she had trouble believing that she found Ted Thomasson so appealing. Would wonders ever cease? She certainly hoped not.

Oregon's coastal Highway 101 stretched along four hundred miles of spectacular open coastline. With her love of the ocean, Caroline had made several weekend jaunts to the area. She never tired of walking the miles of smooth beaches, clam digging, beachcombing and doing nothing but admiring the breathtaking beauty of the unspoiled scenery.

"We'll need to stop in Seaside," she informed him once they crossed the Columbia River at Astoria.

"Why Seaside?"

"Historians agree that the Lewis and Clark trail ended on the beaches there."

"I don't need a history lesson. Unless it's important, I think we should press on."

From the minute they'd left the beach house that morning, he had seemed intent on making this trip a marathon undertaking. He didn't want to travel the freeway, and, to be honest, she was pleased. The coastline made for far more fascinating travel, and she had several favorite spots along the way.

"It's not an earth-shattering reason," she concluded, disappointment coating her tongue. "But Seaside has wonderful saltwater taffy, and I'd like to get a box for my mother. Taffy's her favorite, and she likes Seaside's the best, so—"

"All right. We'll make a quick stop," he agreed.

"Thanks." Sighing, she smoothed her palms down the front of her dark raspberry shorts. She couldn't understand Ted. His moods kept swinging back and forth. Last night he'd been good-natured and patient. This morning he was behaving as if they were fleeing a Mafia gang hot on their tail.

When they reached Seaside, he parked along the beach-side promenade and cut the engine. "I'll wait here."

"In the car?" she asked disbelievingly. "But it's a gorgeous day. I thought you'd like to get something to eat and walk along the beach."

"I'm not hungry."

Glaring at him, she climbed out of the car and closed the door with unnecessary force. Maybe *he* wasn't hungry, but *she* was. They'd stopped for coffee and doughnuts at a gas station hours earlier, and that hadn't been enough to keep her happy. Fine! He could sit in the car if he liked, but she wasn't going to let his foul mood ruin her day. Every stride filled with purpose, she walked to the end of the street near the turnaround and bought a large box of candy for her mother. A vendor was selling popcorn, and she purchased a bag and carried it down the cement stairs to the sandy beach below.

Ted found her fifteen minutes later, sitting on a log and munching on her unconventional meal. "I've been looking all over for you," he said accusingly.

"Sorry." She offered some popcorn in appeasement, but she had no real regrets. "I got carried away. It really is lovely here, isn't it?"

"Yes." But he sounded preoccupied and impatient. "Are you ready to leave now?"

"I suppose."

Back on the highway, he turned and gave her a disgruntled look. "Is there any other place you'd like to stop?"

"Yes—two. Cannon Beach and Tillamook."

"Caroline, this isn't a stroll down memory lane. You must have seen these sights a hundred times. We're in a hurry. There's—"

"Correction," she interrupted briskly. "*You* appear to be in a rush here, not me. I explained once before that I refuse to run away. You can let me off at the next town if you insist on acting like this."

His hands tightened around the wheel until she was surprised he didn't bend it. "All right, we can stop in Cannon Beach and Tillamook, but what's there that's so all fired important?"

"You just wait and see," she said, feeling much better.

Less than a half hour later he pulled into a public parking area near Cannon Beach. While he grumbled and complained under his breath, she found a vendor and bought a huge box kite. Tight-lipped, he helped her assemble it, but then he only sat on the bulkhead while she raced up and down the shore, flying the oblong contraption. The wind caught her laughter, and she was breathless and giddy by the time she returned.

Ted gave her a sullen look and carted the kite to the car, setting it in the backseat next to the box of saltwater taffy.

Caroline wiped the wet sand from her bare feet before joining him in the front seat. Snapping the seat belt into place, she closed her eyes and made a gallant effort to control her tongue but lost. "You know, you're about as much fun as a bad case of chicken pox."

"I could say the same thing about you."

"Me?" she gasped, outraged. She was shocked at how much those words hurt. She swallowed back the pain, crossed her arms and stared straight ahead.

He started the engine and backed out of the parking space. The tension was so thick in the close confines of the car that it resembled a heavy London fog.

Thirty-five minutes later Ted announced that they were in Tillamook. She had been so caught up in her hurt and anger that she hadn't realized they were even close to Oregon's leading dairy land.

She pointed out the huge building to the left of the road. "I want to stop at the cheese factory," she said, doing her best to keep her voice monotone. She didn't bother to explain that her father loved Tillamook's mild cheddar cheese and she was planning on bringing him a five-pound block.

Ted sat in the car while she made a quick stop in the factory's visitor shop. He climbed out of the front seat when he saw her approach. She made only a pretense of meeting his cool gaze.

"Would you open the trunk, please?" she asked with a saccharine smile.

When he did, she lifted her heavy suitcase from inside and set it on the ground.

"What are you doing?" he demanded.

"What I should have done in the beginning." She opened the car door and took out the box of saltwater taffy and the kite, and sat them on the ground beside her suitcase. "This isn't working," she replied miserably. "It was a mistake to think the two of us could get along for more than a few hours, let alone a week."

He raked his hand through his hair. "Just what do you intend to do?"

She lifted one shoulder in a delicate shrug, hoping to give the impression of utter nonchalance. "The Greyhound bus comes through town. I'll catch that."

"Don't be ridiculous."

"I thought you'd be pleased to be rid of me," she countered smoothly. "From the minute we left Ocean Shores this morning, you've been treating me like I was a troublesome pest. Here's your chance to be free. I'd take it if I were you."

"Caroline, listen. . . ."

"Believe me, I know when I'm not wanted." She'd suffered enough rejection when she was young to know the feeling intimately.

"I should have told you earlier," he said with gruff insistence, "but I didn't want to frighten you."

"I told you before, I don't scare easily."

"Do you remember when I gassed up the car this morning?"

She nodded.

"I phoned Randolph, and . . ." He paused, his look dark and serious. "There's no easy way to say this. Apparently there's been a death threat made against us."

Seven

"A death threat." The ugly words hung in the air between them for tortuous seconds. "Who?"

"They don't know."

"So the threat wasn't phoned into the police station? Because they could have traced it then, right? So . . . how—how did Randolph hear about it?" In spite of her calm voice, her heart was pounding so hard she thought it might burst right out of her chest.

"Apparently someone wrote on the walls outside my apartment, as well. This time the message was more than a few distasteful names. The neighbors phoned the police after an article came out in the morning paper."

"Your name was in the paper?" Caroline breathed in sharply and briefly closed her eyes.

"It turns out this is the seventh robbery of a minimart in which the cashier was pistol whipped. The MO's are identical in each case. The paper interviewed Nelson Bergstrom's arresting officer, and followed his case through the trial and what's happened since. The two of us aren't exactly going to be asked to run for the Seattle city council, if you get the picture."

Caroline did, in living color. "I see," she murmured, and swallowed at the lump thickening in her throat. An unexpected chill raced up her spine. "But surely whoever did this wouldn't follow us. . . ."

"No one knows what they're capable of doing." Ted rubbed his face, as if to erase the tension lines etched so prominently around his eyes and nose. "Randolph suggested that we stay clear of your parents' place in San Francisco, as well."

She agreed with a quick nod. "Then where do you think we'll be safe?"

"Brookings. Randolph has some connections there. He's making arrangements for us to rent a secluded cottage. That way he'll know where he can reach us."

No wonder Ted had been so disagreeable all morning. Numbly, she responded, refusing to allow fear to get the best of her, "That sounds reasonable."

His rugged features hardened into glacier ice. "I'm not letting you out of my sight anymore, Caroline, not for a minute. Do you understand?" His cutting gaze fell to her suitcase.

"I wish you'd said something before now. I thought you were sick of my company."

"Never that, sweetheart, never that." He used the affectionate nickname as if it had slid off his tongue a thousand times. Then, with deliberate, controlled movements, he lifted her suitcase and placed it back inside the trunk.

"Ted?"

He turned toward her, the hard mask of his face discouraging argument. "Yes?"

"Would you . . . mind holding me for a minute?" For all her

brave talk about refusing to run away, she was scared. Her blood was cold, and she felt weak with fright. People had disliked her over the years, but never enough to want to kill her.

Ted wrapped his arms around her and gathered her close. The warmth from his hard body warded off the icy chill that had invaded her limbs. She relaxed against him, letting her soft curves mold to the masculine contour of his body. She felt his rough kiss against her hair, the even rhythm of his pulse, and a soothing peace permeated her heart.

"Nothing's going to happen to you." His whispered promise felt warm and velvety, like a security blanket being draped around her. "Whoever comes after you will have to get through me first."

Scalding tears burned the backs of her eyes. For years she'd treated Ted Thomasson abominably. When they were younger, she'd teased him unmercifully, to the point of being cruel. Even as an adult and with the best of intentions, she'd managed to outrage him. Yet he was willing to protect her to the point of risking his own safety. She had never felt more humbled or more grateful. Frantically, she searched for the words to express her feelings, but nothing she could think of seemed appropriate.

"Would you like some cheese?"

"Pardon?" He relaxed his hold and lifted her chin so their gazes met.

"Mild cheddar," she said, and sniffled, though she managed to hold all but a few emotional tears at bay. "I . . . I thought you might like some cheese."

"Another time. Okay?"

"Sure." She wiped the dampness from her cheek with the back of her hand and quickly redeposited her accumulated items inside the car.

Silence reigned as they took up their journey. Finally he

reached for her hand and squeezed it reassuringly. "I should have told you sooner."

"I shouldn't have been so self-centered. Something was clearly troubling you. I was the one at fault for being so oblivious."

"Don't be ridiculous."

"Oh, Ted, how can you say that? I bought the kite just to spite you. I don't deserve anyone as good as you in my life and you certainly rate someone better than a troublemaker like me."

"Maybe, but I doubt it," he answered cryptically.

Before this latest stop she had felt his urgency and resented it. Now the need for haste was in her blood, as well. They barely spoke after that, both of them wrapped up in the troubles of the moment. Brookings represented safety; there were people there who would help them, people who were in contact with Detective Randolph in Seattle.

"Are you hungry?" Ted asked as they approached the outskirts of Lincoln City.

Caroline was convinced he'd asked because her stomach had been rumbling, but the pangs weren't from hunger. She glanced at him consideringly. Although she'd eaten the bag of popcorn, he hadn't had anything today except coffee and a sugar-coated doughnut. A look at her watch confirmed that it was after noon.

"Maybe we should stop."

"Anyplace special?"

"No," she said, "you choose." Lincoln City was a seven-mile-long community, the consolidation of five former small cities, with a wide assortment of restaurants and hotels. Caroline had visited there often on her way to San Francisco and enjoyed the many attractions.

Ted parked in the center of the town. Eager to stretch her legs, she stepped out of the car and lifted her arms high above her head as she gave a wide yawn.

"Tired?" he inquired, and smiled lazily.

"No," she assured him. "I'm just a little stiff from sitting so long." As she spoke, a German Shepherd approached her, his tail wagging eagerly. "Hello, big guy," she greeted him, stooping to pet his thick fur, which was matted and unkempt. "What's the matter, boy, are you lost?" The dog regarded her with doleful dark eyes. "He's starving," she announced with concern to Ted, who had walked around the car to join her.

"He probably smelled the cheese." Absently, he patted the friendly dog on the top of the head. "There's a good restaurant around the corner from here, as I recall."

"What about the dog?" she asked, slightly piqued by his indifference to the plight of the lost animal.

"What about him?"

"He's hungry."

"So am I. If he's lost, the authorities will pick him up sooner or later." A hand at her elbow led her toward the restaurant.

She resisted, shrugging her arm free. "You're honestly going to leave him here?" She twisted around to discover the dog seeking a handout from another passerby.

"I don't see much choice. A stray dog is not our responsibility."

From his crisp tone, Caroline could tell the discussion was closed. Her mind crowded with arguments. But he was right, and she knew it. Nonetheless, there had been something so sad in those dark eyes that it had touched her, and she couldn't put the pitiful dog out of her mind.

Even after they'd eaten and were lingering over their coffee, she continued to think about the lost dog. Neither of them spoke much, but the silence was companionable. When Ted stood to pay the cashier, she placed a hand on his arm and murmured, "I'll be right out front."

As she'd suspected, the German Shepherd was outside the

restaurant, glancing hopefully at each face that walked out the door.

"I bet the smells from here are driving you crazy, aren't they, fellow?" She took a few scraps she'd managed to smuggle into a napkin without Ted noticing and gave them to the dog. He gobbled them down immediately and looked at her for more.

"How long has it been since you ate?" The poor dog was so thin his ribs showed. Glancing around her, she spied a food vendor down the street. "Come on, boy, we'll get you something more."

The dog trotted at her side as she hurried down the block, past Ted's parked car and toward the beach. She bought four hot dogs and found a sandy spot off the side street to feed the starving dog.

After he'd eaten his fill, she regarded the sad condition of his fur. "You're a mess, you know that? What you need is a decent bath. Someone needs to comb your fur."

A flicker from those dark eyes seemed to say that he agreed with her.

"Caroline."

Her name was spoken with such anger that she whirled around.

In her concern for the dog, she'd forgotten about Ted, and he was clearly furious. She forced herself to smile, but her heart sank to the pit of her stomach at the angry twist of his features. She hadn't meant to wander off, but she'd been so busy trying to take care of the dog that she had forgotten he didn't know where she'd gone.

"Just what do you think you're doing? You said you'd be right outside."

Responding to Ted's anger, the dog moved to Caroline's side and took up a protective stance, emitting a low growl.

"It's all right, boy. That's Ted." Caroline gave the dog a reassuring pat on the head.

"I should have known that animal was somehow involved in this," Ted snarled. "Right out front, you said. Can you imagine what I thought when you weren't there? I swear, Caroline, my heart can't take much more of this. What do I have to do? Handcuff you to my side?"

"I'm sorry . . . honestly, I didn't mean to take off, but I couldn't stop thinking about the dog and—"

"Just get in the car. I'll feel a whole lot better once we're in Brookings."

"But . . ."

"Are we going to argue about that as well?"

She didn't want any more dissension between them. "No."

"Thank you for that." He turned and headed toward the car with a step that was as crisp as a drill sergeant's.

Gently patting the side of her leg to urge the dog to follow her, Caroline followed in Ted's wake. The German Shepherd didn't need any urging and trotted along happily at her side as if he'd been doing so all his life.

When she started to open the rear door, Ted cast her a scathing look. "Now what are you doing?"

"I—I was thinking that it might not be a bad idea to take the dog with us. He's hungry and needs a home. And I bet he'd offer us a lot of protection. I'm going to name him Stranger because—"

"We're not taking that filthy dog!" Ted exploded.

"But—"

"You've already managed to accumulate a box of candy, a slab of cheese and a sackful of worthless sea shells, in addition to a man-size kite. I absolutely refuse to take that dog. The answer is no. N. O. No."

Caroline turned away. "I get the picture," she replied tightly. She crouched down on one knee. "Goodbye, Stranger," she whispered to the dog. "I did the best I could for you. You take care of yourself. Someone else will come along soon—I hope."

The car's engine roared to life, and she swallowed down the huge lump in her throat before climbing in beside Ted, who sat still and unyielding, arms outstretched, gripping the steering wheel. She closed her eyes, biting back the words to ask him to reconsider. It wouldn't do any good; his mind was made up.

"Next stop is Brookings," he said as he checked the rearview mirror and pulled out of the parking space.

"Right," she agreed weakly.

Turning the corner, they merged with the highway traffic as it sped through town. Not wanting Ted to see the emotion that was choking her, Caroline turned and stared out the side window. A flash of brown and black captured her attention from the side mirror. Stranger was running for all his worth, following them down the highway. Cars were weaving around him, and horns were blaring.

"Stranger!" she cried, twisting around despite the seatbelt, so she was kneeling in the front seat and staring out the rear window. She cupped one hand over her mouth in horror as she watched the dog, his tongue lolling from the side of his mouth, persistently running, unaware of the danger.

"All right. All right." With a mumbled curse, Ted pulled over to the side of the road. "You win. We can take that stupid dog. Heaven only knows what else you're going to pick up along the way. Maybe I should rent a trailer."

The sarcasm was lost on Caroline, who threw open the car door and leaped out with an agility she hasn't known she possessed.

As if he'd been born to it, Stranger leaped into the open backseat of the car, curled into a compact ball and rested his chin on his paws. Still panting from exertion, he looked up at her with grateful eyes. She sniffled, and ruffled his ears before closing the back door and slipping in beside Ted.

"Thank you," she whispered brokenly to him. "You won't regret it, I promise."

"That is something I sincerely doubt."

The tires spun as he pulled the car pulled back onto the highway. Having gotten her way when she'd least expected it, she tried her best to be pleasant company, chatting easily as they continued south.

He made a few comments now and again, but his lack of attention irritated her. The least he could do was pretend that he was interested.

"Am I boring you?" she asked an hour later.

"What makes you think that? I'm thrilled to know the secret ingredient in bran muffins isn't the bran." His well-defined mouth edged up at one corner in a mirthless grin that bordered on sarcasm.

Fuming, she crossed her arms over her breasts and focused her gaze straight ahead. Ted wasn't pleased about the dog, but he didn't need to pout to tell her that. For that matter, she wasn't exactly sure what *she* was going to do with Stranger, either. But leaving him behind to face an uncertain fate was an intolerable thought. She simply couldn't do it. To be truthful, she had been shocked that he had been so heartlessly willing to leave the dog behind, though he'd redeemed himself by pulling over and letting Stranger in the car. In her own way, she'd been trying to tell him that by being chatty, witty and pleasant. She was tired of arguing with him. She wanted them to be friends. Good friends. "I won't bother you anymore," she grumbled, swallowing her considerable pride.

Ted's gaze didn't deviate from the road, and his quiet low-pitched voice could barely be heard over the hum of the engine. "Not bother me? You've been nothing but trouble from the time we met."

She forced herself to relax against the seat, refusing to trade insults with him, though the words burned on her lips to tell him that he'd been easy to terrorize. That gentlemanly streak of his was so wide it looked like a racing stripe down the middle of his back.

"Has anyone ever commented on how your eyes snap when you're angry?" he inquired smoothly ten minutes later.

"Never."

"They do—and very prettily, I might add."

"You should be in a position to know."

He chuckled and turned on the radio. Apparently listening to the farm report was more interesting than her attempts at conversation had been.

They stopped for gas in Florence, outside of Dunes City. Had things been more amiable between them, she might have suggested that they stop and explore the white sand aboard rented camels. It had always been her intention to hire a dune buggy and venture into the forty-two-mile stretch of sand, but she never had. The camels were a new addition, and she would have loved to ride one. Knowing Ted's preferences, he would have chosen to stand at the lookout point, utterly content to snap pictures.

Thinking the situation over, it shocked her once again to realize how different she was from this man. Even more jarring was the knowledge that it would be so easy to fall in love with him.

"I might have been tempted to stop here and take a few pictures," he confessed, echoing her thoughts, "but I don't think the car is big enough to hold both a camel and a dog." Amusement gleamed in his eyes, and she chuckled, appeased by his wit. He was full of surprises. Until recently, she had thought the highlight of his week was breaking in a new pair of socks. Now she was learning that he had wit and charm, and she had to admit, she enjoyed being with him when he was like this.

They drove for what seemed an eternity. She couldn't recall ever being so comfortable with silence. He was content to listen to the radio. Stranger, who had slept for most of the journey, now seemed eager to arrive at their destination. He sat up in the backseat and rested his paw beside her headrest.

The car's headlights sliced through the semidarkness of twilight, silhouetting the large offshore monoliths against the setting sun. The beauty of the scene was powerful enough to steal Caroline's breath.

"It's lovely, isn't it?" she murmured, forgetting the reason for this exile.

"Yes, it is," he agreed softly. "Very beautiful."

Briefly, their eyes met, and he offered her a warm smile that erased a lifetime of uncomplimentary thoughts.

"We'll be there soon."

She responded with a short nod. The quiet felt gentle. She could think of no other word to describe it. A tenderness was growing between them. They'd both fought it, neither wanting it, yet now they seemed equally unwilling to destroy the moment.

"Caroline," he finally murmured, then paused to clear his throat.

"Hmm?"

"There's something I should tell you now that we're near Brookings."

"Yes?"

Whatever he had to say was clearly making him uneasy. He studied the road as if they were in imminent danger of slipping over the edge and crashing to the rocks below.

"This morning, when I talked with Randolph . . ." He hesitated for a second time. "I want you to know that he was the one who suggested this."

"Suggested what?" She studied him with renewed interest. The pinched lines around his mouth and nose didn't speak of anger as much as uneasiness.

He ran a hand along the back of his neck and expelled his breath in a low groan. "What I'm about to tell you."

"For crying out loud, would you spit it out?"

"All right," he snapped.

Stranger, apparently sensing the tension, barked loudly.

"Tell that stupid dog to shut up."

"Stranger is not stupid." Twisting around, Caroline scratched the German Shepherd behind the ears in an effort to minimize the insult. "He didn't mean that, boy," she whispered soothingly.

"Caroline, listen, what I'm about to tell you is none of my doing. Randolph seemed to feel it was necessary."

"You've said that twice. Would you kindly quit hedging and tell me what's going on?"

"We're going to have to pose as a newlywed couple."

"What?" she exploded, stunned.

"Apparently the people who own the cottage are old fashioned about this sort of thing, but it's safest if we stay together, so Randolph suggested the newlywed thing. I don't like it any better than you do."

A bemused smile blossomed on her lips. "Does this mean I'm going to have to bat my eyelashes at you and fawn over your every word?" She couldn't help giggling. "Will I need to pretend to be madly in love with you?" She was afraid that wouldn't call for much acting on her part.

"No," he returned sharply. "It just means we're scheduled to share a cottage."

"Oh, good grief. Is that all?"

Ted glanced at her sharply. "Well, doesn't that bother you?"

"Should it?"

"You're behaving as though you do this sort of thing often."

She decided to ignore the censure in his voice. "I don't see much difference between sharing a honeymoon cottage and spending the night in your one-bed cabin."

"Well, you needn't worry, I'll sleep on the couch."

"Now that's ridiculous. I'm a good six inches shorter than you. If anyone sleeps on the couch, it'll be me."

"Can we argue about that later?"

Caroline released an exaggerated sigh. "I suppose."

Ten miles later she couldn't stay quiet a moment longer. "You know what's really bothering you, don't you?" There was no holding back her lazy smile.

"I have the feeling you're going to tell me." The sarcasm was back, although he tried to give an impression of indifference.

Reading him had always been so easy for her. She wondered if others could decipher him as well as she could, then doubted it. "The fact that we'll be sharing the same cottage isn't the problem here." His grip on the steering wheel was so tight that she marveled that it hadn't collapsed under the intense pressure. "What's troubling you is that we'd be living a lie. Pretense just isn't part of your nature."

"And it *is* yours?"

"Unfortunately, yes," she admitted with typical aplomb.

Her answer didn't appear to please him. "Then you should take to this charade quite well."

"Probably. For a time I toyed with the idea of being an actress."

"Why didn't you?" He tipped his head to one side inquisitively.

"For obvious reasons." Her fingers fanned the auburn curls falling across her smooth brow. "With this red hair and my temperament, I'd be typecast so easily that I'd hate it after a while."

"That's not the real reason."

His insight shocked her. "No," she admitted slowly with a half smile. "Mom didn't like the idea." It had been the only time in her life that her mother had asked anything of her. She'd been a college freshman when she'd caught the acting bug. A drama class and a small part in the spring production had convinced her that she was meant for the silver screen. As usual, her timing was off. Her mother had taken the announcement with a gentle smile, then nodded calmly at Caroline's decision to enroll in additional drama classes. But when it looked like it was more than a passing fancy, Ruth had taken Caroline out to lunch and asked her to abandon the idea of changing her major to drama. She'd given a long list of reasons, all good ones, but none were necessary. Caroline knew this was important to her mother and had forsaken the idea simply because she'd asked.

The road sign indicating that they were entering the city limits of Brookings came into view, and Ted pulled over to the side of the highway and pulled out his phone, calling up the GPS app.

"What are you doing?"

"Getting the directions."

While he punched buttons, Caroline crossed her arms and asked, "Is there anything else that was said in this morning's conversation that I don't know?"

Glancing up from the screen, Ted regarded her with unseeing eyes. "No, why?"

"You keep dropping more and more tidbits of information. Just how long were you on the phone?"

"Five minutes."

She hated being kept in the dark this way. Circumstances being what they were, she would have preferred knowing what they faced instead of bumping into it bit by bit.

After pulling back onto the road again, Ted took a righthand turn and followed an obscure side street that led downhill as they approached the beach.

Checking the name printed on the mailbox, Ted stopped in front of a white house with a meticulously kept yard. Azaleas lined the walkway, which was illuminated by the porch light.

Eyeing Stranger, Ted murmured, "Maybe you'd better stay here."

"Of course . . . darling," Caroline whispered seductively and batted her eyelashes.

"Don't forget, your name's Thomasson now."

"Naturally." She couldn't resist a languid sigh.

He rubbed his hand over his eyes. "This situation has all the makings of a nightmare."

"Tell me about it," she grumbled under her breath.

She waited with Stranger beside the car, while Ted knocked on the front door of the white house. He was greeted by a short, dark-haired woman with a motherly look. She cast Caroline a sympathetic smile, and when her husband appeared and began talking to Ted, she hurried over to Caroline.

"I'm Anne Bryant. Charles phoned and told us of the unfortunate circumstances of your visit. Now, don't you worry about a thing. You'll be safe here." She smiled curiously at Stranger, no doubt taken aback by his unkempt condition. "And of course your dog is welcome, too."

"Thank you. I'm sure we'll enjoy it here." Caroline liked Anne immediately and wondered if it was because the loving concern in the older woman's eyes reminded her of her mother.

Ted and Mr. Bryant strolled toward the car, still talking. Ted introduced the other man as Oliver. Together the four of them headed down the steep bluff to the cottage, hauling the suitcases, with Stranger traipsing behind on the narrow pathway and the steep stairs that led the last thirty feet.

"We don't have many visitors this time of year," Anne explained. "And none now, so if you see anyone along the beach it might be best to get back inside. No one knows you're here except Oliver and me."

"Unfortunately there's no cell service around here, but if you need a phone, we've still got a land line," the whitehaired Oliver explained.

"What a terrible thing to happen to you on your wedding day."

Ted and Caroline's stricken gazes clashed. She had thought pretending to be a loving wife was going to be so easy, but it wasn't. She hated having to lie to these nice people. Seeming to sense her unease, Ted slipped an arm around her waist and pulled her close to his side. She made the effort to smile up at him, but his mouth curved in an expression that was devoid of enjoyment.

The feel of his arm around her brought with it a welter of emotions. His touch felt warm and gentle, and caused her pulse to trip over itself. When his gaze slid to her lips, she was shocked at the desire that shot through her. She yearned for him to turn her in his arms and kiss her there and then. Mentally shaking herself, she pulled her eyes from his.

"The missus and I feel sorry that things are working out so badly for you two lovebirds."

"Yes," Ted murmured. "We're quite upset ourselves."

"Oliver and I wanted to do something special for you to make your wedding night something to remember," Anne continued. "So we spruced up this cottage and turned it into a honeymoon suite."

"Oh, please," Caroline gasped. "That wasn't necessary."

"We thought it was," Oliver said with a delighted chuckle as he swung open the door to the small cottage.

A fire burned in the fireplace, casting a romantic light across the room. A bottle of champagne rested in a bucket of ice on the coffee table, flanked by two wineglasses.

"Now," Oliver said, stepping aside, "you kiss your bride and carry her over the threshold, and we'll get out of your way."

Eight

Anne's look was as tender as a dewy rose petal when Ted slid his arm around Caroline's waist and effortlessly lifted her into his arms. His lips nuzzled her ear.

"If you ever wanted to be an actress, the time is now," he whispered.

Looping her arms around his neck, she tossed a grateful glance over her shoulder and laughed gaily. "Thank you both for making everything so special."

"The pleasure was ours," Oliver said as he pulled his wife close to his side.

"We'll never forget this, will we, darling?" Caroline batted her thick lashes at Ted.

"Never," he grumbled, then stepped inside the cottage as she waved farewell to their hosts. He closed the door with his foot. Almost immediately her legs were abruptly released. Her shoes hit the floor with a loud clump. "Good grief, how much do you weigh?"

She decided to ignore the question. "This is a fine mess you've gotten us into."

"Me?" he snapped. "I told you, I didn't have anything to do with this wedding day business."

"Whatever." As she stomped into the tiny kitchen, she was met with the most delicious aroma. She paused, closed her eyes and took in the fascinating smells before peeking inside the oven. A small rib roast was warming, along with large baked potatoes wrapped in aluminum foil. An inspection of the refrigerator revealed a fresh tossed green salad and two thin slices of cheesecake.

Silence filled the room, and the sound of the refrigerator closing seemed to reverberate against the painted walls.

A scratch on the front door reminded her that Stranger was impatiently waiting outside with their luggage. By the time she returned to the living room, Ted had let the dog inside and was lifting their luggage.

"I'll put your suitcase in the bedroom," he announced.

She was too tired to argue. As her fingers made an unconscious inspection of her blouse buttons, she said, "Dinner is in the oven."

Being ill at ease with each other was easy to understand, given the circumstances. The intimate atmosphere created by the low lights, the flickering fire and the chilling champagne did little to help.

Ted returned from the bedroom and lifted the champagne from its icy bed. A look at the label prompted his brows to arch. "An excellent choice," he murmured, but she had the feeling he wasn't speaking to her. "I'll see about opening this."

The kitchen was infinitely better lighted than the living room, and she opted to remain where she was. With the honeymoon atmosphere slapping them in the face, it would be too easy to pretend this night was something it wasn't. "Okay," she agreed reluctantly.

After turning off the oven, she set the roast out to sit a few minutes before being carved. A quick check of the living room showed Ted working the thin wire wrapping from around the top of the champagne bottle and Stranger sleeping in front of the fireplace. The dog raised his head as the cork shot out of the bottle, but he seemed to realize that he wasn't needed for anything and promptly closed his eyes.

Looking for something to occupy her time and keep her in the kitchen, Caroline turned her attention to the table. She noted that it was already set for two. She busied herself tossing the already-tossed salad and then set it in the center of the table.

Not knowing what else she should do, she stood in the arched doorway and skittishly rubbed the palms of her hands together. "Stranger needs a bath."

"Now?" Ted looked up, holding two filled wineglasses in his hands.

"Yes . . . well, as you may have noticed, he's dirty."

"But the champagne is ready, and from the smell of things, I'd say dinner is, too."

"I believe you also said something about me needing to lose weight. I'll skip dinner tonight," she said stiffly, her voice weakly tinged with sarcasm.

"I didn't say a word to suggest that you're overweight."

"You implied it."

"In that case, I beg your pardon because—" he paused, appraising her intimately "—you're perfect."

Her feet dragging, Caroline stepped into the living room. The fire had died down to glowing red embers, and music was playing softly in the background. She could feel the romantic mood envelop her and had no desire to fight it any longer. What puzzled her most was that Ted had fallen into the mood so easily.

"We've been through a lot together," he commented, handing

her a wineglass. “Let’s put our differences aside for tonight and enjoy this excellent meal.”

She stood nervously to one side. The warm, cozy atmosphere was beginning to work all too well. “It *has* been a crazy day, hasn’t it?” She took her first sip and savored the bubbly taste. “This is wonderful.”

“I agree,” he murmured, sitting on the sofa beside the fireplace.

Reluctantly, Caroline joined him, pausing to pet Stranger.

Ted’s gaze fell to the dog, and his startling blue eyes softened. “To be honest, I’m glad he’s with us.”

“You are?”

“Yes.” He stood and added a couple of logs to the fire, then knelt in front of it, poking the embers into flames. Flickering tongues of fire crackled and popped over the bark of the new logs. He stood and turned, but made no effort to rejoin her on the sofa. “Are you enjoying the champagne?”

“Oh, yes.” She hugged her arms across her stomach, attempting to ward off her awareness of how close he was to her. She was overly conscious of everything about him. He seemed taller, standing there beside her, and more compelling than she remembered. She could feel the warmth of his body more than the heat of the fire, even though he wasn’t touching her.

“I don’t think I’ve ever noticed how beautiful you are,” he whispered in a voice so low it was as though he hadn’t meant to speak the words aloud.

“Ted, don’t,” she pleaded, closing her eyes. “I’m not beautiful. Not at all, and I know it.” Her hair was much too bright, and those horrible freckles across the bridge of her nose were a humiliation to someone her age. Not to mention her dull brown-green eyes.

“I can’t help what I see,” he murmured softly, sitting beside her at last. Gently he brushed a stray curl from her face, and then his finger grazed her cheek. Her sensitive nerve endings vibrated with the action, and an overwhelming sensation shot all the way to her stomach with such force that she placed her hand over her abdomen in an effort to calm her reaction. "I've thought so since I first met you."

"Oh?"

"You must have known." His voice remained a husky whisper, creating the impression that this was a moment out of time.

Whatever was happening between them sure beat the constant bickering. They'd done enough of that to last a lifetime. "How could I have known?" she whispered, having difficulty finding her voice. "Sometimes things have to hit me over the head before I notice them."

"I know." He bent his head toward hers, his jaw and chin brushing near her ear.

Caroline's stomach started churning again as his warm breath stirred her silken auburn curls. She gripped the stem of her wineglass so tightly it was in danger of snapping.

Ted pried the glass from her fingers and set it aside. "Relax," his soothing voice instructed. "I'm here to protect you."

She closed her eyes as if to still the quaking sensation, but the darkness only served to heighten her reactions. "Ted," she murmured, not knowing why she'd spoken. His mouth explored the side of her neck, renewing the delicious shivers over her sensitized skin.

"Hmm?"

"Nothing." She slipped her arms around him and rolled her head back to grant him access to any part of her neck he desired. He seemed to want all of it.

A soft moan slipped from her throat when his strong teeth gently nipped her earlobe. The action released a torrent of longing, and she melted against him, repeating his name over and over. If he didn't kiss her soon, she would die.

Somehow he shifted their positions so that she was sitting in his lap. "Here's your champagne," he murmured.

She looked up, surprised. She wanted his kiss, not the champagne, but when he raised the glass to her lips, she sipped rather than protesting. When she'd finished, his eyes continued to hold hers as he took a drink from the same glass. As he set the champagne aside, his smoky blue eyes paused to take in the look of longing she was convinced must be written on her face for him to see. He cupped her cheek, his fingers sliding down the delicate line of her jaw to rest on the rounded curve of her neck. Then he dipped his head and kissed the corner of her mouth. She yearned to intercept the movement and meet his lips, but she felt like a rag doll, trapped by her strange emotions.

At last his mouth claimed hers in a study of patience. Her breath faltered; she was choked up inside. The kiss was a long, slow process, as he worked his way from one side of her lips to the other, nibbling, tasting, exploring, until Caroline wanted to cry out with longing. When she attempted to deepen the contact and slant her mouth over his, he wouldn't let her. "There's no hurry," he whispered.

"So . . . dinner?" she mumbled, not knowing why. The only appetite she had was for him.

"More of this later," he promised, and leisurely kissed her again.

His mouth, she decided, was far headier than the champagne and twice as potent.

"You're so very beautiful," he whispered.

"Thank you," she mumbled.

He kissed her again, his mouth lingering on her lips as though he couldn't get enough of the taste of her. She didn't mind. She loved it when he kissed her. He was so gentle and caring that the emotions swelled up in her until she wanted to cry with wanting him. When he raised his head, she noted that his eyes were a darker blue when they met the troubled light in hers. He inhaled, attempting to control his desire. With unhurried ease he carefully lifted her off his lap and set her back on the couch.

"Did you say something about dinner being ready?"

Reluctantly, she glanced toward the kitchen. "It can wait a few more minutes."

"Maybe," he agreed. "But I can't. If we don't stop this soon, I'm going to carry you into that bedroom, and it won't be for sleep."

"Oh," she muttered, and twin blossoms of color invaded her cheeks. She practically leaped off the couch in her eagerness to escape. Hurrying into the kitchen, she went about the dinner preparations without thought. Thinking would have reminded her how much she wanted Ted to touch her, to kiss her. If he hadn't stopped when he did, she would have gone with him into that bedroom. Love did crazy things to people, made them weak—and strong. During all the years of repeatedly saying no to every boyfriend, she had never come so close to surrendering to a man. Heaven knew Clay had tried to get her into bed with him, and although she'd cared for him, she had never been tempted to give him what he wanted most. If he had been more subtle about his desire, she might have succumbed. In the end, when he'd broken off their relationship, he'd used the fact that she hadn't given in to him physically as an excuse, claiming she was a cold fish, not a real woman at all. Challenging her femininity had been the worst possible tack to take if he'd still hoped to get what he wanted. If Ted had lifted her in his arms and carried her into the bedroom, she knew in her heart that she wouldn't have resisted. She'd wanted him and would have willingly given him what so many others had sought.

Ted joined her a few minutes later, standing awkwardly behind her in the close confines of the kitchen. "Is there anything I can do to help?"

For one insane moment she was tempted to ask him to hold her again, kiss her—and make passionate love to her. Thankfully, she suppressed the urge.

The atmosphere at the dinner table was strained. They ate in silence, and although the meal was wonderful, she didn't have much of an appetite.

"Caroline?" Ted said at last, avoiding her eyes as he sank his knife into the roast beef as if he wasn't sure if he should kill it before taking a bite.

"Yes?"

"You mentioned this man you were seeing recently. Did the two of you . . . I mean . . ."

"Are you asking if I'm a virgin?" She would rather swallow fire than admit that to him.

He glared at her, and she nearly laughed. "Are you?"

"That's a pretty personal thing to ask a man."

"But it's all right for a man to ask a woman?"

"In this case, yes."

Caroline sliced her meat so hard it nearly slid off the plate, but a smile hovered just below the surface. "Why do you want to know?"

"Because we nearly . . ."

"Did it," she finished for him. "You needn't worry, I was in complete control the entire time."

"That's not the impression I got."

She ignored that and said, "We make a good team."

"Yes, we do," he agreed, and the amusement in his vivid eyes threw her further off balance then she was already. "And you've already given me the answer to my question."

"I sincerely doubt you know what you're talking about." She swallowed and boldly met his gaze, not giving an inch.

Looking pleased with himself, he pushed his plate aside and leaned back, crossing his arms over his chest. "No woman blushes the way you do if she's accustomed to having a man appreciate her beauty, and you are definitely beautiful."

"You sound awfully sure of yourself."

"Because I am," he said with maddening calm.

Caroline took twice the time necessary to clean the kitchen after dinner. Giving Stranger a bath and cleaning the bathroom afterward took up even more time. By the time she'd finished three hours later, she was exhausted. Avoiding Ted could become a full-time occupation, she realized. But she couldn't trust her reaction to him, and being alone with him in the small cottage made the situation all the more intolerable.

He was watching television when she reappeared with a thick towel draped over her arm. Stranger traipsed along damply behind her and eyed Ted dolefully. The dog seemed to be asking him what he'd been up to while they were gone. The dog paused in the middle of the room and shook his body with such force that water droplets splattered across the room.

"Hey, what's going on?" Ted asked, brushing at the wet spots on his shirt.

"Sorry," Caroline murmured, hiding a smile.

"Things must be bad when you apologize for a dog," he teased. His eyes grew warm and gentle, and she glanced away rather than risk drowning in their deep blue depths. "You look beat."

"I am." She sat on the floor in front of the fireplace, leaned the back of her neck against the couch and studied the ceiling.

Ted didn't continue with the conversation. She supposed that he was caught up in his television program. She opened one eye, noted what was on and groaned inwardly. He was watching televised fishing—and liking it.

"Ted, since we're asking each other personal questions . . ."

"We are?"

"You know, like the one you asked me at dinner."

"Oh. That."

"Yes, that. Now I have a question for you."

"All right."

He was too agreeable, but she didn't want to turn around and read his expression. "Do you remember the night you dropped me off at the apartment and left because of an appointment?"

"I remember." Reluctance coated his voice.

"Were you telling the truth when you said you weren't seeing a woman?"

It took him so long to answer that she grew concerned.

Finally he said, "No, to be honest, I lied that night. I didn't have an appointment."

Caroline straightened, giving up all pretense of resting. "You lied?" She would have sworn that he was the most honest man in the world. To have him admit to lying was so out of character that it left her feeling shocked. "But why?"

A muscle close to his eye twitched as he tightly clasped his hands. "We were both feeling a bit unsure that night, and the truth is, I was afraid if I stuck around much longer, drinking coffee and sharing a meal, I wouldn't be going home until morning."

Abruptly Caroline closed her eyes and resumed her earlier position. The way she'd been feeling that night lent credence to his observation. She'd wanted him to stay so badly. "I see."

"At the time I was sure you didn't."

"I thought you preferred not to be with me."

He draped his hand over her shoulder, and she raised hers so that they could lace their fingers together. "Rarely have I wanted anything more than I wanted to be with you that night," he whispered, and bent forward to kiss the crown of her head.

Caroline's heart beat wildly against her rib cage as her brain sang a joyous song. She dared not move, fearing a repeat of what had happened earlier. The realization that Ted found her physically attractive pleased her, but he'd given no indication that his heart was involved.

"I'm going to bed," she announced on the tail end of a long and exquisitely fake yawn. She needed an excuse to leave and think things through.

"Stay," he prompted gently. "The best part of the program is coming up. In a minute they're going to show how to tie flies."

She grimaced. "Isn't that inhumane?"

"Not those kinds of flies," he chided, squeezing her fingers. He urged her up on the sofa so that she ended up sitting beside him. His smiling eyes met hers as he looped an arm around her shoulders.

To her amazement, the fly-tying part of the program was interesting. Bits of feather and fishing line were wrapped around a hook, disguising it so cleverly that she actually had difficulty seeing the hook. But finally, after a series of very real yawns, she couldn't keep her eyes open a minute longer.

"Go to bed," he urged with such tenderness that she had to fight the urge to ask him to come with her. Struggling to her feet, she paused midway across the room. "Where do you want to sleep?"

Without so much as glancing away from the television, he replied, "The better question would be where *will* I sleep?"

"All right," she whispered, embarrassed. She was infuriated with herself for the telltale color that roared into her cheeks. "Where will you sleep?"

"Here."

He was several inches too long for the sofa, but the choice was his, and she was much too fatigue to argue. Tomorrow night she would insist that he take the bed, and she would sleep on the sofa.

A moment later, sitting on the end of the mattress, she yawned again. She really was exhausted. The day had begun early, and it had been long and tiring. It didn't seem possible that so much had happened since they'd left Seattle.

After gathering blankets and a pillow, she contained a deep sigh as she walked back into the living room and wordlessly set them on the far end of the sofa where Ted was still sitting. He was so engrossed in his program that he didn't even seem to notice.

Back in the bedroom a few minutes later, after quickly washing up, she didn't waste time before putting on her nightgown and climbing between the clean, crisp sheets. Almost immediately after she rested her head on the pillow, the living room lights went out.

"Good night, Ted," she called.

"Night."

A minute later she was wandering in the nether land between sleep and reality. Then the bedroom door creaked open, and her heartbeat went berserk. Had Ted changed his mind and decided to join her? She wanted him. Oh, dear heaven, she wanted him with her. Every night for the remainder of her life she wanted him.

Her courage failed her, and she dared not open her eyes. She would play it cool, she decided, and wait until he was beside her before turning into his arms and telling him all the words that were stored in her heart. But nothing happened. Silence reigned until she couldn't tolerate it a minute longer. As she eased herself up on one elbow, her eyes searched the darkened room. Perplexed, she wondered at the tricks her mind was playing on her. She'd heard the door open. She was sure of it.

A soft whimper came from the floor and, shocked, she tugged the blanket up to her nose as Stranger laid his snout on top of the mattress, seeming to seek an invitation to join her.

"No, boy," she whispered. "You'll have to stay on the floor. This place beside me is reserved for someone else." Then she rested her head back on the thick feather pillow and promptly fell asleep.

Sunlight splashed through the window, and Caroline stirred, feeling warm and content. Long after she was awake, she lay in the soft comfort of the bed and let the events of last evening run through her mind. Ted had held her and kissed her. He'd desired her the other night when he left her, inventing an excuse because he feared he would end up spending the night with her. He'd desired her then, and he wanted her now. Knowing that was better than any dreamy fantasy.

Stranger scratched at the door, wanting out, and she tossed aside the blanket and quickly dressed. A happy smile lit up her face as she pulled jeans up over her hips and snapped them at her waist. She felt rejuvenated after a good night's sleep and was eager to spend the day with Ted. For the first time she looked forward to their time together, almost hoping that days would stretch into weeks. This picturesque cottage by the sea would become their own private world, where they would learn to overcome their differences. "Opposites attract" was an old saying, one she had heard most of her life. The strong attraction she felt for Ted was living proof. They were powerfully and overwhelmingly fascinated with each other. This time together would teach them the give and take of maintaining a solid relationship.

As she entered the living room, the happiness drained from her eyes. The cottage was empty. The blankets were neatly folded at the end of the sofa, and for an instant she wondered if they'd even been used. Then she realized that Ted wouldn't have abandoned her; she knew him well enough to realize that. His sense of chivalry wouldn't allow him to leave her alone and unprotected.

Stranger had gone to sit patiently by the front door, wanting out. Feeling hurt and a little piqued at finding Ted gone, she opened the front door. Surprise caused her eyes to widen when she realized that it had been left unlocked. Anyone could have walked in. So this was the protection Ted offered her!

In the kitchen, she discovered that the coffee was made and had been sitting there long enough to have a slightly burned taste. A note propped against the salt shaker on the table informed her that Ted had gone grocery shopping. She knew it was ridiculous to feel so offended, but she was the one who'd gone through two years of training to become a chef. If anyone should do the grocery shopping, it was her. Or they could have had fun doing it together.

Her appetite gone, she went to try her cell and discovered that the Bryants hadn't been kidding. No bars. She pulled a sweater over her head and hiked the trail up to the Bryants' house.

Anne was outside, on her knees, pulling weeds from the flower beds. "Morning," she said cheerfully, awkwardly rising to her feet. She gave Caroline a wry smile. "These old bones of mine are complaining again, but I do so love my flowers."

"They're beautiful." One look at the meticulously kept yard revealed the love and care each blade of grass and plant was given.

"Can I help you with something? Your husband was by earlier."

For a wild second Caroline had to stop and think of who Anne was talking about. "I'd like to use the phone, if that's all right." In the rush to leave Seattle, she had neglected to make arrangements to have her mail picked up. Mrs. Murphy lived down the hall and would willingly collect it for her. They had each other's mail key for just such instances as this. Normally there wasn't much to worry about, but Caroline had filled out applications for jobs at several restaurants and was hoping employment was in the offing. The sooner she became self-sufficient, the sooner she could prove to her father that she had made the right choice. If she couldn't be reached by phone, then an employer would probably contact her by mail. At least she sincerely hoped so.

"Go right in and help yourself to the phone. It's there on the kitchen wall."

"Thanks."

Stranger followed her to the back door and stayed outside while she made the quick call. Just before she hung up, she asked Mrs. Murphy to mail a smoked salmon from the Pike Place Market to the Bryants as a thank-you for all they'd done. Mrs. Murphy said she would be pleased to do it and didn't mind waiting until Caroline was home to be reimbursed.

On her way back to the cottage, Caroline stopped to chat. Anne explained that Brookings was famous for its azaleas. The flowers were in full bloom in May, and Anne spoke with pride of their beauty. Native azalea bushes covered more than thirty acres of a state park north of town, and Caroline hoped that she would have the opportunity to see them in bloom someday.

The cottage felt empty without Ted. To kill time, she took Stranger for a long walk, trying to teach him to fetch by throwing a stick she found along the way. Anyone observing her would have found her efforts hilarious, she mused sometime later as she sat on a driftwood log, watching the waves come crashing in to shore. No matter how long she stayed, the sight would never bore her. Stranger lay at her feet, panting. Despite that, he was eager for more, as he demonstrated by offering her his stick.

When she heard her name carried by the wind, she turned and waved. Ted jogged to her side, then sank to the sand at her feet. "You weren't at the cabin."

"Brilliant observation," she said with a hint of a smile.

"I thought I told you that I didn't want you running off?"

So they were about to start their day with an argument. She didn't want that. Their time together should be spent building a relationship.

"I didn't run off." The denial was quick, although she strove to appear indifferent.

"I couldn't find you," he returned. The words were sharp enough to sound like an accusation.

"If you were afraid the boogie man was going to get me, then you might have locked the door."

"Caroline . . ." He turned to her in a burst of impatience and rubbed the back of his neck. "Listen to me. I had to get out of the house this morning."

"Why? We would have had a good time doing the shopping together. I like to cook, remember? I *am* a chef, you know."

"I know." He leaped to his feet and began pacing back and forth in front of her. His steps were quick and sharp, kicking up sand. "Listen, Caroline, we're going to have to help one another. I can't be around you without wanting you. If I'm going to resist, then you'll have to help."

A warm glow of happiness seeped into her blood. "But, Ted," she whispered seductively. "Who says I wanted you to resist?"

Nine

"I wish you hadn't said that," Ted said. He stood looking toward the rolling waves that crashed against the beach. "Being together like this creates enough temptations without you adding to them."

He sounded so stiff and resolute that Caroline wanted to shake him. "So what do you want me to do?" she asked, trying not to sound too defensive. "Sleep in the car or camp out on the beach?"

"Don't be silly."

"Me be silly? I thought you knew me better than that." She picked up a handful of the sand and slowly let it slip through her fingers. The grains felt gritty and damp. She'd awakened with such high expectations for this day, and already things were beginning to fall apart.

Lowering himself onto the log beside her, he claimed her hand with his. "The problem isn't you," he admitted with a wry twist of his mouth. "I'm the one having difficulties. It's nothing you've done—or not intentionally, anyway. You can't help it if I find your smile irresistible." He bent his head toward her and tucked a strand of hair behind her ear. "And you have the most incredible eyes."

She could feel the color working its way up to her face but was powerless to resist when he lowered his head and tenderly explored the side of her neck, sending delicious shivers skittering down her spine. Her stomach was tightening as waves of longing lapped through her. Her fingers clawed against the wood as she resisted the urge to slide her arms around him and lose herself in his embrace.

"See what I mean?" he groaned. "I can't even be close to you without wanting to kiss you."

"But I want you to touch me," she whispered candidly.

"I know."

"Is that so bad?" she asked in a prompting voice, leaning her head on his shoulder. "You make me feel beautiful."

"You *are* beautiful."

"Only to you."

"Is the world so blind?"

"No," she returned softly. "You are."

His hand found her hair. Braiding his fingers through the thick length of it, he pressed her closer to him. "That's my greatest fear."

"What is?"

"That what's happening between us isn't real. I'm afraid that circumstances have put us under unnatural stress. It's only logical that our feelings would become involved."

"Are you saying that I'm not feeling what I think I'm feeling?" She cocked her head a bit and grinned. "That doesn't make sense, does it?"

"The problem is that, as a couple, *we* don't make sense."

"Oh." She swallowed down the hurt. "I thought we balanced one another out rather well."

"Maybe, but that's something we won't know until this ordeal is over. As it is, we're playing with dynamite."

"What do you suggest, then?" She was sure she wasn't going to like anything he proposed.

"No touching. No kissing. No flirting."

"Oh." She straightened, lifting her head from his shoulder as a chill that had nothing to do with the weather ran through her. "Nothing?"

"Nothing," he confirmed.

She ran her fingers through her hair, not caring about the tangles. She needed something to do with her hands.

"Do you agree?"

There was little else she could do. "All right, but I don't like it."

"Constantly being together isn't going to make this easy." He clenched his jaw and shook his head. "But that can't be helped."

Ted had made her feel lovely and desirable. When he'd held her, it hadn't mattered that her eyes were dull and her nose had freckles. To him, in those brief moments, she had been Miss Universe. Now she felt as if she had a bad case of the measles.

"I—I think I'll put away the groceries," she said, rising to her feet and pausing to wipe the sand from the back of her jeans. "Is there anything special you'd like for lunch?" She couldn't look at him for fear he would read the misery in her eyes.

"No," he answered on a solemn note. "Anything is fine."

Caroline spent the remainder of the morning in the kitchen, baking a fresh lemon meringue pie and a loaf of braided holiday bread. Heavenly smells drifted through the cottage. She loved to bake. From the time she was a child, she'd enjoyed mixing up a batch of cookies or surprising her mother with a special cake. Kneading bread dough was therapeutic for her restless mind.

She thought about her relationship with Clay and was surprised to realize that the pain of their breakup was completely gone now. She was grateful for the good times they'd shared, but he'd been right—she simply hadn't loved him enough. He'd asked her to prove her love—admittedly, in all the wrong ways—and she'd balked. Her hesitation had caused the split, and for a time it had hurt so much that she had wondered if she'd done the right thing. But she had. She knew that because now she was in love, really in love, with no doubts or insecurities. But Ted doubted. Ted was filled with uncertainties. Ted wanted them to wait and be sure. How like him to be cautious, and how typical of her to be impulsive and impatient.

By evening a plan had formed. Bit by bit, day by day she would prove to him that they weren't really so different. They shared plenty of things in common, and she simply needed to accentuate those. Within a few days he would realize that she would make him the perfect wife. She would cook fantastic meals, be enthralled by what he had to say, and laugh at his corny jokes. Within a week he would be on bended knee with stars in his eyes. In fact, she was shocked that he didn't see how perfect they were together. They'd been meant for each other from the time they were teenagers. Unfortunately, circumstances had led them apart, but no longer.

Dusk had settled when Ted returned to the cottage, hauling in an armload of wood for the fireplace. She had wondered what he'd done with himself all afternoon. He'd eaten lunch with her, then left almost immediately afterward. She hadn't seen him since, but Stranger had gone with him and returned at his side now.

"Something smells good," Ted commented, setting the uniformly cut logs on the hearth.

Wiping her hands on the terry-cloth apron she'd found in a

drawer, she joined him in the living room. "I hope you like pot roast in burgundy wine with mushrooms."

His brows arched appreciatively. "I don't know, but it sounds good."

"I would have attempted something more elaborate, but . . ."

"No, no, that sounds fantastic."

"There's homemade bread, and fresh lemon meringue pie for dessert." After days of traveling and living together, she suddenly felt awkward and a little shy. She hadn't been bashful a day in her life, so this reaction was completely out of character for her.

He didn't look any more confident about their arrangement than she felt. They stood with only a few feet separating them, both looking miserable and unsure. "I'll wash my hands if everything's ready," he murmured after an awkward moment.

"It is."

At the dinner table they sat across from each other, but neither one of them spoke. Caroline literally didn't know what to say. The silence was thick enough to taste. Again and again her gaze was drawn to him, and every cell in her body was aware of him sitting so close, and yet they were separated by something more powerful than distance. Once she glanced up to discover him studying her, and her breath caught. He looked away sharply, as though he were angry at being caught. But if he was looking at her with half the interest with which she was viewing him, then they were indeed in for trouble.

The next morning Caroline woke to find that once again Ted had already left the cottage. The pattern repeated itself in the days that followed. She could sometimes see him working in the distance, chopping wood. What else he did to occupy his time, she didn't know, and she had no idea what the Bryants thought of a honeymoon couple who barely spent time together. Evenings proved to be both their worst and their best times. Since she did all the cooking, he insisted on cleaning the kitchen. At times she was convinced he only volunteered because it limited the time they spent in close proximity to each other.

To their credit, they both did their best to put aside their almost magnetic attraction. And despite everything, there were times when she could almost believe things were natural and right between them. Ted taught her how to play backgammon and chided her about beginner's luck when she proceeded to win every game. Later they switched to chess. Oddly enough, they discovered that although their strategies were dissimilar, their skills were evenly matched. When their interest turned to cards, she insisted that he play poker with her. He agreed, as long as she was willing to learn the finer techniques of bridge. One evening of poker and bridge was enough for her to realize that cards was one area they would do better to ignore.

Some nights they read. Ted's tastes were so opposite to her own that she found it astonishing that she could love such a man. And love him she did, until she wanted to burst. Doing as he'd asked and avoiding any physical contact had proven to her how much she did care for him. He seemed so staid and in control. Only an occasional glance told her that his desire for her hadn't lessened. When he looked at her, all the warmth he had stored in his heart was there for her to see. Some nights she wanted to cry with frustration, but she'd agreed to this craziness, and in time her plan would work. It was taking far longer than she'd expected, though.

Late nights, when the cottage was dark and she lay in bed alone, proved to be the most trying times. They were separated by only a thin door that was often left ajar so Stranger could wander in and out at will. Some nights, when she lay perfectly still, she could hear the rhythmic sound of Ted's even breathing. She wanted to be with him so much that sleep seemed impossible and she lay awake for hours.

Seven days after they'd arrived in Brookings, Caroline had experienced enough frustration to last her ten lifetimes. True to his word, Ted hadn't touched her. Not even so much as an accidental brushing of their hands. He seemed to take pains to avoid being near her. If she was in the kitchen, he stayed in the living room. After dinner, he lingered in the other room so long she had to call him into the living room for their nightly games. It was almost as if he dreaded spending any time with her and each minute together tried his resolve. Yet in her heart she knew that he desired her, wanted to be with her, and hated this self-imposed discipline with as much intensity as she did.

On the afternoon of the eighth day, she was finished baking a cake and had set it out to cool before frosting it. Surely by now he could see what fantastic wife material she was, she thought. If he didn't, then she would be forced to take matters into her own hands. But she would much prefer it if he recognized his love for her without forcing her to resort to more . . . forceful methods.

The sun was bathing the earth in golden light when Caroline pulled on a thin sweater. In moments she was on the beach, where Stranger came racing to her side, kicking up sand in his eagerness to join her.

"Hiya, boy." She sank to her knees and ruffled his ears as he demonstrated his affection. From the way he was behaving, an observer would have assumed they'd been separated for weeks.

More by accident than design, Stranger had become Ted's dog. In the beginning she hadn't even been sure he wanted the dog tagging along after him. He neither encouraged nor discouraged the dog. Stranger simply went.

What Ted did during the days was a thorn in Caroline's side. Not once had he mentioned where he went, although she had phrased the question in ten different ways and with as much diplomacy as possible. He would smile and look right through her, then direct the conversation in another direction. Her curiosity was piqued. There was nothing to do but wait impatiently for him to explain himself in his own time, which he would—or she would torture it out of him.

Petting Stranger, she noticed that he was wearing a collar. She did know that Ted had taken the dog to a veterinarian in town one afternoon and she'd been pleased to learn he was suffering no ill effects from his days as a stray. Later she'd discovered a doggie toy that Ted had obviously bought.

"Stranger," she whispered, elated, "I love him. I really do. I think it's as much of a surprise to me as anyone," she said, and ran her hand through the dog's thick fur. "You love him, too, don't you, boy?"

The dog cocked his head at her inquisitively and she thought how strange it was that she could talk so freely to him.

"Come on, let's go for a walk." Agilely, she rose to her feet. Maybe she would stumble on Ted and discover his deep, dark secret. Surely he spent his days doing more than chopping wood. By now he'd chopped enough to supply the cottage for two long winters. After an hour's jaunt up and down the sandy shore, Caroline was convinced he wasn't anywhere around.

As she started back to the cottage, Anne waved to her from the top of the bluff. The two often shared a cup of coffee in the afternoon, and Caroline waved in return and started up the creaky walkway.

"The salmon arrived this afternoon. I can't thank you enough."

"Ted and I wanted you to know how much we appreciate everything you've done."

"You're such a sweet couple. It's obvious that you two were meant to be together."

Obvious to everyone but Ted. "What a nice thing to say," Caroline murmured, glancing at the green grass between her feet.

"At first I was concerned, I don't mind telling you. It didn't seem right that a honeymoon couple spent so much time apart. Your husband painting, and you down there in that cottage cooking your heart out."

So Ted was painting. Probably helping Oliver out every day just so he could avoid being with her.

"He's so talented. When I saw the beach scene he did of you and the dog, I was utterly amazed. Oliver offered to buy it, he liked it so much. But Ted refused—said it wasn't for sale."

Caroline's head shot up. Ted was an artist! He'd never said a word to her, not a word. So that was what he did with his time. And he'd shown Anne his work, but not her. An unbearable weight pressed against her heart, and she swallowed back the bitter taste of discouragement. "He's wonderful," she agreed weakly.

"Do you have time for coffee?"

"Not today, Anne. Sorry."

"Thanks again for the salmon."

With her hands buried deep inside her pockets, Caroline started walking along the top of the bluff. If Ted was painting, he was probably doing it from this vantage point.

"Caroline!" Anne called, pointing in the opposite direction. "Ted's over that way."

"Of course, thanks," she returned, and gave a brief salute.

Stranger raced on ahead. She rounded a curve in the windswept landscape and hesitated when she saw Ted. He was so caught up in what he was doing that he didn't notice her until she was only a few feet away. When he did see her, he glanced up and a look of incredible guilt masked his features.

"Is anything wrong?" he asked.

"No." She laced her fingers in front of her and looked out over the beach below. The cottage was in clear sight, and there was a long stretch of beach on either side, so that no matter where she walked, he could see her. "It's lovely from up here, isn't it?"

"Yes," he said and swallowed. "It is."

"I hope I'm not interrupting you," she lied.

"No, not at all." He set his easel aside and stood so that he was blocking her view of the canvas.

Caroline got the message louder than if he'd shouted it. He didn't want her looking at his painting any more than he wanted her to be there. "I just came up to say hello, and—and now that I've done that I'll be on my way."

"You can stay if you want."

She didn't believe a word of his insincere invitation. "No thanks. I've . . . I've got things to do at the cottage." Like count dust particles and watch the faucet drip.

"I'll be down in time for dinner."

Her answer was a hurried nod as she turned sharply and retreated with quick-paced steps that led her away from him with such haste that she nearly slipped on the path leading down the bluff to the cottage.

Stranger elected to stay with Ted, seeming to sense her troubled mood and her desire to be alone. The pain of Ted's simple deception hurt so much she could hardly bear it.

All this time that they'd been together, she'd been open and honest with him. She trusted him implicitly. While waiting for him to make his moves in chess, she'd shared her dreams and all the things that were important to her. One night in particular, when neither of them had been sleepy, they'd sat in front of the fireplace, drinking spiced apple cider. They'd ended up talking away half the night. She had never felt closer to anyone. That night had convinced her that what she felt for Ted was a woman's love, a love that was meant to last a lifetime. Unwittingly she'd given him her heart that night, handed it to him on a silver platter. Not until now did she realize that she'd been the one doing all the talking. He had shared a little about his life; he'd spoken of his job and a few other unimportant items but revealed little about himself. He certainly hadn't mentioned the fact that he painted or even that he appreciated art. She'd admired the canvases on his apartment walls and realized with a flash of renewed pain that he'd probably done those, as well. Anne was right. Ted was a talented artist.

He found her about four-thirty, sitting on the beach, looking out over the pounding surf. He lowered himself beside her, but she didn't acknowledge his presence.

"You're looking thoughtful."

"I'm bored," she murmured. "I want to go home."

He forcefully expelled his breath. "Caroline, I'm sorry, but we can't."

He'd probably been talking to Randolph again and not telling her about it. Ted liked keeping secrets.

"Not we—me! I'm the one who's going."

"What brought this on?"

Staring straight ahead, yet blind to the beauty that lay before her, Caroline shook her head. "Eight days stuck in a cottage with no contact with the outside world is enough for anyone to endure."

"I thought you liked it here," he countered sharply. "I had the impression you were having a good time."

She leaned back, pressing her weight onto the palms of her hands, and raised her face to the sky. "I told you before I was a good actress."

"So this whole time together was all an act." A thread of steel ran through his words.

"What else?" She could feel the hard flint of his eyes drilling into her.

"I don't believe that, Caroline, not for a minute."

She gave an indifferent shrug. "Think what you want, but I'm leaving."

"No you aren't."

Clenching her jaw so hard that her teeth hurt, she refused to argue. She would leave. Finding someplace else, any place away from Ted, was essential. He had discovered a place within her where only he could cause her pain. If he'd wanted to punish her for the sins of her youth, he'd succeeded. She'd never felt so cold and alone, so emotionally drained or unloved. She had given him a part of herself that she had never before shared, only to learn that he didn't trust her enough to trust her with that same part of himself.

When she chanced a look at Ted, his expression of mixed anger and bewilderment tugged at her heart. The best thing for them both would be for her to leave as quickly as possible before they continued to hurt each other.

"I'll go wash up for dinner," he announced, rolling to his feet with subtle ease.

She refused to look up at him. "I didn't cook anything."

"I'll do it, then."

"Do whatever you want, but only cook for one."

He ignored the gibe. "Come on."

"Where?"

"You're coming to the house with me."

"I thought you said you were going to fix your own dinner?"

"I am, but I don't want you out here alone."

"Why not? You leave me alone every day."

His hand under her arm roughly pulled her up from the sand. "I'm not going to argue with you. You're coming with me."

Jerking her arm aside to free herself from his touch, she took a step backward. Stranger gave the two of them an odd look, tilting his head, unaccustomed to their raised voices.

"You're confusing the dog," she said.

"The dog?" Ted shot back. "You're confusing *me.*"

"Good." Maybe he would feel some of the turmoil that was troubling her. Trying to give an impression of apathy, she rubbed the sandy grit from her hands, feeling more wretched every second.

"Good?" Ted exploded. "Why do you want to do this to me? Just what kind of game are you playing?"

"I'm not playing a game. I just want out." To her horror, her voice cracked and tears welled up, brightening her eyes. She shoved her hands in her pockets and started toward the cottage.

"Caroline."

She quickened her pace.

"Caroline, stop! You're going to listen to me for once."

"I'm through listening!" she shouted, wiping away a tear and fighting to hold back the others. When she heard his footsteps behind her, she started to run. She didn't have any destination in mind, she only knew she had to escape.

His hand on her shoulder whirled her around, throwing her off balance. A cry of alarm slid from her throat as she went tumbling toward the sand. Ted wrapped his arms around her and twisted so that he accepted the brunt of the fall. Quickly he changed positions so that she was half-pinned beneath him.

"Are you all right?"

A scalding tear rolled from the corner of her eye, and she averted her face. "Yes." Her voice was the weakest of whispers.

Gently, with infinite patience, he wiped the maverick tear

from her cheek. His hands were trembling slightly as he cupped her face. "Caroline," he whispered with such tenderness that fresh tears misted her eyes. "Why are you crying?"

Unable to answer him, she slowly shook her head, wanting to escape and in the same heartbeat wanting him to hold her forever.

"I don't think I've ever seen you upset like this." He smoothed the hair from her face. "You've got to be the bravest, gutsiest woman I've ever known. It's not like you to cry."

"What do you care if I cry?" she sniffled, shocked at how unnatural her voice sounded.

"Trust me, I care."

Not believing him, she closed her eyes and turned her face away from his penetrating gaze. Her hands found his shoulders and she tried to push him away, but he wouldn't let her.

"Caroline," he groaned in frustration. "I care. I've always cared about you. I want you so much it's tying me up in knots so tight I think . . ." He didn't finish as his mouth crushed down on hers, kissing her with a searing hunger that left her breathless and light-headed.

"Ted," she groaned. "Don't, please don't." Having him touch and kiss her made leaving all the more impossible, and she had to go. For her sanity, she had to get away from him before he claimed any more of her. She'd already given him her heart.

"I've wanted to do that every minute of every day." Again his mouth claimed hers, tasting, moving, licking, until she feared she would go mad with wanting him.

"Ted, no . . . you said . . ." But her protest grew weaker with every word.

He cut off her protest by pressing his lips against hers, tasting them as though they were flavored with the sweetest honey.

The urgency was gone, replaced with a gentleness that melted her bones. She felt soft and loved, and he was male and hard. Opposites. Mismatched. Different.

And yet perfect for each other.

But not perfect enough for him to share a part of himself, she remembered. No, he didn't need her—not nearly enough. With a strength she didn't know she possessed, she pushed against his shoulder, breaking the contact.

Stunned, he sat up, while she remained on the sandy beach, lying perfectly still. Every part of her throbbed with longing until holding back the tears was impossible. She covered her face with her hands.

"I thought you said you wanted me?"

"No," she whispered, sitting up beside him. She looped her arms around her knees and took deep, even breaths to calm her heart.

The muscles in his jaw knotted. "That wasn't the impression you gave me the other night when you invited me to your bed."

"That was the other night." Another lifetime, when she'd felt they'd had a chance.

"And this is now?" he asked with heavy sarcasm.

"Right."

"You don't know what you want, do you? Everything is a game. It doesn't matter who's caught up in your—"

Caroline had heard enough. She put out a hand to stop him from talking, and then, with a burst of energy she struggled to her feet and rushed inside the cottage. Stranger was lying beside the fireplace, waiting for her.

"You stay here with Ted," she told the dog as she hurried into the lone bedroom and dragged out her empty suitcase.

"I told you I wouldn't let you go," Ted said, his large frame blocking the doorway between the bedroom and the living room.

"You don't have any choice. Please, Ted," she pleaded. "I don't want to argue with you over this. I'm leaving."

"But why now?" he asked firmly. "What makes today any different from yesterday?"

She could hardly tell him the truth, that her heart was breaking a little bit more every day as it became clear that he would never feel about her as she felt about him. "Because I'm bored, and if I spend one more minute cooped up in this place I'll go crazy," she lied.

Ted ran his fingers through his hair in agitation and then curled his hand around the back of his neck. "I'm sorry. I guess I haven't been very good company."

"That's not it. For Tedious Ted, I'd say you did a fine job, but I want out. Now." Delaying the inevitable would only prolong the pain. She opened the suitcase and began dumping her clothes inside.

"I'm sorry, Caroline, but I can't let you go."

"You don't have any choice." She would have thought he knew her better than to lay such a challenge at her feet.

"If I need to, I'll tie you up."

"You'll have to."

"I won't have any qualms about doing it."

Her eyes sparked with determination. "You'll have to catch me first."

Ted's gaze hardened. "I can't believe you're doing this."

"Believe it," she said, then slammed the suitcase shut and swung it off the bed.

A loud knock at the front door diverted their attention.

"Stay here," Ted commanded. He checked the window before swinging open the door. "Hello, Oliver, what can I do for you?"

"There's a call for you. Detective Randolph."

Tossing a look over his shoulder at Caroline, Ted nodded. "I'll be right there." He closed the door and turned to face her.

"Go answer your important call."

"I want your promise you won't try to sneak out of here while I'm on the phone."

Her mouth thinned to a brittle line. "My promise?" He had no right to bring up promises. He'd said he wouldn't touch her, and then he'd kissed her until she'd thought she would die from wanting him. Childishly she crossed her fingers behind her back in an effort to negate her words.

"Caroline, promise me you won't try to leave. Either do that or I'm dragging you up that path with me."

"All right, I won't leave." Her heart ached with the lie.

His facial muscles relaxed. "Thank you. I'll be down to let you know what's happening as fast as I can."

It didn't matter, because the minute he was safely out of sight she was leaving. She didn't like breaking her word, but he had forced her into it.

Emotion clouded her eyes. Checking her purse for cash and credit cards, she decided the best thing to do was to take her chances walking along the beach. For the first few hours she would need to avoid the highway. Eventually she could find a town and rent a car.

She paused only long enough to say goodbye to Stranger and assure the dog that Ted would be good to him.

Her heart tightened as she took one last look around the cottage. She would always remember these days with Ted as a special time in her life.

She wasn't more than a few feet out of the door when a shadowy figure moved from behind a large rock.

Her heart rose to her throat, and fear coated the inside of her mouth, as the brawny, angry man she'd seen in the courtroom with Joan MacIntosh stepped directly in front of her.

Ten

Caroline felt her panic rise. She was alone and defenseless. She'd intentionally left Stranger inside, afraid that the dog would follow her down the beach. Ted and Oliver wouldn't hear her cries, and, from the size of this man, she doubted that she could outrun him. Her hands felt weak, and she dropped her suitcase to the sand.

He seemed to sense her fear and took a step toward her.

Raising her hands defensively, she met his glare head-on. "I would advise you to leave now. I've taken karate lessons," she said with as much bravado as her thumping heart would allow. She didn't mention that she'd quit after three classes. Her breathing was shallow as she edged backward with small steps, praying he wouldn't notice that she was working her way toward the bluff. If he raced after her, she would have more of an opportunity to escape. At least if she got above him, she would be able to kick at him. In addition, there was a chance Ted would hear what was happening. Somehow, some way, she had to warn him. Otherwise he would come down the bluff to tell her what was going on and walk into a trap.

The man shifted slightly, and his dark shape was outlined by the sun, making it impossible for her to see his face clearly. He looked around, but she couldn't tell what he was thinking. Why had she left Stranger in the cottage? She wanted to reason with her attacker, plead for him to understand, but alarm clogged her throat, and the words tangled helplessly on the end of her tongue.

"Where's Ted Thomasson?"

The heel of her tennis shoe hit the edge of the bottom step, and with a frenzy born of fear and determination she turned, grabbed a handful of sand and threw it in his face. Taking the creaky wooden stairs two at a time, she ran from him, screaming for Ted at the top of her voice.

"Ted! Ted!"

She heard Stranger begin barking wildly and scratching at the front door to get out.

"Caroline!" Miraculously, Ted appeared at the top of the bluff.

"He's here!" she cried. "He found us!" She was trapped between the two men, positioned halfway up the stairs. She turned toward Joan MacIntosh's companion. From this height, she could better see the bulky man. He looked surprised, almost stunned.

Ted raced down the bluff to Caroline's side. "If you've touched a hair on her head," he called to the other man, who hadn't moved, "you'll pay." He put his arm around her, his fingers biting into her side. "Are you all right?" he whispered near her ear.

"Fine, I think," she whispered back.

He attempted to step in front of her, but she wouldn't let him.

"Caroline," Ted groaned with frustration as they juggled for position. "Let me by."

"No," she argued, stepping one way and then another on the narrow stair, blocking him.

"If you two would stop being so willing to die for each other, maybe you could listen to what I've come to say."

"You listen!" Ted shouted, placing his hands on Caroline's shoulders and holding her still. "I just finished talking to Detective Charles Randolph from the Seattle police department. They've caught the man who's responsible for the attacks."

"Was it Nelson Bergstrom?" She twisted around, needing to know.

Ted didn't seem to hear her; his gaze was focused on the man below. She returned her attention to him as well.

"I know!" he shouted up at them. "I've come to try to make amends to you for everything I've done."

"You mean you don't want to kill us?" she asked, her tensed muscles relaxing in relief.

"Don't act so disappointed," Ted said in a low murmur as he smoothly altered their positions so that he stood directly in front of her.

"So you're the one who kept calling us?" Ted asked.

"Yes." The stranger laced his fingers together in front of him and looked almost boyish as his eyes shone with regret. "And I was the one who spray-painted the outside of your apartment and made those threats." He swallowed and lowered his chin. "I want you to know that I'll pay for any damage."

"We can discuss that later," Ted replied. "For now, it would be best if you returned to Seattle. I'll contact you once we return."

"I *am* sorry."

Caroline felt compassion swelling in her. "I can understand how you felt," she told him, and was rewarded with a feeble smile.

"It's the most helpless feeling in the world to have something like that happen to the person you love most in the world.

However, that doesn't make up for the things I did to the two of you. Venting my anger and frustration on you was wrong."

"I understand, and I accept your apology," she said.

"Thank you for that. But I'm ready to pay for what I did, even if that means going to jail. I deserve it for having put you two through so much. If it's any consolation now, I want you to know I didn't mean any of those threats. That's all they were—empty threats."

"It took courage to come here and face us."

"I had to do something," the man continued. "You can imagine how I felt when the police contacted Joan. The attacker made a full confession. If it had been up to me, I would have condemned an innocent man."

"We did the right thing to let Nelson Bergstrom off," Ted informed her—needlessly, since she'd already figured that out.

"Oh, thank God." Relief washed through her until it overflowed. The guilt she'd experienced when another woman was attacked had been overwhelming. She'd tried to convince herself that following her conscience was the important thing. But that knowledge hadn't relieved the weight of the albatross that had hung around her neck—until now.

"I'll be leaving now. When you want to contact me back in Seattle, the name's John MacIntosh." He turned away and started walking down the beach.

"John!" Ted called, stopping him. "How did you know where to find us?"

Caroline had been wondering the same thing herself.

"Miss Lomax's neighbor told me the address."

"I see," Ted said slowly.

His look narrowed, cutting into Caroline as she searched for the words to exonerate herself. "I gave it to her so she could mail the salmon to—"

"What salmon?"

"—Anne and Oliver as a thank-you for all they'd done."

"You told someone where we were?"

"Just Mrs. Murphy, but I assumed that—"

"I can't believe you'd do something so incredibly stupid. So . . . insane."

"Stupid?" she sputtered almost incoherently, her temper rising. "The dumbest, most insane thing I've ever done is take this crazy trip with you."

"I couldn't agree with you more." Ted stalked down the stairs, leaving her standing there, feeling both humiliated and ashamed. All right, she would concede that giving Mrs. Murphy their address wasn't the smartest thing she'd done in her life, but it was far saner than falling in love with Ted.

He stopped outside the cottage doorway when he found her suitcase in the sand. He hesitated, as if stunned, and a renewed sense of guilt filled her.

He turned and gave her a look of such utter contempt that she knew she would remember it the rest of her life. "So you were planning to leave anyway." He stopped to study her flushed, guilt-ridden face. "Even after you'd given me your word."

"Yes," she admitted, and her chin rose a notch. "Not that it matters anymore. Now that everything's been settled, there's no reason for me to stay." Her lips trembled as she struggled to regain her composure. Without knowing why, she followed Ted inside the cottage and watched as he took out his own suitcase and began to pack. His movements were short and jerky, as if he couldn't finish the task fast enough. He was normally so organized and neat, but now he merely stuffed the clothes inside, then slammed the lid closed.

"I'll tell the Bryants we're leaving."

"Not together we're not," she corrected him briskly. "I'm not going back to Seattle."

"Just where do you plan to go?"

"San Francisco." The name came from the top of her head. Her parents' house would be empty and cold, but she couldn't remain with Ted. She had too much pride for that, and too little self-control. He had to know she loved him. She'd done everything she could to prove she wanted to be his—everything except propose marriage. From the things she'd realized lately, she recognized that he simply didn't want her. The knowledge seared a hole into her heart. She would recover, she told herself repeatedly as she picked up her suitcase and followed him up the creaky old stairs. But her heart refused to listen.

Caroline had assumed that familiar surroundings would lessen the void in her soul. She was wrong. A three-day stint alone in San Francisco had taught her that she couldn't return home like a little girl anymore. She was a woman now, with a woman's hurts. She'd wandered aimlessly around the empty house, and all she could think about was Ted.

He had dropped her off at the airstrip in Brookings and left almost immediately afterward, with Stranger looking forlornly at her from the backseat of the car. She hadn't heard from him since, not that she'd really expected to.

Her return to Seattle a couple of weeks ago had been uneventful. She found part-time employment the first week. Having a job lent purpose to her days and proved to be her salvation.

Her mother telephoned, full of enthusiasm after they returned from China, but for the first time in her adult life, Caroline couldn't bare her soul to her mother.

"For a minute when I walked in the door, I thought you might have come for a visit."

"I *was* in San Francisco, Mom."

"When? Why?"

"It's a long story."

Her mother seemed to sense that Caroline wasn't eager to share the events of her latest escapade. "You don't sound like yourself, honey. Is something wrong?"

"What could possibly be wrong? I've got the very thing I've always wanted. I'm working as a chef and loving it."

"But you don't sound happy."

"I'm . . . just tired, that's all."

"Have you seen any more of Ted Thomasson?"

The pain was so intense that Caroline hesitated before speaking. "No, not for a couple of weeks now." Two weeks, four days and twenty-one hours, she mentally calculated, glancing at her watch.

An awkward silence followed. "Well, I just wanted you to know that your father and I arrived back home safely, and that China was wonderful."

"I'm pleased you're home, Mom. Thanks for calling. I'll give you a ring later in the week."

"Caroline, don't you want to tell your father about your job?"

"You can go ahead and tell him, if you want to."

It wasn't until she hung up that she realized her mistake. At any other time in her life, she would have been puffed up like a bull frog at having achieved her goal of working in a restaurant kitchen. Now her profession was nothing more than a means to fill the empty days.

She'd barely finished the conversation with her mother when a hard knock sounded against her front door. She glanced at it, inexplicably knowing in her heart that Ted stood on the other side. The entire time she'd been back, she had subconsciously been waiting to hear from him. Now, like a coward, she waited until the hard knock was repeated. Forcing a brittle smile to her lips, she finally turned the lock and opened the door.

"Hello, Caroline." His eyes caressed her like a warm, golden flame.

"Hello, Ted. How are you?" Pride demanded that she not reveal any of the emotional pain these weeks apart had cost her. He looked wonderful. Everything she'd remembered about him seemed even more pronounced now. His features were even more rugged and compelling. His eyes were an even deeper shade of blue, if that were possible. The strong, well-shaped mouth that had shown her such pleasure slanted into a half smile.

"I brought your kite and your other things."

The instant she'd seen what he was carrying, she had realized with a sinking heart that the reason for his visit wasn't personal. "How's Stranger?"

"Fine. My apartment doesn't allow pets, so I had to find a home for him."

"You gave Stranger away?" She breathed in sharply, unbelievably hurt that he would so callously give up their dog.

"Could you take him?"

Her apartment building had the same restriction. "No," she admitted, subdued. "You . . . did the right thing. Is he happy in his new home?"

"Very."

Her smile wavered, and she murmured with a breathless catch in her voice, "Then that's what counts." Realizing that she had left him standing in the doorway, she hurriedly stepped aside. "Come in, please."

"Where do you want me to put all this?"

"The kitchen counter will be fine. Thanks." She threaded her fingers together so tightly that they ached. She knew her features were strained with the burden of maintaining an expression of poise. She tried unsuccessfully to relax.

"Do you still make that fancy coffee?" he asked softly.

"Yes . . . would you like a cup?"

"If you have the time."

Time was something she had plenty of these days. Time to remember how his mouth tasted on hers. Time to recall the velvet smoothness of his touch and how well their bodies fit together. Time to compile a list of regrets that was longer than a rich kid's Christmas list.

Their gazes held for several seconds. "Yes, I have the time," she murmured at last, breaking eye contact.

He followed her into the kitchen. "How have you been?"

"Wonderful," she lied with practiced ease. "I have a job. It's only afternoons for now, but I'm hoping that it'll work into full time later this summer." Actually, she'd taken the first job that was offered, even though she would have preferred a regular forty-hour work schedule. But anything was better than moping around the house day after day.

"I'm pleased things are working out for you."

"What about you?" She couldn't look at him, knowing it would be too painful.

"I've been fine," he supplied, leaning against the kitchen counter.

She put as much space between them as possible in the cozy kitchen. Her gaze centered on the glass pot, praying the water would boil quickly.

"We need to talk," he said quietly. "You know that, don't you, Caroline?"

She gripped the counter so hard it threatened to break her neatly trimmed nails. "About what?" Wildly she looked away as her heart jammed in her throat.

"About us."

"Us?" She forced a laugh that sounded amazingly like a restrained sob. "Within two hours we were at each other's throats. How can you even suggest there's an 'us'?"

"That's not the way I remember it."

The minute the coffee finished brewing, she filled two cups and handed him one. He immediately set it on the counter. "Coffee was only an excuse, and you know it."

She took a quick step away from him. "I wish you'd said something before I went through the trouble of making it."

"No you don't."

Without her noticing, he had moved closer to her, trapping her in a corner. Mere inches separated them. Her breathing had become so shallow it was nearly nonexistent.

"I thought I'd give myself time to sort out my feelings." He lifted the luxurious silky auburn curls away from the side of her neck. Her pulse hammered wildly as his thumb stroked her skin. "Every time I was close to you, I had to fight to keep myself from kissing you."

Magnetically, Caroline's gaze was drawn to his eyes. "It's only natural that under the circumstances we—we feel these—these strong physical attractions."

"Problem is," Ted said softly, his breath caressing her face, "I'm experiencing the same things now, only even more powerfully, more intensely, than ever."

"That can't be true," she insisted, too afraid to believe him and seeking an escape. Abruptly she turned and reached for her coffee, nearly scalding her lips as she took a sip. She clenched the mug with both hands. "What we had on the beach wasn't real," she said in a falsely cheerful voice. "You warned me that things would look different once we returned to Seattle, and now I'm forced to admit that they do."

"Caroline," he said her name with a wealth of frustration. "Don't lie to me again."

"Who's lying?" Her voice cracked, and she struggled to hold back stinging tears as she chewed on the corner of her bottom lip.

"Is your pride worth so much to you?"

Unable to answer him, she stared into the black depth of the coffee mug.

"Maybe we should experiment."

"Experiment?"

"Let me kiss you a couple of times and see how you feel." He took the mug from her hands and set it on the counter.

"There isn't any need. I know what I feel," she argued, knowing that if he touched her, she would be lost. With her hands behind her, guiding her, she edged her way along the kitchen wall.

"It may be the only way," he continued, undaunted. "It seems that we've come to different conclusions here. There's too much at stake for me to let you pass judgment so lightly."

"I know how I feel."

"I'm sure you do." He cupped her shoulders with his hands, halting her progress. "I just don't think you're being honest with yourself—or me—about your feelings."

"Ted, please don't."

"I have to," he breathed, bending toward her.

She averted her mouth, so that his lips brushed her cheek. "Please," she whispered. "It won't do any good."

His hands slid from her shoulders up her neck to her chin, tilting her face to receive his kiss. The pressure of his mouth was as light as the morning sun touching the earth. Soon the magnetic desire that was ever-present between them urged their mouths together in a kiss that left Caroline clinging to the counter to stay upright.

"Well?" he asked hoarsely, spreading kisses around her face, pausing at her temple.

She kept her eyes pinched shut. "That was . . . very . . . nice."

"Nice?" His hands slid around her waist, bringing her to him until she was pressed hard against his chest. "It was more than nice."

"No," she offered weakly, pushing against him.

He kissed her again, only this time his lips stayed and moved and urged and tested. Caroline was lost. Her arms rose from his chest to link around his neck, so that she was arched against him. Softly, she moaned, unable to hold back any longer, clinging to him, weak with longing and desire. Again and again his mouth met hers, until she saw a glimpse of heaven and far, far beyond.

When he broke the contact, she buried her face in the curve of his neck. The irregular pounding of his heart echoed hers.

"Does that convince you?"

"It tells me that we have a strong physical attraction," she answered, breathless and weak.

"More than that. What we share is spiritual."

"No." She tried to deny him, but her feeble protest was broken off when he raised his mouth to hers and kissed her again. The kiss was tempestuous, earth-shattering.

"Don't argue," he said with a guttural moan. "I love you, Caroline. I want us to marry and give Stranger a home."

"I thought you said you gave him away." It was far easier to discuss the dog than to think about the first part of his statement.

"No, I didn't." Tenderly he kissed the bridge of her nose, as if he couldn't get enough of the feel of her. "I said I found him a home. And I have. Ours."

"Oh." She pressed her forehead to the center of his chest as she took in everything he was saying. She loved him. Dear

Lord, she loved him until she thought she would die without him. But sometimes love wasn't enough. "I—I don't think anyone should base something as important as marriage on anything as flimsy as making a home for a stray dog."

"I love you," he whispered against her hair. "I think I've loved you from the time I first saw you."

Slowly she raised her eyes so that she could see the tenderness in his expression and believe what he was saying. Her fingertips traced the angular line of his jaw.

"Why didn't you tell me?"

"That I loved you? Honey, surely you can understand why, given the—"

Her fingers across his lips stopped him. "You're an artist, aren't you?"

He blinked and captured her hand, then kissed it. "So that's it." He forced the air from his lungs. "I should have told you, but to be honest, I was wary. I was afraid that if you saw my work, you'd think it was another one of my interests, like dancing lessons, that always made you think less of me."

"You thought that of me?" she asked, forcibly trying to break free. It hurt to believe that he saw her as so insensitive.

"Listen to me." His hold tightened, not allowing her out of his embrace. "That was only in the beginning, before I realized how much you'd changed. Later, I thought I'd surprise you with the painting and make it a wedding gift."

"That's why you didn't want me to see it that day on the bluff?"

He wove his hand into her hair, running her fingers through her curls. "The only reason."

"Oh, Ted." She pressed her head over his heart, hugging him hard. "I was so hurt . . . I'd talked for days and days, sharing the most personal parts of my life with you. And when . . . when I saw that there was a part of yourself that you hid from me, I felt terrible. I lied about being bored. I loved being with you every minute that we were together. It nearly killed me to leave you."

"I knew you were lying all along. What I couldn't figure out was why."

"I lied because I thought you didn't care. But . . . how did you know?" She had thought she'd given an Academy Award–winning performance.

"No one could shine with as much happiness as you did and be faking it," he replied, smiling tenderly.

She closed her eyes, holding on to the rapture his words spread through her soul. "You're sure you want to marry me? I'm stubborn as a mule, contrary, proud—"

"Headstrong, reckless and overbearing," he interrupted with a chuckle. "But you're also warm, loving, creative and so many other wonderful things that it will take me a lifetime to discover them all."

"I'll marry you, Ted Thomasson, whenever you want."

His gaze took in her happiness. "We're going to have some fantastic children, Caroline Lomax."

They kissed lightly, and Caroline grinned. "I think you may be right," she whispered, bringing his mouth down to hers.

★ ★ ★ ★ ★